CW01192342

*A Dark Intelligence Has Been
Poisoning Carefully Selected Lives.*

The Con Man: 'Reverend' Joe McGill claims he's a healer, but he's chosen the wrong man to con.

The Psychotic Gangster: Arthur Bewlay has cancer eating away at his face. He's in no mood to be messed around—either by fake miracle workers or his dead brother Tommy—and he'll stop at nothing in his desperate desire to live.

The Eccentric Recluse: Maryam Clemenceau is just what both McGill and Bewlay need—a real miracle worker with a bona fide gift. But it comes at a considerable cost.

The Architect: The sinister link between Maryam's Gothic apartment block, and Bewlay's boarded up, abandoned Victorian pub—buildings that are contaminated with fear and the echoes of old and ominous power.

BABY STRANGE opens with Joe beaten and bound in the back of a car, on his way to an appointment with a cement pit under a Glasgow flyover . . . this is not to be the lowest point of his day.

Baby Strange

To Winnie,
Willie
Maxi
Maria,
Louisa,
Cassie,
Charlie

Hope you enjoy it!!

Jim xx

Baby Strange

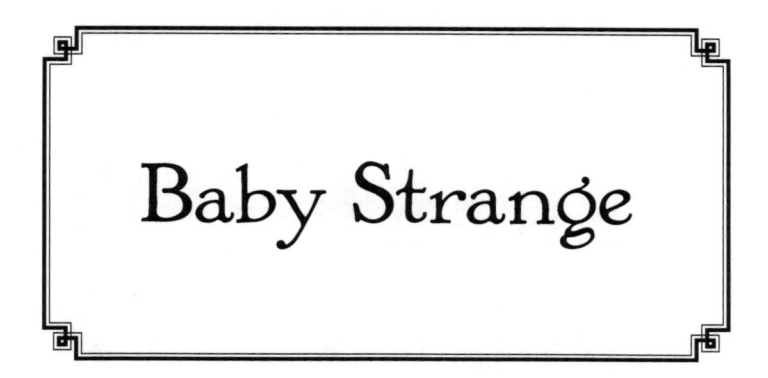

Jim Shields

2014

BABY STRANGE
Copyright © Jim Shields 2014

COVER
Copyright © Ben Baldwin 2014

Published in April 2014 by PS Publishing Ltd. by arrangement with the author. All rights reserved by the author. The right of Jim Shields to be identified as Author of this Work has been asserted by him in accordance with the Copyright, Designs and Patents Act 1988.

FIRST EDITION

ISBN
978-1-848637-63-4
978-1-848637-64-1 (Signed Edition)

This book is a work of fiction. Names, characters, places, and incidents either are products of the author's imagination or are used fictitiously. Any resemblance to actual events or locales or persons, living or dead, is entirely coincidental.

Design and Layout by Aaron Leis.
Printed and bound in England by T.J. International.
Set in Sabon and Colwell HPLHS.

PS Publishing Ltd
Grosvenor House / 1 New Road / Hornsea, HU18 1PG / England

editor@pspublishing.co.uk
www.pspublishing.co.uk

Baby Strange

For Linda, Natty, Harry and Alec

1

Through the mirage haze of the gasoline fumes, slow motion stick figures were now heading toward him. The small lake of petrol he was lying in made him gag, and the lorry which had run over his legs had somehow managed to come to a scraping halt against the ribbed concrete sides of the underpass without sparking. What had hit the car?

In those brief seconds, it had looked like an old man had suddenly landed on the windscreen from the sky with an almighty bang, cracking and smearing it with a paint splash of blood before just as suddenly disappearing again; the world's unluckiest bungee jumper.

Joe thought of a Biblical plague—old geezers simply dropping from the clouds in showers, like frogs or fish, but no other old guys had arrived so it must have been a one-off. He managed to lift his head to look at the bodies of the odd, heavy men still in the mangled car he'd been thrown from. None of them were moving. He sincerely hoped they were dead and that they'd died in squealing horror. He dared a look down below his waist and knew that he'd never be able to use his legs again. He couldn't feel anything so far but on a purely visual level, Joe could tell that this wasn't going to be fixable. It didn't really bother him yet, though. At the moment it felt like a great big pause button had been pressed, giving him time to observe.

There . . . splayed out on the road behind the Merc was the old guy, ribs erupted through his chest, a fat bubble of blood expanding into a dome just below his collarbone. Did that mean his lungs were still working? He couldn't still be alive, surely? Joe hoped not.

The guy was wearing a hat which had somehow remained firmly wedged on his head, tilted Sinatra rakish. Was it a Fedora maybe? Homburg? Who knew hats these days? The old geezer had obviously reckoned that some form of head gear was indispensable for dropping onto a dual carriageway. Joe looked up. Some way back, there was a thin pedestrian footbridge over the road. He must have fallen from there.

The old guy's expanding blood bubble burst then, spotting his face. Another started to form immediately.

◆

Above this section of motorway, which ribboned through a deep cut in the city centre of Glasgow, Maryam Clemenceau stood at her bedroom window. She and Grace lived with their father in the Victorian grandeur of their sprawling two level apartment at the very top of the Charing Cross Mansions. The gigantic clock with the signs of the Zodiac around its rim directly below Maryam's bedroom windows said it was a minute to eight. Below the clock was a bas relief of a scowling, mustachioed face, glaring out at the city. This was alleged to be the face of the architect who'd designed the place, but no one really knew for sure. The whole structure covered most of a city block and looked not unlike New York City's Dakota Building. Maryam's clients loved it because aside from anything else (its grandness, its solidity... its vibe of old money spent well) the whole 'Rosemary's Baby' thing really rather seemed to suit her line of business.

Consequently, Maryam hated it.

She put on a pair of dark glasses (thick, round and black enough to observe a solar eclipse through) and pulled the net curtains aside to try and get a better look at what on earth was causing all the racket down below. But her hooded eyes—even protected by her shades—began to water in the bright sun of the morning and she gave it up as a bad lot. Pulling her cashmere wrap around her bony shoulders she hobbled painfully back to bed. Her grey, frizzy hair bent itself like wire wool when she settled against the pillow behind her.

Carefully, she removed the dark glasses, squinting deliberately so that her pink-hued eyeballs could gradually accustom themselves to the dim light inside her room once more. After a few moments, her hands came into focus and she found herself staring at the wet, yellow patches staining the palms of her white cotton gloves. The hands were leaking again.

There was a light knock and Grace arrived with breakfast on a tray. Maryam, pursing her thin, cracked lips, watched her walk around the mahogany footboard at the bottom of the bed. Wearing a cream silk kimono tied tight round her slim waist, her sandy blonde hair tied in a hank and bouncing behind her as she strode through the room, she made Maryam think of a Shetland pony; healthy, vigorous and cute.

Grace arrived at the bedside, humming happily to herself. As well she might, thought Maryam. What did she have to worry about? Maryam's sporadic cystitis jabbed at her momentarily and, grimacing, she placed her spindly hand over Grace's wrist. The humming stopped. Maryam took in the freshly washed face, the clear complexion. Not a blemish on her. Not even a freckle.

'Try not to annoy me Grace.'

Grace looked Maryam straight in the eye, chin jutting slightly forward in an attempt at defiance.

'It's omly music. I ammem't noying you . . . not reliberately.'

Maryam decided to ignore the speech impediment, although she had told Grace only last night that she was sick to death of hearing it. After intentionally not speaking for ten or so seconds, during which time she could see Grace's defiance ebbing away, Maryam slapped Grace as hard as she could. Her grip did not slacken, and in a short while, Grace lowered her gaze and that was that—all over, lesson learnt. Maryam let go.

'Empty vessels make the most noise dear,' she said, 'and I wouldn't want you to get into the habit of inanely broadcasting that fact. Humming the latest from the top ten will only annoy clients. No salon . . . no money.'

'But it's is'mt a salom day, Maryam . . .'

Grace sounded hurt, but Maryam was no longer listening and had set about unfolding her napkin, looking down at the bowl of salted porridge on the tray before her. It was, she noted, in Grace's 'Batman' bowl.

'What age are you supposed to be?' said Maryam.

Grace looked between Maryam and the offending bowl, tongue-tied.

'Speak to me—why am I eating from this *toy*?'

'Sorry . . . I dibm't do the dishes yesberday . . . s'was the omly cleam plate this mormimg . . .'

'If this ever happens again I shall drop it on the floor, breakfast and all, and break it into pieces. Do I make myself clear?'

Grace nodded. The sound of ambulance and fire engine nee-nawed up from below and, excited, she started over to the window as Maryam closely examined her spoon for cleanliness.

'There seems to have been an event on the road, dear,' she said. 'Switch on the radio so that I don't have to listen to the emergency services whilst I eat.'

Grace stopped, halfway to the window and its promise of a rare glimpse of something exciting happening in the world outside.

'Camn't I just look Maryam . . . please?'

'Radio first, Grace. Don't be selfish.'

Grace stood still. Maryam could see that she was torn but, as was usual, obedience won. Grace sloped over, defeated, to the old radiogram in the corner to switch it on . . . but then stopped suddenly before she could reach it. She mumbled something. Maryam sighed, annoyed.

'Speak up!'

She suddenly turned and Maryam gasped, despite herself, looking at her sister and realizing—Bad News.

'What's happened Grace? What is it?'

She stumble walked to the edge of the bed and murmured incoherently, banging her shin on the sharp corner. She didn't seem to feel it, although Maryam could see the scrape start to well up with pinpoints of blood.

'For heaven's sake, what *is* it, Grace? What have you seen?'

Grace steadied herself on the bed board, gripping it tightly, her knuckles white. Her voice came out strangely, like she was calling from a distance.

'Papa,' she said.

A chill froze Maryam's heart. Oh Jesus, she thought, what was the ghastly old wretch doing *now*? She realised that she hadn't heard him at all this morning—there had been no noises of muffled padding about from his room, none of the usual quiet, irritating murmuring of his prayers—and she knew that this hadn't been because he was asleep. He never slept anymore.

'What about him?' she asked, her voice sounding very fragile to her. Grace spoke again in that distant, strangulated tone.

'He's killed some people . . .'

It took Maryam a few shocked moments to get a response out.

'He's *what*?' she said. 'Where? For heaven's sake—who?'

'. . . by accidemt . . .' said Grace. '. . . amd he's . . . he's . . .'

Grace's eyes suddenly rolled up in their sockets showing only the whites. She opened her mouth wide, as if she were about to scream, but Maryam could only hear a thin whistle of air escaping from her lungs.

◆

The sirens were cutting through Joe's accident bang tinnitus. The old guy's head had just . . . slumped to one side. The blood bubbles had stopped.

Another boy for Jesus, thought Joe.

He wondered if the old guy had made sure he was wearing clean underwear before he left the house this morning—or did that rule only make sense if you actually survived an accident? Would morgue technicians have the same delicate sensibilities about unclean underwear as ambulance men were alleged to? Mother never said.

Joe giggled as random, nonsensical thoughts like these crowded in on him, desperately running interference against what was really happening . . . but they were losing the fight. Then he heard the sound of a young woman screaming at the top of her lungs, like she was aiming to rip her throat inside out.

Strange.

It was only when the paramedics started tourniquet procedure on his legs that Joe McGill realised he was the one who was screaming.

2

IN HIS SET OF ROOMS ABOVE THE PUB ARTHUR BEWLAY LOOKED at his face in the mirror. Yon McGill fellow absolutely had a way with the words, no doubt about it. Looking at it objectively, Arthur reckoned that what was left of his nose did indeed—as McGill had unwisely stated—resemble the inside of a red pepper. The brown and yellow tumour clusters were like seeds suspended in the vermillion hole in the middle of his face. Immediately below this was his mouth, filled with his immaculately brushed teeth, and between both holes there was a thick flap of skin that still functioned as a rudimentary top lip. Arthur thought to himself that this is probably what mankind would have looked like had they been descended from crabs.

He turned away from the mirror, deciding he'd had enough objectivity for the day. He removed the silver hipflask from his pocket, unscrewed the top and took a necessary swig of the morphine mixture inside. Christ almighty; he despised the taste of that stuff. It was, however, preferable to the pain.

The sound of hurried footsteps coming up the narrow staircase from the pub below drew his attention. His door was knocked brusquely but Big Ian entered before Arthur could say anything. The cross-hatching of old machete wounds across the big man's face stood pink and livid against his already reddened skin and he was panting and perspiring freely. He really shouldn't run up stairs, thought Arthur. Not carrying the weight of several decades' worth of deep-fried chip shop suppers he shouldn't.

Big Ian paused for breath and leant against the doorframe, his strange-looking thumbless hands by his sides.

'The guys taking McGill up the quarry are all in intensive care,' he said without preamble, trying to control his breathing. 'Some kind of smash up on the M8. They were lucky but there was other people killed.'

Big Ian also had a very high-pitched voice. A lot of people seemed to find that comical—but he usually persuaded them that there was nothing at all funny about it. If pressed, Arthur would have described him as sounding not a kick in the arse off Minnie Mouse.

Big Ian began detailing the injuries received by the boys; there had been punctured lungs and a smashed pelvis for Dumplin', broken arms and jaw for Ralph, and internal injuries, severed windpipe and significant head trauma for poor Terry.

'What about McGill?' interrupted Arthur.

'Sorry Arthur—McGill's still alive. He's pretty fucked up, though . . . '

'How fucked up? Can he speak? Is he expected to live?'

Big Ian paused for a second. He hated giving Arthur bad news.

'As far as they can tell, aye.' He continued. 'His legs got run over by a truck and that kind of . . . burst them and sealed them at the same time. Lost a lot less blood than he should have. Sorry. That was all I could get on him.'

'What'd Sergeant Wendy have to say?'

'She says the straight cops don't know anything about him. They're going to pay you a visit to ask if you know who he is and what he was doing naked in a motor with our guys.'

Arthur nodded to himself. That would be an easy explain— he'd just deny knowing anything and then they would fuck off. He'd probably get a visit or two from the press as well though, he thought, what with the, um, unusual nature of the men in the car and his own current state of health. Human interest . . . gangland figure . . . Mis-Shape men—he could see tabloid appeal, but wee visits were not a problem. McGill still alive and able to make some kind of statement was a problem. Arthur still had all of McGill's clothing and personal items in a black polythene bag stuffed into the airing cupboard in the hall. He'd wanted to play with them for a while, but now it looked like he'd have to have it all burnt. Pity.

The expected fuzziness from his medicine was starting to make its presence felt as the warm glow spread from his stomach. He became aware that Big Ian was talking again. He supposed he'd better get the wheels rolling on this situation before he was too stoned to think rationally. He lifted his hand and Big Ian shut up.

'Repeat, please,' said Arthur, quietly.

'Sergeant Wendy says they're waiting to get word from the hospital when he regains consciousness.'

'Ok, then make sure you get him first,' Arthur said.

Big Ian didn't say anything. Arthur frowned.

'Would you like me to repeat it for you, Big Ian?'

'That's a hard call, Arthur. He'll be surrounded by doctors and nurses and that . . .'

'So?'

Big Ian shut up. Arthur was staring at him, eyes unblinking, and Big Ian knew better than to say or do anything to upset or annoy him when he was like this. Arthur continued speaking as if Big Ian hadn't said anything at all.

'Make sure he suffers as much as you can make him suffer under the circumstances, alright?' he said. 'Use the rough sponge if you think you have the time . . . do it to him under the sheets. Something they won't find immediately and if he regains consciousness when you're working on him, all the better.'

Arthur then turned his back on him and although Big Ian hated the gesture, he was kind of glad to not be looking at that face any longer. Not because it repelled him, but because it made him sad to see the boss in this sorry state. Big Ian would have done anything for Arthur—he had more than enough to be grateful to him for—and the boss's mental and physical deterioration was starting to become more than he could bear. He'd sworn to himself that he would never *ever* let on to Arthur about his own distress. The boss had enough to contend with without having a crybaby working for him. Arthur, still with his back to Big Ian, cleared his throat and spoke again.

'Are you needing directions to the hospital?'

'No Arthur. I know the way to the hospital.'

Arthur barely noticed him walk away. He wondered to himself—had he been *too* harsh with young Reverend McGill? After all, the man had only been trying to make a living, hadn't he? It wasn't as if he had wished deliberate harm upon the person of Arthur Bewlay, was it? But . . . as amusing as the fellow had been, as presentable as he had been—in fact, as droll and entertaining as he had been—Arthur could not countenance the idea of being taken for a sucker. It was not good for any business, never mind *his* business. McGill had to be made an example of or what was left of Arthur's own life would not be worth living. Not if people were going about saying he had completely lost the plot.

The warmth of the drug had spread all the way through him and he noted with mild surprise that he was now lying on his sofa. He had no memory of having gotten to this side of the room, nor of lying down. It was like time travel using this stuff, he thought. No wonder all the little smackheads would do literally anything for their low-rent version of it. The constant background wasp buzz of his pain was completely gone and he hoped that he hadn't drunk too much from his flask—he wasn't ready to die yet. He lifted his hand and watched his fingers ghost before his eyes as he slowly waved them about. For some reason, it made him think of joke shop X-Ray Specs, and it made him laugh.

Jokes, he thought to himself with satisfaction, he could take. He was not a humour free man and he prided himself that he could find the fun in even the grimmest of situations. Like when he'd buried his wee brother, for instance.

◆

It had been raining heavily the day before the funeral. As the cortege was winding its way up boot hill bringing wee Tommy to his final resting place, two sad-sack gravediggers shuffled off behind the nearby ash tree where they'd planked their litre of supermarket vodka. Council overalls were not acceptable for Arthur and he had told the nervous funeral director that any and all graveside operational staff be dressed 'respectfully'. Dressed in suits hastily purchased from Oxfam, the gravediggers—now mud caked from their labours—looked like they'd both recently been disinterred.

The funeral director stood nearby, visibly anxious, and not just because of the current state of the gravediggers. It was who they were planting today that was his concern. He had the gnawing fear of someone who felt they may just have made a terrible mistake. For a start, the coffin was not balanced well, what with no one having actually found Wee Tommy's missing head yet, and what with a couple of taped together bags of sugar having been substituted for it. (The funeral director hadn't been able to source an adequately proportioned sandbag and had reasoned—correctly—that an open coffin would probably not be on the cards for the vigil, so he'd risked sending the Goth Who Was Always Drinking Cider to the shop next door for an acceptable substitute.)

His main problem though wasn't the bags as such, but the fact that they were not attached physically to the mortal remains of Wee Tommy in any way, shape or form. He shuffled from foot to foot, hoping for the best.

It was not to be.

Terry the Driver was one of the pallbearers, and he had no proper hands as such, but fat, twin-digited flipper type appendages at the ends of his arms. Arthur hadn't really thought it was a good idea for Terry to be on the burial team, but had let it go, not wanting to disappoint him—the boy had been keen to show that he could contribute. Besides, Big Ian was chief pallbearer and Arthur couldn't be seen to favour one strangely extremitied soldier over another.

And at least he wasn't a midget like Wee Tommy.

As Arthur's soldiers began lowering the child-sized box into the hole though, Terry's bare and rain-soaked flipper hands slipped. The sugar bags inside shifted suddenly. The coffin's centre of gravity shifted with them and the entire coffin suddenly upended as it dropped into the hole. Tommy's coffin was left standing upright, tiny inside the comparatively huge grave. Another tick in the 'mistake' column for the funeral director.

For some very long moments, no one said a thing. All, including Father Monty, looked to Arthur terrified at what he might do.

The funeral director was now running away in an insane panic, sliding down the muddy lee of the hill, desperate to get out of range of Arthur and party.

Arthur eventually drew his eyes up from the coffin and looked over at the petrified gravediggers, both holding the vodka bottle in mid-pass between them like a pair of freeze-framed zombie alcoholics. One of them immediately fainted, banging his face against the rough bark of the tree trunk as he fell, peeling skin like orange rind from his cheek on the way down. The other one necked half the bottle in one go, unable to take his unblinking eyes from Arthur. A crow cawed. Distant traffic splashed through far away puddles.

Arthur had eventually smiled. There was no way he was going to let some funeral director's idiocy spoil Wee Tommy's day, and if there was one thing he knew, it was how to relieve a difficult moment of tension.

'It's alright boys, don't worry about it.'

He'd looked around at the other mourners, giving himself a moment before his punchline.

'Tommy always was a stand up guy.'

Arthur began to laugh and everyone glanced at each other sideways—should they join in or not? At that point though, the little coffin had simply toppled over and smashed face down into a layer of muddy water that geysered over everyone, making them squeal. Their faces and clothes dripped, wet and filthy as if someone had just discovered oil here and they all looked down at Tommy's coffin again, now half in/half out of the water like some grim novelty float in a bleak, tiny swimming pool.

In the sudden silence you could just about hear the fizz of dissolving sugar from inside.

Wiping watery mud from his cheek, Arthur had simply laughed harder, and everyone had nervously joined in again. They laughed until they cried, mostly with relief. Arthur was still laughing when he'd come back a week later to see how the runaway funeral director was getting on after spending two days buried alive in the wet ground, up to his neck in Wee Tommy's grave.

How was he doing? Not well at all, was the answer.

When Arthur had arrived, the funeral director's wife was kneeling beside him, freezing wet from the constant drizzle, trying to get him to drink some Lucozade. Arthur stood looming over her, hands deeply embedded in the warm pockets of his thick winter Crombie coat, a nice woolly scarf round his neck. She was obviously a loyal sort, coming all the way out here in this sort of weather. He liked that. Never give up, that was his motto. He cleared his throat and she jumped back, petrified.

'He'd be better off drinking tea or something hot, darling. Have you not got a thermos at home?

She looked up at him, bug-eyed and terrified out of her mind. She was about to speak, but Arthur cut her off. He knew she was only going to make bleating noises about letting her husband go.

'You fuck off home, dear, to those two wee boys of yours. I've just got one thing to do with your man here, and then my boys'll dig him out.'

She stared. He smiled pleasantly at her.

'Go on, hen. Off you fuck.'

She backed away from him and Terry took hold of her elbow with one of his flippers, leading her away gently. Arthur stared down at the very sorry looking head sticking out of the black, wet dirt, and sighed.

The man was moaning, unable to form coherent words, and his face and bald head were an unpleasant blue colour. He didn't look natural at all. He was trembling uncontrollably and obviously suffering from hypothermia. There were some small, blood crusted indents around his forehead and eyebrows—probably made by crows.

Terry, whose own punishment for letting the rope slip in the first place had been to keep guard come rain or shine until Arthur showed up, obviously hadn't been putting his bucket over the man's head when he went for food breaks and such.

Sloppy.

The man was being severely punished as it was—there was no need for him to risk losing his eyesight to the local wildlife.

Arthur got on with his visit. He calmly stated that he didn't mind people making mistakes. That was only human, after all. What he minded was people not doing the decent thing and owning up to them. He especially minded a person legging it and leaving innocent parties like his poor gravediggers—ordinary, hard-working men—to take any flack. Tut tut. He said all of this as he squatted over the barely conscious man's head taking a shit on him.

Oh yes, Arthur could find humour in even the grimmest of situations.

By coincidence, it was the day after that when he had started feeling the first pains in his nose.

◆

Arthur was drowsing himself into a nap. He remembered a time when his sheer bulk would have made even attempting such a thing on this sofa a slapstick comedy. Now? He felt like it could swallow him up. It was a terrible thing really, he thought as he closed his eyes, to have one's faith in a person comprehensively destroyed—the image one has of them thoroughly debunked by, for example, the chance overhearing of an offhand remark.

The Reverend Joe McGill had been doing so well. But . . . fallen idols, feet of clay, he thought. Even though he'd hardly known McGill, Arthur had actually liked him and had come round to believing his pitch. Or, at least, wanting to. And that was half the battle, wasn't it? Faith was supposed to be able to move them mountains. Shame, really. He thought that to have hope introduced to one's life only to then see it blow away like dust really was a hard thing to bear. He would bear it better though, knowing that the young reverend had already suffered terribly and, with luck, was going to have his last moments on earth made unendurable.

3

Joe lay on the bed in the glass walled Intensive Therapy Unit, which was tucked away in a dogleg corner of a mixed ward, barely noticing he was covered in wires and tubes. It was night now, and he felt absolutely fucking terrific. He was vaguely aware, though, that if he wanted to stay happy, he really shouldn't try to move (or even look down at) his legs. Admittedly he knew enough about narcotic analgesics to also know that this relaxed feeling of well-being was due entirely to the drugs he was receiving. He rationalised, however, that he might as well enjoy it while he could because nothing this good could possibly last forever.

It felt like he was on a very comfortable but slow moving train and memories came drifting back to him, voices and faces from the ambulance and hospital admission; a pale doctor speaking from somewhere a hundred miles above his head, theorising that 'the legs' could be 'partially retained'. Not saved, Joe noted—'retained'.

Partially.

Somewhere outside of the chilled out zone he was currently occupying, a tiny voice was telling him that although 'partially retained' was better than 'not retained at all', it still wasn't very good.

Something else chuffed by . . . the old guy; the 'leaper' the nurses had called him. He'd heard one of them say the guy was French? Or, at least, he had a French name? The circumstances of Joe's rescue from Arthur's oddly-shaped men became ever more bizarre. What was a Frenchman doing leaping from pedestrian flyovers in

Glasgow? Maybe it was raining frogs after all? He laughed aloud. A wave of euphoria hit him and he closed his eyes, enjoying the dry orgasm of the morphine.

. . . vibrant stripes were replaced by jiggling dots and one on top of two on top of green on top of red. His ears felt somehow full up, completely different sounds in each one, all made by the dust swirling around in the sunlight of the barn. A girl was singing and he was in love. How many telephones are there in the world, exactly? The nurses specifically stated that it was just too fucking bizarre for words—a crashed car full of seriously injured Thalidomide-affected adult males. What the hell were they doing—going to a convention? . . . dad held his hand as he walked him on to the plane . . . Pin perfect silhouettes of Stan Laurel and Oliver Hardy began to laugh. But not in a nice way and a curtain kept swishing open and closed . . . open and closed . . . open and closed . . . when he opened his eyes again . . .

. . . it was afternoon, although really much closer to evening from the way the light was brawling horizontally into the place. Simple as that—one second he was completely out, the next he was wide-eyed and alert.

He tried to shift his weight on the bed and an express delivery of pain hit him so profoundly that Tiger Woods swinging a five iron across his teeth would have been a blessing. He had to stay still—perfectly, perfectly *still*—to let the feeling that his legs were caught in two rusty, grinding bear traps abate.

Through the smoked glass and partly open slat blinds, he could see through to the rest of the ward outside. Other patients in other beds were being hugged and given magazines and candy by visitors. Except they called it 'sweeties' back here in Scotland, didn't they? He smiled, his spine now beginning to undulate pleasurably as another burst of the drug kicked in some more. His eyes closed . . .

He forced them open again—no way was he going to just keep drifting off uncontrollably. He had something important to do, if he could only remember what it was. Now there was a man out there in the main ward looking straight in at him—someone he knew? Maybe, probably, perhaps . . . although where he knew him from, Joe couldn't pinpoint with any accuracy right at the minute. Things were foggy. The guy was a great big fella though, giant head with a tiny childlike face in the middle of it, which looked like it had been through a bacon slicer and then glued back together again. This guy appeared very pleased to see Joe and waved at him, before indicating his watch. Looked like he was trying to say he'd be back later, mouthing the words *'when it's less busy'* to him from beside the nurses' station.

Joe thought it was like watching a cartoon. He smiled pleasantly and nodded, giving the guy an agreeable thumbs up, but for some reason, this seemed to upset him . . . and that's when Joe realised why he was thinking of cartoons—it was the friendly guy's hands. He only had four fingers on each one. Shit! He knew him now! Shit shit shit shiiiiit! It was Arthur's big mutant psycho! Joe could see in the big man's eyes that he knew Joe had recognised him.

Big Ian nodded, smiling and delighted—*aye! It's me! Coo-ee!*—and drew a finger across his throat, winking at Joe before leaving the ward. It took a moment before true panic set in. Joe grabbed his sheet and pulled it, his escape systems on automatic, desperate at any cost to get out of there. But this time when the wave of pain and nausea hit, it totally overwhelmed him and his body switched off all the house lights.

◆

On his way out of the hospital, Big Ian snatched some shrink-wrapped janitor's overalls from a small pyramid of them on a broken armchair, smiling broadly to himself.

Didn't look like McGill was going anywhere in a hurry. Good.

4

THE BLACK CAB RATTLED AND VIBRATED NOISILY OUTSIDE THE rear entrance to the Mansions. Maryam had insisted on leaving via the back way, since at this time of night on a Friday, the front of the buildings (Sauchiehall Street, lined with pubs, clubs and fast food) would be full of drunken, barely dressed children making pests of themselves, vomiting in the gutters, jabbering inanely and walking heedlessly onto busy roads as if indestructible. Grace was disappointed—she liked looking down on the street scenes at night from her window, and would have quite liked to actually stand among people her own age—even though it also frightened her. But Maryam wouldn't have it.

'It's for your own good, Grace dear,' she'd declared. 'Young people change at night. They become animalistic and venal and all they care about is sex. It wouldn't be safe for someone like you. Tell the cab man to pick us up around the back.'

Grace opened up the cab door for Maryam who, stooped and in some discomfort, brusquely told the driver where they were going. Even though it was night, she was wearing her 'showbiz' dark glasses. They were white framed and huge (they had been Mama's, and she used to call them her 'Jackie O's'). She had a cream silk scarf tied round her head at the chin, as if she were just going for a wee run down to Monte Carlo in an open-top sports car. She had an ankle-length, ratty, brown fur coat buttoned up to her neck and white opera gloves. Completing the ensemble, oversized sheepskin slippers were secured around her feet with string and her scarlet lipstick looked like a laceration across her paint-white face.

Grace could see the driver staring at Maryam in his rearview mirror taking this in, his startled expression making her smile a little. Grace slammed closed the door behind her and the cab light went out—a blessing as far as the driver was concerned.

'What are you waiting for?' asked Maryam, tapping his window with her stick and the cab duly pulled out onto the road. Maryam sighed and spoke to Grace without looking at her.

'This is all Papa's fault. I don't see why I should have to discomfit myself and risk exposure.'

'It's the right thimg to do, Maryam.'

'What would you know? Besides, when did Papa ever do the right thing for me?'

Grace took a deep breath.

'If we hadm't . . . if you hadm't helped Papa, this wouldem't have happemmed.'

Maryam stared at her, completely aghast.

'If I hadn't helped Papa? Well what was I expected to do?'

'I ammem't sayimmg it's all your fault . . .'

'*None* of it is my fault!'

The taxi driver looked over his shoulder for a moment. Maryam lowered her voice.

'So why don't I just go round the whole hospital, hm?' she hissed. 'I could go to all the wards and sort *everyone* out! That would be fun wouldn't it? Why just him?'

But even at the asking, she knew why. Grace looked frightened when she replied.

'Because *I* heard him screamimg Maryam, up *here* . . .'

She indicated her head.

'. . . I heard *his* voice, not emmyome else's . . . it must meam *somethimg* . . .'

She looked down at her hands and spoke very softly.

'Everythimg means somethimg.'

Maryam looked at Grace's profile against the streetlights and the raindrops streaming on the cab window. Grace's 'gift' was random and unpredictable, not like her own, and Maryam took her episodes far more seriously than she ever let on. They were very . . . left of centre, and they sometimes gave Maryam oddball glimpses into things she would really rather not have to think about. In fact Grace's occasional turns had actually disturbed her once or twice—although she would never ever let Grace know that. Not too long ago, she had told Maryam she'd heard the screaming of a baby coming from 'imside' a schoolgirl in the supermarket. Grace had said it was crying '. . . *ascause it didem't wamt to die*'.

Maryam had had no idea what to say to that.

Thinking along these lines always unsettled her and she decided to take control of the conversation once more. Besides, most times Grace barely even knew when she was having an event herself; she really did seem the embodiment of the adage about empty vessels making the most noise.

'I will try my best tonight Grace, but if this fellow is to die, then I *will not* help him and you will not whine at me for not doing so—understand? If he is to die, then so be it. You know why. Now tell me, am I making myself clear?'

'Yes, Maryam.'

'I really shouldn't be doing this at all,' she muttered, aware that she was fussing and repeating herself like an old woman but unable to stop. 'None of this is my fault—*none of it.*'

But Maryam could see that Grace's limited attention span had played out as far as this particular subject went. The cab had made its way out of the quiet road at the back of the Mansions and had pulled onto Sauchiehall Street proper and Grace was already gazing excitedly out at the city's busy Friday night streets and at all the youngsters buzzing about. Maryam tutted and tried to make herself a little more comfortable.

The taxi stopped at the lights. A young couple were kissing in a dark doorway next to Mister Chips, both still with their bags of food in their hands.

Grace smiled a big, happy smile for them.

◆

Big Ian was dressed in his stolen overalls outside Arthur's pub, working his way through a bag of chips with his usual unusual four-fingered technique. From a distance, it looked like he was holding bunches of particularly thick cigarettes and cramming them into his mouth, humming tunelessly along to an old Cher record belting from the jukebox inside.

The pizza delivery moped pulled up and Skinny sat there gripping the handlebars, waiting for Big Ian to climb on behind her. She cursed quietly to herself as she watched him ball up his chip paper and toss it into the gutter.

Skinny was meant to be going out tonight on a long fought for date with her new friend Mandy and—aside from being horrendously late already—knew that her clothes were now likely to stink of vinegar and fat wherever Big Ian put his paws on her for support on the ride over to the hospital. She hoped it would be around her waist because then she'd have some chance of covering the stains and smell with her jacket.

She knew she was very lucky indeed to have found Mandy—a good-looking girl who seemed willing to put up with the fact Skinny only had one eye. She didn't want to push it by smelling any worse than she had to. She also didn't like that Arthur had specifically wanted her in on this although she supposed that with the others in hospital he really didn't have much choice. Still, it was never good to be the object of his attention and she tried not to read anything sinister into it. Any thoughts she'd recently had on the subject of Arthur Bewlay and his fitness for purpose had been entirely kept to herself, so as far as she was concerned, she had nothing to worry about . . . apart from smelling like a fucking chip shop on the first date she'd had for a year.

Big Ian climbed on behind Skinny . . . putting his greasy hands on her shoulders. He could feel her stiffen beneath his touch.

'Something up?'

His weird lady voice also put her on edge these days.

'Let's just go,' she muttered.

She started the engine and they roared off into the night, wobbling on the bike, looking for all the world like Stan and Ollie on a tiny scooter.

Georges I

The Devil is the glue, he thought. The glue that binds man to God.

For without the Devil there was no evil and with no evil . . . well, how could there possibly be good? But which of them, Georges Clemenceau wondered, *had come first?*

And who, really, had been first to decide which was which?

Georges was already beginning to feel the flesh being persuaded from his bones by rot and gravity, his stomach tense with bloat and ready to split inside him—the very particular sensations of still being alive inside one's own dead body.

He had stood leaning over that peeling, rust-bubbled handrail, looking down at the constant, roaring stream of rush hour traffic on the motorway below, and had simply leaned further and further over until his balance had finally been tipped. By the time he'd realised he was making yet another stupid mistake, it was too late.

He knew he had no right to feel shame. He had done too much and committed too many sins, for want of a better word, to have any rights left to him at all. Besides, to feel shame you had to be human, didn't you? But now he was inevitably to become like them—the ladies and the gentlemen who used to meet at the Architect's apartments all those years ago. Gathering innocently enough in the beginning merely to drink tea and eat scones with jam and cream and to indulge in jolly fancies of imagining what they would do if their lives were eternal. Such fun. They were all dead now, of course.

But they'd stopped being human long before that.

◆

The Architect had found them by attending odd gatherings; spiritualist societies, public post-mortems, lectures at the university halls on documented and provable galvanic episodes—anywhere in fact one might be likely to find persons with a more than passing interest in the afterlife. He had met them individually and in married pairs and had cast them for his 'society' as a director might a play. Discreetly arranged meetings in the public tea houses were parlayed into regular evening gatherings at the Architect's apartments in his brand new and much sought after Charing Cross Mansions.

Soirees were spent on the Ouija or in theorising the finer points of the afterlife and the spirit world. There were small controversies over ectoplasm and much lively discussing of degrees of knocking and such—the debates growing more passionate, the theories more outlandishly outré as other enthusiasts joined the group. The Architect told them all that there was a hunger in the world for something other than cold science of Darwin and the empirically provable facts of their industrial age. They were in an era where, for people such as they at least, the mundane necessities of existence—food, drink, shelter—were taken care of and the true destiny of mankind could begin. They were present at the golden dawn and there was no reason why, he declared, that with the correct application of spiritual will, the base metal that was man's current earthly span of years could not be transformed into the gold of eternal life.

The gathered ladies and gentlemen were thrilled to be in the presence of one such as he. He seemed more than a man—he was a prophet.

Gradually the evening gatherings became overnight stays.

Weekend 'Jollies' turned into week long retreats of contemplation, which began to stretch to months... until finally the ladies and the gentlemen had cut themselves off from any form of significant contact with the outside world. What vestiges of normal and business life that were still necessary to them were dealt with via intermediaries—solicitors, notaries, business partners, concerned in-laws and such. These good-hearted people, often hoping against hope for their clients and relations to recover their senses and come home, would oft times be kept for hours outside the apartment's door in the common hallway, waiting in miserable suspense for a decision on this, or a signature for that. Contact such as it was took place through the letter box; correspondence and speech both, until eventually the Followers of the Certain Path, as they had now named themselves, had entirely relinquished all of their responsibilities and saw no one at all anymore. They were determined to concentrate only on achieving eternity without decease! Life everlasting! Not for them anymore the promissory notes from the Holy Bible about the kingdom of heaven—that ragbag of children's stories and IOUs from God that their contemporaries put such stock in. They wanted surety . . . and if they followed the Architect's instructions to the letter, he assured them, they would have it . . . for the lives of the wretched and the meaningless were to be erased so that the Followers of the Certain Path might live forever.

As often as a victim could be sourced for them—a foundling or an injured worker from the Architect's hospital in the south of the city perhaps, or sometimes an unaccompanied traveller snatched from one of the lonely backrooms of the Architect's coaching house on the great East Road out of town—the ladies and the gentlemen would sacrifice.

And in the apartment's grand hall, beneath its magnificent stained glass dome in the powder blue ceiling high above them, each victim, regardless of age or gender, would first be passed around in turn from Follower to Follower, used by them all to their own particular satisfactions, afterwards to be suspended from the iron hook in the bathroom and bled until death.

But with time and dreadful repetition, the sacrifices somehow ceased to have any end result in the minds of the Followers at all and became merely an end in themselves—simple relief from *the diseased ennui of their uncountable days in the apartment and their growing, dazed horror at what they beheld if ever they dared look into a mirror. They became less certain of the Path they were following. They would wander through the rooms naked; some of them covered in their own filth, coupling with each other in various jaded combinations, performing degrading acts upon and with each other, any notion of actual, genuine pleasure having long been superseded by a basic compulsion to merely act.*

To do is to be.
Nothing means anything.
Everything means something.

The Architect observed their gradual loss of even the most fundamental of human decencies, until the day came when he upped and left them to their own devices, advising them with a cheerful smile to forget about sacrifices, encouraging them instead simply to murder each other.

In the main they had been relieved to do so.

They were long gone now, their scandal successfully buried along with their disease-ravaged, starved and filthy bodies. The dreadful wounds they had received from each other—some evidently postmortem—and the terrible, chilling grins frozen on each and every one of their faces would stay forever in the minds of those unhappy constables who had broken down the doors to discover them. The corpses were soldered into lead caskets and removed at midnight and relatives of the deceased were discreetly advised not to rake over any coals. The Mansions was one of the finest architectural achievements in Glasgow, and the city council would be damned if they were going to allow the depraved deaths of those weak-minded enough to fall into the company of mesmers and spiritualists to cast their degenerate shadows across the second city of the empire.

The place had been quietly cleaned and a dreadful chapter in the city's history had been closed, and kept a complete secret. Those who had, of necessity, known about what had been found there kept their oaths of silence and when they died, the story of the dead at Charing Cross Mansions died with them.

After that, there had been no one resident in the top apartment at all for almost a century . . . until Georges Clemenceau had moved in.

◈

Georges realised now that he had wasted his life away in a futility of expectation . . . that what he had been promised was hollow and meaningless—a putrid con. Suicide, Georges had thought, empowers mankind because it is the only real statement of independence and control a human being has over their own destiny. But he knew that he was theirs now—that death was not the gift he had wished it to be, and that his naïve attempt to escape them had only hastened him into their grasp. He could feel their anger at him for his disrespect.

They would want to teach him a harsh lesson. He knew they would.

5

THE VICTORIA INFIRMARY ON THE SOUTH SIDE OF THE CITY HAD originally opened in 1890 as a standalone building, capable only of handling up to 84 patients; built on the slope of a steep hill overlooking the site of the battle of Langside (the area was actually named Battlefield). Mary Queen of Scots' armies had been resoundingly crushed here by those of her cousin Elizabeth . . . a defeat which had led ultimately to her beheading.

A famous site then, and one visited in the months after the event by certain members of the English Queen's court. Among them was one of the more minor apprentices to Doctor John Dee, Gloriana's chief astrologer. This apprentice had claimed, amongst other things, that the secrets of the spheres could be divined via drinking the correct combination of ram's urine and crystallised fat rendered from the corpse of a sea elephant. His attempts to explain that these ingredients were symbolic—the 'ram' being Aries, the fish being Pisces—had fallen on disinterested ears and the results of his research went unrecorded. The astrologer's apprentice never returned to court, and was thought to have been bled for sausage in the more savage parts of Scotland. He was not missed.

His stay there had begun a tradition, however, of crudely built 'lying in houses'—the earliest form of hospital—dispensing rude medical welfare to the destitute and the diseased, which became a tradition at Battlefield, with new structures regularly being built over the remains of old, until in Victoria's reign, the first real hospital had been constructed there.

The architect of the 'Vicky', as it came to be known had given his services for free in a typically philanthropic display of Victorian largesse towards the eternally poor. If, however, one were to look at records for this building, the name of this architect would be nowhere to be found. Only the name of the firm chosen to oversee its construction can be seen on the plans and blueprints—unusual for those times when responsibility for charitable works was keenly sought and claimed. There were not many other buildings designed and built in that era which were 'unauthored' in this manner—but if one were to start looking, *really* looking, one would be able to find a significant few.

Like the Mansions at Charing Cross, for instance.

The Infirmary had been variously extended and added to over the years, growing in fits and spurts until it now sprawled haphazardly over one entire side of the hill. The original building lost at its centre, black with grime and dirt, was untouched by the sandblasting frenzy which had gripped the 'Smiles Better' Glasgow of the 1980s. It seemed that someone somewhere had thought there was no point in having that lowly part of the hospital cleaned—no one would see it after all, surrounded and towered over as it was by all of the subsequent developments on the site. The old building also has a rare feature on its roof which is—unusually for a structure not a church or cathedral—visible only from the air; a glass-paned dome, around which are carved, like numerals on a clock face, the twelve signs of the Zodiac.

Now, a new Victoria Infirmary had been built across the road from the old one and the complex of original hillside buildings was in a state of partial shutdown (being closed and abandoned section by section as facilities were moved to the new place), existing as a hybrid of the derelict and the functional, with warrens of darkened corridors existing alongside the still working wards.

At one of the now unused side entrances to the old Infirmary complex, a rotund woman with perfectly smooth, pale skin hurriedly stamped out her cigarette as Grace helped Maryam from their cab. The woman went to Maryam and curtsied before her, taking a gloved hand and kissing it. Maryam pulled away.

'Get up Lizzy, you big oaf. I haven't got all night.'

The rotund woman, clearly nervous in front of Maryam, nodded and smiled tremulously before unlocking the door leading them all to the dark corridor inside. The cab driver, his meter left running as instructed, had been getting more and more weirded out as he'd watched.

What the fuck was that meant to be all about?

❖

Maryam and Grace were led into the quiet ward by Lizzy. She was head supervisor and had already told the Kenyan night staff girls to go get themselves some coffees, that she'd look after their ward for half an hour so's they could have a break, phone their boyfriends or home or whatever. She'd thought of her African girls, she'd said, what with them being so far from their families and all. As a further inducement, she'd also left a box of doughnuts in the staffroom and told them they could help themselves.

Nurse Ojomo had raised an eyebrow, because if Lizzy had been thinking of them benignly at all, it would have been for the first time. But she hadn't objected—it would be late afternoon back home and she'd like to speak to her mother. She wasn't going to be touching any doughnuts though—she thought Lizzy was unusual and didn't really trust her. Besides, just because the thought of a box of doughnuts sent Lizzy into spasms of delight, didn't mean it did the same for everyone. Nurse Ojomo thought it typical of the woman that she would presume her likes or dislikes to be universal.

Also, she'd always thought that Lizzy's skin looked funny—*too* clean, if such a thing was possible; like the look a vagrant had when they'd been taken in and scrubbed up and sent back out into the world again. She didn't like standing too close to her, but thanked her for her generosity and told her they'd be back in twenty minutes.

Lizzy knew this was a big risk—a job loss type of risk, in fact—but she would have done almost anything for Maryam. She had been thrilled to bits when her phone had rung and Grace had asked her about the admissions from that day's monster traffic accident. Normally Lizzy only saw Maryam at the salon sessions, and even then very briefly with as few words as possible spoken. She had asked why they were showing such interest, but had been told to mind her own business. No big deal; she could swallow Maryam's rudeness. The woman was her guarantee of a normal life and Lizzy was determined to stay on her good side.

Maryam and Grace now stood on either side of Joe's bed, looking down at him. He was certainly one very handsome young man and, although unconscious, Maryam thought she could see in the line of his mouth a latent sliver of good humour—kind of like he might break into a smile at any second. He looked confident, even in his sleep, and she couldn't help smiling back at him. She wondered what he sounded like. She looked over at Grace . . . who stood there staring down with her mouth wide open, and all her simple, straightforward emotions on display like toys in a shop window. Maryam cleared her throat.

'Grace . . .'

Grace looked up at her sister as if woken from a dream, eyes like saucers, whispering reverently in the presence of a god.

'He's beautiful, Maryam. Look at him—he's *beautiful*.'

Lizzy stood by looking at Maryam, barely able to contain her own excitement. This was going to be a really big job. *Really* big—and she was going to get to see it! The patient had been brought in looking like a half squeezed tube of tomato puree and the surgical team were going to have to operate before morning. They hadn't reckoned on Maryam though, Lizzy thought, just about ready to burst. Maryam had needed a favour from *her*—and now Maryam would *owe* her! This could be a big step towards erasing the uncertainty of these stupidly irregular salons. If she were to become 'friends' with Maryam—sharing this experience could only bring them closer, she thought—then she would be able to pop up and see her when she needed to, without the agonies of waiting for the phone to ring!

Maryam could see the strange expression on Lizzy's face and frowned. This fat oaf had better not be lying to her.

'You told Grace that this man was not going to die. Now tell *me*. Is this man going to die, Lizzy?'

Lizzy was startled speechless by Maryam's frosty tone.

'*Well?*'

'No . . .'

Maryam looked at her long and hard. She hated that her livelihood depended on creatures such as this—human leeches who cared not at all that they were draining the life from her, as long as their own stupid, petty troubles were taken care of. They had helped make her what she was, and she despised all of them.

'I'm going to ask you just one more time. This is your last chance,' she said. 'Are they expecting him to make some sort of recovery from these injuries or are they waiting for him to expire? Tell me the truth.'

'I promise you, Maryam, faithfully and truly—I promise. He isn't expected to die, only to lose his legs.'

Grace was pulling at Maryam's sleeve, breathless and excited.

'Hurry *up*.'

Maryam pulled herself together. Stay calm—no good upsetting yourself, she thought. This young man before her (and Grace was right, he was beautiful); he hadn't asked for this and Grace *was* technically correct . . . this *was* kind of her fault. If only she hadn't helped Papa.

'Go away now Lizzy and fetch me a wheelchair.'

'But . . .'

'And be swift! I don't believe I'll have much time.'

Lizzy reluctantly waddled off, clearly disappointed at being sent away. Good, thought Maryam. The woman was a ghastly individual and if she'd had any choice in the matter, she would never see her again.

Grace, oblivious to anything else but the handsome face in front of her, touched the bridge of Joe's nose with her fingertips. Maryam could see what she had found. The perfect face had a flaw—an old injury, but one which had not quite healed perfectly.

'He's had a rokem nose, Maryam,' she whispered, almost in awe.

'Broken, Grace. It's broken.'

But Grace wasn't listening and babbled excitedly.

'Will you fix that, too? Because if he diddem't have a . . . if he diddem't have it . . . his face would be just *perfect*.'

Maryam looked at her sister's soft hands. *They* were perfect, unlike her own wrinkled and leaking ones. The comparison made her feel sad. She despised being sad.

'Shut up Grace and leave him alone. He is not a toy.'

◆

Joe was hearing female voices—reverbing madly like he had his very own Phil Spector production going on in his brain. An effort with his eyelids, a crack of light . . . and then he saw them.

'*He's awake, Maryam. He cam see us*! *He looks like a fillem star. Do you thimk he's a fillem star? Do you thimk he was visiting to make a fillem before Papa fell om his car?*'

He focused—on one side of him was the speaker; a gabbling girl who looked like the prettiest, healthiest cheerleader he'd ever seen in his entire life, rosy-cheeked and smelling absolutely wonderful. Across from her was someone whose closest match in an ID parade would be Bette Davis after her stroke.

His eyes moved back to the cheerleader as fast as he could move them. Ms. Davis, however, seemed to have different ideas. She put her gloved hands on either side of his head and turned him back to look at her before placing her palms directly over his face, covering it entirely. He didn't like it. He mumbled through her fingers at her.

'Please don't do that ma'am . . .'

Except it came out as: '*Psshashh dummmn dunnn m'naam . . .*'

It didn't have the desired effect. Shit. He'd have to try again, and this time he'd concentrate harder on what the fuck he should be saying.

'Please stop,' he said, 'your hands . . . they smell bad. I mean, really bad.'

'*He's Americam, Maryam!*'

The gloved hands, which he could now feel were trembling, were also kind of warmly damp, like they were exuding . . . something. The palms pressed down hard on the middle of his face. There was an internal 'crunch' and he felt like his nose had just been hit by a house brick. He cried out, muffled beneath the gloves.

The cheerleader seemed unable to contain her excitement.

'Maybe he *is* a star!'

Joe was starting to feel smothered now, a hateful sensation. There was a ringing in his ears, growing louder and louder and then suddenly a huge roar—like a train going through a tunnel.

'What—the—*fuuuuuck*!!!?'

Then the deafening noises suddenly stopped, and Joe's pain left him as swiftly as it had appeared, leaving a small burst of warmth where it had been. In the echo memory of the noise, he heard an unfamiliar voice—female, but deep and distant.

'Do you thimk his thimg is big?'

Startled, Maryam stared at her sister.

'Grace! Where on earth did *that* come from?'

Grace, momentarily lost for words, stared back. Her voice had come out different, somehow ... but when she spoke again, she once more sounded like she normally did when she was excited—like a kid on Christmas morning.

'Just hurry *up*, Maryam!'

'We'll discuss this at home.'

Maryam moved down to Joe's feet. She didn't like how Grace was starting to behave and could see that she would have to exert some control.

'Go and hurry Lizzy along with that wheelchair. This will take a lot out of me and I'll need help to get out of here when I'm done.'

Grace did not move. Maryam glared at her.

'Are you deaf? *Now*, stupid. Immediately.'

'... but I always watch you do it, Maryam.'

'Yes, but normally when I 'do it' we're in the privacy of our home and holding a salon, not trying to get it 'done' as quickly as possible before someone catches us! Now get going.'

'No, Maryam, I wamt to see you do it. Dom't worry—if you faimt I will catch you and I will hold you umtil the chair gets here for you. I wamt to see him get better.'

Maryam's fury came out in the icy, controlled tone that usually terrified her sister ...

'Do not disobey me Grace.'

. . . but not this time. Grace stood her ground defiantly.

'I dom't care if you hit me . . . I wamt to see him get better.' She took a deep breath. 'I . . . love him, Maryam.'

Maryam stared at her in disbelief.

'You . . . *what*? What is *wrong* with you?'

'I love him and I wamt to see him get *better* . . .'

'Shut up you simpleton! You don't even know who he *is*! I will make your life complete hell for this Grace, I promise you.'

'I dom't care, Maryam. I love him and I wamt to see him get better. He spoke to *me*! He called to *me*! He shouted im *my* head for *my* help! *Me*!'

'Don't be an idiot!' Maryam snapped. 'He didn't shout for you—he doesn't *know* you! He simply 'shouted', or whatever, in his pain and you heard—there's a difference!'

'Everythimg meams somethimg!'

'*Grace*! Stop saying that! You are a liability! This is not a film on the television. You don't love him—now or at any time!'

'You better do it *right away* Maryam before the murses get back. *I wamt to see him get better. I love him!*'

Time seemed to stand still for Maryam for a few moments. She had never seen Grace like this before—never. She was mentally and emotionally stunted, Maryam knew—a grown woman who acted like a child, and although sometimes Maryam was irritated beyond human capacity for patience by her childishness, she was used to it. Perhaps now, though, Grace was finally reaching her own, delayed version of adolescence? Perhaps these were going to become her rebellious years? Perhaps she would start smoking cigarettes and stealing drink? Staying out late and bringing home boyfriends?

And at the thought of this, Maryam found herself feeling happy for Grace.

She stopped herself, annoyed at having let her imagination run away with the fairies. Thinking such things implied that Grace was capable of developmental progress. It was ridiculous. Grace had done all the growing and developing that she was going to. She wasn't a child *or* an adolescent—she was a grown woman and an idiot. She lived in a world of television soap operas and afternoon weepies and Maryam suddenly felt more than willing to abandon her here—in a hospital ward in a strange part of the city with a lot of explaining to do. No money to get home, no brains, and no grip on real life, she'd drown in her own tears. Better all round for Maryam to just get out and return home. There'd be less hassle for her, less strain, and less risk of discovery. In fact why the hell was she here in the first place? None of this made the slightest sense! What on earth had possessed her to potentially expose herself like this? For the sake of someone she didn't even know and who wasn't even going to pay the fee for her considerable troubles? She must have gone mad.

But *something* was stopping her from leaving.

She looked down at the young man's face . . . and again simply felt herself *wanting* to do this thing for him. It wasn't his fault he was here, his poor body in this terrible state. But this was no salon day—no case of eczema or arthritic hips. Doing this for him would take a lot out of her for sure, maybe too much for comfort, but if she was quick—if she acted *now*—then she would at least be able to get away without being discovered. Maryam had lost her doubts. She was going to help him.

She hadn't noticed how intently Grace had been staring at her as her mind had ricocheted around the situation.

Maryam looked up at her sister, still standing there, still refusing to budge—the threat of some kind of full blown infant's tantrum hanging in the air between them. She suspected that it would take dynamite to shift her and she determined to let Grace think she'd had her little victory—what did it matter? She could make her life as miserable as she liked once they were back home and safe again.

'I am going to do this Grace, and I'm going to start now because we don't have much time . . .'

Grace merely stared her out, defiant.

'. . . but believe me I will make you suffer for this later, I promise you.'

'If you like, Maryam'

Maryam pulled the sheet away from Joe and both of the women gasped at the sight of his ragged, lacerated body. Aside from the horror of his legs, huge areas of skin on his torso had been torn away from him in strips. There were deep cuts and gouges everywhere. Maryam felt her eyes begin to tear.

'I'll fix everything for you,' she said quietly to him. 'Everything.'

◆

Joe's feeling of sea sickness had dissipated and he managed to lift his head up a little to see that the old woman was now standing at the bottom of his bed, her hands placed on his ankles. Oh shit, he thought, oh fuck, what the hell was she going to do to him now? Her gloved fingers began to manipulate his toes and he started feeling waves of increasing pain as she pulled and tweaked and began running her hands slowly up the length of his legs. The horrible noises started up again, this time even louder, right inside his head.

'... hey ... whoa ... stop that ... stop; for God's sake ... please ... no more ... ohhh Jeeee-suuuus ...'

This was worse than the accident. The room was spinning, going alternately dark and bright and he could feel sharp, jagged ... *stuff* on the insides of his legs; serrated things moving around. It was like hundreds of broken coral fragments, cutting their way out of his flesh ... no, not out of it—*through* it, like they were *wriggling* inside him. The tendons on his arms stood out like cables as he gripped the sides of the bed, his back arching and his teeth gritted.

'Oh God, please ... why are you *doing this*?'

Grace brought her face very close to his, so close he could smell the soap on her skin, the sweetness of her breath, the tip of her button nose almost touching his. Her eyes shone, clear and blue and she was so beautiful that it actually caused him an ache to look at her. She was a high school sweetheart, the tiniest breath of cool wind on a sweltering day, the girl you glimpsed on the street or the bus or in the coffee shop and who you fell in love with and who you never, ever saw again—

'We'm very sorry ...' she whispered softly, her breath gentle on his skin, '... it was our Papa's fault. Maryam made him well. We're makimmg it up to you ...'

—she was an oasis to him, making the pain briefly bearable.

'Shut up Grace! This is hard enough as it is without you gibbering!'

The girl was suddenly gone and the pain was back. In heaps. It was travelling up his legs as the old woman ran her hands along them, making them feel like they were being fed into a grinding, chomping garbage disposal inch by agonising inch. He wondered if it were possible to throw up and faint at the same time.

'Oh in the name of Christ please *no more*!' he gasped, now barely able to pull breath into his lungs. Maryam carried on regardless, ignoring Joe's weeping, her own breathing ragged with effort.

'It's nearly done!' she gasped '... so ... stop ... crying ... like ... a *baby*!'

She stopped when she reached the tops of his legs, her fingers gripping his thighs. She could feel the shards of bone swimming around under his skin—like shoals of fish—meeting, re-forming and knitting together. She was looking directly into his dark eyes and panting, desperate to catch her breath and she could feel that her trembling had changed into a hard uncontrollable shaking and knew she had passed the limits of her strength. She collapsed upon him, falling on his chest, the remains of everything she had left in her healing the deep cuts on his torso, and she had the same strange, rush feeling she got whenever she did this. But it had somehow intensified this time round—as if her bloodstream was being turbocharged in quick bursts—she felt a huge pleasurable buzz ... and she started to cry.

◆

Through his blurred watery vision, Joe saw the old woman's face as close to his as the cheerleader's had been, and that from behind her ridiculous sunglasses, rivulets of blood were running down her cheeks.

Gasping for breath, she remembered when being exhausted used to feel this good. When she had been at school and she'd been training for the cross-country events. She had loved it. She would run herself into near collapse and had once stopped and lain down in a cold stream, letting the freezing water run over her, feeling more alive than she'd ever felt in her life before . . . the dizziness passed and she realised that she was still embracing this handsome young man, her fingers gripping his broad shoulders.

She found herself reluctant to move away.

Even though he was still in agonising pain, Joe felt like he wanted to say something to her . . . he felt sorry for her and wanted to tell her . . . he didn't know what. Anything comforting. Then a new sensation engulfed him. It was like a warm shaft of sunlight bursting through clouds and onto his legs. He closed his eyes . . . and could have sworn that he felt actual sunlight hitting him . . . that he could *see* its brightness through his closed eyelids and feel its warmth on his face . . . it was wonderful and . . .

. . . he was standing beneath the tree and a girl, the prettiest girl he had ever seen in his entire life, had just fallen down from it and straight into his arms, wham bam. She was laughing . . . she was lucky he'd been there, and he'd been lucky to catch her . . .

The sound of Maryam dropping in a faint to the floor and Grace's unsuccessful attempt to break her fall sounded very far away.

6

ARTHUR BEWLAY WAS PROUD OF THAT ELEMENT OF HIS GANG who'd been born differently from the regular herd and he knew that he'd made a wise choice in promoting their interests more favourably over others. His brother's physical disadvantages had been the spur for conceiving this way of working and Arthur knew how Wee Tommy's life would have been so much the better had the world been a more understanding place. His rule was: anyone who wanted a chance, no matter what they looked (or sounded) like, got one. If they fucked up, of course, then the consequences would be the same as for anyone else—but at least they'd been given an even playing field.

After all, who else was going to give these people a leg up, as it were?

And besides, apart from bringing its own advantages in the sphere of work (who would really suspect a nice, friendly, physically disadvantaged person to be on the rob, or capable of extreme violence or dealing?) it also brought loyalty. And Arthur valued loyalty above anything else. He knew that Big Ian, for example, would have no hesitation whatsoever in risking his life for him were it to be necessary.

Arthur opened the sitting room door onto the corridor and stepped out. He had been restless since he'd sent the big man on his mission and wouldn't sleep well until he knew for sure that McGill had been taken care of. There was no way Arthur was going to spend his last days on earth in court, in custody or incognito somewhere, hiding from the cops like some kind of fucking criminal. The reverend had to go.

He assured himself again that it wasn't a matter of vanity—that it wasn't what McGill had actually said that had bothered him (he prided himself on never having been vain)—it was a matter of *respect*. Even now, in the twilight of his time here on earth he couldn't risk letting one person's *dis*respect mutate into general dis*regard*. Lessons had to be taught and, more to the point, be seen to be taught. And it wasn't only for his sake, he had his people to think of. Other gangs were already eyeing up his field of operations and eager to take over all his stuff when he expired. Things were probably getting quite bad out there for them as it was, without it being put about that he was weak enough to be muscled out prematurely.

The irony was that he didn't actually mind having the piss taken out of him, especially if it was funny. He'd heard (or, rather, had heard *of*) worse comments than McGill's about his ravaged face from his own people, and those involved in the merriness had only received a stern ticking off from him when he could easily have been much more severe with them. (The individuals concerned had been fractured, rather than broken, as it were.)

The thing was, Arthur knew that good, honest slaggings were DNA deep in the culture of this fine city, and he appreciated that. It was the kind of thing that kept your feet firmly on the ground and there was also a certain honour in being able to take—with a smile—the honest mockery of ones help mates in the workplace. It meant you were the type of person who could face your enemies and not go to pieces—the bigger man, or bigger than they were. If he'd ever passed anything worthy on to Tommy when he'd been alive, it was surely that.

'You have to be the bigger man, Tom.' He'd said without irony, sitting on the corner of his brother's child-sized bed. 'Take your punishment if it's deserved; there's *honour* there, and you need to have honour. Without honour man is just a beast that can walk on two legs.'

But, Arthur knew there was no honour *whatsoever* in a person laughing up their sleeve at someone they'd just promised to help—no honour in that at *all*. Reverend Joe would be learning that lesson right now.

As he stepped forward into the hallway, the creak of a floorboard under his foot accentuated the silence inside the building. Apart from the constant hum of the fridges, there was no noise at all coming from the empty pub below. All activity had ceased at least twenty minutes ago. The doors had been closed and all the broken noses, gin blossoms and underage pool players had gone their own ways.

It was still an age before official chucking out time, but Arthur had felt the urge come upon him again to converse with Tommy and he had shouted down the staircase and into the pub, telling the staff to clear the place. They were good boys and girls behind the bar and Arthur often wished he could bear to spend more time downstairs with their youth and health. He rather enjoyed watching them strain to not be anything other than delighted in the company of his face.

He reached along the wall and switched the lights off, abruptly plunging the whole place into total darkness. That was much better. He began feeling his way down the corridor towards Tommy's old bedroom, running his fingertips along the painted woodchip wall like he used to when they were children, when the orange glow from the streetlamps outside would illuminate the wallpaper in oblong patches, the shape of the light warped by the imperfections in the cheap glazing. Except there wasn't any orange glow from outside nowadays, and no glazing either, for that matter.

Not since he'd had every window in the place bricked up.

He was amazed, really, that people still bothered coming to the Pretty Blue Fox for a drink at all, given that not one pinpoint of daylight had been allowed into it for . . . well, quite some time now. But, as publicans and brewers the world over knew, wherever there was a bar, there would be drinkers crowding into it – *always*, even if it were in Hell.

Arthur and his brother had been brought up here, in this apartment above the pub. He had built his empire from here and, unless a miracle happened (like the miracle Reverend Joe had promised him? Hah!) he would soon die here.

He stopped at his brother's bedroom door, bringing a trembling hand to its central cruciform panel and stretching out his fingers, straining to feel the words 'Tommy's Room' carved into the wood. He had engraved this for his beloved brother on the occasion of Tommy's twelfth birthday. He'd used a Stanley knife and had cut through the paint and wood by flickering candlelight, during the dark days of the three-day week and the power cuts of the early seventies, when the only thing electrical that worked in peoples' houses was the battery-powered transistor radio. The BBC had still broadcast through the cuts, and he and his brother used to listen to the radio avidly in Tommy's room ('thrilled *stupit*', as Tommy would say) if ever Bowie or Bolan came on.

Arthur now found that he couldn't bear to have any 'proper' lights on whenever he went to Tommy's room. He liked the darkness. It gave him comfort and made him feel secure—just like when he'd been sharing those good times in the dark with Tommy.

From a young age Arthur had hung around downstairs in the bar whilst his beloved brother had remained up here, incarcerated in this tiny box room. Arthur had always felt guilty about the amount of freedom he'd had compared with poor Tommy, and about his natural intelligence—which he had been careful to underplay in the early days of his career. (He hadn't wanted to be alienating potential allies with his erudition and was more than capable of lowering his IQ and raising the severity of his accent, depending on whose company he was in.)

Whilst he'd still attended school, Arthur's IQ had registered off the scale and he knew, just *knew*, that if only Tommy had been given a chance to even *go* to school, he would have been the same. But it was not to be; Da was determined never to let the wee man out.

So Arthur had been a solo operator down among the adults in the pub, getting to know the dealers and their customers, gleaning the economics of his future trade from these fucking jerks as they had come and gone—and all under Da's nose. Even if Da had realised what was going on, Arthur wasn't sure there would have been a whole lot he could have done about it. He was that drunk most of the time, he hadn't a fucking clue that his pub was the main marketplace for drugs in the whole area. Vitamin deficient, side-breezered hard men with George Best haircuts, tank tops and Zapata moustaches were the dealers of that era, every one of them a complete and total anus.

Even in Da's last days, when Arthur had—at fifteen years of age—taken over the running of the pub and the plain facts of the matter were undeniable—groups of people were actually taking taxis from town to come and score before returning to their Friday night out. Da didn't seem aware of what was going on around him at all. He would wander about drink sodden and apologising to Arthur for what he had done, in the general way that guilty drunks apologise for everything and nothing, the nub of what they're really guilty about hidden deep and undiscoverable. Arthur didn't really care—he was just waiting for Da to peg out so he could really spread his wings.

And of course, once Da was gone there was no one to stop Tommy getting out anymore. The day that Da had haemorrhaged to death on the toilet, his every orifice expelling his life's blood as his body finally gave up on him, Arthur had released his brother, and he'd done it even before the withered remains of his father had been taken away.

Arthur had cried on and off through most of that afternoon—because Tommy was out and about at last and could now lead an actual life and make friends! Tommy's friends, of course, had had to be made for him by Arthur, but that wasn't a chore. In those days of good health, there were plenty who wanted to stay on Arthur's good side. Plenty. Poor Tommy, of course hadn't had any chance to develop any social skills during his years upstairs and occasional social . . . errors had been made—mainly involving girls. But that was alright too. Arthur could get hold of plenty of girls.

As far as the business was concerned, Arthur had seen the job grow from mainly small time dope, acid and speed in the seventies, exploding into smack in the eighties and then, via the gradual normalcy of coke use in everyday people's lives, settling into the kind of regular, almost legitimately accountable (i.e. by an accountant) white powder trade of the here and now. Of course there were other, new and synthetic, powders and physicks available these days, but they were invariably light on profit margin and Arthur had decided that until the day methamphetamine managed to take a real hold, he would stick to coke.

He'd also traded porn from the prehistoric era of dog-eared mags and super 8 reels through the boom years of video cassettes and into DVD, although there wasn't much profit in that for him these days. Not with sex flicks on the internet and blank discs costing eight pence each and the top shelves in newsagents being full of the kind of stuff he would have been put away for only a short number of years previously... that, and ordinary punters making and sending each other live rape movies (for *free*, for Christ's sake!) on each other's phones. Besides, the porn had been more Tommy's thing.

Arthur took the key from the chain round his neck and opened the bedroom door, hesitating for a few moments before going in, always respectful of his brother's privacy.

'Tommy?'

Silence.

'You awake?'

Arthur could feel the breath from the hole in his face bouncing back at him from the door. It felt cold to him, as if he was already dead and his lungs were somehow being made against nature to carry on functioning anyway. He was glad he couldn't smell it.

'Tommy?' he whispered, hoarsely.

A fox screamed a few streets away.

'Wake up Tommy. Can I sit and chat for a wee while?'

Not a peep, but Arthur wasn't discouraged. Tommy *was* dead, after all.

'Please Tommy. I wouldn't disturb you if I wasn't feeling so down.'

Then, there was a soft rustle from inside the room, like a light breeze over dried autumn leaves. Arthur, turning the key, smiled to himself, and slipped in closing the door behind him with a gentle 'snick'.

◆

Wee Tommy's reappearance in Arthur's life had been a beautiful miracle. He had awoken early one morning, the sunshine cloying hot and brown as it had fought its way through the heavy curtains of the sitting room. He'd taken a swig of the vile painkiller from his flask and was prepping his atomiser to spray antiseptic into the cavity in his face, noting that his bathrobe was hanging embarrassingly huge on him. He knew the 'Big Arthur' who had attended his brother's funeral was gone forever, and had been replaced by this wretched old man he had to look at every fucking morning in the mirror.

He was straining hard to prevent thoughts of just ending it all fight their way up from his subconscious when there had been the noise from outside—a very individual noise. Arthur was so used to hearing, variously, the huge plastic sacks of well-fired rolls being tied to the handles of the pub doors, the palettes of meat for Wok My World being smacked down across the way at the Parade, the shouting of the fish people and the potato men further down at the chippy, shrink-wrapped crates of booze being slid along greasy cobbles and down the chute into the cellar—in fact any and every early morning delivery sound you could ever conceive of, Arthur had heard it at some time outside this pub since his childhood. But *this* sound? It wasn't spectacular, it wasn't loud—it was just... unusual enough for him to notice. Two dull thuds. Something hitting wood, and then landing on the ground.

Door to paving stones? Thu-*thud*.

And a very slight crackle.

He listened intently, and although there was no repeat of the sound, he found it playing over and over in his head. What *was* it?

(Thu-thud... crackle)

It gave Arthur a feeling.

(Thu-thud... crackle)

It could have been anything, of course, but Arthur somehow felt it was very important that he know *exactly* what it was.

(Thu-thud... crackle)

The crackle sounded like dried leaves being stepped on, but it wasn't autumn. Was it? Had he lost all sense of time in his illness?

He'd made his way down the stairs and shuffled across the empty bar to unlock the front doors. There was no need to switch off burglar alarms because there weren't any. The simple fact of this being Arthur Bewlay's pub and domicile was deterrent enough for any young badhats from the surrounding scheme if they'd ever thought of breaking in.

(*Thu-thud . . . crackle*)

What was it about that bloody noise that drew him? Why was it getting so under his skin?

He undid the bolts and swung the doors open.

It's a strange sensation feeling the warmth of sunlight on a part of one's body never meant to feel such things. Arthur tended to stay away from daylight as much as possible because of that. He didn't like it—he had enough to contend with and didn't need a new carcinoma added to the tumours he already had. Exposing one's skin to direct sunlight was bad enough for you, so how much worse would it be to let it shine on the inside of your head? It didn't come any more exposed than that. He instinctively shielded the hole in the centre of his face with his hand and he looked down.

There at his feet, through the open top of a very old Co-op carrier bag, he could see short, black matted hair, glistening with tiny ice crystals. He knelt and gently rolled the sides of the bag down from around the spherical object inside, peeling the plastic away with a crackle of ice. He knew immediately that it was Tommy's head. Had to be.

How many other people did he know who'd been buried without one?

His brother's face looked as if it had collapsed in on itself, a bit like how newborn—*brand* newborn, no more than minutes old-babies looked, their faces still all squinched up from having been in the womb for all that time. Babies' faces, of course, had elasticity and would sooner or later form into more pleasing, recognisably facial shapes. Tommy's wouldn't. The skin had a greenish hue, apart from around the eyes, which were purply and puffed like a boxer's after a rough bout. Icicles hung from his brows and nostrils.

What was all this about? Had Tommy's head been in someone's freezer all this time? Over a year now his brother had been dead and that was a hell of a long time to be dark and cold. Tears welled up in Arthur's eyes. Tommy hated the cold. Arthur resolved there and then to never let his brother be cold again.

He pulled the bag back up over Tommy's squashed up, frozen, green and purple face and lifted it from the ground, hugging it to his chest. Whoever had killed Tommy had obviously grown weary of looking after his head and had simply decided to return it. Maybe the guy's missus was sick and tired of having it in the freezer and needed to make more room for the lamb chops. It was that or something like it, thought Arthur, because if it was some kind of a message or a warning to him, it was a bit fucking late.

It could have been a lone, random psycho nut job who'd gotten Tommy in the wrong place at the wrong time and who now had lone, random psycho nut job weirdy reasons of their own for returning the head.

Arthur found to his surprise—and it probably had something to do with being so close to death now himself—that he actually didn't give a fuck any more about the who, where or why. He had his brother back! *That* was what mattered! He felt insanely, gloriously happy and hugged the head to his chest even more tightly, unable to smell the defrosting beginnings of decay starting to puff upwards invisibly from the bag. Even if he could have, he wouldn't have minded. He was crying as he whispered to his brother.

'Welcome home, Tommy. Welcome home. No one will ever hurt you ever again. Never.'

He stepped back into his pub, closing the door behind him and by the end of that week; every single window had been bricked over. Arthur had made the pub the dark sanctuary he felt he and his brother required.

7

JOE WASN'T SURE IF HE WAS AWAKE OR ASLEEP—HE FELT . . . peculiar. His body was tingling all over and there was a painful pressure somewhere between his thighs. Without a second thought he sat up straight and swung his legs from the bed. The wires and suckers popped from his body and his penis yanked about unpleasantly of its own volition. Joe yelped in surprise and pain and he looked down to see an opaque plastic tube sticking out from the top of his dick.
  Penis.
  Catheter.
  Hurt.
  Shit shit shit shit shit.
  Slowly and oh so carefully, he gently tugged at the tube—*easy now, easy easy* . . . fucking hell, didn't they use *any* kind of lubricant with these goddam things? It felt like he was pulling an open cocktail umbrella out of there.
  Dammit!
  He held his breath as he worked on getting it out of his body, frowning in concentration, keeping his hands as steady as was humanly possible, eventually extracting the slim tube free with a (*nearlythere*) . . . very . . . (*that'sit,justcoming*) . . . small . . . (*come on come on come on*) . . . 'pop'.
  !!!!!!!!!!!!!!
  Fuck! Shit! . . . it felt like he'd just turned his dick inside out! Recovering from the highly unpleasant sensation, he now realised

something else. His feet had made contact with the floor. He looked down. He'd been so busy having fun playing with himself, he hadn't noticed that his legs were perfectly fine.

Perfectly. Fine.

He could actually *see* the muscles under his skin—healthy and robust, like they'd been when he was a teenager. He could wiggle his toes. What the hell was going on here?

Had all of that stuff actually just happened? Where were the two weird chicks? Had he just been miracled or something? Not that he was unhappy about it, but it was a lot to take in.

Miracled.

If it wasn't actually a word, it should be. He could maybe use it in the act. He felt woozy again and giggled. He'd been doing a fair bit of that recently and he knew (deeply buried in some area of struggling rationality inside him) that he still wasn't quite right yet, head-wise. Obviously. Never mind, he—of all things, now that the goddam catheter had been yanked out of him—needed to take a leak. However, he supposed that a simple project like that would keep him busy and give him some direction. Need to take a leak, need to take a leak, need to take . . . tum te tum . . .

He stood up and immediately felt nauseous again and dizzy. He grabbed the drip stand, waiting for the feeling to pass, his head clearing momentarily as it did. That was good—a clear head. He needed a clear head. He needed to steer his brain in a more constructive direction than just going to the goddam toilet. What the hell was he doing? He had to get a grip . . . had to think . . . there was something important happening or going to happen. *Think*. Facts.

He was very weak; he knew that. The state his legs had been in, they must have been going to operate on him so he'd very likely not had anything in his stomach for at least a day. Ok, that would explain a lot of the dizziness. Also, he'd been shot full of morphine pretty much since he'd been scraped off the road. Those two things, plus whatever the hell that woman may have done to him . . . well it was no wonder that he felt pretty Kevin.

He meant spacey.

He got the giggles again.

Well feeling Kevin Spacey or not, life went on and he still needed a piss. He stood gently away from the bed, his nausea having passed, and looked round for a toilet. Peeing through his rawed out urethra was very probably going to burn hellaciously, but it had to beat hands down feeling like there was a rusty screwdriver stuck down his cock.

He concentrated on putting one foot in front of the other . . . and was pleasantly surprised to discover that not much effort was required and found himself actively enjoying the simple sensation of walking. The terror he'd recently had of moving his legs in any way whatsoever had given way to a childish joy at every little movement they made. Whee.

He walked unsteadily out of the glass walled room—not noticing that there were no nurses at the station at the far end of the ward—his backless, green, papery gown swishing slightly at each step. He began searching the adjoining corridor for a bathroom, putting aside that not so long ago (how long ago? He couldn't quite remember) he'd wanted to—*needed* to—think about something . . .

Something very important.

❖

Big Ian had left Skinny outside by the pizza bike and was now pulling on his special gloves as he strode into the lift. He liked these—they'd been Skinny's idea when she'd still been friends with him. She'd stuffed both the thumbs with wads of cotton wool wrapped round the broken halves of an ice lolly stick and the appearance and feeling they gave of a fifth digit on each of his hands always made him feel good. That, and the idea that someone had cared enough to bother making the effort for him. Recently though, she hadn't been talking to him so much—he had no idea why—and that made him sad. He didn't really want to ask her about it though, just in case she told him something he didn't want to hear. Putting the gloves on made him happy again, like he had her back as a friend. He missed her friendship a lot.

Before getting into the lift, he'd passed a strikingly pretty young girl and a big, fat woman who were pushing an old biddy in a wheelchair out of the hospital. He'd felt like telling them they were travelling in the wrong direction. By the look of her, the old one (splayed across the wheelchair, head lolling to one side) should've been going *in* to the hospital. He hadn't said anything though, not wanting to attract too much attention to himself. He knew his voice would make them stare. But he did think that a hospital shouldn't be letting someone in that state out of its doors—there was blood smeared over the old woman's cheeks from behind her white framed sunglasses and she looked to him like she'd just had a stroke.

He'd suddenly realized that he'd been gazing—hypnotised—at the space where these women had just been, even though they'd already left the building. He felt odd...but snapped out of it. There was stuff to do.

He paused in the empty corridor and pulled out the palm-sized piece of wood from the box in his jacket pocket, being very careful not to let the small shards of razor blade that had been embedded into one side cut him. This had actually been Arthur's invention, but he had charged Big Ian with its construction. Arthur had always tried to encourage him to learn to do more with his hands, and Big Ian had spent an entire Christmas Day carefully breaking a whole, brand new packet of razor blades into pieces, and embedding the shards into the soft wood with tweezers and superglue. Not easy for someone with no thumbs, but worth it in the end.

It had been like having a hobby and the making of it had given him a pleasant feeling of well-being—much better than jigsaw puzzles and less depressing than porn. Arthur had christened the finished item the 'rough sponge' and these days the boss especially enjoyed patting stray dogs with it. Their jaws had to be well taped together first though.

Big Ian slid the thick elastic attached to the back of the piece of wood over his gloved right hand, where it now looked like a deadly horse brush. He'd have to wad up a spare sheet or something and stick it onto McGill's crotch when he'd finished giving him his rub down, so the blood wouldn't be seen too soon. He'd also have to cover McGill's mouth well with the black tape he'd brought. There'd be a fair bit of screaming being done, he expected.

❖

Grace and the driver were loading Maryam into the back of the cab. Lizzy was near hysteria.

'Will she be alright?' she babbled. 'Will she be alright? Her eyes . . .'

'You get back upstairs case he wakems,' Grace replied. 'He might have a pamic. You hold his hamd—tell him he's goimg somewhere good with me am' Maryam. I'll be back up to help you carry him.'

'But . . . does *Maryam* want me to do that?'

'. . . Yes.'

'Are you sure, dear?'

Grace turned on her.

'Shut up Lizzy! I dom't care if Maryam doesm't wamt you to do it! *I* wamt you to do it!'

Lizzy blinked dumbly in surprise. She had never seen Grace being so forceful before. In fact, she had no idea that the girl possessed any sort of personality at all. She found herself smiling, as if at a child, and spoke gently, but firmly, to her.

'Grace, dear, I think you're maybe getting a little above yourself . . .'

Grace actually *hissed*, making her draw back a little.

'If you amen't goimg to do it, I will make sure that you dom't get past our door whem we have a salon!'

Grace's eyes were wild and flecks of spit had sprayed from her mouth.

It struck Lizzy then; the girl was Maryam's sister, after all, and although Maryam clearly didn't like Grace very much, she was more likely to feel closer to her than she was to Lizzy. And Lizzy knew if she was barred from the curative salons, that it wouldn't take long for her to return to how she'd been . . . the psoriasis had once covered every part of her skin, even the rims of her eyelids. Her life had been a total misery from her teenaged years onwards. Nothing she had tried had ever worked—until she'd found Maryam.

After her very first curative, she'd had clear skin for the first time in her miserable existence and it had changed her utterly—overnight she found that she was living a normal life. Not long after that, she had met her Derek at the Christmas dance and although he was no one's idea of a catch, he was plenty good enough for her. They had gotten married within eight months and Derek, of course, had no idea of what she would really look like without Maryam.

And now this wee bitch might actually fuck everything up. Her new husband, a normal life... Lizzy realised that she couldn't possibly risk it. She would have to swallow her pride and do as Grace was demanding.

◆

Big Ian had been unsure exactly how to proceed once he'd gotten to the floor where they were keeping McGill. There would be nurses on duty for sure, but he'd thought he might get away with the fact that the ITU was in a dogleg corner of the ward.

These old buildings sometimes had strange nooks and crannies like that.

If he was lucky and could stride across the fifteen feet or so of open ward area from the double doors, he would be able to make it to the dogleg and sneak into the ITU and if the slat blinds were down, then all the better. He would close the door, tape up Reverend McGill's cake hole and proceed. The rough sponge would take no time at all in destroying McGill's chances of reproducing and Big Ian would then simply walk out and let him bleed to death.

He felt no qualms whatsoever about doing this—he had a talent for being able to hurt people and not feel anything afterwards. Or during. It was to him the same as cutting cheese from a block or picking his nose. It simply was. He didn't derive any sadistic pleasure from the things that Arthur told him to do, nor did he dwell on them.

Arthur had said he was 'autistic about violence' and had been very pleased with him in that department ever since rescuing him from his previous existence on the streets.

When he got to the ward, there were no nurses around at all—result! Also, by good fortune, the slat blinds were already closed, so most of his job was done. However, because they were closed, as he entered the ward Big Ian couldn't actually see into the ITU—not until he was already inside the small room and by then it was too late. All McGill's wires and bits were loose and scattered across the bed but there was no McGill.

Must be getting his operation, thought Big Ian.

He was standing there wondering how long McGill would be when he heard the swift footsteps of the two Kenyan nurses returning and hid the rough sponge behind his back just as they arrived, speaking over each other at him.

'Excuse me? What are you doing in here?' said one. 'Who are you?'

'. . . where's the patient?' asked the other.

Big Ian thought quickly. Something unusual had clearly happened here—McGill was gone and the nurses didn't have a clue where. So?

So that meant that these two were no use to him and that there was no point being here anymore. But they were at the doorway, blocking it. The more confident looking of the two had stepped forward. She was clearly a brave sort and Big Ian liked that. He supposed that that was why he liked Skinny so much. She was pretty fearless as well. Big Ian looked at the nurse's name badge—'Hilary Ojomo'.

He liked that too. He bet it sounded nice when spoken aloud.

'Who are you?' she said. 'What do you want here?'

Big Ian just wanted minimum fuss but knew he had to say something. And then they would hear his voice . . . but he knew there was no way to avoid it.

'Excuse me I have to leave now,' he said.

They stared at him, wide eyed disbelief on their pretty faces. Nurse Ojomo looked him up and down. A patient with liquidised legs suddenly disappears and now a giant of a fellow speaking with a woman's voice was here in his stead.

'Ring security, Dorothea.'

The other nurse ran to the station for the desk phone. Big Ian headed for the gap left by her departure to walk straight out of the ITU. Nurse Ojomo started grabbing for him in a kind of 'not so fast' type motion—her continuing bravery just pleasing him no end—but then her eye caught the flash of Big Ian's rough sponge, still in the palm of his hand, and she shrank back, making a small 'oh . . .' sound.

Big Ian looked at her.

'That's right—'Oh',' he said, gently moving her aside with his free hand. 'You've got the right stuff, Nurse . . .' he couldn't help but try saying it aloud, '. . . Hilary Ojomo, but don't pick this fight or you'll be sorry. And that would make me sorry.'

She stepped away, giving him clearance. But resentfully. He headed off and she shouted after him, afraid now . . . but not for herself, he was pleased to hear.

'What have you done with him? Where have you put him?'

Big Ian kept going, faintly hearing Nurse Dorothea shouting down the phone and the murmur of the other patients waking up, their lamps being switched on. Big Ian knew that security, such as it was, would be lax, given that it was being split between both the old and the new hospital, but he started to run off at a brisk trot anyway. No point taking risks.

Lizzy was approaching along the corridor heading back to the ward. Nurse Ojomo shouted a warning over at her.

'Lizzy! Keep away from that fellow—he's got some kind of weapon in his hand!'

Alarmed, Lizzy pressed herself against the wall and let Big Ian jog past.

◆

Joe was listening to this scene at the bathroom door, kneeling and looking through the keyhole. He could see the head of the stairs and caught sight of the shape of Big Ian lumbering down three stairs at a time.

Joe cursed his still foggy brain. He knew that he wasn't fully *compis* yet, and that took a huge advantage from him. If only he could get a clear head, he'd be able to figure an angle out. At the minute, the most he could plan was getting the hell away from this place ASAP before either the big guy came back—maybe mob-handed—or those nurses pulled him back to his room.

He quickly weighed up his immediate options. Although, of course, torture and death at the hands of Arthur Bewlay would be worse, it was a pretty close run thing between that or having the hospital bringing in the cops to find out what was what with their mystery guest. If that happened, they'd want to know who he was, where he was from, what he was doing in this country. It meant that he'd have to explain things . . . and he didn't want to have to explain things.

Joe emerged from the bathroom and ran away from both the ward and the main stairwell that Big Ian had just run down. To one side there was a set of double doors blocked by a trolley with only three wheels to it—a crude barrier that he dispensed with easily. He pushed through the doors and found himself in almost complete darkness. He stood still for a moment to let his eyes adjust to the very low lighting here. This part of the hospital looked like it had been abandoned. As his eyes got used to the gloom, he could make out scattered x-ray plates on the dusty floor ahead, various overturned boxes and the general detritus of someplace that had been extremely busy right up until the last minute before it had suddenly been just walked away from. What the hell kind of hospital was this?

He could, in the distance behind him, hear the fat woman, who'd just arrived, now in tears explain how sorry she was to have left the ward; telling them she felt really *stupid* . . . and the rest was lost to Joe as he saw just ahead of him in the gloom, a fire escape door wedged open and the dimly lit top of another stairwell. He strode over to it and began running down the stairs, looking over his shoulder and trying not to let panic completely take him over.

❖

Nurse Ojomo was—while trying to not actually touch her—comforting Lizzy who was repeating over and over, as sorry as anyone could possibly be, that she'd only gone out for a quick fag. She'd been trying to give them up for years, but she was weak-willed, she *knew* that she was . . .

Lizzy also knew she deserved an Oscar. She might get into trouble for this, and there might well be suspicions as to why she'd sent the two nurses away ... but then, they were the ones who were supposed to be in the ward, not her. She didn't give a flying fuck who the big ugly guy with the 'weapon' was or who the mystery patient was anymore—let them sort all that out themselves. All she cared about was that she no longer had to either kidnap the guy for Grace or have to explain to the night staff how come he'd been miraculously cured on her watch. Now that circumstances had helped her out of this completely unexplainable situation, she couldn't possibly do any more. Thank God for that.

Both nurses abandoned her and started looking uselessly around the rest of the ward for any signs of their missing patient, when Lizzy saw Grace arrive at the top of the stairs in the corridor outside. She was flushed and excited, and clearly expecting Lizzy to start heaving the mystery leg guy all the bloody way down to the taxi with her. Well that's just too bad for you, Miss Gracey.

Pretty, snotty Grace, thought Lizzy. She could take her threats now and go fuck herself.

Lizzy quickly walked away from the ward, indicating for Grace to stay hidden and mouthing '*He's gone*' to her, just about managing to keep the smile from her face when she did so. Grace looked thunderstruck, as if she was about to start crying. That gave Lizzy a little satisfaction, but she knew she had to get her away from here.

'*Where did he go?*' whispered Grace.

'I don't know darling. The girls back there are saying that some person with a knife or something was here looking for him.'

Lizzy had grabbed her and pulled her down the corridor, far and away from the two panicking nurses, whispering urgently and feigning concern.

'I think that maybe he's not such a good person, this man, if he has people with weapons after him. Maybe him running away is just the thing—it's not a good idea to take a strange man home with you, after all, is it? Think of Maryam, dear. She needs her privacy above all else, doesn't she?'

Lizzy saw to her satisfaction that Grace had gone from wilful martinet to a panicked frightened child and started ushering her off.

'There is nothing to be done here anymore, Grace. You'd better go and look after Maryam now.'

Grace suddenly ran away, like she'd been naughty and didn't want to be told off, and Lizzy finally allowed herself that smile.

❖

Joe was in Hell again—a disorienting, half abandoned hospital. Was this a dream or was it real? His head felt like soft, melting fudge. He was starving, dehydrated and very probably still off his face on morphine—he'd just been running (well, staggering) down what felt like hundreds of stairs. The descending square circles made him dizzy, his vision started to blur and darken around the edges as he ran and ran until he could barely draw a breath into his lungs. It was fair to say, he thought, that he wasn't tip-top at the moment, although he was dimly aware of a rational, working part of his mind—envisioned by him at this point as being peanut-sized and surrounded by the pink fluffy marshmallow of stupidity that was currently the rest of his brain. It was screaming at him to keep running, to get out. Anywhere, just do it immediately, it screeched, because if you're caught here by the lady-voiced freak guy with the hacked up face, there won't be anyone to help and there won't be any second chances.

He was in a fire escape stairwell. There had been a door only on every other landing and each and every one of those doors had been locked from the other side . . . and he could *hear* the big guy lumbering down after him, that weird lady voice of his now the soundtrack to Joe's living nightmare—screaming for him and telling him he was going to die . . .

. . . and suddenly Joe lost all sense of space and time and he was completely naked and trying to feel his way through Bewlay's foul smelling dark pub again. All the doors had been locked and he was playing a horrifying game of hide and seek in the bowels of Hell. He could hear Bewlay taunting him—and the big guy with the scarred face and all the other little helper imps in the darkness around him—they all had flashlights trained on him and had the advantage of knowing every square inch of the place.

Joe stumbled into things, dashing his shins off wrought iron table legs, treading on the shards of broken bottles and the shattered beer glasses that they'd thoughtfully scattered on the floor for him. The broken pieces were grinding and slicing agonisingly into the soles of his feet or slashing into his legs if he stumbled and fell. And he was being sporadically slapped across the bare buttocks and the backs of his thighs by the flat of a machete, feeling his own warm blood turning cold as it hit the air and ran down his legs to his heels, making him slip and skid about on the floor.

'Give his bum another skelp!' shouted Bewlay, 'but don't slice him too deep. I don't want him bleeding to death before he gets to the quarry!'

Joe prayed for his eyes to get accustomed to the dark, so he could at least try to avoid the agonising obstacles and blows, but his tormentors would shine their flashlights into his face whenever they sensed he was starting to get his bearings.

Flash!

Straight into his eyes, the sudden glare dazzling and hurting them—stripes and dots and blurs of green and red from the after images. They would grab him then. They would spin him round until he was dizzy and boot him into the darkness once more, to crash about on more broken glass, getting more 'skelps'. At one point, he had tried to pick up a piece of bottle to use against them, but it had been kicked from his hand and his tormentors had redoubled their efforts against him. He'd hurtled against the bar and had clung to it like shit to toilet paper. It was something solid, a geographical point of reference—at one end or the other there might be a door. He had chosen a direction to flee in at random, skittering quickly down the bar's length, his toes banging painfully against the support struts for the brass foot rails on the floor as he went.

The attacks ceased then and there was silence and he should have realised that this was a trap or a trick of some sort, but his panic had seized him completely and all he could do was struggle blindly on, desperate for advantage, feeling the dirty, sticky surface of the wood beneath his fingers, fumbling as a blind man would.

Suddenly, the surface of the bar beneath his hands just disappeared, like he'd stepped off the edge of a cliff, and he fell painfully straight down for a foot or so, before banging his arms against flat wood again, the impact jarring his teeth together and making him nearly bisect his tongue. The sudden burst of laughter from those bastards around him almost deafened him. He hadn't realised that they'd all been so close. All the flashlights came on at once and he saw the cause of their mirth. At this end of the pub—where, he noted with dismay, there *wasn't* an exit—the bar didn't disappear suddenly, it just dropped in height before carrying onwards to the wall. Placed in front of it were several barstools, which had also been cut down in height, or manufactured, to match up with this scaled down bar.

What the fuck was this? The circus midget section?

He was pulled away from this temporary respite and hurled into the centre of the room once more, for the merry-go-round to begin again. The torture halted only when a telephone began ringing loudly. Everyone stopped having their fun for a moment as the sound echoed through the bar. Bewlay picked up and answered softly before hanging up.

There was a long pause and Joe crouched there, beaten and bleeding, the backs of his hands criss-crossed with cuts from where they'd tried to prevent him protecting his crotch, holding himself and shivering.

Bewlay hung up and told them that Terry had finished putting the plastic sheeting down inside the Merc and that they'd better take Reverend McGill out to the quarry and plant him like the graveyard guy (whatever that meant) but in slate chips instead of nice, soft dirt. And no bucket either (whatever *that* meant), because Reverend McGill wouldn't be coming back.

Bewlay had wanted to come out and visit personally, but it was too sunny this morning—he would like a wee video diary kept of the occasion, though, so that he could enjoy it at his leisure. Joe had begged Bewlay for mercy. What had he done wrong? They had left on the best of terms not too long ago! They'd just made *an arrangement*, for Christ's sakes! Surely they could work something out?

Bewlay said that he didn't think so and that he wasn't one for mealy-mouthed politicking. He was an honourable man. You *do* something dishonourable, you *say* something dishonourable—you take your punishment like a man.

Them's the rules.

Off you fuck.

◈

Joe opened his eyes, seeing once more the reality of the hospital stairwell around him, the involuntary remembrance of the pub nightmare now gone; his nausea passed. He saw he'd been gripping the banister so tightly that his hands were white; so white they were almost luminous.

The marshmallow part of the McGill consciousness kept telling him to just stay the hell down here, on these nice comfy concrete stairs—take a breather, smell the flowers—because there *was* no one chasing him. There was no noise around him—it was just his imagination . . . but the peanut ignored it and kept on screaming at him to keep moving.

He had a vague notion that this was probably primeval survival instinct. But who was right—peanut or marshmallow? Even though he couldn't hear any footsteps—no feet, no breathing, no doors slamming, no whiny woman voiced giant psychopath with halitosis and a Picasso face—he decided to go with peanut.

8

Big Ian was now striding over to Skinny at the moped. She threw her fag away, ready to leave—that'd been quick, even for him. She might just make it for her date with Mandy after all. She'd tried ringing her whilst he was gone, desperate that this beautiful girl shouldn't be thinking that not only had she gone to a lot of effort for someone as borderline not really worth it as Skinny, but that she'd also been stood up by her.

Skinny'd had no luck, however. Her phone was currently a bit fucked—had been since she'd gone flying tit over knob from a skid on the pizza bike last week, trying to avoid some twat who'd opened their car door right in front of her. She had somersaulted and landed right on top of her phone, with the net result that not only did the stupid thing now work only intermittently, its screen cracked and blank, she suspected that the imprint of the keypad would be forever embossed on her arse. Big Ian arrived in front of her, vexed.

'There was no guy there anymore, Skinny. He's disappeared.'

Skinny smiled. Result.

'Oh dear. Let's just go home then?' she said.

Skinny moved off toward the moped, but Big Ian wasn't following. She sighed and returned to him. He was frowning.

'Arthur sent me to do the guy.'

'Yes, but he's not here is he?'

'No.'

'No what? Because if the guy's legged it and knows that Arthur wants him dead, he's going to run and keep on running, isn't he? Let's just go, hm?'

'No, Skins! He couldn't run anywhere. His legs were fucked! I saw that when I visited earlier—they were totally *totally* fucked. The other patients were telling their visitors in the ward; he was going to have his legs off . . .'

He was frowning again, but more in concentration, she knew, than in anger. She watched him standing there, thinking. He wasn't completely unintelligent, she thought; he just thought things through in a different way from other people. Skinny sighed and lit another fag—looked like she wasn't going anywhere.

'You smoke too much Skinny.'

'So?'

'So, you'll get cancer, that's so.'

He clammed up again, looking over at the hospital entrance.

'. . . someone must've took him,' he said, eventually.

She smiled. How long had it taken him to reach that conclusion?

'This guy must be shit hot fun to be around,' she said 'Everybody wants to take him places.'

Big Ian wasn't laughing; he was ploughing this particular furrow of thought with a keen blade.

'Whoever took him'd have to carry him—no way could he've been able to move himself. So that means he's working with other people. Arthur won't like this. Did you see any cars or taxis leaving?'

'It's a hospital, Big Ian,' she said patiently. 'Of course I did. Hundreds of them. People come and go all the time.'

'It's shutting down soon, but.'

'Even with only half of it working, this is still a hospital. A *big* hospital. There are other entrances.'

He clammed up again, thinking more thoughts. She took a draw on her fag. This wild goose chase Bewlay had sent them on—this was the kind of thing that'd been disturbing her for a while now. She'd been actively attempting to drink less and had been spending evenings thinking about how she might—if at all—start turning

Bewlay's condition to her advantage. At the very least try and ensure that if the ship went down because Bewlay was indulging in the carelessness of the insane, that she wouldn't end up sinking with it.

Skinny had heard that over the last few months, since large portions of Bewlay's nose had seriously begun to drop into his soup, all sorts of vile shit had been occurring up in the pub. Really vile shit. She'd heard rumours of wee junkie lassies, and boys too, going in—staying up there in that evil smelling flat with him. And not coming back out. She hated being in that place. Absolutely fucking hated it. It had always smelt bad—decades of dodgy sell-by date bar meals, chip oil and body odour—but these days it smelt of actual rot, like a dead animal on a garbage dump.

The last time she had been there—inside, as opposed to her preferred option of waiting in the street for her delivery instructions—some old jakie had voided his bowels right in front of her while standing at the bar. He'd just stood there, letting it all go—lumpy, vile smelling brown liquid running down his trouser leg and *pat pat patting* onto the floor, pooling at his feet—before ordering another cheap Chinese whiskey. No one had batted an eyelid, never mind fetched a mop.

The staff, such as they were, looked more and more to her like people desperately trying to get through each day without incurring serious injury or death. She used to wonder why they stayed at all, before she realised that they very probably had no choice. If Bewlay liked someone, then they were 'his' forevermore, like it or not. Also, he had a way of tracking down people who displeased him and his 'staff' in the bar would likely be shit scared of offending him in any way. Not so much that they'd wipe a customer's diahorrea off the floor though, she'd noted. Although maybe they'd been instructed not to. Maybe Bewlay thought it added to the ambience of the place—projecting an image of total couldn't care less craziness maybe being a good way of keeping threats at a distance. No wonder even cops were afraid to go in there. She was amazed that it still had customers at all; especially considering the place was also now sealed up like a reactor at Chernobyl.

She sighed to herself. She needed Bewlay's money, but she was sick and bloody tired of having to work for him. He was going downhill rapidly for absolutely fucking sure, behaving like an emperor in the last days of Rome, and it looked like Big Ian was just happy to be skipping down that road with him.

She used to like Big Ian more than she did now. She'd felt sorry for him and she also knew that—for Christ knew what bizarre reason—he carried a torch for her. But she'd gone off the big fella in a major way since she'd been hearing about the recent comings and goings at the pub. He was Bewlay's bag man, in all senses of the phrase, and she had not really passed anything like a friendly word with him in quite a while. Skinny had wanted to distance herself from all of that shit.

And recently, she had also started thinking endgame.

What would happen the second after Bewlay died? Who would fill that gap? Not Big Ian, that was for sure—at least, not on his own. But whoever did take over would benefit a great fucking deal from having Big Ian by their side. Maybe tonight would be a good opportunity to test the water on a few things. She put herself on warning though; tread carefully. Big Ian interrupted her thoughts.

'Maybe he's still about. Let's search.'

He started walking off, but Skinny grabbed him.

'Hang on,' she said 'Have you any idea how long that'll take? This place is huge, and he's probably miles away by now.'

'I don't see how,' he said. 'He was in intensive care and his legs were going to be chopped off. You don't just get a taxi away from that.'

She spoke softly.

'Let's just have a wee talk—you and me.'

'What about, Skins?' he said, and she could detect a small note of petulance in his voice. 'You not being friends with me any more?'

'Of course I'm friends with you,' she said.

There was awkward silence for a moment.

'I've just been a bit . . . worried about stuff, that's all,' she said. 'Preoccupied.'

'What stuff, Skinny? What's wrong? Can I help?'

He was suddenly genuinely concerned for her—she could see it in his eyes; hear it in the tone of his voice. It was like a switch had been pulled.

'I don't know, Big Ian . . . it's complicated . . . I don't know if I should say . . .'

She looked steadily at him, knowing she could be about to make the biggest mistake of her life. She could back out now or plunge in.

'Just tell me Skins. I'd help you do anything . . . you know that.'

She could see that he meant every word, the big sap, so she decided to plunge in.

'Tell me,' she said, 'why are we after this guy?'

'Cos Arthur wants him dead.'

'Why?'

'Because he insulted him.'

'Because he insulted him.' She didn't even try to keep the mockery from her voice. Big Ian looked uncomfortable. Skinny sighed.

'Big Ian, there was a multiple vehicle smash up during rush hour on the city's busiest road. Our team was wiped out. D'you not think that enough damage has been done because he 'insulted him'?'

'What do you mean?'

'I mean, why are we doing this at all? It's stupid and pointless—what does it matter?'

'He might grass on Arthur—tell the cops it was Arthur that wanted him done in.'

'So?'

Big Ian was about to reply but stopped, mouth half open. She could see her simple question was working on him. 'So?' indeed. She pressed on.

'Arthur is dying,' she said. 'He doesn't have very long left so what does any of this shite matter? Hm? What does *he* matter?'

He looked at her for a long time, his face completely impassive.

'What are you saying?' he said.

'I'm saying that we need to deal with this . . . situation with the boss.'

'I don't know what you mean, Skins.'

'Yes you do. He's getting worse. In the head.'

There was another awkward silence. She pressed on.

'He's talking to all sorts of weirdos and strangers, isn't he? He's trying to find some miracle way of stopping his cancer. I mean fair enough, nobody wants to die but who's he had up there? Crystal healers? Psychics? People in wizard hats practically, and other people just off the fucking street—like this guy with the sore legs we're out here looking for . . .'

'They weren't sore legs—they were totally destroyed. The guy has no right to be up and about . . .'

'Yeah yeah, whatever—that's not the point.'

'What is the point then, Skins?'

She decided to just say it.

'What if he ends up talking not just to himself but to these other people? What if he starts telling them stuff? About us . . . about what we do for him—stuff we wouldn't want other people to know about? And then what if they just go and tell the straight cops?'

Big Ian was intentionally not looking at her. She pressed on.

'What if the cancer doesn't get him before he takes everyone down with him? He's off his nut on morphine all the time now anyway. He doesn't give a single soft shit whether you or me or anyone else lives or dies, does he? Not anymore—he's too far gone. It honestly wouldn't make any difference to him . . . and you can see that. How much concern did he show for our guys in the car accident? None, right? And that's starting to make a difference for you . . . isn't it?'

She put a hand gently on his arm and squeezed it. He tentatively put his huge, meaty four-fingered paw on top of her hand and squeezed back. Simple as that. She wondered if he'd ever received anything like affection in his life and suddenly she was convinced that this mad idea of hers could really work. Big Ian's oddly high voice was very quiet when he replied.

'I'm praying for him to die,' he said. 'For *his* sake, Skinny. Every night. I *want* the cancer to take him . . . before he loses any more of his mind.'

Skinny found that she couldn't speak. Christ almighty things *must* be bad—way worse than she could have imagined probably—if Big Ian was saying things like this out loud. Bewlay was well on the way out for sure, the business was in disarray, three of the guys were in intensive care as of the morning's accident and she knew of others who were AWOL, already drifting off to other gangs, or making arrangements to do so. Arthur Bewlay liked to spout off about loyalty and his team—but he was also completely off his trolley and couldn't see everyone quietly drifting and making arrangements for how their lives would carry on without him. But they would come back—if there was still money to be made once Bewlay was gone, they *would* come back. And Big Ian was more than just holding her in high esteem—she could see now that he was, in his own way, in love with her.

She reminded herself though that this guy was also very, very dangerous. He would snuff anyone, anyone at all, if Bewlay told him to. And he wouldn't show the slightest concern when he did it, offing someone as easily as he would go to the corner shop for a plain loaf and bottle of milk. It literally meant nothing to him.

That was his talent and that was what Bewlay valued in him. But his lack of, what was the word . . . empathy . . . was selective. He never went out actively looking for trouble—never killed anyone for *sport*, as it were—he only did as Bewlay told him to. He was the embodiment of the phrase 'only obeying orders'. As cold blooded murderers went, she supposed Big Ian wasn't so bad. Put another way, he was not a leader, but would *need* a new leader soon. So why shouldn't it be her?

Her decision was made. And if she had to fuck him twice a day to keep him on her side, then she would. She'd been fucked by men before. It wasn't the end of the world. She stood closer to him, looking up into his eyes.

'Look Big Ian—I'm smart. I'm very smart—you know that.'

He smiled broadly, nodding, his face very open and childlike to her now. She would never ask him to really hurt someone, she decided. She would just use him as a threat until she'd made enough money to get the hell away from here for good.

'I know everyone and they know me,' she continued softly. 'I can do more than just courier grams of Charlie around on a shitty pizza bike. I can do deals, *big deals*, and I can run business. All I need is you behind me. The other guys—the ones that are left—they'll go wherever you go . . .'

'You mean when Arthur dies?' he said. 'We? You and *me*?'

She was watching him carefully. He seemed to be taking this in ok. In fact, more than that, he seemed to rather like the idea. There was a light in his eyes and he seemed to be processing new possibilities—entire worlds, perhaps, that he'd never dared imagine. Mentally, she took a deep breath. Here goes . . .

'Why wait at all?' she said. 'That's what I've been telling you—he's *already* lost it, Big Ian. We can't just hang on, hoping he doesn't do something really stupid before he pegs out, pulling us all down . . . *we* have to do something . . . *to* him. It would be for *his* sake, like you said . . . it would give him peace . . . a mercy . . . we have to—'

She gasped as all the air suddenly left her body. She flew backwards about eight feet straight, crashing loudly into the huge aluminium waste bins and falling to the ground like she was made of absolutely nothing.

Big Ian had punched her as hard as he could in the stomach. She clutched herself, her cheeks blowing in and out comically as tears flowed freely from her eye. He strode calmly over to her and she fought the excruciating pain and tried to get up, to back off, to squirm the hell away from him, clawing and sliding in the deep grease, which was laked around the bottom of the bins beside her, slathering around, unable to breathe properly or gain any purchase on the slippery ground before giving in to her body's need to vomit.

Big Ian stood over her as she sicked up uncontrollably. His voice was sorrowful.

'That was for your own sake, Skinny,' he said softly. 'If you'd said what you were going to say, I'd have had to tell him, word for word. You know I would. And then he'd have asked me to kill you.'

He took a deep breath, which caught a little in his throat.

'Probably worse. I don't want to do that.'

She was gasping great scoops of air into her lungs, barely able to see him through her tears, but still angry enough to spit out: 'But you'll . . . stand by . . . and watch him melt down? Maybe drag . . . everyone down with him? Me . . . and you . . . going to fucking jail when he's going to be dead soon enough! *What's the point in waiting?*'

'There's a line, Skins, between brave and stupid. Don't cross it.'

He smiled, an unpleasant duty now over with, and she could tell that the thorny subject of disposing of Bewlay didn't exist for him anymore.

'Tell you what,' he said, 'maybe you're right about the preacher guy. He'll be well away from here already if he's got people to take him, won't he? So maybe we shouldn't look so hard—he just seems to upset Arthur anyway. I'll just take a quick walk round the perimeter, though, and try my luck with a few back doors, eh? Just so's I'm telling the truth when Arthur asks if I searched. That ok with you?'

Big Ian chuckled, like he was sharing a warm, homely secret with a beloved family member, and not a girl half his size he'd just hit hard enough to send to Cuba. He hunkered down on his haunches next to her and made to touch her hair with his fingertips, but thought better of it. He smiled shyly.

'Don't worry about giving me a lift back, Skins. I'll just get a cab when I'm done, you go off on your wee date—see you tomorrow eh? Enjoy yourself. Don't do anything I wouldn't do. If you can't be good be careful.'

And then he stood up and walked off, just like that, as if it were actually feasible for her to go on a fucking date now.

Skinny managed to haul herself up on one elbow, the immediate agony just beginning to abate, but she could feel the start of what promised to be a truly terrible ache deep in her abdomen, like maybe something in there had been ruptured. She began suddenly to dry heave, which turned into a cough she found she couldn't stop. She hacked uncontrollably for as long as it lasted, having no choice but to ride it out.

Jesus F. Christ, she thought, I'm in the grounds of an effing hospital and I'm vomiting and coughing myself inside out. Anyone on duty? Hello?

When her body eventually gave up on trying to find stuff to eject, she eased herself upright and sat with her back against one of the huge bins. She noticed—distractedly, as if it had nothing much to do with her—that she was trembling all over.

The dog seen a ghost, she thought.

That was something she and her cousin used to say when they saw the cowed and trembling strays on the scheme standing shock still before bolting off somewhere, tails between their legs, for no good reason that anyone could fathom.

The dog was trembling because it just seen a ghost.

Her legs were splayed out before her, and she sat there not caring that her clothes, already sodden with her own sick and the filthy cooking grease from the ground, were getting filthier. She looked like she'd been shat out of something's arse. She laughed. It hurt. She stopped. She got out her pack of cigarettes and one handed lit up a greasy mutant, bendy fag with her Zippo. She exhaled. Well, that was that—she was on her own. So fuck you, Big Ian and fuck you too, Arthur Bewlay.

No bad dream fucker was going to bring *her* down.

9

Joe was at the very bottom of the stairwell and there was a huge set of grey, double swing doors directly in front of him. He'd been shivering the rest of the way down here, but found that he was getting warmer now. There was a constant roar from nearby. Incinerators maybe? He was getting worried about freezing to death on the outside in this dumb paper gown.

He pushed through the doors and found himself nearly walking straight into a dimpled cinderblock wall. It was so close to the doorway, it only just about gave the swingers clearance, and he had to let them close behind him one at a time just so that he could get through. Wiring in primary colours hung down from dented metal brackets running the length of what was basically a corridor. Too bright fluorescent strips made his eyes hurt. To one side, about thirty yards away, was a dead end with two ramshackle looking cage pallets on wheels filled with huge yellow plastic waste bags. Along the other way, the corridor space stretched on for a bit before merging in to what looked like—of all things—an arched stone doorway. It was the only other way out of this corridor, apart from the way he had just come in and he headed straight for it.

This was the kind of architectural anomaly, he knew, which happened a lot in old, municipal buildings. Extensions were built, and old parts were abandoned or blocked off and forgotten. Maybe there was a storeroom or something down there and he could steal some overalls or find a way out? This looked like a very old part though, and not too promising for an exit door . . . but he really didn't relish having to go all the way back up those stairs again.

He went along to the arched doorway, carefully opening up the ancient looking and peeling door, and found himself looking down a long, vaulted and dimly lit corridor; with hundreds more yellow plastic hospital waste bags piled chest high along its walls on either side. Waiting to be incinerated he presumed.

The walls in here, what he could see of them, were black tile and there were old fashioned wire covers on the irregularly spaced lamps. He could also see that nearby to each lamp there were sawn off, truncated copper pipes. He stared at them in fascination for a few moments. What were they all about, he wondered. Then it hit him . . . they were sawn off outlet pipes for gas lighting. *Wow*. Gas lighting brackets? This was about as Victorian as you could get without actually wearing a stovepipe hat and beating children.

He could just about see, *hallelujah*, an exit light at the far end through the leaning walls of yellow bags. As he began heading for it, he noticed that some of the bags were open and even in this weak light he could see that they were full of clothes. This was weird. It was starting to feel like this was somehow supposed to happen. Every time he needed something, he got it, albeit in a very perverse and mean way.

He needed rescue from Bewlay's men, he got it; via a car crash that killed some old guy when it should have killed him.

He needed healing, he got it; from someone who looked even sicker than he did.

He needed clothes—and here they were; bloodstained (it looked like) and from dead people (probably), but clothes nonetheless. What had made him such a magnet for this fucked up Twilight Zone good luck/bad luck voodoo shit?

He tentatively peeled a bag a bit further open, and the abrupt, rank smell of ammonia and excrement made him reel back. Jumping Jesus, no wonder they were going to burn these. They were probably covered in diseased sputum, HIV, MRSA, C Difficile, Heps A, B, C and all the other goddam letters of the alphabet for all he knew. What the hell else could be on the menu down here? Ebola?

How desperate *was* he?

Desperate enough to wear something from the hospital's autumn collection, he knew. Ok, so he had to get organised here. For a start, he would certainly stand out in a bus queue if he was to wear a selection from *this* bag.

He held his breath like that was going to help and tentatively opened a different sack. This didn't stench nearly as much but the clothes inside were still badly fucked up. He had to presume that all of the bags were going to be pretty much the same and that he might have to spend time actually going through all of them to pick out the least toxic apparel. He told himself to stop bitching. All that the clothes had to do was fit reasonably well and not stink too bad—he was on the run here, not going to the fish and goose soiree at the Algonquin. But even if he did find a white tie and tails, he thought, where the fuck was he going to go anyway?

He only had one option as far as he could see—Trudy. He thought that he could just about remember the number he'd gotten for her, or at the very least remember enough of it to eventually get through to her without too many tries. But then what?

'Hi Trudy! Remember me?'

That would be just terrific—showing up completely out of the blue wearing dead peoples' clothes, with no money, and smelling of shit and disease. Oh, and with a psychopathic gangster wanting him dead. She'd obviously be glad to welcome him with open arms.

Just fucking terrific.

He decided that he didn't want to think about it any more, for the time being at least. He was feeling dizzy and weak again and he agreed with himself that he would simply have to get on with the task at hand. Every journey began with but a single step and you could only take your life one day at a time, *sweet Jee-zuss*, one day at a time.

The snatch of song in his head, unasked for but gratefully received, cheered him minutely.

He lifted his gaze up from the bag he was holding and looked down the length of the corridor, the walls lined with a seeming infinity of these yellow waste bags. It looked like either there had been a *hell* of a lot of accidents and deaths at this hospital recently—or the lazy sons of bitches in maintenance hadn't been remembering to do their incinerator duties for the past few, oh ... years? He could sympathise. It wasn't a glamour profession down here that was for sure.

While he wasn't looking, something had moved inside the bag he was holding open. He stared down into it, hoping that this small but potentially significant event hadn't actually happened—it had been glimpsed out the corner of his eye, after all. It could have been a tic.

But then whatever was in there had the bad manners to move again and he jumped away from it with an involuntary yelp. Nothing happened for a few seconds. Then, whatever was inside the bag started moving yet again, making the clothing rustle against the plastic of the bag with a slithery sort of sound. Oh crap. There was for sure something inside there, he thought, moving about in a plastic disposal bag full of dried bodily fluids.

For God's sake, he thought. Did this never end? His life had become hard enough recently, without having to wrestle hospital bag dwelling critters for rights of ownership to dead people's clothes. He wanted then to just head to the exit and get the hell out, not particularly caring any more that he was wearing a backless green paper gown. He'd have pulled on a nurse's uniform if there'd been one handy.

He sighed, bone weary—get a goddam *grip* McGill! He began assuring himself that it would have been more of a surprise if there *hadn't* been any vermin down here. Fortunately, he had no real fear of rats. It wasn't that he wanted to spend time cuddling them or would like to have a basket of them drop on his head unexpectedly, but he didn't have a phobia about the damn things. They were just big fuck off rodents and there were only two rules to them—don't let them bite you and don't drink their piss.

He figured it would be safer to pick up the waste bag from the bottom and tip its contents out onto the floor, rather than just stick his hand inside. This would give ratty a chance to make a getaway as well. Go on, little guy, run free and wild in the meadows.

Gingerly, and with his face well away from the opening of the bag, he gently tipped the contents out on to the damp floor ... which he now noticed was actually very old, much worn black cobblestone. Good gravy, how old *was* this place down here? The more his eyes got used to it, the older it seemed to get. With its floor sagging in the middle, it actually looked like a cobbled lane, built over and forgotten about (apart from by the yellow waste bag guys, of course, to whom this unofficial dump was obviously a godsend for finishing shifts early). He looked down at the pile of clothing and felt his heart begin thudding faster in his chest. There, among the pile of tipped out clothes, was a Homburg.

Or was it a Fedora?

Whatever, this was a hat he knew . . .

Oh for Chrissakes, if he wasn't afraid of rats, why should he be afraid of hats? They were terrific for passing round. Normally though, he thought as an obscure panic began to grip him, hats didn't move around of their own volition . . . like this one just had. It had been another 'did I just see that?' moment.

'No it hadn't', he said to himself. The lights are so dim down here, he thought, and my vision is affected by my lack of food and my exhaustion and shock and . . . and . . . and . . .

And the hat moved again.

Then Joe realised that Mister Ratty must be beneath the goddam thing.

Dammit, he was sick and tired of this. Getting angry with himself for being afraid and with the rat for managing to spook him—again—he stepped up to it and gave it the mightiest kick he could manage.

Surprisingly, it exploded with a ghastly, loud wet pop squelch . . . and a burst of warm and stinking fluids splashed onto his bare legs and face. It wasn't a rat after all. It was a big goddam toad. It was completely white. He'd split its fat, wrinkled, bag of guts body apart with his kick and its slimy, glistening, insides were now its outsides—and they were all over him. They were also an odd, fish belly white—not the kind of Technicolor you would expect from exposed internal organs—with a translucent, gel membrane around them, networked with criss-crossing red, thread veins. It smelt absolutely disgusting.

It was still alive, its horrible little arms grasping feebly at the air, legs jerking spastically. Its head turned. It seemed to be looking at him. This was really creeping Joe out now—it had a . . . a look on its face . . .

Wait . . . just wait a goddam minute, he thought. This was insane. It *didn't* turn its head—because it *couldn't* turn its goddam head because toads don't have necks to turn their heads *with*. They just had heads! The same way that it hadn't had a 'look' on its face either. Toads couldn't give 'looks' because toads didn't have faces! Not really . . . not like a real face, a *face* face.

(Like, for example, the face of the old guy that had caused the accident?)

Joe told himself that he was just projecting. Hunger, weariness and what was left of the morphine in his bloodstream were ganging up on him. This was the old dead guy's hat and Joe's mind was making up a dumb story to fit this toad into it somehow. He supposed he should be grateful, really, for a brain that was constantly trying to impose some form of logic on the situation. It wasn't unusual, he rationalised, to have amphibious creatures dwelling in damp, dark areas. That was their habitat, for god's sake. As an occasional watcher of wildlife series, he knew that.

Its whiteness was easily explainable also—that would be due to the fact that it lived in the dark. Obviously. Everything was explainable. He had once had to hide out from a family of Nazi Christian fundamentalists—unhappy with a phoney astrology shtick he was peddling at the time—in a desert cave, and he'd had to share it with a big colony of albino, almost translucent, chuck spiders. It was horrible, sure, but it was *explainable*.

The toad's mouth suddenly hinged open then, and through an abruptly cascading foam of sickly pink bubbles spilling out from it, a helium scream emerged.

No it didn't, Joe commanded himself, fighting hysteria. It's just the air escaping from its toady goddam lungs—like what happens when live lobsters are stuck in a pot of boiling water and all the air escapes from their little living, scuttling, scrabbling, boiling alive bodies. It was something like that, he told himself. Except with toads.

But the scream was getting louder now.

Because, he thought—grimly hanging on to his thin thread of logic—whilst it might just feasibly be argued that there was a case for toads to have necks... or faces, even ... toads with *actual vocal chords* with which they could *scream* were most definitely *not on the cards*. That was not possible. That was *not* reality.

Mister Toad, however, was rather inconveniently showing no signs of sticking to the rules, reality-wise. But it's a *toad*, Joe thought. It couldn't have that much fucking air in its lungs to begin with for God's sake—they must be absolutely tiny! He thought, then, that it was screaming at *him*... it was getting louder and screaming and crying like a goddam baby! *And he'd squished it!*

It was when he thought he could discern something like speech starting to form, from some place far, far down from inside the toad's body, that he unfroze and stepped over the damned thing and walked briskly away from it as fast as he could toward the exit door at the far end of the corridor, wishing—dream or no dream—to not ever see or hear anything like this ever again. His bare skin was scraped at by the sharp edges of the heavy duty plastic bags as he strode through them, trying not to let his growing panic turn into screaming flight. He was failing and he picked up the pace, stumbling into a half run and knocking one of the bags down onto him, the foul clothes spilling out, making his flesh crawl.

He made himself stop. Blind panic was of no use to anyone, he thought, especially not in his current situation. He made himself stand as still as he could and tried to control his breathing.

He'd get a grip of his emotions and then he would calmly—but quickly—just get to that good old exit door there, open it up and step out into fresh, sane, air. He was sure that he could find more clothing elsewhere in the building. It was a hospital, after all, and hospitals were big places. Maybe he could just steal a live patient's clothes from a bedside locker or something? That was the logical thing to do; that would be just the ticket. That was when he heard the scuttling claws. He could hear them arriving behind him- coming out from beneath all these bags, making the thick plastic crinkle and scrunch.

Rats, he thought. Real rats. *Actual* rats.

Suddenly what he'd been thinking earlier by way of rodents and their activities didn't really apply any more, because the idea of rats did bother him now. The idea bothered him *a lot* . . . because it sure sounded like there were a lot of *them*.

And not only that, he thought, what if *they started screaming and talking too*?

He went running to the door in a terror, looking over his shoulder but able to see only the high corridor of plastic bags crowding in behind him, stumbling on cobbles as he fled. He suddenly hit the exit door full on and bounced back from it, dazed. He got up again and scrabbled for the bolts top and bottom, catching his fingers painfully on them but not caring. He was shaking as he put his hand on the door handle, and felt it starting to turn on its own beneath his palm. Then there was a pressure on the door from the other side. Shit. It was being pushed open! The door abruptly jerked toward him with a nerve-scraping creak, the dry hinges screeching for oil. Who would be pushing open a door into this place unless it was someone sniffing around, searching?

Joe put all his weight against the door, desperate to get it closed again. He snuck a look over his shoulder, down the length of the bag lined walls and suddenly felt conned—like a lab specimen in the simplest maze in the world, one with no way back, cajoled into finding either his reward or punishment. He thought he could hear a muffled grunt—the person outside surprised at the resistance to their pushing . . . it was a high pitched sound, like a girl's. Oh my God, it was the psycho! Joe turned, his back against the door, ready to try running the length of the corridor back to the stairwell—but there were more and more rats arriving; it sounded like a cacophony of screeching and scrabbling . . . and, faintly, he could hear the toad screaming . . . being ripped apart, still alive. He felt everything crowding in on him, the screaming and tearing seemed to be right inside his head, his eyes felt hot and dry and small and he was dizzy and nauseous and he hadn't eaten and he was drugged and he had to hold on very, very tightly to any kind of logic that he could. Well fuck this. He'd rather step outside and take his chances than remain in here for one goddam second longer. He looked around for some kind of weapon—anything at all, iron bar, stick ... *anything*. But there was nothing to hand except a beaten, plastic charity can on the floor at his feet—a slot at the top for the coins and the hospital's name now barely legible across the outside.

The door was being pushed towards him again. Well, so be it. He grabbed up his pathetic non-weapon, holding it aloft as threateningly as he could manage.

'Ok you goddam freak show ape, fucking *go for it*!'

He wrenched the door open.

Standing there was the cheerleader.

'Do you like music?' she said. 'I like music!'

Grace smiled the biggest smile Joe had ever seen on anyone's face, totally unfazed by the sight of him—the most bizarre charity collector in the world about to leap onto her and beat her to death with his can.

Behind him, a savage feeding frenzy was happening. Joe could hear the toad creature being pulled apart, screaming and bleating horribly, being eaten alive by the rats. Grace looked concerned and tried to see over Joe's shoulder to what was occurring indoors, but he blocked her view, suddenly concerned for her safety above anything else.

'Don't look in there ...' he croaked.

She smiled at him again.

'Grace,' she said, helpfully.

'Grace. It's a ... bad thing in there ...'

'Ok, I wom't, mister ... ?'

She waited.

'Joe,' he said.

She nodded cheerfully, and thrust out her hand for a friendly shake.

He fainted and fell into her arms.

10

Maryam's eyes were jammed uselessly shut against the oncoming, unstoppable migraine. The touch of her clothes against her skin made her want to scream and every gear change or movement of the vehicle felt like a personal violation against her. She realised that she was too exhausted by the epic healing she had performed to do anything other than just breathe to stay alive.

She opened her eyes, which still felt sticky with blood and matter . . . and saw that she and Grace were not alone.

His head was resting against Grace as she stroked his cheek, and he had an odour about him like fish guts or similar. Maryam's voice came out like an angry croak.

'Why is he in this cab with us?'

Grace at least had the decency to sound sorry.

'I'm apologise for this Maryam, but we better take him with us.'

'Are you completely stupid? *Why* for God's sake? There's nothing wrong with him! *I* am the one who needs nursing!'

Grace held the young man's head tighter to her, resting her cheek on his forehead.

'Too much queschims would be asked if he stayed im the hospital,' said Grace, simply. 'Like how he got healed up amd what if emmyome saw us there.'

Maryam's anger dissipated. Of course. Why hadn't she thought of it? Take him away with them—it was the only thing to be done! That would keep her involvement secret . . . but what to do with him now that they had him? They couldn't just keep him indefinitely, could they? He would wake up and he would want to leave. He'd want to go back to his own family. Or whoever. Wife and children, maybe. He would blab, wouldn't he? She and Grace knew nothing about him. In fact he could be a journalist for all they knew. And now he would know where they lived! Maryam knew she was going round in circles here, her head a pinball table with lots of balls going simultaneously. How had she let Grace persuade her to get into this? Was she losing her marbles, along with every other rotten thing that was wrong with her? The situation hadn't gotten better after all—it had gotten worse! Damn you Grace!

Maryam glared over at the young man and found herself wishing . . . that she was the one holding him.

◆

Joe had a vague, almost not there, awake dream feeling of dislocation. The cab was turning a corner and the centrifugal force was lightly pressing his head further into the warmth of the cheerleader's breasts—an incredibly pleasant sensation, and one which could, if bottled somehow, give Valium a run for its money as a nerve soother. But the peculiarity of looking out of a car window from low down—a view usually to be seen only by a child, he thought—and up at the corner of a vast red sandstone apartment building as the cab drove around it, made him felt like time was standing still. This was compounded by the fact he was looking at a clock; like the face of a giant looking over the city. And he noticed that around its face, between each of the Roman numerals, there were symbols. Signs of the Zodiac? He smiled to himself about how odd his life seemed to have become. What on earth else could happen to him?

◆

Maryam knew that she had been staring at the young man's face in the hospital like a love struck teenager as much as Grace had. Just as she was staring at it right now. She couldn't stop staring at his face. Why? What right did she have to be looking at someone so beautiful?

She thought again of how Grace seemed to be turning into a troublesome teenager. Maybe adolescence was a virus, she thought.

Maybe it was catching?

11

ARTHUR SAT ON THE EDGE OF TOMMY'S BED, HIS ARMS RESTING on his knees. He had lit the stubby candles he'd taken to keeping in his brother's top drawer—just like he used to when they were kids—and the constantly flickering light gave him glimpses of the masses of Biro handwriting all over the wallpaper. He knew that if he ever turned on the electric light in here, he would see it all—blue, black, red and green ball point pen scrawl covering every square inch of Tommy's walls, skirting board and all, floor to ceiling.

Arthur had decided never to bother trying to read what his brother had written. They were his private thoughts and should be kept that way, like a diary—but it *had* been a comfort during Tommy's temporary absence from his life to come in and just sit here to be with the words. There were so many of them.

He looked at the severed head on the pillow—the dancing shadows from the candlelight were playing across Tommy's features, making him look like he was pulling faces. Despite the twice daily applications of moisturiser, though, there was no getting round the desiccated look his brother's face had when viewed close up—like a mummy's.

It was all over for Tommy now, Arthur thought. He had gone through death and now he didn't have to worry about it any more. Arthur had it to look forward to. It worried him. He worried a great deal. His face was eaten away as if he were already a corpse, the hideous agony of his cancer only barely held in check by the ever increasing doses of the morphine. He would give anything not to die like this; *try* anything not to die like this. Literally anything.

'I know I was being stupid, Tommy,' Arthur said. 'Stupid and gullible.'

He reached out and chucked his brother gently under the chin.

'He caught me at the right time,' Arthur continued, 'I was getting depressed, really, really down, and this guy, Reverend Joe, showed up saying he had something to tell me that would be to my advantage . . . you know, about the cancer.'

There was a rasping noise, throaty and dry—a noise that still thrilled Arthur whenever he heard it.

'*Tell—me—all—about—it,*' said Tommy.

So Arthur did.

◆

Big Ian had been standing guard at the door. Bewlay was lying on the long sofa—legs covered with a blanket, his face in shadow. Joe McGill was on the threadbare armchair opposite, hands folded patiently across his lap and a serene expression on his face. He was dressed stylishly in black—a silk-lapelled drape coat and bootlace tie combo making him look a little like a riverboat gambler.

'Reverend McGill?'

Joe extended a friendly hand and a broad grin.

'Call me Joe.'

Bewlay ignored the offered hand, preferring to puff spray the hole in his face with his antiseptic aerosol. He noted an involuntary moue of disgust register on his guest's face.

'Not exactly Chanel Number Five, hm?' Bewlay smiled 'Not that I can smell it, of course.'

He then unscrewed the cap from his silver hipflask and took a swig, grimacing at the aftertaste.

'So, let's get down to it *Reverend*, hm? You've been pestering me by phone for days now and I told you several times that I already tried God and it didn't work. You persisted. I've relented. Tell me why—and don't bore me.'

'This may surprise you, Mister Bewlay,' Joe said, 'but whether or not you believe in God is immaterial to my presentation this morning. To be frank, I am not entirely convinced of his existence myself.'

'Then what the fuck are you doing here? I was under the impression you were to cure me by means of faith.'

'You don't need faith for my cure, sir. Only money,' Joe grinned. 'I am a reverend merely insofar as it helps me introduce my cure to the credulous. In other words, some with faith prefer to have it confirmed by my methods . . . but what I have come here to offer you today works just as well without it.'

Joe became serious.

'Now don't take me up wrong Mister Bewlay—Jesus Christ existed, sir. I certainly believe *that* . . .'

'Really?' said Bewlay. 'Then how . . . ?'

Joe interrupted.

'—but he was a man like you or I; a man who walked the dust of the world as we do every day, and who lived and breathed as we do every day and who was most probably as much like you or I as we could imagine—just ordinary folks . . . apart from one important aspect. He had the restorative gift sir—he could heal . . . of that I have absolutely no doubt.'

Joe leant over and took Bewlay's hand. Big Ian started forward, but Bewlay stayed him with a look.

'Now Mister Bewlay—all the son of God stuff?' Joe said, gently turning Bewlay's hand palm upwards. 'Maybe that was added to the stories afterwards because there was no other way in those times of explaining what he could do. But I can take it or leave it because it is irrelevant to what I am offering you.'

'Which is?' asked Bewlay.

Joe opened Bewlay's palm, lightly pressing a fingertip down into it.

'Are you familiar with the term 'half-life', sir? It refers to how long radiation clings to a place or an object before it eventually diffuses and becomes harmless . . . well, Jesus Christ of Judea was a veritable nuclear power station of *positive healing* radiation, sir and everything he ever touched holds the dying embers of that power yet—kinda like plutonium, but in a nice way. From whence this power came, or why—who knows? Maybe we are all born with such powers to a greater or lesser degree? Maybe it doesn't come in exact proportions like cake mix and some of us are lucky enough to receive a surfeit of this energy of the universe?'

'I believe that this is the first time I've ever heard the words plutonium and cake mix mentioned in the same breath,' said Bewlay, not unamused.

'Maybe,' said Joe. 'Personally, I don't care—all I care about is results.'

Joe began to press his fingertip harder down into Bewlay's palm.

'You feel this?' Joe asked. 'This is the ghost of an approximation of what Jesus felt that day on Calgary as the soldiers drove the spiked metal into his flesh.'

Bewlay stared down at his hand, Joe's finger unrelenting in its pressure.

'I have in my possession a rough-hewn, pig iron nail, black with age and blood,' he said. 'It is one of the Roman nails that pierced the actual body of Jesus Christ. It was bought originally by Mister Howard Hughes for a paltry thousand dollars from Muhammed edh-Dhib, child discoverer of the Dead Sea Scrolls, who found the nail amongst the scattered pots in that barren place. It was stolen from Hughes on the very day he died by an employee of the Sands hotel in Las Vegas . . .'

Bewlay's fingers began to curl as he felt Joe pressing harder and harder.

'. . . It fell into my hands when I bested this decrepit bell hop during a week-long debauch of blackjack, rye whisky and cocaine in that dreadful city of night. I am not ashamed to say, Mister Bewlay, that the relic is better in my possession than his, for I can spread its wonder to those who need it and can pay for it. I have seen it with my own eyes cure the liver, pancreatic, oesophageal, penile, brain, lung, spinal and eyeball cancers to name only the few I have faced down so far.'

'It didn't do much for Howard Hughes, did it?'

'Did you not hear me sir? I said it was taken from him on the day he died. Had it not been, who knows? It is my understanding that during the man's autopsy, many black tumours were found within him—tumours that should have killed him long before his actual expiration date, as it were.'

Bewlay remained silent, glancing down at Joe's fingertip still pressing into his palm.

'I am not telling you that you won't die, sir,' said Joe. 'Just that you won't die *yet* . . .'

'If this works so well, why haven't I heard about it?'

Joe smiled.

'I choose my clientele very carefully Mister Bewlay. They are a select bunch—moneyed and discreet. They have to be, for there is only a finite amount of this, um, *material* to go around. The Romans made their nails big—big enough to hold the weight of a man suspended, but every sliver I pare from this object to help a client reduces it permanently by that amount. Do you see? It is a disappearing commodity, like oil, but infinitely more precious.'

Joe let go of Bewlay's hand and sat back, a beatific smile on his face.

'There are others who would gladly grasp this chance with both hands sir. I have appointments to keep up and down the length and breadth of this good nation and across mainland Europe with people equally in need. I may well not pass this way again.'

Arthur had been aware of Big Ian looking intently at him, waiting for the signal to pick up the Yank and throw him out on his arse. But Arthur hadn't given it. Instead, he'd sat forward and stared intently into the young reverend's eyes, barely concealing the hope welling up from inside of him, his voice barely there when he finally managed to speak:

'How much?'

◆

'So—how—much?' croaked Tommy.

'Two hundred grand.'

Tommy laughed as well as he was able. After a moment, Arthur nodded.

'I was off my face, Tommy boy, I'd probably had a wee bit too much of the OraMorph, hm.'

'... you—were—being a—total fanny ...'

Arthur was lying on Tommy's bed, his head next to his brother's. His sense of smell was all gone, but he could taste on his tongue the rot in the atmosphere of the room. There had been no fresh air in here for ... well, since the pub had been sealed up anyway.

'Thing is though, I liked him,' Arthur continued, ignoring Tommy's observation. 'He was cheeky. He was confident. He was a good salesman and you know what? Even though I knew—and I really did, deep down—that he was talking shit ... that wasn't the point. I actually thought, why not? Nothing else I'd been trying was working. What was to lose? Money? Ha.'

Arthur was staring up at the ceiling. He hadn't noticed before now that there was writing up there as well. It went in a longhand, scrawled spiral around the base of the lamp hanging from its ancient and dusty, worn flex. Tommy's wee stepladders rested against a corner on the door side of the room. They were a fluorescent yellow, which stood out in the gloom—but it wasn't a happy yellow. Arthur had never liked that colour.

'I reckon there was a wee bit hypnosis in there too—all that hand grabbing stuff. He'd obviously banked on me being desperate enough to believe in anything that might help me.'

Arthur could hear the shallow, dry clicking from his brother's atrophied voice box as he made the effort to speak once more. He knew that this was a huge effort for Tommy, and he appreciated it. He drew his attention away from the writing above him, thinking that he probably hadn't seen it before because he never usually went around looking up at the ceiling.

Arthur pulled himself up on one elbow. Carefully, though—he didn't want Tommy's head to roll off the pillows again. Last time that had happened, he'd had to spend a couple of hours carefully picking all the carpet fluff from Tommy's face. It was harder to do round the eyes because the eyeballs had collapsed in on themselves and the lids were thin and tricky to handle without tearing.

That was when he'd decided to buy Tommy the glass eyes—and he was glad he'd done so, because even though they gave Tommy an unnerving, permanent goggle eyed stare, Arthur thought it was better than his brother looking like he was asleep all the time.

He concentrated on listening to Tommy, who was struggling with every word.

'. . . *you don't want . . . some cunt . . . taking . . . advantage of you, but . . .* '

'No Tommy—that's just it! I know this sounds stupid, but I would've given anything not to have known for *sure* that McGill was just a fly man! I wanted something to believe in! That's how these guys get away with it, isn't it? They know that somewhere deep down you know that it's bullshit—all they're waiting for is the okay to go ahead with the scam. It's like lottery tickets. You know it's a total con, but you do it anyway . . . because someone's got to win.'

'. . . *Do . . . they . . . ?* '

Arthur lay back again, resting his head on the pillow. His brother could be hard work sometimes. Tommy was right to be cynical, he knew . . . but then it was easy to be wise after the fact, and Tommy wasn't the one facing imminent death, was he? Tommy spoke again.

'*So—what—changed—your—mind about the rev-rend?*'

Arthur sighed.

'I sent Big Ian and Terry to follow him. I'd have been happier if I hadn't.'

❖

Arthur explained to Tommy that McGill had been trailed to his budget hotel, somewhere between a set of on and off ramps on the M8. It was a squat, puce bricked building of only two storeys and McGill's room had fortunately been on the ground floor. Terry and Big Ian had obtained the room number from the terrified Bosnian receptionist and as Big Ian had headed to the door, Terry had nipped round the back to the window to make sure McGill wouldn't try and do a runner that way. It was Terry who had heard snatches of the phone call McGill had made just before Big Ian had kicked the door in and it was Terry who had reported McGill's words verbatim to Arthur when they had returned empty-handed (apart from the unconscious body of the reverend draped over Big Ian's shoulder, of course) half an hour later. Big Ian had turned McGill's room upside down and been unable to find any fucking Roman nails or anything to do with Jesus and his fucking cross.

❖

'I was just after the relic Tom,' said Arthur. 'I knew it probably didn't exist and I was quite prepared to let the reverend off with a mild face kicking from the guys—as I said, I liked him, and he was only trying to scam me. But when Terry told me the things he'd said—I couldn't just let it go. If it had only been Big Ian who'd heard, he'd have kept his mouth shut, but you know what Terry's like—a total blether. I had to show that no one—not even a charming reverend—could get away with any of that shit or it would have spread all over that I was a total fud.'

'So what—did—he—say—about—you?'

Arthur shifted uncomfortably and told his brother that Terry had heard McGill saying that he would soon have 'the money'. That he was working a 'dude' who was the ugliest motherfucker he'd ever seen. He also said that the inside of the dude's nose looked like a split open red pepper and stank like a blocked drain. That he must go through some amount of Kleenex and that 'this dude' was so desperate for a cure he'd have listened to a cat farting in a box if he'd thought it was going to help him.

Tommy snickered.

'That's—quite—funny—'

'Doesn't *matter* if it's funny, Tom!' Arthur shouted. 'That's not the point, is it? I wasn't telling you to give you a fucking laugh, was I? For God's sake don't be such a fucking obtuse fucking wanker and concentrate on the fucking point I'm making—what matters is that I was looking weak! And that will never be allowed to happen; you of *all* people know that!'

There was silence from Tommy. Arthur stopped himself from ranting any further, getting a grip on his temper. He'd thought that he was over all of that childish, sibling bickering shite with Tommy, especially now that he was dead, but sometimes the old brotherly thing could still wind him up.

Tommy still said nothing. Arthur sighed and carried on, managing to put a more civil tone back into his voice.

'I had no choice from that point on, Tom. McGill was the author of his own downfall.'

Arthur looked at his wee brother's head on the pillow, resolutely mute now. Arthur hated it when Tommy went into a huff and gave him the silent treatment. His head just resting there made him think of Tommy as being lifeless as opposed to merely dead, and that depressed him. He knew from experience that once Tommy decided to dummy up there was very little that he could do about it. Best just to leave him for a while and let him cool down on his own. He hoped Tommy wasn't too upset about being shouted at . . . but he really should know better by now. How one is perceived can really affect one's business.

There was a banging on the downstairs door.

'*Arthur? It's me!*' called the familiar, high-pitched voice from below. '*Can I come up?*'

'That's Big Ian, Tommy.'

Arthur rose from the bed, feeling awkward now and ashamed of himself for his outburst against his poor brother. What had he been thinking, giving the kid a bollocking for daring to laugh at something that was actually funny? Just because the joke had been on him? Christ knew, Tommy got little enough entertainment up here, the state he was in. He couldn't exactly skip out for a night at the dancing, could he?

'Listen Tom, I'm sorry. Thanks for chatting with me, I feel better for that.'

The walk to the door felt long and lonely and Arthur was nearly there when Tommy started speaking again, but his voice was more raggedy and . . . well, *drier* would be about the only way Arthur would have described it. Individual words began coming out more slowly, and with ever larger gaps between them. It was a bit like receiving a particularly slow message on a Ouija board, being read aloud by a disgracefully pissed Stephen Hawking. Not that Arthur was complaining—it was a fucking beautiful miracle to be talking to Tommy at all.

'If—you're—that concerned—then—finish the—fuckin'—job— properly and don't—fuckin' shout the odds at me ya—ugly— wanker. Job's no'... done yet...... cuntface...'

The effort was clearly draining his brother, but Arthur had to ask.

'What d'you mean Tom?'

There were some long moments as Tommy was gathering what strength he had to reply. When he did, Arthur jumped back a little at the ferocity of his response.

'Use—your fuckin'—dome, Arthur! Who—else—is—involved? Look at his... phone. Who—the fuck—did—he—call?!'

Arthur felt like slapping his own forehead. The reverend's phone! Of course. Who the fuck *had* he been calling? And what might they know about Arthur Bewlay's private business? McGill was an American, wasn't he? So he *had* to have someone working with him in this country, probably the same person who'd tipped him off about the opportunity to exploit his cancer in the first place!

Arthur felt like a total dickhead, although to be fair he reckoned that it was probably the amount of drugs he was taking that clouded his brain enough to prevent him doing the obvious first time round. Tommy was, as usual, a genius.

'You make me feel totally thick sometimes, Tom, you really do. Why didn't I think of that?'

'Cos—you're—stupit and your face—looks like—an alien's cunt,' Tom offered. He sounded amused, but his voice really was almost played out as far as this wee session went.

Arthur was still laughing heartily at his brother's wit as he locked the bedroom door. Not that Tommy was going anywhere, but his return home was still Arthur's secret. The business was already on a bit of a shaky peg, what with his illness, and he knew that people wouldn't understand his new relationship with Tommy. Or *choose* not to understand it. It wouldn't be beyond someone,

Arthur thought, to take unscrupulous advantage of the situation for their own ends by maligning his mental health.

Being viewed as unpredictable and strange wasn't a disadvantage in his line of work, but it wouldn't do to be known as being completely beyond the pale—and Arthur well appreciated that perception was often much more important than reality in this game. Consequently it was *very* important to be perceived in the right way. If you weren't, and you let rumours fly around you, you were headed for a fall.

Arthur had sacrificed a lot in his life already—a *lot*—to ensure that he *was* and *continued to be* perceived in just the right way; as an iron man, certainly—hard but fair and whose extremes of violence and retribution were always perfectly justifiable. Any private habits that he had remained just that—strictly private. And he knew that, painful and heartbreaking as it so often was, sacrifice was something that had to be borne—regardless of the consequences.

The door downstairs was knocked again, or rather it was slapped vigorously with that peculiar flat of hand way that Big Ian had.

'Hold your horses, Big Ian!' he called, 'I'll be down in a tick!'

Arthur placed the bedroom key around his neck once more and turned the hall light back on. The bare bulb's glare showed the narrow, colourless corridor with its row of closed doors and its nylon carpet worn shiny. His own bedroom was opposite Tommy's—another room absolutely never entered by anyone but himself. About twelve feet or so further down on the same side was the locked door of what used to be Da's room. That was where both he and Tommy had been born and where Ma had died after (as Da used to say) shitting Tommy out into the world.

Arthur used it as his guest room these days.

Opposite that door was the sitting room where he spent most of his time, and ten feet beyond that at the end of the corridor was the narrow stairway leading down to the pub. A simple dwelling, but one that suited him. There was a magic about this whole place for Arthur. He liked its age, the fact that it had been standing here for over a century, long before any of the surrounding scheme had been thrown up around it. It was originally a coaching house on the great East road, it had been built by its Victorian architect to *last*. It was as solid as a fortress and so secure did Arthur feel there, that he had very rarely spent more than a night or two away from the place. He looked at Tommy's bedroom door and an unwelcome thought flitted butterfly like through his brain, alighting softly on his synapses.

Was he worried about Tommy getting out?

The thought flitted off again and he let it, before heading down the narrow, wonky stairs to greet Big Ian and all of his undoubted good news about the slow, unpleasant death of the Reverend Joe.

◈

Joe was being half-carried/half-dragged out of an ancient brass cage elevator by Grace, who was struggling and breathless under his weight, but gamely refusing to give in. This beautiful girl was determined and amazing, he thought. He would like to have helped out by taking more of the strain and standing on his own two feet, but his body seemed to have put itself on some kind of minimum power setting. Possibly it had had enough for one day.

Coming through the front door from the beautifully tiled but comparatively cramped communal hallway, he wasn't prepared for the huge chamber he now entered.

His first thought was that he'd been taken to some municipal public meeting hall or Victorian swimming baths. The ceiling was incredibly high for an apartment. The place was two storeys, with a gallery around the upper level. The walls on the ground level were lined with high bookshelves and full rows of ancient looking volumes. There were a couple of low, heavy oak tables, – sprayed with dusty, unread magazines and pushed against the bookshelves. There was an odd array of various types of different sized chairs dotted around that made Joe think of a group of disparate strangers forced together for shelter. In the centre of the ceiling, way above him was a beautiful dome of stained glass, each curved and acutely pointed pane displaying a sign of the Zodiac. Joe was still staring up at it when he stumbled and fell to the floor and,

99

as Grace struggled to pick him back up, he noticed for the first time that resting on two wooden trestles right in the middle of this room was a highly polished coffin.

Funny how sometimes a person couldn't see the wood for the trees, he thought. How the hell could he have missed *that*?

She chivvied him along past it to the far end of the chamber, and they struggled to clamber up the wrought iron spiral staircase to the gallery level. They had just made it, with poor Grace gasping and panting for breath, when Joe heard a distant door banging closed below. Grace left him leaning precariously against the handrail whilst she opened a door onto a bedroom behind him and he saw Maryam enter the hall—very unsteady on her feet. She looked up, having to stop for a breather, her face a grimace of discomfort and anger, her elbow resting on the polished coffin lid. Idiotically, Joe raised his hand and, grinning like a dope, waggled his fingers at her in the friendliest way he could manage. She had saved his legs, after all, and he was very grateful to her.

'Grace!' she screamed, ignoring him. 'You left me *downstairs*! I am more important than he is! I provide the money to run this place and to keep our lives! You will suffer for this, I *guarantee* you!'

He was pulled backwards, away from the balcony and the momentum carried him through a doorway, his arms weakly flapping to try and save himself from falling, before he found himself suddenly lying on a bed with the room spinning around him. He closed his eyes and the spinning stopped. He decided that he would try his best to never open them again.

From outside, the traffic's low roar worked hard at sending him off to sleep and made him think of a distant seashore heard at night. Or was it more like slow breathing?

He drifted off, feeling the hospital gown being tugged gently from his body by soft, friendly hands.

◈

Maryam lurched away from the temporary support of the coffin, hoping to reach the safety of her bedroom before she collapsed.

The heat from her hand had left a palm print on the surface of the dully shining wood that evaporated before she'd even reached the bottom of the iron staircase.

12

Skinny sat and smoked fags in the sex room at the back of the house. Naked and still wet between her legs, she ran her hand though her cropped black hair and looked at Sergeant Wendy lying face down in the single bed. She was hypnotised by the blackhead on the dozing Sergeant's shoulder . . . but decided not to squeeze it. That would have woken her up and Skinny could live without chatter for a while.

The state she'd been in, there had been absolutely no point in even thinking of seeing Mandy, and she hadn't wanted to be by herself, so she'd come here;—the sergeant was always good for a comfort shag. Maybe though if truth be told, Skinny thought, she didn't really mind missing out on her date. If only because it meant she wouldn't have to face up to the horror of being rejected. Maybe taking the coward's way out was better for everyone all round.

Standing up, she swigged the last inch of vodka from the bedside half-bottle, stepped over the sex toys and padded down the bare floorboard corridor to the bathroom to turn the taps on. She'd decided to clean Sergeant Wendy's bath for her. It was still ringed with all the garbage grease they'd both scraped off Skinny earlier, before their mutual need to have someone to pretend to love for a while overtook them.

She looked at herself in the full length mirrored bathroom cabinet and took in the wide, multicoloured bruise across her abdomen where Big Ian had punched her. She covered it with both hands, barely, and looked the rest of herself over . . . and saw once more exactly why she would never ever be able to keep someone like a Mandy, even if she could actually get her to agree to another date. She was rake thin, for a start, with absolutely nothing in the way of breasts and no hips to speak of. She looked like a teenage boy, even down to a big pair of size nine feet at the ends of her legs. God almighty, she thought, what a freak. She should have been a boy for fuck's sake! Not that she actually wanted a penis, but her life perhaps would have been simpler if she'd just had one to begin with. But that wasn't really the main thing she had going against her, was it?

She looked at her artificial eye. How she hated it.

Skinny presumed there was still some kind of market for the videos—once they were made, they were there forever after all. Who knew—perhaps the last tape she'd been forced to make was still doing the rounds out there somewhere? Even after all these years.

She remembered the feeling of warm liquid from her burst eye running down her cheek and into her mouth more than the actual pain itself. That one must've sold a million by now and Skinny wished she could trace every single person who'd ever watched the fucking thing.

She could sure do with the royalties.

Her phone started to ring. Fuck it; it was still in the back pocket of her jeans—probably coated with grease. She sighed, fumbling around in the heap of sodden denim on the floor, frankly amazed that the damn thing was still capable of ringing. Got it.

Urg.

The screen, aside from having a thin film of slime across it, was cracked and blank from the pizza bike accident . . . but she supposed that smacking it off the ground after Big Ian had punched her wouldn't have helped much either. She pressed 'Answer' and brought it to her ear, holding it a little away to avoid the grease.

'Hello?'

There was a long pause. She could hear breathing and started feeling uneasy.

'Hello?' she repeated. She suddenly recognised who it was and it felt like her insides had frozen. There was no one else who breathed like that.

'Hello, Skinny. Arthur Bewlay here.'

Shit! She thought. Sober up! Why was *he* ringing her? Had Big Ian spilled? Fuck! She made herself sound as normal as she could.

'Hello Mister Bewlay. How are you doing?'

'I'm fine Skinny, absolutely fine. Aside from dying of cancer, of course. I was just ringing to see how you were and to thank you for taking Big Ian to his hospital appointment. It wasn't very successful, I gather?'

'No, Mister Bewlay . . . did Big Ian not tell you?'

'Yes, he did. Listen, you're not thinking of going away anywhere soon, are you?'

'What do you mean? Where?'

'Nowhere specific. I'd just like to know that you're around the place, in case I need any other errands or things like that—we're a bit short-handed as I'm sure you know. You don't mind, do you? You weren't going on any trips to the polar ice caps or anything, were you?'

He laughed and Skinny pulled a face despite herself. Polar ice caps? What the fuck was that about? She hated this, she fucking hated it. At the best of times she never knew what this psycho fucker was thinking, never mind now that he was in the dog days of his sickness. She made herself put a smile in her voice.

'No boss! No ice caps, as far as I know.'

'Good. I'll give you a bell if I need you. Thanks very much. And do make sure you're round on Friday for your regular money, won't you?'

'Sure.'

He hung up abruptly, but that didn't necessarily mean anything. He did that anyway . . . but Skinny could feel the start of a sick, creeping panic. What had *that* been about? Had Big Ian blabbed? She shook her head, disgusted at her own naiveté.

Of *course* he'd fucking blabbed. She was such an idiot! What the fuck did she imagine she was doing, telling Big Ian what she was thinking!? She was disappointed in herself. *Obviously*, Big Ian was going to tell Bewlay.

Dummy!

She thought about her options—could she actually get away and manage to stay away until such time as Bewlay had snuffed it, however long that took? Would that even be any use? Bewlay had a long reach, especially if he felt personally slighted. Maybe that was what he was saying with the ice caps shit—reminding her that he was good at finding people?

Or maybe he was just being fucking random and bizarre like the complete nut job he was. It was time to leave, even if she had no chance, because by avoiding being in the same city as him she had a much better calibre of no chance. She decided she'd better see what clothes she could nick from Sergeant Wendy and just go now. If the sergeant woke up, Skinny would ask her for money. If she didn't, she would just take it. She preferred the second option because Wendy—although generous in many other ways—was tight as fuck about money and would almost definitely say no.

13

Joe was sitting up in bed looking around him. The dope seemed to have worn off and he was feeling pretty straight again, if hungry and a little dizzy. The walls of the room were covered in crucifixes of all sizes, and the headboard and footboard dripped rosary beads. There was a chorus line of freestanding crucified Christs along the tops of the drawers, the bureau and the bedside table and for good measure, there were posters of The Sacred Heart and a big reproduction of Dali's Christ of St John of The Cross pinned to the ceiling above his bed. Someone round here was into God in a big way, Joe thought.

Good. He could use that.

A little chill went down his backbone. This was the first time for what felt like an age that he'd been considering angles, and at that moment Joe knew that his mind was back in the office, feet under the desk and open for business. About goddam time.

The door was lightly knocked and the cheerleader—her name was Grace, he remembered—walked in without waiting for a reply, a tray in her hands. He could smell strong tea from the little china mug that had a '*Batman*' logo on it.

'This is Papa's old room, Joe,' she said, her smile dazzling and beautiful and all for him. 'I'm makimg a special supper amd you cam wear what you wamt from Papa's wardrobe because he ism't here emmymore.'

All of this just kind of washed over him as he sat up straighter in bed and stared at her. He couldn't remember ever being as struck by a girl's beauty as much as this before in his whole life. Everything about her, physically at least, was just . . . perfect. She had the kind of fresh face that modelling agencies would chop each other up for and an unaffected sort of innocence that he hadn't encountered since high school. He could also see, however, that she was mildly retarded in some way . . . but it was only noticeable when she spoke, because she sure as shit didn't look it.

With the crook of her elbow she phalanxed a bunch of crucifixes together to make room for her tray—ignoring several that fell heavily on to the floor—and as she laid it down she admitted bashfully that she had washed him when he was asleep. She held his gaze as if this revelation should hold some significance for him. He noticed that she had a deep bruise round her wrist and when she saw where he was looking she pulled away.

'I cam't stay im here alome with you,' she said.

He smiled at her, unable to disguise the fact that he was genuinely puzzled.

'Why not, Grace?'

'Because she said you would wamt to have sex with me and that I might let you amd that you would kmow that I might . . . and you would wamt to. But Maryam's a old poo . . . amd I love you.'

She then, seemingly unable to contain her excitement at her own daring, stood before him and twirled around in her loose summer skirt, showing him her legs and pants before stopping and giggling happily and smiling that brilliant, open smile of hers again.

'I fell from the tree—me, me, me. *I* fell from the tree . . . and *you* caught me.'

Joe searched in his mind for a suitable response, but found that there wasn't really anything he could say to that . . . but there *was* a memory there somewhere. From when he was in the ward . . . a dream? Girl falling from a tree? But how would Grace know that?

'Whem I was washimg you,' she said softly, 'your thimg got big amd hard. It still is.'

She twirled around again, her arms outstretched, her palms up, smiling smiling smiling before she stopped and gently shook her head at him, bringing a finger to her lips.

Shhhh.

She blew him a kiss and he watched her turn and bounce happily from the room, banging the door closed behind her. He could hear her humming tunelessly to herself as she receded from earshot.

He genuinely hadn't noticed his erection until she'd pointed it out, and had no idea whether that was a good or a bad thing. In fact he wasn't exactly sure quite what had happened there, but there *had* been mention of supper and that could only be good.

He looked down at his legs.

This was way better than 'retained'.

He'd never known or even heard of anything like it, and he'd been in the game since he was twelve. The old woman had done the most incredible thing. She was for real . . . and she surely was worth *a lot* of money. If she could cure him, she could cure other people—if she wasn't doing so already. Her power was truly staggering. What he could *do* with what she had! He felt like he'd stuck a pickaxe into dirt and oil had come bubbling out.

He got up from the bed and walked over to the massive wardrobe by the window for a squint at 'Papa's' clothes. He paused, curious as to where he was, and pulled the roller blind aside slightly. His breath caught in his throat.

He knew that he was looking down almost directly on to the motorway he'd been smashed up on. The old man. The leaper. The coffin. Frogs. 'Papa' . . . ? What had Grace said at the hospital—something about 'Papa' *causing* the accident? *He* was the leaper and this had been his room. It had been *his* hat that the, um, amphibian had been under. But that had been a hallucination, seen when he was still out of it from the drugs!

No, he corrected himself.

The *toad* hadn't been a hallucination—it'd had a perfectly legitimate reason to be there. It was the toad screaming like a girl in a horror film and attempting to *speak* to him that had been the hallucination.

Hallucination or not, though, he was now looking at the wardrobe apprehensively. It had better not be full of moving hats, he thought. If he was to see anything like that again, he'd be opening up the goddam window and doing some leaping of his own. It looked like some kind of black, upright sarcophagus and it wouldn't have surprised him in the least if he pulled open the doors to see a bandage swathed Boris Karloff reaching out for him. He pulled open the doors anyway and saw merely a pretty good selection of suits. Old fashioned, to be sure, and on the large side by the look of them but pretty stylish in a retro kind of way. He reached in and started looking through them, another hat panic over.

So . . . time for a little inventory. What else did he have to worry about?

He had no doubt that Bewlay would be aware of his disappearance by now and would have his bottom feeders out there scouring the streets for him. This apartment seemed the safest, in fact the *only* place to be, until he could source the capital to finance an escape. And Maryam would be that source.

He started pulling on the first shirt he could grab. It was time to see what was what, here at home with the Munsters. He felt bad that he hadn't actually gotten round to raising Trudy. Very bad, but the fact was that everything had turned to shit now and there was absolutely nothing he could do about it. Besides, she probably wouldn't have wanted to see him again anyway, even if she did recognise him.

Why the hell would she?

❖

Maryam had lain in her bed, drained, ever since they'd arrived back, alternately trembling with a bone deep inner cold or sweating and kicking the sheets from herself, her internal thermostat doing its own thing while her body tried to recover from the epic healing she had performed. She was completely exhausted—what she had managed to do for this American was the biggest thing she had ever tried and she knew now that she had been wise indeed to not ever have attempted anything like it before.

She had just reconstructed—from what was, after all, largely wastage and raw meat pulp—this young man's legs. Tiny shattered fragments of bone had been knitted together via her power, torn veins had been reconnected and burst arteries made whole. Nerve endings and muscles, which had just been so much slurry, could now be used for walking, running, jumping and *living*. But doing it had taken too much from her; it was as if her own life force had been sucked right out and it now made her wish, not for the first time in her life, that it could all just be over. Her life would be so much the simpler if she were dead.

She knew her eyesight was deteriorating (bleeding from the eyeballs clearly didn't help much in that department) and wondered how long it would be before she ended up shambling around the place blind, having to depend even more on that idiot Grace; leading her around the house, taking her to the toilet and such. It would be bloody awful.

And the thought of Grace attempting to *read* to her . . . ? Well, that was more than she could possibly bear. Braille would have to be learnt.

And yet she had truly loved living once—when her running had been as important and as natural to her as breathing—and when John had been both the centre of the life she'd had and of the life she had been looking forward to.

It was amazing really, that happenstance and the actions of no more than a few seconds could completely alter the course of someone's life, forever and ever and with no redress or right of appeal. She knew, she did, really, deep down she knew, that it was unfair to blame Grace, but if her younger sister hadn't been so foolish . . . so selfish . . . then Maryam might never have found out about herself and none of this would have happened.

But Grace had only been twelve years old.

She couldn't have known what she was doing.

Maryam told that to herself again and again, whenever the ghosts of the past would creep up on her, their spindly, shit covered fingers messing with her head, always seeming to be at their worst when she was alone. Grace had only been a child. And the fact that she would always pretty much be a child meant that she deserved

Maryam's sympathy and her care and her love—not this . . . this *venom*. Maryam, however, couldn't help herself.

Even though her sister's beauty—and let's face it, she thought, her *grace*—was a tragedy of potential never to be fulfilled, Maryam's life was a similar tragedy was it not? In fact her tragedy was worse, because she knew and could appreciate what she could have had and what she had now lost forever. Grace didn't and never would know any better. Blessed in her ignorance she could feel sad all she wanted to, but it would be the sadness of a child denied a toy or a chocolate bar, perhaps deeply felt but soon enough forgotten—Grace would never know *real* sadness.

If only Maryam had realised what it would lead to, how it would shape her life, she would never have exploited her ability. She would have walked away. Yes. From John, too. He had eventually walked away from her, after all, hadn't he?

Maryam was in such a state of decrepitude now that she surely would not be able to last much longer. And what would happen to her simple-minded sister then?

Who would look after her?

Who would look after her?

14

ARTHUR BEWLAY WAS STARING AT THE MOBILE PHONE IN HIS HAND.
'You'd never lie to me, would you?' he said.
He looked up, smiling, at Big Ian who was almost standing to attention at the door. Arthur thought he could detect worry in the big man's posture.
Big Ian shook his head solemnly. Arthur nodded. If he had faith in anything at all, it was that.
'This, Big Ian, is one of Reverend Joe's mobile telephones.'
Big Ian nodded. Fair enough.
'He had several, as you might expect from someone in his line of work, but this one seemed to have been special. It had only one number on it. Strange, yes?'
Big Ian shrugged, but he could see that this was going to be about more than just the numbers McGill kept on his phone. There was a look on Arthur's face that was starting to make him feel nervous.
'Well here's the news,' Arthur continued, 'I've just dialled the number on this phone.'
He manoeuvred himself onto the threadbare sofa, settling back and making himself comfortable as he opened his silver flask for a swig.
'But you just rung Skinny, Arthur,' said Big Ian, not really comprehending.
'That's right,' Arthur said, 'I've just rung Skinny.'
He looked at Big Ian evenly.

'Anything you want to tell me about?' Arthur drank from the flask, grimaced, and then took another swig. Big Ian remained impassive, despite feeling like he'd just received a kick in the nuts.

'She obviously knows him,' Arthur said, 'and knows him well enough to be the only number on this telephone. How has this come about, Big Ian?'

'I don't know Arthur . . . how would I know?'

'Because you're very close to her. You like her. She's your wee sweetie, isn't she? A wee hard-boiled sweetie.'

Big Ian didn't know what to say, so he said nothing. Arthur stayed looking at him, grim faced.

'My theory is that she was the one who informed Reverend McGill of my current health troubles and of my disposable income and of what a good target I would make for his con game,' he said. 'It makes sense—how, otherwise, would he have been able to pick me out from the herd? What on earth could have led him to *my* doorstep, if not a tip off? My question to you is, how much do you know about all this?'

'*Me?* Nothing Arthur, I swear . . .'

'Are you sure?'

Arthur sounded dangerous. Big Ian knew that whatever he said to him from this point on had better be the absolute truth.

'All I know is that we went to the hospital. Like I said—I went upstairs and he was gone. When I came back Skinny was still standing exactly where I left her. She didn't even want to go looking for him.'

'Maybe because she already knew where he would be, Big Ian. Just as a matter of interest, what *did* she want to do?'

Big Ian squirmed. Skinny hadn't *really* meant what she'd said. Had she? He would just have to hope that maybe his punching her in the gut might satisfy Arthur as being punishment enough. That was why he had done it, after all.

'Big Ian . . . ?' said Arthur. 'If there is something you want to tell me, I suggest you do it now.'

'. . . She wanted to talk about you.'

'Yes? About me? In what sense? My ears are ablaze.'

'I'd rather not say.'

'You'd rather not say.'
'I don't want her in trouble.'
'You don't want her in trouble.'
Big Ian shook his head, starting to feel ridiculous.
'What's the problem, Big Ian?' Arthur continued. 'Are you feeling conflicted? I hope not. You've never disappointed me in your life and to think that you might do so now gives me real pain. And you know that I'm in enough pain already, don't you?'

Big Ian nodded, miserable and guilty. Arthur had enough shit happening in his life as it was and he didn't want to add to it . . . but he didn't want Skinny in trouble either! Why did she have to start telling him what she was thinking? Why did things always have to go wrong? Always, always, always! People fell out with each other or they killed each other or themselves or had accidents or were born funny and nothing was ever straightforward and plain and simple—*everything* had a corner, *everything* had a complication—there was *always* a hidden secret that everyone seemed to know but him!

Arthur was watching the big man carefully. He was as easy to read as a Janet and John book. He decided to go a little more gently.

'I've always found it better to have things out in the open, Big Ian. You end up having sleepless nights otherwise. Why don't you just tell me about it?'

After a long time staring down at his feet, Big Ian knew he would have to tell on Skinny. Every instinct of loyalty to Arthur made him. He had no choice.

'She wanted us . . . she wanted us to . . . to help you die.'

It was as if every sound in the room had abruptly been sucked into a vacuum. There was a silence so perfect that the sudden barking of a stray dog miles away made Big Ian jump. Arthur was frowning and half smiling at the same time and he was looking with honest to goodness puzzlement in his eyes at Big Ian, who could see that the concept of what Skinny had been proposing was so outlandish to Arthur that he really couldn't believe it.

'. . . help me die?'

Big Ian couldn't look at him any more, an agony of guilt on his face. Arthur got it then and began laughing heartily—great rasping barks from his lungs, finding a strange, wet echo as they came simultaneously from the cavity in the middle of his face.

'You mean kill me? And this would have been for my own good, I suppose?'

Big Ian nodded.

'I had no idea she was such a humanitarian.'

Big Ian said nothing.

'And what exactly did you say to that, Big Ian? Please speak in a loud, clear voice.'

Big Ian said nothing.

'Keeping schtum isn't an option.'

'I didn't say anything, Arthur. I hit her to shut her up.'

'Good for you.' Arthur laughed again, delighted. 'Good—for—*you*!'

'She was more joking than anything else, probably. She was a bit drunk, I think.'

Big Ian was grinding his calloused palms together—a sign of frustration and confusion that Arthur recognised.

'She drinks too much,' Arthur said, 'you've said so yourself. And when drunk, she's unreliable and mouthy . . .'

'But that doesn't make her bad, Arthur . . . she didn't mean it . . .'

Arthur turned on Big Ian and in that moment all of his old energies seemed to have come flooding back to him, his face and his eyes suddenly animated by hate.

'Get a grip of your *fucking* brains you *fucking* moron!' he shouted.

Big Ian clamped it immediately, only recognising now just how furious Arthur actually was.

'Are we or are we not just after trying to kill Reverend McGill for shooting his mouth off about me?'

'Yes Arthur.'

'*Yes* Arthur! So are we saying that different rules apply for fucking one-eyed dyke fucking friends of yours?'

'No Arthur.'

'That's right—*fucking 'no, Arthur'*!'

Arthur was almost screaming. Flecks of brown sputum had flown from his mouth and nasal cavity and onto Big Ian's face. Big Ian knew better than to attempt wiping them off and he tried to remain as impassive as he could. Arthur abruptly turned away from him, taking deep breaths through his mouth, calming himself down before speaking again. Big Ian didn't take his eyes from him. He'd done that only once before when Arthur had been in a temper and had paid for his inattention with a bottle smashed across his face.

'Now, let's think this through, shall we?' Arthur breathed, starting to sound more normal. 'Let's try and figure out what is actually going on here, hm? She's with Reverend McGill somehow. We can both see that, can't we? Do *you* not think that she might be hiding him?'

'But I don't see how . . .' Big Ian said, '. . . he was gone by the time I got there—by the time *we* got there. How could she have taken him? Where?'

Big Ian was looking almost comically perplexed.

'Whoever's got him would have to own a private hospital or something,' he continued, 'because the guy was in intensive care and he was totally and completely fucked, Arthur. And even if he'd not been injured in the crash at all, he'd still be absolutely fucked up after what we done to him in the pub!'

Big Ian realised he was beginning to sound hysterical. He shut up and Arthur regarded him coolly for a few moments.

'The human body can continue to function through some amazingly traumatic events,' he said quietly. 'Believe me. I've seen it. And recently too.'

He smiled sadly. Big Ian wondered what he was talking about. Whatever it was, it was giving him a bad feeling.

'Don't get all het up,' Arthur said, brightening suddenly. 'I apologise for shouting, old friend, I genuinely do. I don't really believe that you have anything to do with this situation . . . your face is an open book to me. And it's not your fault you carry a torch for the treacherous wee lezzy Cyclops—you're not the first good man to have his head turned by love. Look at Samson and Delilah, hm?'

Arthur took a small handful of paper tissues from the open box next to his puffer spray and began to wipe the wet spots from Big Ian's face for him. The big man stayed as still as he could while Arthur continued to talk.

'Obviously she wouldn't have been able to carry him from the place herself, would she? Not if he was all fucked up like you say. So she must have accomplices. That's the only logical answer, isn't it? She'll be working in tandem with another firm. Guggan and his crew maybe, looking to muscle in before I'm even dead. Or the cops, even? Some kind of bizarre sting operation? Those are the only sorts of things that make sense here. Otherwise, what are we saying happened to Reverend Joe? That he ascended up to the heavens?'

Arthur laughed. Big Ian smiled as best he could manage. He knew where this was going to go now and the thought made him sad.

'But all isn't lost, is it?' said Arthur, 'Because although we don't know where *he* is, we certainly know where *she* is, don't we?'

Big Ian looked down at the floor. He prayed that Arthur wouldn't suggest he bring her over for a 'wee stay'. He wasn't actually sure he could bear that. Not Skinny. Arthur paced for a few moments. Then, he suddenly stopped and smiled a weird kind of half smile, and Big Ian knew he was pretending he'd just thought of something.

'I'll tell you what,' Arthur continued, 'let's have Skinny over for a wee stay. She'll tell us what she's got to do with all of this, and then she'll tell us where to find McGill and then we'll find him and then we'll all be happy at last and for good, what do you say to that? Hm?'

Big Ian knew what he should say—he should say: *'Sure Arthur. I'll go get her.'*

. . . but he didn't want to. But he didn't know what to say instead, either. He knew that Skinny's involvement in the disappearance of the Yank was impossible. That this was all some kind of insane coincidence—a mistake that was beyond his ability to grasp at the moment, but which he was sure *could* be explained, somehow.

Arthur headed for the door.

'Help me clear the spare room out for her,' he said, smiling happily, 'so that we can make her comfortable whilst she's here. It won't be for long, I'm sure . . . and I'll bet you'd be glad of a chance to spend a little time with her, hm? *Quality* time to discuss your 'relationship'? Time that you wouldn't normally get to spend with a woman, Big Ian. At least not one that you really like and that you didn't have to pay for. And believe me; time spent well is so rare.'

Arthur put a chummy arm around Big Ian's massive shoulders and whispered conspiratorially.

'Time spent well . . . *and with no consequences.* Trust me, there's nothing like it.'

Big Ian tried not to let himself think about what was being suggested. As far as Arthur was concerned, he knew, Skinny's betrayal meant that she was dead already and Arthur was taking it as read that Big Ian understood and went along with this—the suggestion being that he might as well have 'fun' with her before she was killed.

Big Ian didn't want that—not any of it. His mind started running away with him. He couldn't say no outright because if he wouldn't do what Arthur wanted, he knew that there were other men who would—strange, mentally diseased men scattered in odd bolt holes throughout the city; men protected by Arthur who owed him for that protection. They were men whose lives should have been snuffed out at birth and whose dark and ghastly appetites were fed and encouraged by Arthur. He was keeping them 'in the bank' for such times as when he might need something *really* special done for him.

Whatever happened, Skinny was a goner.

Big Ian knew he had no choice in the matter, but at least he could make sure she didn't die slowly. He could just snap her neck if it looked like Arthur was going too far and he would make sure she suffered as little as possible—and to hell with what Arthur wanted. It was the least he could do for her.

The very least, he thought.

'Are you . . . crying Big Ian?' said Arthur.

Was he? He hadn't noticed.

'Please don't be such a baby. Let's get that room cleared out.'

15

JOE EMERGED FROM THE CRUCIFIX BEDROOM ONTO THE GALLERY landing. The jacket of the vintage, grey worsted Hardy Amies suit he'd chosen from the wardrobe had hung on him like a circus tent, so he'd dispensed with it before finding a belt (he'd opened a drawer that looked like it was full of dead snakes) to hold the huge, waisted trousers up. The plain, white cotton shirt he'd chosen was equally voluminous but he found that rolling the sleeves up and some judicious tucking in made him look a little less like he was in a Spandau Ballet tribute act. The dead man's shoes, however, fitted perfectly and although delighted by this as far as having comfortable feet went, he didn't want to dwell on it as a concept.

'Papa' must've lost some hellish amount of weight before he'd decided to leap onto the road, he thought. Some kind of cancer probably. Joe had seen a lot of it and knew that the amount of pain it eventually involved could drive anyone to suicide. He sure knew *that* for a fact.

Above him, the stained glass dome in the ceiling glowed weakly from the city light bouncing down from the dark orange clouds above. Whoever had designed this place was sure into astrology, he thought, and although nowadays to most people Zodiac just meant '*your lucky star signs!*' and a couple of lines of one size fits all about your love life, the people who were into it when this place had been built took it a lot more seriously. Obviously. Because stained glass domes in ceilings didn't come cheap, even in the days of little match girls and infant chimney sweeps. And he could see enough of the terrific workmanship involved in the frame and glass to surmise that this vast late Victorian apartment—which looked to him so far to be in pretty excellent condition—could well hold more of the kind of esoteric, fin de siecle arcanery that some collectors were really nuts about. Nuts enough to pay well over the odds.

He'd been inside enough old wealthy people's houses to develop a pretty good eye for what would be valuable and what wouldn't and he knew a more than fair amount about antiques and art—he had made it his business to. He had, in fact, suffered through a straight job for nearly six months at the Barrington auction house in Elizabeth, Alabama in order to train up.

After all, hard cash wasn't the only thing one could be paid in.

Specialist dealers, Joe thought, would love to get in here and do a forensic pass for anything old school mystical or occult—a particularly lucrative market since the turn of the new century; stuff from the days when tables levitated or fairy photographs developed and ectoplasm could be obtained from the cat. Those times were, after all, the wellspring for pretty much every cult, alternative religion or crackpot sect that had happened afterwards. There was even some sort of astrological link between the world's number one all time favourite money spinner—Jesus—and the Zodiac. He'd looked into it a while back but hadn't really found an angle in it worth exploiting. At least, not yet, anyway. But he was sure that if he put his mind to it, he would. And anyone, he thought, who was unable to make money from Jesus in *some* way had to be a complete idiot.

Joe caught himself smiling. Well he'd sure woken up, hadn't he?

He got moving again.

Across the canyon of the great hall, a Victorian splendour of brass fittings, copper pipes, real porcelain and dark hardwood could be glimpsed through the half open bathroom door. He could just see Grace standing over there, performing the unmistakable motions of hair brushing on Maryam. He walked around the gallery toward them, hearing Maryam complain in a low-level war of whispering attrition against Grace and her flair for tugging. Every other door on the way round the gallery level was closed and, much though he'd have liked to nosy around some more, there was no point in risking upsetting Maryam prematurely. He was sure he'd know everything of value here soon enough.

The coffin, he noted, was still on the trestles downstairs.

So what had happened with dear Papa, he wondered. Why hadn't Maryam cured him? Maybe she couldn't do terminally ill people—or 'terminals' as Phil K, Joe's IT contact from Massachusetts, had called them. (This was when he'd been compiling his buckshee list of Scottish incurables for Joe to visit and had been in a punning state of mind.)

Phil K's hacking skills tracked down high dosage morphine based prescriptions (for a fee of course), which Joe would then follow up. The simple equation was: a dying mark got a lot of dope to help them slide down the plughole and the high-strength pain relief kept the worst effects of their condition at bay . . . which helped render the 'client' pliable to the word of the Lord. Or whatever it was they could be made pliable to. But of course there were exceptions. Like Bewlay. And Brewster, too . . .

Joe stopped that thought dead right there.

He wasn't about to start thinking about Brewster. Not right now.

He needed to start thinking about Maryam and what she could do because she surely to God was worth a hell of a lot of money and he was going to make sure a share of it came to him.

He reached the open bathroom door and Grace saw him at the same instant he saw her. A wild mixture of expressions ran across her face like cloud shadows crossing a hillside in a high wind; surprise, delight, desire . . . The girl seemed to have absolutely no censoring mechanism in her at all to prevent people from seeing directly into what was going on in her mind. That would come in handy, he thought, as far as getting the best out of this situation went. Whatever this situation actually was.

He stepped into the bathroom and Maryam spoke without turning.

'Grace tells me it's Joe. Is that correct?'

'It is, ma'am. And you are Maryam?'

She gave him the briefest of curt nods, her back still to him.

'Is that all there is?' she said.

'My full title is the Reverend Joseph O. McGill, but do, please, just call me plain Joe . . .'

He'd put his best, most sincere sunshine into his voice but he could tell Maryam's thermometer wasn't climbing any. Never mind, he'd just have to try harder.

'I would like to thank you, Maryam,' he said, 'from the bottom of my heart for what you've done for me. It was the most remarkable thing—an honest to goodness by God miracle . . . you saved my life.'

She was already waving his gratitude away with a bony, glove sheathed hand before he'd finished speaking.

'No, I did not. Your life was in no danger—at least, it better not have been. I simply saved your legs.'

That stopped him. *Simply?* God almighty.

'Nevertheless . . .' he began.

'So, a "reverend",' she interrupted. 'Aren't we the blessed ones, Grace? We've got a reverend as our guest.'

Grace had forgotten all about hairdressing by now and was staring at Joe instead, very evidently enthralled by him—her slim, elegant fingers half embedded in the grey, split end halo around Maryam's head.

'And what is your church?' said Maryam.

Excellent, thought Joe. She seemed ok with the notion of having some kind of minister in the house, so he'd give her the works.

'Baptist,' he said. 'At least, originally—but during my travels I expanded my outlook. These days I cover a broad church. I spent some time on a mission in Lima, Peru and from there paid visits to most places of note in that region. I have extensively travelled the continent of Africa, I have hidden in the banned and forbidden Christian enclaves of North Korea in the shadow of their nuclear ambitions; I have been to many wild and still untamed places, but also to Hong Kong, Australia, the subcontinent of India . . . I depend on the charity of my fellow man to help me wherever I go and I have seldom been disappointed.'

He spread his arms and smiled his best gosh darn it smile.

'Case in point . . .' he beamed, making a play of looking around him.

'You like the sound of your own voice, don't you?' said Maryam.

Joe laughed, but it was genuine enough. The old lady was a tough cookie, but she spoke as she saw and that was cool with him.

'An occupational hazard, Maryam—I do apologise.'

Grace had been looking more and more thrilled at Joe's travelogue of exotic destinations, barely noticing Maryam taking her by the wrists and removing her hands from her hair. Maryam finally turned, but with an effort, to face Joe.

She took in his outfit for a moment before ignoring it.

'So what brings you to this country?' Maryam continued. 'Have we become so depraved and godless that we need missionaries?'

'Well, that depends on your point of view . . . but that's not why I'm here. Now you probably wouldn't believe it,' Joe said, making himself even more toothsome for her as he came further into the bathroom, 'but I'm a native of this very land. In fact I was born in this city . . . generations of my family were raised in this old town . . .'

'I don't care, and I didn't ask about your family, I asked about you. Why are *you* here? What is the purpose of *your* visit?'

'Maryam!' Grace cried, 'Dom't be so rude to Joe!'

'It's alright Grace,' said Joe. 'I'd be nervous of a complete stranger in my house too—she's just looking out for the both of you, and that's ok. I wish my mom had looked out for me as much when I was younger.'

The change in atmosphere was as immediate as it was chilling. Grace was all of a sudden staring at the floor and Maryam was looking at him like he'd been dipped in yak shit and served up as the evening's entree. What had he said? Maybe she wasn't Grace's mom? An aunt, then? Maryam smiled abruptly. It was broad but there was no humour in it.

'I am not Grace's mother, Joe,' she said, her voice sounding carefully neutral.

'Oh,' he said. 'Well, I'm sorry if I've offended you . . .'

'You haven't. I know exactly what I look like. I'm just not used to hearing it spoken aloud, that's all. My other visitors are very careful not to bring the subject up.'

'Well, um . . .' he said, 'what relation are you? If you're a relation?'

'I am her sister,' said Maryam.

Joe paused for a moment before replying, looking between both the women.

'I see.'

'No, you don't,' she said. 'How could you? Look at me. I'm separated from Grace by decades and you're wondering by how many and how it came to be.'

'Well, I'm sure it's not uncommon for siblings to be separated by, um, several years.'

Maryam stood then, raising her hand once more to silence him. He supposed she didn't want him to start guessing how many years. He was relieved.

'Please pardon my abruptness. I'm not used to intelligent social company—as you can probably tell,' she said, indicating Grace, who didn't look like she minded the slight at all. Maybe she wasn't aware there had been one, thought Joe. Maryam continued.

'Let's get back to our little Q and A, could we?' she said. 'Why are you here?'

'Call it a vacation, if you like,' he said. 'I just felt a need to re visit the old country. I suppose I felt I could reconnect with the land of my birth . . . '

Maryam sighed.

'Shut up, please,' she said.

He shut up. His smile remained fixed. This didn't seem to be going well at all. He wondered if he could go out, come back in and start over again.

'Are you grateful for what I've done for you, 'Reverend'?'

'Well, yes. Of course I am!'

'Then please stop putting on your act. I don't know exactly what kind of bullshit you're trying to give me, but I do know that it is bullshit. Please, just behave yourself and act like a real human being.'

'*Maryam*!' said Grace.

Maryam ignored her.

'I'll start you off if you like. There was a man looking for you in the hospital with some kind of weapon,' she said. 'And even if you were the worst churchman in the world, a midnight assassination in an intensive therapy ward is taking atheism to an over enthusiastic extreme, d'you not think?'

Joe shifted uncomfortably. So she knew about the big guy. That wasn't good.

'Try again, Reverend. Last chance. The police are just a phone call away, and we've already established that you're not exactly on the straight and narrow.'

'Really?' he said, striving for amused bafflement and failing. 'Well, I don't think that 'we' have established anything of consequence Maryam.'

'Let me guess what you're thinking now—you're thinking who would get to the telephone first. You? Me? Or the idiot girl with the hairbrush? You're thinking that you would win hands down and so you would. But what then? Would you keep us prisoner here? For how long? You would have to sleep sometime and keeping us locked in a room while you did so would become wearying. Or perhaps it would be better to simply murder us? What would happen when we got visitors? What would you say?'

'I'd say you're maybe getting a little bit carried away,' he said.

'Maybe I am. Maybe you're not so desperate as I imagine. Maybe you wouldn't stoop to threatening two women to save your own skin from whoever is after you.'

She smiled at him.

'Maybe.'

Her teeth looked greenish and loose, their edges chipped . . . but he found himself smiling back at her.

'Thanks for the benefit of the doubt.'

'All I want is for you to tell me the truth,' she continued. 'I deserve at least that. If we are to be hiding you then I would like to know exactly why we should be doing so.'

'I'm not hiding anything, Maryam—I have no idea what you're talking about. As far as I know there's no one after me . . .'

She raised her hand and he shut up again.

'Please have no worries about my discretion. I have absolutely no desire at all to let the outside world intrude on me, but I am not going to allow you to stay here for one more second unless I know for sure that you are not going to bring disruption and danger to us. Why are you here and why is someone after you?'

Joe sighed. He was finding it harder to resist her interrogation and was beginning to consider whether he actually *should* resist any more.

'Well?' she said.

'Look . . . the less you know the better,' he said. 'Honestly.'

'Well that's a step forward. At least you're admitting that there *is* something to know. I'm very encouraged by this Joe. Please continue.'

He shook his head.

'No?' she said. 'Let's try again. The less I know the better? I disagree. The more I know, the better protected and prepared I am. Tell me the truth.'

He took a step over to the clawfooted, enamel bathtub, sitting down as wearily as he could in *faux* defeat. He would get her off his back with a version of the truth. Who knew? It might even help.

'I'm a faith healer . . .'

Maryam merely blinked at him.

'A faith healer . . . ?'

Joe nodded and continued on, aiming for humble sincerity and succeeding.

'The person who was, uh, after me? He was a dissatisfied customer. Or, at least, a dissatisfied customer's representative. They were bad people and I wish that I'd never gotten mixed up with them, but my calling is to help the sick where and when I can in my own small way. Nothing like what you can do of course. Happy?'

'Do I look happy?'

'It's really hard to tell Maryam.'

'Believe me Joe, when I'm happy you'll know about it.'

'So you're not happy. There's nothing much I can do about that. I've told you everything.'

Maryam looked at Grace.

'Observe this Grace—how lies spring naturally to the lips of men like him.'

'Are you a healer like Maryam?' asked Grace, eyes wide.

Joe shook his head.

'No, Grace. Not like Maryam. I'm more of a . . . well, as I say—I do *faith*.'

'No, indeed,' said Maryam, dryly. 'Most definitely not like me. You're a con man, aren't you? You take advantage of the sick.'

He smiled a little tightly.

'That's a matter of opinion.'

'There's quite a lot about you that's a matter of opinion. Is there nothing solid about you Joe?'

'I'm really starting to feel not too good, Maryam,' he said.

His voice was sounding clipped to him. His throat was dry and he cleared it awkwardly.

'You take advantage of the sick and most probably the dying, too,' she said. 'I should have guessed you were that sort of person from the moment I saw you.'

Grace nervously tried to interrupt her.

'Maryam . . . please dom't . . .'

'Shut up Grace. People are talking.'

Maryam pressed on, staring directly at Joe.

'You're the perfect specimen for such a low practice. Your face is like a great big ice cream—sweet and appealing to draw one in, but basically just fat and water.'

There was a silence for a few moments.

'I wouldn't go shouting too loudly about people's faces,' Joe said quietly. 'No offence.'

'None taken. As I've said already, I'm perfectly aware of what I look like. So how do you do it? Do you tell them that God works through you?'

'I see what I do as being of help and comfort to people who need it.'

'But you don't actually cure anyone, do you?'

'I believe I already said something to that effect earlier, ma'am. I provide faith.'

He was starting to feel depressed now. He thought that maybe he'd been too sure of himself too soon after the horrific trauma he'd just been through. Leaping out of bed thinking that he could just own this place by sheer force of his irresistible personality—how ridiculously egotistical was that? He should have just stayed under the blankets—Maryam could clearly smell blood.

'Terminally ill people are the best customers in the world for your sort aren't they?' she continued. 'Because they consist mainly of hope—and hope is, after all, your stock in trade, isn't it? The deep down inside hope that the impossible will happen; that they'll just wake up one morning inexplicably cured, or that an undiscovered genius in a lab coat will take all their troubles away with a hypodermic full of miracle goo—or that someone like you will be able to keep your promises,' she said. 'I mean, that's why someone was after you, wasn't it? You disappointed the wrong person, Reverend McGill, didn't you?'

Maryam began to laugh to herself.

Now he felt *really* down. Said aloud like that, it really did sound reprehensible, and he knew that it wasn't—mostly. These people didn't need their money anymore, did they? And it wasn't as if he was taking everything from them and robbing their families, was it? They were going to die anyway, for God's sake. All he was doing was making their lives more hopeful before the inevitable happened, and what the hell was wrong with that? Sure, he did it for profit, but then lots of far worse things were done in the world for profit. Far worse. What he did was between him and the client and he was, truly, never greedy; he asked for and got fair dues and in return, he *did* give them hope, and in many cases good cheer . . . and nine times out of ten he gave them good old fashioned Holy Biblin' entertainment—or similar—along with it, if that was what they were into. He had natural abilities he could be proud of, goddam it.

. . . *although*, a small voice in his head said to him . . . *what about the one time out of ten when you didn't give 'good old fashioned entertainment' in return for the 'fair dues'? What about that one time in ten that forced you across the goddam Atlantic Ocean, all the way back to this rainy, cold, shithole country? Made to flee before the cops grabbed you for the old hippy's death? Forced to hide behind your citizenship over here in this blighted* city—*desperate enough to go to a goddam gangster to make a quick score? What about that time, Country Joe, good ole boy, everyone's friend, wouldn't harm a flea?*

Joe shut out that part of his mind. Brewster hadn't died *because* of him. Not really. He was going to die anyway. That was the whole fucking point. All he'd done was . . . help him. He'd never done anything violent (*Never, Joe?* the small voice said). Ok then, *intentionally* violent in his life.

Brewster had *wanted* to die.

He had said time and time again that he welcomed death. . . . and Joe *had* been reluctant, of *course* he had, but Brewster had offered him a lot of money . . . so much money . . . and all simply to help him stop breathing.

Goddammit, he thought. Why the hell was he thinking about all of this *again?* Didn't he have enough to worry about without that old fuck Brewster sneaking up and sandbagging him? Besides, it wasn't murder—you can't be accused of murdering someone who'd asked you to kill them—at most it was . . .

'Assisted soomicide,' said Grace.

He looked up, startled. Had he been speaking out loud? What the fuck?

'Who said anything about that?' he said, hearing a nervy tremor in his voice.

There was silence in the room. Grace's breath was coming in short, sharp pants, like she was afraid. Maryam's was slower, more controlled. There was the occasional wet, buried gurgle from her chest; like she had phlegm trapped somewhere deep down there.

'That was interesting,' she said. 'Are you aware that you haven't said a single word to us for at least a minute?' She smiled at him. 'Penny for your thoughts.'

'What's going on?' he asked quietly, glaring at them both.

'We both have a gift, Reverend McGill,' she said. 'You already experienced mine at the hospital. This one is Grace's.'

'What? Mind reading?'

He was gripping the sides of the bathtub, hard, and he realised that he was straining to not get up and just run out of there. One second he'd been sitting, his mind on the matter at hand and the next his head had gone wandering off somewhere else—somewhere he didn't want it to go.

'Not really mind *reading* . . .' Maryam continued, 'it's more of a . . . oh, I don't know how best to put it. More of a *joining up* with someone's mind. Being inside their head with them, for a very brief period of time, as far as I've been able to work out. Her descriptions of these episodes aren't very detailed, which isn't surprising, given the way her brain works. Or rather doesn't.'

Maryam was being light about it.

'I'm not finding this funny,' he said.

'Not everything is, Reverend. Look, don't worry. It's random, unpredictable and usually very brief. She rarely comprehends what she sees or feels. Do you, Grace?'

Grace spoke quietly.

'Did I saym somethimg Maryam?'

'Yes dear. You said 'assisted suicide'.'

Joe groaned inside, growing tenser. He wanted out of there.

'I dom't know what it meams,' said Grace, very shyly.

Maryam stood abruptly at that point, giving Joe a start. She stepped over to Grace, taking her gently by her wrist.

'Did you experience Mister McGill's mind?'

Grace looked down at the floor as if she'd done something shameful.

'Go on dear, speak up,' said Maryam.

'Yes Maryam. I did.'

'What did it feel like?'

'Like the first time, whem he had his accidemt. He was frightened.'

Maryam smiled over at him and he thought he could detect . . . was that triumph on her face?

'Don't look so worried,' she said, 'I really don't think she gets any more than an emotion at most. Sometimes just a phrase . . . she could just as easily have said 'rotary lawnmower' or 'cheese and onions' . . . had you been agitated about such things.'

Joe wasn't sure if Maryam was doing a number on him or not. Grace looked at him, her eyes wide with terror of chastisement, her hands clasped together tightly as if in prayer.

'However, without context, the random means nothing, don't you think?' Maryam continued. 'Grace does not have the capability to comprehend what she feels or sees when she's having an event. She has neither a precise gift nor a precise mind and expecting sense to come from what happens to her is like sending someone who speaks only Cantonese to report on the Parliament of Sweden.'

'It seemed pretty precise to me,' he said.

'Believe me,' said Maryam, 'if Grace had an ability to read people's minds at will and with any kind of precision she would be the one performing like a circus freak for a living, and not me. I would make sure of it.'

'Please Joe, I'm sorry,' said Grace suddenly, on the verge of tears. 'I dom't meam to do it. It just happems.'

Joe said nothing.

'She's sort of like a radio, I suppose,' Maryam continued. 'A receiver, of course, not a transmitter. As I say, she only manages to tune in when someone is 'shouting' loudly or intensely enough. In fact it's a bit of a nuisance—she hears all sorts sometimes when she's out getting the shopping. Apparently unborn babies in the wombs of unfortunate schoolgirls make a *lot* of noise.' She smiled at Joe. 'Who knew?'

He glared at her.

'So . . . would you care to explain the term 'assisted suicide'?'

'The term seems pretty self-explanatory,' he said. 'If you're having any problems with it, I'd suggest investing in a dictionary.'

'I was meaning specifically as it relates to you,' she said.

'It doesn't relate to me. Whatever you're thinking, you're mistaken.'

'Is it part of your scam?'

'No.'

'I'll have to take your word for that, won't I?'

'You don't have to take anything,' he said. 'Your house, your rules. You can throw me out on my ass if you want.'

'This person who was after you in the hospital . . .' she said, ignoring this, 'perhaps now you'll be less coy about him and why he was after you. After all, I think I know you a lot better than I did five minutes ago.'

Joe suddenly decided that he had had it with this pair. First, he starts opening up when he doesn't need to, spilling the beans to these two weirdos on how he earned a living. Next thing he knew, goddam Grace was running around barefoot in his fucking head, picking up his thoughts like daisies in a fucking meadow. *Dammit! Why* had he started opening up like that?

'Thanks for the clothes, I've got to go,' he said. 'I'll send you some money for them when I get fixed up.'

He stood and walked from the room. Grace gasped, about to run after him, like a child who's puppy was being taken away.

'Joe . . . Joe . . . I wom't do it agaim I wom't I promise!'

Maryam grabbed her arm, and although she didn't have much strength, Grace had learned a long time ago to respond immediately to her sister's touch. She stopped and saw that Maryam was smiling.

'Shhh, Grace, there's a dear,' she said reassuringly. 'He isn't going anywhere.'

❖

Joe strode along the landing in the semi-dark, grabbing at the banister to better swing down the spiral staircase more quickly. Maryam waited until she heard him reach the bottom before shouting through the open bathroom door.

'Good luck, *Mister* McGill! I hope that you find somewhere suitably warm and comfortable to shelter you tonight . . . and I hope that your hospital friend doesn't find you! But if you wouldn't mind sending us your forwarding address—just in case we meet someone who's looking for help committing suicide. We could recommend you!'

Her words had stopped him dead. He was at the bottom of the staircase, his hand gripping the black, wrought iron banister. He looked up at the balcony above, at the harsh electric light spilling out from the open bathroom door. What the hell was he doing? Where did he think he was going to go? And what was he going to use for money when he got there?

He was trapped.

Maryam shouted out to him once again, although her tone had become much softer.

'If you do decide to stay a little longer, Joe, you would be most welcome to have dinner with us. Grace, I believe, has already made something especially. If you wish to make yourself useful, you may lay out the cutlery on the dining room table!'

There was quiet then, for a moment, before he heard her speaking conversationally once more to Grace.

'I'm feeling a little chilly now, dear. Please button me up.'

He thought over his options. It didn't take long. He guessed he'd better go locate the dining room.

16

Big Ian was tamping down the wet earth with a shovel. He was humming quietly to himself and remembering the day his mum had been buried. He had cried a lot the night before the service, but from then onwards, he'd never cried ever again about anything. Until now. He still missed her, most of all on Sunday nights when he would tune in to the radio to see if there was a play on, just like she used to. There usually was, and he would sit back and close his eyes and keep them closed all the way from the announcer's introduction through to the last credit and music's end. He seldom understood or was even interested in the drama being played, but that wasn't the point. He wanted to connect to his childhood and to when he'd felt the unconditional love of his mother, sitting on her lap as she had listened. She'd always preferred the radio to the telly, saying that it took her back to the days when she was a wee girl and they didn't have tellies. She said that the pictures you could see in your own mind were always a million times better than the ones other people made for you to see.

Big Ian had to take that on trust.

In fact, Arthur often said that Big Ian didn't have any imagination at all and that was why he was so good at the jobs he did for him. He could never see the other fellow's point of view, Arthur said. Therefore no matter what amount of pleading or begging, Big Ian was simply incapable of—what was the word Arthur said?—of *emp-a-thighs-ing* with anyone. It was Arthur's opinion also that

Big Ian had a medical condition that made this so and that he was born that way, but Big Ian knew that wasn't so. He hadn't been like that when he was wee. He *did* have an imagination—it was just buried somewhere inside him under the tons of rubble caused by the life he had lived.

He liked the feeling of continuity he got from listening to the radio now. Both he and his mum had ending up doing not only the same things for comfort in their adulthood, but for essentially the same reasons. His Auntie Pauline would sometimes come over to see mum and they would all sit there quietly, sipping their tea, listening to the voices coming from the wireless, all in their own way dreading the sound of the door opening and the return of his father. Auntie Pauline was long gone now, as was her daughter—Fi—for whom he'd harboured an unrequited crush. And now Fi's daughter, Ella, was also gone, being buried here by him, along with her dickhead boyfriend Jackie, in this wasteland of giant weeds and abandoned mattresses.

Big Ian stood up, his back aching from the constant freezing drizzle soaking through his clothes and the work of shifting shovelful after shovelful of damp earth, first of all out of the ground and then back in again over the tops of the two bulky black bin liners. They had been sealed around the tops with red and white Christmas themed sellotape—the only roll to be found in the kitchen drawers of the pub flat.

He hadn't liked looking at them laid there in the hole. The bags had looked too small, as if they'd contained children.

But they didn't, he told himself. And he didn't want to go thinking of them like that. Ella and Jackie were (correction, *had* been) adults, not kids, and big enough to make their own decisions and mistakes. It wasn't his fault that they were junkies. Besides, they were going to die anyway, and sooner rather than later, with all that crap they were injecting into their bodies. Ella's life had been over from whatever moment it was she'd started sticking that fucking Afghani poison into her veins. And even if she'd lived, he told himself, even if she had come off the smack and recovered, her life—the *real* life she'd once had the potential to live—that would never be. The drug had long broken her inside and she was better off dead.

That was what Arthur had said anyway.

Big Ian looked over at Arthur across the waste ground, standing leaning against the bonnet of the car admiring the orange flames roaring from the Grangemouth oil refinery across the bay, a place that was at once both gigantic and distant, like the busiest factory in Hell.

Big Ian didn't like what had happened to his niece. She hadn't deserved to die like that. No one did.

❖

Back at the pub, when the guest room door had been opened by Arthur so that they could 'clean out' the room for Skinny, Big Ian was as close to being shocked as he had ever come. He saw instantly that Ella and Jackie were already dead, having served their time as Arthur's guests. From the way the bodies were splayed out, Arthur had clearly been busy with them right up to their last moments and probably beyond.

There had been surprisingly little blood though, and Big Ian saw that Arthur had actually been stitching up whatever wounds he had created on them. Seeing that Big Ian was staring at his handiwork, Arthur had matter of factly explained that he'd been sewing them up as he went along, so that no wound had been open for longer than he'd needed it to be.

The lumps and bumps of the objects he had been inserting into Ella and Jackie whilst they were still alive could clearly be seen; misshapen and poking against their emaciated and stretched pale skins. There were dozens of . . . things inside them. Nearly all in their torsos, although Jackie seemed to have had something inserted into his scrotal sac that enlarged it grotesquely.

It would have been unbearably painful—all of this, for both of them—Big Ian thought, even with the constant medication of the heroin Arthur said he'd been giving them. Big Ian didn't know what to think or how he should react. Arthur was blithely gabbing away at him, and all Big Ian could do was stand and stare at these two emaciated bodies. He was dazed, he supposed. It was one thing, he knew, to torture some stray dog, or some cunt that'd crossed you or owed you and who deserved it. It was one thing to kill someone, or several people. It was one thing to bring people up here for bouts of Arthur's own particular brand of sex. Big Ian had done all of these things for Arthur.

But nothing like this.

Big Ian stood in the doorway, looking down at the hideously disfigured and abused corpse of the sole remaining member of his family, and her useless, stupid boyfriend—jammed with his back into a corner of the room, as if he'd been pushing himself away from whatever had been happening in front of him—and started wondering about the choice he'd made to be loyal and faithful to Arthur.

Surely he wasn't feeling anger? Not towards Arthur? Arthur had done everything for him and Arthur was in charge and Arthur was always right. That had been proved time and time again. But . . . maybe this time Skinny was the one who was in the right? Maybe she'd actually had a point after all? It was the old Arthur—the Arthur who hadn't had the cancer—who had always done what was right. Perhaps *this* Arthur, the poor Arthur driven to distraction by his pain and the fact of his death, had gone too far? And if he had, did that mean he shouldn't be in charge any more? Skinny's motives had been selfish, but Big Ian knew that his wouldn't be.

He could do it right now, he'd thought, here in this room.

Then it would just be a question of disposing of three bodies instead of two. Or maybe he would wait until they got to the dumping place. Less dead weight to carry. Arthur Bewlay was physically half the man he'd been even a year ago, the disease having very efficiently eaten him up from the inside out. It would be a mercy killing. What was to stop him?

The idea had turned in his mind a while as he'd let Arthur continue with his discourse on what he'd been up to in this room with these two teenagers. He explained that it had been part of an experimental cure for his cancer. Silly, he knew, but there were more things on heaven and earth etcetera, weren't there? And who knew what would work really, when you came down to it? People regularly went to Lourdes, didn't they? And he had, after all, been prepared to put faith in Reverend Joe and his holy energy nail, hadn't he? This particular curative with the wee junkies, however, was just something he'd read about during his ongoing research into how to not die of cancer and he thought he might as well give it a wee go—after all what did he have to lose? It was done for the terminally ill in Haiti, although usually with pigs or monkeys, but he had read that it became a more powerful spell if performed with humans.

The internet surely was a wonderful thing.

It had been a toss-up for Arthur between this or a form of Muti from South Africa. The Haitian cure won the toss only because the African thing would have involved actually eating parts of the intestines and genitals of both victims and Arthur hadn't fancied that. He was ill after all, and he was never sure of keeping anything down for long, so he didn't see the point in potentially ruining a possible cure just because he couldn't control his tummy.

Over a period of two weeks, there had to be lots of different items placed inside the living bodies of the 'charm carriers' as they were known, for the spell to have a chance of working. Items of importance to the patient's life, like photographs or actual pieces of loved ones, or precious gifts such as glassware (that could be broken into fragments before insertion if the object was too big to fit in one piece), or ornaments or jewellery. Things like that. And Arthur'd had *lots* of items—some small, some large—that he simply 'popped' inside each of his 'carriers', one per day.

It was actually hard work, Arthur had complained as he'd watched Big Ian bagging up the corpses. He wasn't a fucking surgeon after all. But . . . he'd done the best he could with the anatomical diagrams he'd printed off from a medical website and after about the third day, he was pleased to note that he could pretty much guess the depth of the derma and fat layer (not that there was much fat on these two) to scalpel in to, so that the day's chosen object could be easily tucked in between the outer layers of skin and the internal organs, and not plunged bluntly into a rope of intestine or such. That way, the amounts of actual blood—and writhing around—he'd had to deal with had reduced considerably.

One amendment that Arthur had added to the proscribed method of procedure, though, had been to place each of the next day's objects into the room with the 'charm carriers' the night before. That way, they could look at the next day's incoming object overnight—be it man made, natural, plastic, steel, glass, whatever—and contemplate what was going to happen to them in the morning when they were to be 'operated' on again.

He'd taken this idea from his research on the Muti spells, where torture and fear allegedly added greatly to the potency of the hex. Arthur had enjoyed the process very much—it had given him something of interest to get out of bed for of a morning, and he thought that he could understand now (in his own small way) what it was that drove the great men of science in their quests.

◆

Hefting the shovel over a shoulder, Big Ian could feel fragments of wet dirt falling down the back of his collar as he began the walk over to Arthur and the car. His assumption that Arthur had merely wanted the pair for sex was why he hadn't been too bothered about getting Ella involved in the first place. She had needed money for smack and was already working the streets to get it anyway, so why (he'd figured) should he give the gig to some other girl?

At last, he'd thought, he was a family connection worth having.

He'd realised that it wasn't exactly like being head of a bank and giving his niece a job at the firm, but had felt good about being able to help out a little, even if her boyfriend was a dickhead.

He had naturally presumed that Arthur would let them go after he'd had his fun. He had even anticipated some complaints from Ella and the dickhead on their release—for Arthur wasn't one to hold back when sex was involved—but Big Ian was prepared to give her a little extra money from his own savings to compensate. In fact, he thought Arthur *had* let them go and had for several days been expecting a phone call or a knock at his door from them after they had calmed down a bit; not realising that he'd only stopped hearing the thumping and grunting noises from the guest room whenever he went up to see Arthur because they were already dead.

It was only when Big Ian had started lifting them up that he'd noticed that their lips and eyelids had been sewn shut, and their ears stuffed with wadded up paper with weird writing on it. Part of Arthur's 'spell' he'd supposed. Still, at least that part had happened after they'd died. Must have, he knew, because there was very little blood around the suture punctures.

It occurred to him that the last thing they'd ever seen in their lives had been the inside of that room with the bricked up window. The bare lightbulb in the ceiling had been on when Arthur had opened the door, so he figured that Arthur had just left it on all the time during their stay. He wondered if he thought he was doing them a kindness or not? He wondered if it would have been preferable for them to have just lain there in the dark, unable to see the face of the lover they were trapped with. Did it help to see that face—the person who was sharing your misery—day after day? Was there some mutual comfort to be found in that? Or did it just make it worse?

It made Big Ian despair that Arthur had done what he had to these two, even the wanker boyfriend. Worse still, the spell or whatever voodoo shit that was supposed to have happened hadn't worked out. According to Arthur, these two had been dead three days already, and the cure was supposed to have occurred by the end of the first.

Maybe that explained Arthur's mood. Maybe it wasn't a good idea for someone in Arthur's position to be given any kind of hope. The disappointment obviously chipped away at whatever life force was keeping him going.

It had all been a big waste of time. Maybe his niece *might* have recovered from her addiction, if she'd dropped the boyfriend. She *might* have gotten away from the smack . . . somehow. People did. Sometimes. She might have been one of those people.

And she might have just stayed off it and gotten a normal life together. Maybe gotten a job. Maybe had a kid. Maybe.

Maybe he hadn't done her a favour at all by getting her the gig with Arthur.

He was thinking that he would for definite be there in the room when Arthur was talking to Skinny; and he would make sure that things didn't go too far. In fact, he would make sure that things wouldn't progress, at most, beyond raised voices. Okay, she didn't feel anything for him, but so what? That didn't mean he couldn't feel anything for her. He could if he wanted to. He liked being with her more than he had ever liked being with anyone else in his life. There was nothing to say that everything had to end badly, was there? Maybe there were happy endings. Or, at least, happi*er*. Arthur was wrong about him in one major respect, he now knew. He *did* have an imagination, and he could imagine Skinny laid out like Ella, folded and lifeless and not able to move, or see or laugh or take the piss or talk to him anymore, and he didn't like it. Not one tiny fucking bit. He didn't want there to be a world with Skinny not in it. As he got closer to the car, he could see Arthur was watching him intently.

'Sometimes I wonder what goes on in that massive head of yours, Big Ian. I really do.'

Arthur tutted and got back into the car.

17

She prepared herself mentally for dinner. She didn't have to sit in front of her mirror to know that she had a sagging face and lifeless grey skin—the look on her guest's face when he saw her close up would be mirror enough. She didn't care. There was nothing she could do about the way she was and, unlikely as it seemed, she was very much looking forward to sitting at the table with the handsome man, Joe.

Maryam peeled off her white gloves and threw them into the little wicker laundry bin, suffering the usual painful ripping of her skin where the sticky fluid at the palms had crusted and dried.

He had been correct at the hospital, of course. Her hands did smell abominably. It was as if they were prematurely dead and beginning to rot away at the ends of her arms.

As if that wouldn't be enough for him to contend with at the dinner table, the recurrent dry, stiff clicking of her jawbone whenever she chewed made her sound like a cement mixer any time there was a meat course, but she thought that this would not necessarily impact adversely on what she had decided to propose to him this evening—he would either go with it or he wouldn't.

Had he been just a normal person, she wouldn't have dared even contemplating what she was going to do. She suspected though, that fate might have dealt her a winning hand, because he seemed to be very much *not* a normal person.

She would ring the bell in a moment so that Grace might come in to clean her palms and put a fresh pair of gloves on her for dinner, but first she wanted to have a few moments by herself to enjoy the alien sensation she was feeling—anticipation.

The last time any man other than Papa had sat at the dinner table in this house had been five years ago. The day after her twenty-first birthday.

◆

Joe was sitting in the largest chair at the head of the table, listening out for either of the women approaching. He'd heard the faint tinkle of a distant bell not too long ago followed by swift, almost silent, feet hurrying up the iron staircase and guessed that Grace had been summoned to help Maryam in some way. Since then, nothing. Grace's little trick, alarming as it had been, hadn't materially changed his situation. He still had to get out of the country and he still needed money to do it.

Meantime, he was virtually a prisoner in this place.

Joe sighed. There was no point trying to blank it out any more, especially not now that Grace had dragged it into the light. Besides, things stuffed away in the backs of closets tended to moulder and smell after a while so—even if only to get a clean break from what had happened—he knew he needed to confront his old 'pal' Mister Emile Brewster.

The old man had been a glorious one off—a living relic from the days of genuine freedom, complete with snowy white plait-ponytail and stories to tell about drug busts, free love and fighting against 'the man'. He was also dying of liver cancer—a fact Joe knew only too well when he had come rolling up to Brewster's place.

It was called the Rainbow Angel Wing Commune, forty or so miles outside the happy rural community of Hidsell Farnham Flats near Greystoke, Alabama—'the Woodstock of the South' (which still had on the trim lawn of its town square, however, a civil war cannon pointed ominously North).

It was basically an old barn, converted in '67 into a hippie heaven of hessian and wood and which had subsequently dissipated into museum piece status long before Joe had even been born. There was the rusted skeleton of a once psychedelically day-glo painted Cessna Skyhawk in the tall grass out back, with its propeller now fixed above the barn door like the bleached bone of some giant beast, and the place only continued to exist at all by virtue of Brewster's constant efforts as sole caretaker.

Phil K had sourced the old hippy's high-end meds records and as Joe's next mark, the guy had seemed very promising (ex-flower child? check; new age lifestyle?; check), but Brewster had made it clear in the first few minutes of meeting Joe that he wasn't buying any crystal skull shards from the Andes, nor scraps of Atlantean mummy wrap from beneath the Sphinx. Nor, indeed, had Brewster been in any way enthusiastic about the dried particle of alien blood in a test-tube stolen by a disaffected USAF corporal—later assassinated by the CIA—from Area 51.

He had, however, congratulated Joe on his imagination. He also told him that he already had bookshelves groaning under the weight of that kind of stuff, most of it the same horseshit as Joe was spouting. But some of it was interesting . . . and a very small percentage of it fascinating. Joe was welcome to read them all if he thought anything would help him rook more civilians at county fairs, but personally speaking, Brewster didn't need any extra map reading thank you very much. Besides, he'd much prefer to spend what time he had left getting high and experiencing the wonders of the universe first hand.

He also told Joe that if he needed a place simply to rest up awhile, he was more than welcome to stay and help an old, dying hippy maintain a big old, barn-sized chunk of American history. Maybe even learn something about life?

Joe had cheerfully assented. Why not? He was nearly out of money anyway and needed a place to stop awhile.

It had seemed like a good idea at the time.

He enjoyed his weeks spent at the barn, helping to preserve its fading psychedelic paint job. On the sunnier mornings its interior had danced with motes rising through the warm air which, he had imagined, would look under a microscope like snowflakes made of wood. Walking through the broad shafts of dusty light made Joe feel like he was able to see the very atoms of the universe.

Brewster had laughed at this. Back in the day, he said, he *had*. In his time he'd flown pretty much every place and had dropped acid with anyone who was anyone, including that whiny little prick Manson (when he'd been a wannabe Beach Boy) and Cary Grant . . . although not at the same time. Mind you, he'd added, his expression darkening a subtle notch, with LSD 25 it could be argued that *everything* happened at the same time. And at the risk of sounding naïve and gauche to the modern ear, not to say embarrassing, Brewster let Joe know that he had once experienced the 'one-ness' of the universe—for *real*—while taking the drug. It had been truly terrifying and he had never dropped acid again after that.

Joe listened politely to his host's notions of 'The Universal'—that we have a life force within us that arrives when we are conceived and then returns again to the universe when we die—but Brewster had desisted from going into too much detail when he'd seen the soporific effect he was having on his young guest, preferring instead just to drink beer with him after a long day's work.

He had been a charming and erudite friend and the only time that Joe had ever seen him feeling in any way down—until his sudden decline that was—hadn't even been about his condition. Well, not as such. Morose and a little drunk, Brewster had been depressed about having to face death when the world at large had completely and utterly failed to become a better place during his four score and ten. Peace and love may have been the answer, but it hadn't really caught on, had it? It had all seemed so promising in the 60's, he sighed. The entire planet really had kind of felt like it was ready for change—it was in the music and the art and the movies and it *should* have changed!

Joe had sipped his beer, happy at least that of all the things Brewster could have been worried about, not having hippies rule the world was a fairly benign one.

The next day, everything had gone completely to shit.

All of a sudden, Brewster's meds were simply not working for him and the effects were horrendous. Jagged, wailing agony abruptly spiked into Brewster's placid existence and all Joe could do was stand by, helpless, sometimes holding him, sometimes singing to him—whatever the fuck the he wanted—feeling incredible pity for the old, lifelong doper for whom 'real' drugs were very evidently not working. The cancer must be way aggressive, thought Joe, to fight all the morphine Brewster had been taking, and the only thing he'd been able to offer him had been words of comfort. Joe was very good with words, and proud of it, but when Brewster was suffering they felt like ash in his mouth. Then, the crashing waves of excruciating pain washed away and the old man, weak and sodden with the aftermath of his agonies, could again be 'normal' for a while.

He said he'd been thinking about something ever since Joe had arrived and now he was sure he wanted to do it. He wanted Joe to 'assist' him to die. Joe—although genuinely sympathetic—began to gently sidestep the subject . . .

But then Brewster had offered Joe all of his money.

He told him that he had the legacy of many plane drop dope deals, and he had used his profits to obtain bearer bonds—anonymous and easy to exchange for hard cash anywhere; bonds were the Holy Grail of money launderers the world over. These things were the genuine article, like in the heist movies, he said, and literally *untraceable*. Joe needed money and Brewster needed someone he could trust absolutely to help him. Joe could have them all . . . if he would simply help an old dying man through the out door.

There would be no paper trail to him, no property deeds transferred, no recently signed wills for 'the man' to examine . . . so no blame. Besides, Brewster had no living relatives, so where was the harm? And Joe was no saint, was he? He hadn't rolled up here to sell girl scout cookies, after all. Brewster needed help . . . and all he was asking for was that Joe help him take an overdose and sit watch with him as he slipped away, talking to him, just being with him. Like things used to be when acid was special, like a sacrament, and trippers needed companions to help guide their 'trip'. Brewster wanted his death trip to be like that, if Joe was willing.

Joe's first instinct was to walk straight out the door and not look back. His mantra was: never get involved with a mark, it only led to discovery and ruination. But Brewster had never really been a 'mark' had he? And common sense and logic were being seduced by emotion. Also Joe had, for what was really the first time (possibly *because* of his relaxed time at the barn) begun to consider giving up his travelling life. With a good stake, he could find a nice place . . . and he might even put his talent for oratory to best use and become a *real* pastor of some sort. Well, real enough to start his own church and make (reasonably) straight money. A nice storefront Baptist offshoot in a small town somewhere, with a neatly swept sidewalk and a basket of fresh flowers out front every day—any actual belief in God optional.

Well for him, at least.

And if that happened, he'd thought, then he could try—just try, mind you—to contact Trudy. He would get Phil K to track her down if he could, probably through UK medical records (a virtual ton of them had gone 'missing' from an ill-conceived Brit IT project a few years back and were available for a price on the Chinese black market).

He'd often fantasised that she was alive and well and that she would be delighted to hear from him . . . and equally delighted to drop everything and come over to the States where they could keep their stupid promise to look after each other. But he really wanted to know, more than anything else, that she was alright.

He realised that this was not a very likely prospect. That given her background and living where she lived, she was probably a beaten wife, in jail or a junkie by now. Or dead.

But the prospect of an actual place of his own and the glimmering of a determination to settle down had shone just a little tiny bit of sunlight on the dreams he didn't realise he still had . . . and if he had to stick a needle into the withered arm of an old man and inject him with a massive overdose of his medication to get more of that sunlight, then he would. If he then had to grab a pillow and hold it over the nice old man's face because even the massive overdose wasn't working quickly enough to dull the extreme pain of the cancer then he would . . . .

. . . *Brewster had been screaming and screaming and begging for Joe to kill him, just for God's sake kill him—the drug wasn't working and he couldn't take it any more; please please please just kill me Joe I can't take this any more . . . you'll be safe with the money, there's enough just put me out of my misery I'm begging you . . . and he screamed and screamed and screamed . . .*

. . . if he had to hold the pillow down as the old man's body reacted against him, the feeble arms with his ancient Haight Ashbury 'love' tattoos now wrinkled and stretched by age almost beyond recognition, clawing at him, his body striving yet for life although his mind had begged Joe for release from it, then he would. He would hold it down over the nice, old man's face until the nice old man stopped his struggling and his muffled wheezing—until the nice, old man's already weak grip on Joe's wrists lessened and his wiry, liver-spotted hands slipped away.

◆

Afterwards, Joe had cried.

More for the terrible situation he and Brewster had been in, though, than for what he'd actually done. After all, he had only helped a poor, old man, his *friend*, whose illness had been beyond medication, hadn't he?

He must have been completely out of his fucking mind.

Because after Joe had dropped the tear and phlegm-soaked pillow to the floor by his feet and staggered downstairs to the floor safe, his arms tense and aching, he had opened it up to reveal that there were no bearer bonds inside.

There had been no mistake—Brewster had been unequivocal on the subject of their whereabouts. And Joe had believed him. He'd been expecting bonds and a clean and immediate getaway. Now he had nothing.

He ran out to his car, stuffing what little shit he'd brought when he'd first arrived back into the trunk, and raced back inside, the engine still running. He figured on giving himself maybe twenty minutes tops for his search to try find out exactly what the fuck was going on around here before he had to pull out.

As it turned out, it took him less than two. The first drawer he busted open, next to Brewster's bed, had pretty much all the documentation he needed.

After reading it he thought he was going to throw up. He physically couldn't see or think straight for a solid minute. He felt like some dumb first time hooker who'd been cluster fucked by the football team and left on a desert highway to thumb it home without clothes or money.

Brewster had spent every cent he had on medical and hospital bills. He had also borrowed on the barn and now it was being taken away by the bank. Or the 'man' as Brewster would have it. Joe guessed that any alleged bearer bonds had been long since cashed and spent.

And finally, at the bottom of the little pile that had been locked away all this time in Brewster's bedside drawers, there were the insurance policies. They were made out to a woman. Joe could only presume she was Brewster's wife. Or ex-wife. Or daughter. Or sister. He didn't much care at that point, nor did he have to read them through in any detail to know that as standard they did not pay out on suicide.

Homicide, however, was a different matter.

No wonder Brewster had welcomed him in with open arms.

Joe checked out the hypo Brewster had given him with the 'fatal dose'. It had been filled from a bag of saline solution in the bathroom. That meant a coroner would find no trace of an overdose—simply homicide by asphyxiation.

At the bottom of the drawer had also been a small, handwritten note in Brewster's pain wracked and shaky hand.

Sorry Joe, but I had to take the opportunity. When you came I asked myself the same question you should ask every time you meet someone who isn't kin to you: What do they want?
If you can get the true answer, you'll stay out of trouble.

Joe briefly considered the note's potential as exhibit 'A' in any defence but quickly dismissed it. Out of context it would be virtually meaningless. Besides, months could be spent trying to prove that it was even the old bastard's writing. He'd known when he was smothering Brewster that he was in deep trouble, but at least he'd been in trouble with a huge amount of money coming to him. Now he was just heading for the gas chamber.

Motherfucker.

What was it the Sex Pistols had said? Never trust a hippie? Damn fucking straight. He got into his car and drove as far and as fast as he could out of there.

There was nobody he could turn to and the furthest place he could escape was the small, cold country where he'd been born and where he was still—technically—a citizen. And he knew that he was very lucky to have that option.

After that, the plan was simple enough—make as much money as he could in as brief a time as possible in Scotland and then get the fuck out—go to somewhere that still retained a bit of Old World lawlessness and where money would buy him a new name. Somewhere that didn't have a one sided treaty for handing over suspects to the US under the auspices of Homeland Security. Eastern Europe, probably.

He knew that he was simplifying things to a ridiculous extent. Eastern Europe wasn't the Wild West. They had police forces too, after all, but it had to be easier to hide someplace where the black economy was bigger than the regular one. Besides, migrating *in* to Eastern Europe was going against the tide, and cheap property and a willingness to bend rules might see him into a comfortable, anonymous retirement.

But first, he'd had to find the dying Scotsman.

He'd gotten on to Phil K, while waiting for his flight to Prestwick, and having sourced details of high dosage people in this part of Britain, he'd downloaded back issues of local newspapers—they would reveal whether any of these people had potential. If they had money, they might be mentioned for big charity donations and such. It wasn't foolproof, but there was a good chance of getting a broad result. Before he'd even really started, however, one name had leapt up shouting 'Me! Me! Me!'

Mister Arthur Bewlay, gangster.

Jackpot.

Crooked earnings—an excellent source of nice, instant hard cash. No bank drafts, nothing traceable, just solid crime proceeds in notes he could use to get out of Scotland without leaving an online trail. The guy would probably still be dangerous, he'd thought, but as desperate as anyone else for a chance to prolong life.

With Phil's help, once he'd actually landed at Prestwick (having spent his entire flight paranoid and wall-eyed with fear), he had also managed to track down Trudy. She hadn't visited a doctor since her late teens and Joe could read in those files an awful catalogue of self-neglect. He remembered how they had clung to each other before and after. Especially after. They would cling and they would whisper that they would take care of each other, that they loved each other. They would live together in a place with a garden they could look after and a horse to ride and feed hay to.

He had tortured himself over the years with visions of her life being hopelessly bleak... but for all he knew she *could* have gotten out. She could be happily married with fourteen kids and a dog and a cat and be living in a Disney picture. He hoped so.

He hoped that she had survived the past better than he had. He also knew that, consciously or not, pretty much every decision he'd ever made in his life had had some relation to their bad stuff. He knew, deep down, that Trudy was the root cause of why he always went for a certain type of woman. It was a recognised syndrome—bird with a broken wing. Joe had a better way of putting it—atonement. Always something wrong with every woman he'd ever been with... and always unfixable.

Finally though, when it had come down to it, he hadn't the courage to ring her, pretending to himself that he'd decided not to until he'd successfully gotten Bewlay to take the bait and pay up; telling himself that he would wait until he had money to give her (if she needed it) before he called.... but really, he knew, his nerve had failed him. What if she spat in his face? She had every right to.

More selfishly—what if stuff had happened to her in the years since he'd last seen her that had been so awful, he wouldn't be able to bear hearing about it?

Joe looked around at the dining room. Sitting here on this ancient chair in this weird house waiting for the Dolly Sisters from Loonyville to arrive, he figured now he'd never contact her.

How could he? What would he say? Besides, doing so would just drag her into this world of pain he'd managed to get himself in to (he'd realised that it must have been his foolish, triumphant call to Phil from his shithole hotel room about Bewlay's 200K that had led to his death sentence).

He had fucked it all up again, and not just for himself.

Maybe he was doing it subconsciously, so that he'd never have to face her?

He heard the sound of feet behind him shook and himself from his thoughts. He turned to see Maryam standing in the doorway. It took him a few seconds to completely register her.

Aside from the constant of her opera gloves, she had changed her 'look'. She was wearing a halter top maxi dress, made from some sort of thick, nylon looking fabric, its spiralling, predominantly green and ochre swirling pattern assaulting his eyes. Her hair had been corralled into a kind of frizzy beehive and the whole ensemble was completed by her huge, white sunglasses. She clearly didn't get out much, he thought.

She spoke first, clearing her throat, making a sound so dry it was like hearing a twig breaking.

'I've made an effort this evening, since we never have guests,' she said, indicating her outfit. 'This was my mama's favourite dress. She wore it to parties when she was younger.'

'It's lovely,' said Joe.

She smiled, and for a second he wondered if she actually believed him.

'Perhaps you'd be a gentleman and lead me to my seat?' she said.

Maryam placed her hand on his arm and he recoiled involuntarily. It was very slight and he recovered swiftly, but it was clearly enough for her to register because he could feel her eyes boring into him from behind the dark glasses as she took her hand away.

He would have to make up for that, he thought. He would turn on as much charm as he could muster for this woman and her talent and all of the money he could make from it. But before he could say something—anything—Grace arrived at the door, carrying a tray of steaming plates and looking almost inhumanly cute in a gingham pinny, like she was making a guest appearance in 'I Love Lucy'.

'Time for supper, Joe!' she said, flashing her perfect teeth. Behind her, in the great hall, he could just see their Papa's coffin on its velvet draped trestle stands, the shiny wood gleaming dully.

Maybe not 'I Love Lucy', he thought.

Unless it was an episode by Edgar Allan Poe.

18

Maryam looked down at the cubes of beef in gravy on the plate in front of her.

Stew.

Aside from looking like it had come out of a can labelled 'dog', it was, she thought, as if Grace had deliberately set out to make the most unsuitable meal possible for this evening. But Grace was as capable of malice or forward planning as an oyster and had probably just opened these particular tins because the colours on the labels were pretty.

Besides, Maryam thought, the ordeal and humiliation of having to eat like this in front of this man would actually help her to get everything out in the open—lay it all out on the table before him, warts and . . . well, more warts. She had to make sure he would be under no illusions when she made her request. That was the important thing. Not that he was under many illusions anyway, she thought. When she had given his arm an exploratory touch he had recoiled like she'd been wired to the mains. Not a good start, but she still felt confident about him.

She had not pressed for any further details on his means of making a living and had noted that he seemed grateful for this. Clearly, he wasn't going to volunteer any more about himself and, in truth, she had heard pretty much everything she'd needed to.

She hadn't at all been expecting one of Grace's little episodes, but had been grateful for its timely intrusion nonetheless. No one was entirely without sin, after all, and at least 'assisted suicide' as a phrase was better than 'multiple axe murderer'. It had a humanitarian ring to it.

He was not a violent psychopath, then, nor did he seem to be an intentionally malicious sort. He was merely a crook, and one who looked like he'd gotten involved in something that had been too large for him to handle. He seemed the kind of man whose intelligence was generally pressed to the services of his own selfish needs and whose morals were adaptable—ideal, in other words, for her purpose. He had already asked her about how she earned a living and had seemed disappointed by what he seemed to see as the small scale of her 'operation'. She wondered when would be best to tell him why she was so 'small'.

He was speaking to her between mouthfuls of the brown gunk on his plate, and making a good fist of not looking like he wanted to be sick.

'I can't believe you're not world famous by now, Maryam. At the very least, a millionaire. Your gift is unbelievable.'

'I prefer to keep my head below the parapet,' she replied.

'Why?' he said. 'Have you never thought of all the good you could do?'

'All the good I could do . . .' she echoed quietly. 'All the good I could do . . . that's an interesting thought, Joe. What good could I do, do you think?'

'You are unique. You have the power of a god. There are people who live their lives entirely without hope. You could give them that hope.'

She snorted a laugh.

'Oh? What's this?' she said 'Are you pretending to be an honest and good sort of person now?'

Grace piped up, offended.

'Maryam, dom't be rude . . .'

'Eat up your dinner Grace.'

Grace clammed up. Joe shot her a consoling smile and she beamed happily at him.

'Don't be such a bully, Maryam,' he said

'Let me put it this way, Joe,' Maryam continued, ignoring this. 'Can you imagine what would happen were it to be proven as *fact* that there is someone on this planet who can genuinely cure people by the touch of her hand? No flimflam. No credit cards by phone. No stooges in the audience throwing away their crutches and praising the Lord.'

She looked over the tops of her dark glasses at him and he could see that eye make-up had been attempted. It hadn't really helped.

'What do you think would happen,' she continued, 'if the world found that I could mend its broken bones or cure its blindness, stop its internal bleeding, banish its migraines? Think about it for a moment. Seriously, think about it.'

'You'd be pretty busy, huh,' he said.

'There would be a cry for me to heal the entire world all by myself,' she said. 'I am cursed, not blessed. I would either be given no rest until the day I died . . . or I would be given too much rest . . . in some bleak government facility, kept like a lab rat. A place where they could constantly test me and probe me and eventually no doubt cut me open to see how I do the things I do.'

'I guess I can't see further than the end of my nose,' Joe said. 'I apologise . . .'

She nodded.

'But that isn't to say that I agree,' he continued, grinning at her. 'After all, you could be discreet. All you'd have to do would be to pick your clientele very carefully. Even one person, if they were wealthy enough, would be enough to set you up for life.'

'What happened to 'healing the world', Joe?'

'We are not little children, are we? If you're worried about being hounded down for your gift, let me tell you that rich people can be very discreet. And if *you're* very rich you can be extremely anonymous.'

She sighed as he pressed on.

'You are the genuine article, Maryam, there's no getting round that. Don't waste away here in this cold, grey country,' he said, 'There are very, very rich people in the world—unbelievably rich. So rich as to not fully be living on the same planet as us. People who would pay a hell of a lot, and I mean *implausible* amounts, to stave off the inevitable. And I can't tell you this enough—incredibly rich people are more than capable of keeping secrets, especially secrets that benefit them. That's how they got to be rich in the first place. You stop the right billionaire from popping his clogs, and we'll be set for the rest of *our* lives.'

'I don't heal the terminally ill, or anyone who is supposed to die,' she said, 'I have that in common with you, Joe.'

He laughed aloud, genuinely amused. She might be a bitch, he thought, but at least she was funny with it. He realised that he liked her. She smiled at him, wiping her lips with her napkin.

'Well,' said Joe, 'I'm sure that there are plenty of wealthy people with arthritis or other aches and pains you could cure who would pay equally large amounts for treatment.'

'There probably are. I don't move in those circles.'

'You don't have to. I could source the client base for you and all you would have to do was fix them.'

'And how would you 'source the client base'? Hang around outside private hospitals with a questionnaire for everyone who comes and goes? *Excuse me sir or madam, how much did you earn last year and what's wrong with you?*'

'That's pretty much what happens at hospitals anyway, isn't it?'

'Not in this country.'

'Not yet.'

'You're not answering the question.'

'I have a contact in the medical records line. He can find the right sort of people who are ill and then I'll do the rest. We'd need to give him a small cut for his data, of course.'

'Is this a genuine business proposition you're making me?'

'I don't see why not.'

'Can I ask why?'

'Are you serious? To make money.'

'For?'

Joe looked at her.

'For the good life, Maryam. To live well and be worry free.'

'You make it sound very simple. To be worry free, I mean.'

'It is.'

'All you need is money?'

'Pretty much.'

Maryam laughed. Joe really did have the most beautiful eyes she had ever seen in a man.

'Just think about it Maryam,' he smiled. 'That, as they say, don't cost nothing.'

He returned to his dinner and there was a reasonably comfortable silence around the table.

It almost felt normal.

Maryam laid down her knife and fork. In truth, she knew she was unlikely to be eating any more of this stuff. She already had butterflies in her stomach, fluttering all over what appetite she had left. But . . . the last thing she had been concerned about—how she would actually approach him with her proposition—had just been given to her. By him. She should start now, she thought anxiously, before nerves made her change her mind.

Never mind dinner, never mind politesse—do it and do it now, she thought.

She turned to Grace, smiling pleasantly at her.

'Go and fetch me a glass of fresh water, Grace. Now, please. And do run the tap for a couple of minutes. I need it to be nice and cold. It burns up more calories that way.'

Grace nodded demurely. Joe watched her leave for the kitchen.

'Doesn't look to me like you can afford to lose too many calories, Maryam,' he said. 'If you don't mind me saying so'

'Don't be dense. I sent her away because I have something to ask you. Something extremely serious.'

He raised an eyebrow.

'Shoot.'

'This business deal you have in mind. I am the one who would be doing the work—and believe me, you have no idea how much this work takes out of me. But what would you be doing? Aside from breaking the law by 'sourcing the client base'.'

'I'd keep things discreet and . . . I would be like a manager. Or an agent.'

'A pimp.'

'No!' he said, 'for God's sake Maryam, lighten up!'

'Shhh, Joe. I don't mean to be nasty to you. I like you. But I would need more than what you're currently offering me to agree to your proposal. A lot.'

She removed her sunglasses, folding the legs over and placing them down onto the table in front of her.

'You've seen who I am, and what I am. You know what I look like and how I behave. I am never going to be anything else. There is no good side to me and in order to show you that, I have not curtailed my behaviour or what I am like in any way this evening. I wanted you to know that,' she said.

He started feeling anxious.

'Why?' he said.

As she leaned forward into the flickering candlelight, he could see a faint, yellowish crusting around her eyelids.

'Because the romantic ideal is to be loved for oneself—how one actually *is*.'

There was a silence between them. Joe worked hard at keeping his expression neutral, his mind boiling furiously.

Romantic ideal, she'd said.

Oh fucking shit.

'What if I wished you to give me something, Joe?'

He found to his surprise that his voice was quite steady when he replied.

'That would depend on what that was Maryam.'

'Something that I could never say out loud. Never. Because if I did . . . it would suddenly make . . . the thing . . . not worth having anymore.'

She brought her gloved hand closer to his, but stopped short of touching him.

'There are certain times when if you ask for something too plainly, the . . . magic disappears,' she said softly. 'In fact, if one were to simply ask outright for certain things, then there would be no magic there at all . . . merely a transaction.'

She placed her fingertips lightly against his.

'And I need magic, Joe. I need it badly.'

No point in being shy now, she thought. He would or wouldn't understand; agree or not agree.

'Joe, your plan,' she said, 'it's a good one. I haven't . . . branched out before with my gift as you suggest because I was under the control of my father. He is no longer with me so I am free to do what I like. I would like to try your arrangement . . . with you. In return you would have to help me.'

He remained silent. She hoped that he wasn't deliberately teasing her. Refusal and rejection she could live with—torture she could not.

He swallowed, hard.

'I'm still not sure I understand exactly what it is we're talking about here . . .'

He saw a change come over her face then. In the blink of an eye, she became way less hardassed and looked more . . . vulnerable. He could see need and want in her eyes and they suddenly didn't look old to him anymore. She looked sad and trapped and he could see that she was fighting against appearing this way and failing.

'We're talking about a dream . . .' she said, 'and I would like to live it Joe, as if it were real, even if only for just a little while. But to help me believe in it, it has to just . . . 'happen' to me. I have to believe that you want to . . . to . . . that you *really* feel that you . . . please don't get me wrong—it's not about sex. Not really, it's about . . . I need . . .'

She tailed off. She had run out of ways to express herself. She spoke again, very quietly.

'Who in the world would not like for someone to be in love with them? Do you understand now?'

There was a very long moment. She wanted to die there and then. He would laugh at her, she knew; laugh loud and long, before getting up from his seat and walking from the room. He owed her nothing—he hadn't asked for her intervention, after all. This whole enterprise was stupid and humiliating and . . . Joe put his hand over hers. It was the simplest of gestures, but it made her suddenly feel as though she were running again, running fast and sure. The energy that coursed through her body didn't feel natural. He brought his face closer to hers and spoke very softly.

'You only have one life,' he said.

She was breathing a little faster, not sure now what might be happening.

'Don't you agree, Maryam?'
She realised that he was waiting for her to respond. She had to respond! For God's sake say something, she thought.
'Yes, Joe . . . yes, I . . . agree . . .'
She was confused and thrilled and very afraid. Had he started yet? Did this mean he had understood what she'd meant? Was this him doing it for her? She didn't know! What was he doing?
'I believe that you should take your happiness where and when you can—whatever the price,' he said.
She didn't say anything, still confused.
'Whatever the price, Maryam?'
And then she knew.
It was happening. For her. At last.
'Whatever the price,' she repeated, softly.

◆

Outside the dining room, Grace stood shock still, a glass of freezing cold water in her hand. Tears were filling her eyes and she looked suddenly over her shoulder and hissed in an urgent whisper.
'Shut up! I'm tryimg to listem.'
She turned her attention back to the door again, whispering all the while from the corner of her mouth.
'I cam't ummerstamd what she's sayimg to him!'
She listened for a moment at the door, but then turned to look behind her again, angry.
'No! No! It *ism't* that—amd he wouldem't do it! Shut up! He's marryimg *me*! *You said!*'
Something shoved her forward and she resisted—a petite, pretty girl all by herself, stumbling over nothing and spilling water from a dirty glass on to the floor.

◆

He felt like they were in suspended animation, their breath colliding in the air between them, both their mouths open like a freeze-frame parody of a Hollywood moment, except he was the pretty girl and she was Bela Lugosi. He could hear a parched click from inside her mouth, and a quick glance down rewarded him with the sight of her lipstick flaking off on pieces of her dried out skin. *Get through it, Joe!* He commanded himself, *Think! Work it! She could make you a fortune!*

But still, even with all of the riches of the world dancing before his eyes like Vegas showgirls . . . he couldn't seem to manage to close that tiny air gap between their lips.

Maryam could feel his hesitation and she panicked—she wasn't going to let this go! Not now! She brought her hands round behind his head, but stopped short of urging his lips forward on to hers. She couldn't kiss *him*. That would destroy it! *He* had to kiss *her*, he *had* to! He had to love her—he had to come to her and make her feel loved and cared for and wanted . . . but looking into his eyes, she knew then that he wouldn't. She knew it had been a stupid idea.

◆

He could feel her ebbing in his arms—he realised she could feel his hesitation now. She was starting to think rationally, realistically again. Regaining her senses. He had let himself fall at the first goddam hurdle.

'I'm sorry, Joe,' she said, sadly. 'I should have known . . .'

She pulled away from him, her hands fluttering as she groped for her sunglasses on the table, her voice so low he could barely hear what she was saying.

'The threats I made earlier, upstairs . . . I didn't mean it. Not really. If you're in trouble, I'll help, if I can. I'm afraid I don't really know what I was thinking . . . I'm very sorry . . .'

She was giving up.

If that happened, he would have lost this opportunity! Sure, she'd probably give him some money, maybe even let him stay here for as long as he needed to . . . but she wouldn't owe him. If he did this for her, she would *owe* him, *big time*, and he would be able to make her do what he wanted with her remarkable power.

He told himself again—she could make him an unbelievable amount of money.

And all he had to do was tell her he loved her.
What the fuck was so hard about that?
She was staring at the sunglasses she was holding in both her hands. She sighed and started lifting them up to her face again. Joe reached out and halted her, gently taking them from her trembling fingers and putting them back down onto the table. Maryam remained silent, but was looking at him with such pleading intensity that he almost felt guilty.

Joe thought of Grace then, and in doing so knew that she had been at the back of his mind ever since he'd realized what Maryam was asking of him. He knew he would have to call on her; he just hadn't faced up to it until now.

She had to be one of the most spectacular looking girls he'd ever seen in his entire life.

She should be on magazine covers.

She should be right in front of him right now and he should be kissing *her*.

He closed his eyes and found that he was. The flaking skin round the lips, the loose and yellowed teeth, the uncommon dryness of Maryam's mouth—the smell of her breath—all of these things were no longer apparent to him as he imagined he was kissing Grace.

◆

Outside, the dining room door begins to open and Grace scampers hurriedly away, her pretty face twisted in fear and hate, her vision blurry with tears. She makes it all the way to the end of the great hall and into the cloak vestibule, hiding behind Maryam's fur coat before Joe or her sister can see her.

She listens.

Maryam is whispering to Joe that Grace is a very simple creature and will have forgotten all about them. Maryam looks around.

See? she says, no sign of her.

She'll have been distracted by something and then gone to bed without giving them a second thought, she says.

Grace was screeching inside her head.

Lies! Maryam was *lying*! She wasn't an idiot! Joe could see that—he knew that! He was kissing *her*, not Maryam!

She saw it im his head!

But Joe—*her* Joe says nothing! Nothing!

Why doesn't he tell her she's wrong!

Why doesn't he say he loves *her*, not Maryam!

The Ladies amd the Gememtlemem said that he *would*!

They *said*!

Maryam continues whispering to Joe. She tells him she is aware that Grace might have a wee crush on him, but she is, she says, like that all the time; she gets these . . . enthusiasms, but they soon melt away as if they'd never existed. If it hadn't been Joe it would have been some dark-eyed actor on a soap opera, or a picture of the latest heartthrob in one of her glossy magazines.

Grace watches as Maryam leads Joe up the spiral staircase, their feet clanging dully on its black wrought iron lace. She watches as they reach the gallery level and Joe lifts Maryam up into his arms . . . and begins to carry her to the bedroom. *Maryam's* bedroom.

The door is closed softly behind them.

◆

The hall is still and quiet. The sound of the night time traffic way down below is a sleepy murmuring drone and the metallic tick of the clock in the study measures out its constancy.

Suddenly . . .

Grace pell-mells out from her hiding place, pulling her own hair savagely, twisting and turning as she grips at it. She screams and shouts and yells and kicks—a child's tantrum writ large, her face reddened with rage, the veins on her neck and arms bulging out. Her hands let go of her hair and claw at the air like talons, as if raking at an invisible wall and she stretches open her mouth wide to scream like a fury—wide enough to split the corner of her mouth, a red pearl of blood forming there as she screams and screams and screams . . . but all completely without a sound. A totally silent frenzy of wrath, which suddenly stops as abruptly as it began. She silently mouths words to the air in front of her, her gaze darting around accusingly, the blood from her lip now running down her chin.

'*I dom't wamt to speak to you, you said I'd marry him, you told me, you said I would marry him amd he's gome away with her he's gome away with her! I dom't wamt to speak to you—*'

She turns and mouths over her shoulder as if she were being crowded: '*I dom't wamt to speak to emmy of you ever agaim! You're liars! You're liars!*'

She stops herself, head cocked as if she were listening to a reply. She looks around in a daze, and then down at the floor, thinking...

She stares at Papa's coffin, slack-faced, for several minutes before shuffling dully into the kitchen.

If she was to disappear forever, right now, the only trace of her ever having been here would be a small puddle of water spilt on a carpet. Eventually that would dry out and then there would be nothing of her anymore.

Nothing at all.

Georges II

HOW AMUSING FOR THEM, THOUGHT GEORGES.
They had let him experience living, breathing life once more... but as a low beast on the wet stinking floor of that hospital corridor—and had then torn him apart for sport. They had taught him his lesson, after all, had they not?

But at least that pain, terrible as it was, had been real. A physical and mental sensation to actually experience, and not this endless nothing that he had around him now. He was trying to remain 'human' but it was a losing battle. His dissolution was, he knew, unstoppable and all that he had left to anchor him to what he had once been were memories—

Also disintegrating.

He could remember nothing of his childhood, nothing of his mother and father. He couldn't even remember meeting Louisa or how they had ever come to be together as man and wife.

But he could remember what had brought him to this.

He could remember when he had despised his family, the freezing rain was sweeping along towards them in vast sheets, continuously rolling through the orange brightness of the streetlamps wobbling violently in the wind they were the only people out at 3 a.m. himself, Louisa and little Maryam wrapped in the worn, cheap, quilted anorak Georges had stolen from the charity shop all of them struggling through this deluge along the wide, deserted road to the Victoria Infirmary the hospital's yellow lit windows were just visible through the rain, at the end of this long, long street impossibly far away Louisa's waters had broken in the damp of their smelly single room an agonising half an hour previously and they had no phone and no money and there had been absolutely nothing else for it but to walk.

Maryam was crying and kicking against him, beating his face with her chapped, frozen little hands, the pouring rain as cold as ice water streaming down her cheeks and making them scarlet with pain. Louisa was moaning, clutching at him tightly and having to stop every few yards to scream into his sodden coat. He was half dragging and half carrying her and he found himself wishing that he were dead—finally at rest and away from this screeching baggage to whom he had shackled himself and from the biting, crying, misery of a child wriggling in his arms. He cursed the unborn baby fighting its way out of Louisa's fat, stupid, ugly belly—all set to bring more misery into his already miserable life.

By the time they reached the gigantic, towering black hospital it looked like it was melting, there was so much water running down its walls. Even when they finally drew close to the Accident and Emergency doors, Georges could neither see nor hear any sign of life in the place at all. He wanted to turn tail and run away. He felt like he was a traveller seeking shelter at the keep of some prince, and not at all sure if he should accept it.

The illusion was shattered when the doors had swung open and a surprised off duty porter had dragged them all in to the welcome heat and bustle of the A and E, with its strong, reassuring smell of disinfectant and the comfort of seeing other people's concern for them. It meant that someone gave a shit about them. Maryam was whisked away for rough towels and dry clothes and Louisa was rushed to the nearest available private area—a curtained examination booth. Georges, left to fend for himself, shambled over to a cracked, plastic seat and looked down at the shine on the red linoleum floor (were all floors red at hospital entrances, he wondered?). It felt like he'd barely managed to close his eyes before he was being shaken by a smiling nurse and her happy news.

It was a girl.

The duty doctor regretfully explained to Georges that the child had been born with the umbilical cord wrapped tight around her neck (the image of a snake had immediately sprung, unbidden, into Georges' mind). The loss of oxygen had been relatively brief, but it meant that there was a strong possibility of brain damage. The doctor was sure that this would only manifest itself in an extremely minor way, but Georges knew better. He recognised that this was more of the shit luck that had been the substance of his life since the day he'd been born. He not only had a brand new baby to pay for, the damn thing was a retard.

Georges was losing concentration he was drifting off and he couldn't let himself drift off to the nothingness he could feel himself recoiling from his thoughts—a repulsion with himself at this memory of how he had been all those years ago . . . and that was good . . . that was good . . . even someone who was repulsive had at least been a someone, a living breathing person and not this nothing he was now he was losing concentration and he had to concentrate he had to use his memory to stay focused and stay present stay a sentient being with thoughts and feelings and not an emptiness concentrate, concentrate, concentrate . . .

Louisa had been happy enough; she had even come up with a name for the pug-faced, mewling object—Grace, of all things—but Georges barely managed a word to his wife or the cheery porter and nurse as they travelled all the way up seven floors to a curtained-off bed in the dogleg corner of a high ward.

Maryam was brought to them in borrowed pyjamas, dry and warm and sleepy-eyed. With baby Grace in her incubator and Maryam allowed to cuddle into her exhausted mother on the bed, Georges was left feeling surplus to requirements. He looked at the three of them, all sleeping and at peace.

His family. His obligation. How he hated them.

He could, he thought, just walk out of the door and keep on walking and leave all of the shit behind him, he thought. Let the DSS look after his wife and kids—he certainly couldn't. And he didn't really want to either, he found. He was bone weary and he just wanted out of it. Out of it all.

Georges was aware that someone else was there before he saw him. When he turned around, the old man's horsy face broke into a pleasant grin as he thrust his hand forward, introducing himself in polite, measured tones. The name had escaped Georges almost as soon as the old man had said it, telling him he was from an 'administrative' part of the hospital. Georges, exhausted, yawned pretty much in the old man's long face, not caring if he was being rude or not.

'You will grow fat, Mister Clemenceau,' the old man said.

Georges looked at him. Pardon?

'I'm a physician, or was,' the old man continued, 'and I have enough experience of physical types to know, when I see it, a body that will run to fat if left to its own devices. A man's lifestyle preferences however are his own, sir, and if that man chooses to sit still and eat and drink as much as he wishes then it is no business of mine or any doctor's. Whatever pleases the individual is surely the thing to bring him peace. Perhaps I'm old fashioned but I cleave to the dictum—do what thou wilt. We walk this earth and breathe this sweet air around us for so brief a time it does seem absurd to not be able to enjoy ourselves whilst we are here, n'est ce pas?'

'I won't be growing fat anytime soon,' said Georges, annoyed. 'I've not had a full meal for two days.'

'That will change, sir. I feel it. The sad events of this evening will have an unexpected benefit for you. Come with me, will you? I believe your elder daughter's clothes will be dry by now.'

The old man smiled again and walked away from Georges who, amused, decided to follow—if only to find out what the hell the old guy was talking about. What else was he going to do, after all?

'I understand Georges, that there has been the loss of a small but significant percentage amount of oxygen supply to the brain of your infant.'

Georges grunted a sullen assent.

'A tiny happenstance,' the old man said, 'but one which, as I understand it, has robbed the poor little thing of any sort of normal life. She is likely, as it used to be put in my day, to be simple-minded. The poor little mite will very probably never mature mentally and *will most likely be looking at the world through the eyes of a child until the day she dies.'*

The old man stopped suddenly and turned to face Georges, grinning his long-toothed horsy grin once more, and Georges suddenly noticed that they were halfway down one of many flights of progressively dimly lit stairs. How had they gotten here so quickly? Why had he not noticed?

'Think of it, Georges,' the old man said, interrupting his thoughts. 'A child forever. Would that be wonderful . . . or terrifying?'

Georges shrugged, at a slight loss. The old man laughed good naturedly and turned away once more, positively leaping down the spiralling stairwell, nimble as a goat. They continued downwards the basement, the noise of huge, industrial tumble dryers a constantly increasing thrum.

'Do you have any interests Georges?' he asked.

Again, Georges didn't know what to say.

'I'm interested in many things,' the old man continued regardless. 'Medicine, architecture, chemistry—anything that can increase knowledge can only be good, do you not think? Did you know, for example, that on or around the age of ninety-three, one simply stops ageing?'

No, Georges said, he didn't know that.

'It's true!' the old man chuckled. 'You are no more likely to die of old age when you're one hundred and nine than you are at ninety-three. Other things, you can die from, of course, one is not indestructible—but not old age. In fact, if one was to be disease and injury free, the body one inhabits could in theory live to be one hundred and seventy years old before finally giving up the ghost, as it were.'

He chuckled once more.

'This is a fact.'

Georges had made interested noises and nodded dumbly. Was it? he thought. So what?

As they entered the laundry room, all of the drying machines switched off at once, the abrupt silence pressing heavily in Georges' ears. The old man explained with pride that they were entering the original hospital—its very oldest part. Georges felt strange.

Not uneasy, exactly, just... insulated. Wrapped in a blanket? Distanced. Like it wasn't really him down in the basement with a complete stranger.

As he handed over Maryam's warm dry clothes, the old man explained to Georges that he was retired—his once sure grip now too unreliable to handle even the lightest of the new, modern scalpels. Not that he liked them much—they looked more like craft knives than proper instruments. He supposed that a lot of his old equipment would be regarded as antique nowadays; of interest to collectors only and to be found in dank flea markets and such.

Georges shook himself from his dwam. What, he asked the old man, had he meant upstairs by 'unexpected benefit'?

They were now walking out of the laundry room, but instead of heading for the stairs again, they were walking the other way, down a dark-walled, arched corridor of sorts. It looked like he was walking on shiny, much worn down cobbles.

'The old man told him not to be alarmed. He just needed a few private moments with him to discuss the matter of recompense for the 'accident' with his daughter. Legally, it was an open and shut case—the damage had occurred to a little baby in the hospital's care. Law suits were not out of the bounds of possibility, but he would like to think Georges would want to avoid that sort of thing.

Unofficially, of course, and very much to his benefit.

There was a peeling green door ahead, ajar, a flickering light inside the room, like a flame. Georges could hear the hiss of gas.

The old man offered to personally compensate him for this unfortunate event. But rather than money, he had an idea for something that would be a lot more use to Georges and his family, and which would appreciate in value as the years wore on. In lieu of any claims against the hospital, he said that Georges could have the use of his personal apartments in perpetuity. A grand mansion in the middle of the city—the roof apartments at Charing Cross Mansions to be precise. Wouldn't that be something?

Georges was astounded. Suing the hospital? He hadn't even considered it. The chances of success would be zero anyway. The *offer of a free house, however, sweetened the pill of having an idiot child!*

'I currently reside there myself, Georges,' the old man said, 'and have done for a great number of years, but I'll be leaving soon to a temporary accommodation. Moving into this very room, in fact....'

He pushed the door fully open and indicated that Georges might enter.

Georges found that he didn't want to.

'... and I shall dwell here—and hereabouts—until such time as I obtain my next, um, property to occupy.'

The room smelt of gas and what Georges could only have described as burnt air. The small open flame at the end of the ornately twisted metal pipe was hissing and flickering away, its glass bowl lampshade almost completely scorched black with age and use. And he could see through the partially opened door the bottom end of an extremely old, black iron bedstead. There were frayed pieces of rope tied at the corners and what looked like a huge, dark stain—like something had burst on the mattress. The old man clapped him on the back.

'The apartments are a palace, Georges,' he said. 'A very desirable property. There is a stipend attached that will keep you and your family clothed and fed until your daughter has reached her majority, thereafter a means of earning a good living will be provided for you. What do you say? No work for the rest of your life and you and yours taken care of?'

Georges was about to ask the old man a lot of questions. How did he know who he was? How had he known where he would be? Why was he offering him all of this—a town apartment, money for his keep, a 'means of earning a good living'... all of this when Georges hadn't even raised the possibility of suing the hospital and in fact doubted very much whether such a thing would even be feasible—all of these things were pressing at the window glass of Georges' mind banging against the thick pane screaming to be heard, but visions of the free house and the unearned income grew larger and larger, muting them. Besides, he had something important to do he knew as he and the old man had sat down on either corner of the old iron bed, where on top of a damp threadbare blanket between them now lay baby Grace. She was sleeping. She looked so clean and healthy. Georges was staring at her perfect and beautiful little face, wondering vaguely how she had come to be down here with him and the old man.

He was having trouble in fact, recalling where they actually were.

The gas lit room had an ancient fireplace in the corner, its jade green tiles broken and scattered across its hearth, and a dark pool of what looked like candle wax and the remnants of something fibrous burnt across the grate.

No one had lived or slept in this room for a long time, he thought. It felt odd. It could have been anywhere. This being near the hospital laundry (was it? still?), Georges supposed that it must be an old, disused janitor's accommodation or something. He noticed the overcomplicated wallpaper, the window blind pulled down against the night outside (in a basement?). He looked to the door, but instead of the hospital corridor, he caught a glimpse of a huge grand hall and he realised that they had all moved in to the promised apartments already.

How could he have forgotten that?

The old man was talking again and Georges decided he'd better pay attention. He was getting a house from him after all and he didn't want to appear rude. The old man was explaining that 'hatpinning' had been devised by Victorian surgeons as a means of discreetly practised infant euthanasia.

Using a long thin needle, he explained, the fatal wound was rendered to the infant's heart, ingressing via a small puncture made at the armpit. The bleeding was internal and discreet and—as the surgeons of those times reassured those fathers who were bothered about it—quite painless. After all, a babe born with deformity, mental or otherwise, simply does not understand pain they said, not in the way healthy people do, and would neither comprehend it nor feel it.

Such was God's mercy for even his low creatures.

And since most women were temporarily deranged at birthing time anyway (and likely to cause an unpleasant scene with their attachment to their infant—deformed or not), the mother in these sad cases was seldom informed that the procedure had even taken place. Instead, having been taken away from her at the cutting of the umbilicus, the tot would be returned once more a short time after the process, dead or dying, placed into the loving mother's arms that she might appreciate the fact of its deformity, and therefore be better able to accept not only that the child had been too enfeebled to live but that God's will had rightly prevailed.

The procedure was . . . a necessary evil. In fact it was surprising, the old man said, just how much evil was actually necessary in the world.

Any medical man even in those far off times, he continued, would have been aware that partial strangulation by the birthing cord—such as of the type that happened to Georges' poor daughter—inevitably led to brain palsy and varying degrees of idiocy. Hatpinning a child such as Grace would not have been uncommon. The old man assured Georges that she would feel little discomfort.

Georges thought their conversation ridiculous, veering on the outlandish. How had he come to be discussing seriously the murder of his baby daughter?

'It is unfortunately the only way,' the old man continued, as if Georges had spoken aloud, 'and unpleasant as it will be at the time, she won't remember it once she has been healed.'

'Healed?'

'But of course, Georges,' the old man said, 'she won't actually die. What do you take me for? This is not 1890, after all. This is just a very discreet means of bringing her to the point where she should die, after which I will fix her, don't worry.'

The Architect, smiling benignly, had produced a hatpin.

'And then one day she'll marry someone very special, and the whole world will be a different place,' he said. 'Won't that be something?'

❖

It was like old, brittle film going through a hot projector, Georges thought. Again and again until it frayed and jammed and *disintegrated. Soon there would be more holes than substance. Soon he would have nothing left but himself.*

19

Skinny had stayed too long. The sun was coming up and she was still staring out of the window of her flat at the top of the block. All night she had been sitting there looking at her reflection, smoking and sipping cornershop vodka until she'd realised that if she was really going to leave, she'd better start sobering up. She'd watched her face in the window pane grow fainter with the dawn's light until she was only half there, her features superimposed over the expanse of city before her.

She'd been thinking all night.

And she had realised that this life she thought she'd carved out for herself wasn't really any kind of life at all. She had no lover, no friends, no family worth mentioning and no reason to stay.

This hell hole flat, smack bang in the middle of an area with the highest murder rate in a city of pretty high murder rates ('hard to let' had been the euphemism used by the housing office) had been her only home since she'd gotten out of the care system. And she'd been lucky to get it. Despite its disadvantages, she had gotten used to actually having a place of her own, but really—when she looked at it objectively—it was just another rat trap. If only Big Ian had gone along with her (admittedly rough) idea. She could have been running the whole drug end of things. And why not? Someone would have to when Bewlay was dead, so why *not* her? She had a good brain . . .

She suddenly stopped that line of thought dead in its tracks. Who did she think she was kidding? Her mind was going round in self-deluded pointless circles of drunkenness. For a change. The drink did this to her, she knew. It gave her visions of grandiose schemes and plans that would be coming up roses anytime now. Yeah, right. What had she thought was going to happen? That Big Ian would just decide *yes, ok Skinny, I'll help you bump off Bewlay and then we'll both take over things and be the king and queen of coke shifting and everything else in this part of Glasgow*? She was disgusted with herself.

She thought she'd left any naivety behind her by the end of that first hellish month in the care home. Clearly not. Big Ian had been Bewlay's man for his entire life, and she was a one-eyed lesbian with the build of a pipe cleaner and a drink problem. She wasn't even a fucking dealer. She was a dealer's runner.

A plane flew low overhead, seeming to just suddenly *be* there, its jets abruptly screaming at her from nowhere; the volume control turned up to full from dead silence. It sounded like it was only twenty feet or so above her roof—a weird aural trick these flats played on the ears. She barely noticed. It happened pretty often on this flight path. It would be full of passengers, she thought, families going off on holiday, two weeks in the sun enabling them to play at being rich for a while—giving them a keyhole glimpse into the lives of the truly well off. Living on the top floor of a high-rise block of flats was the nearest she had ever been to a plane. Pathetic.

On arriving home in Sergeant Wendy's clothes and making a thorough search, she'd discovered that she had what amounted to about twenty grams of coke lying about in odd places—little bits she'd been skimming occasionally from her deliveries, put by for a rainy day. Not much, and she should have had more, but the bent cops knew she was a good source and (despite their 'official' payments and freebies in kind from Bewlay) would turn up at all fucking hours to get a wee pick me up from her for free. Even the fleas had fleas, she knew, and it was the kind of drug that no matter how much you'd already had, there was always room for more. She never touched the stuff now, not since she'd tried it, *a lot of it*, at a party and had seen herself turn into a complete slut, rubbing her fanny practically anywhere that had a surface. There was a lot of coke about that night and the other girls there had been equally jazzed by it, she was sure, but Skinny had been the one to take it to extremes. As fucking usual.

That stupid party had been a chance to actually get to meet someone and she had blown it. She had rubbed herself wet in the bathroom and had gone back out, her fingers shiny, and shaken hands with the girl she fancied. Ew. She had no remembrance of why on earth she had ever thought that this would be a good idea, but the ingenious plan hadn't worked. Every time she remembered it, she hated herself more.

She threw her glass at the wall where, instead of breaking, it bounced feebly and landed, upright, on one of her columns of pizza boxes. She stared at it, mildly amazed, and realised that she was sick and tired of sitting here, playing ping-pong in her mind with all these should she/shouldn't she what ifs. There was always something to make her change her mind—a maybe this or a perhaps that or a 'give it a few more minutes and it'll change'. She'd been like this since she was a kid—why couldn't she just make a fucking decision and stick to it? Well this time, she would. It was definitely time to go.

She figured she'd be able to get on a train and travel along the winding strip of decaying seaside towns that ran up and down the West Coast, connected by a long curl of road, like they were all just part of one big, linear, pastel-coloured conurbation. She could cut her already adulterated twenty grams into an even weaker fifty odd for starters (if she made them short weights as well), and start selling in the desperate, peeling pubs and clubs in the backstreets of these seaside shanty towns to kids that wouldn't know any better. She'd make a couple of grand, maybe a bit more—*easy*. But what then? She'd be leaving a trail, she knew. This was no movie—there'd be no idyllic escape into the Big Country where she could get good and lost—the ratty wee dealers in these places wouldn't take kindly to someone new selling on their patch. There would be enquiries made, a description given. Word would get back to Arthur Bewlay and if he wanted her he would get her. Even though she could say she'd been at the vodka whilst waiting for Big Ian at the hospital—maybe try to pass off what she'd said as a drunken joke—she knew that if Arthur had made up his mind she was a goner.

She would have to keep moving and be on the lookout for anyone staring at her for too long or surreptitiously taking photos of her on a mobie. Ultimately though, she had to have a destination. Not one of the islands, that was for sure. On an island you stuck out like a sore thumb and ultimately if things went wrong, you were pretty much trapped. Besides, they talked funny. Maybe Ireland? Or did you need a passport for there? Liverpool, perhaps. Maybe she could start again? The pizza bike scam had been a good one and it could work pretty much anywhere—all she had to do was nick a moped with a carrier box, paint it red, wear a matching cagoule and she was suddenly invisible; free to go where and when she pleased, at all hours of the day or night and no questions asked.

That was how she had 'auditioned' for Bewlay and Big Ian in the first place, simply arriving at the pub and going upstairs to the flat—past all of the mutant security in the bar—with a pizza box she'd nicked and straight in to the living room without knocking. No one had noticed her and in fact no one had known she was even a girl until she'd pulled the helmet off. After his initial shock—she could have been there to kill him, after all—Bewlay had 'hired' her. She was lucky and she was glad; she had needed to start making money and knew two things about the only sort of 'normal' jobs she could have gotten—one, she couldn't have stood the idea of being behind a counter punting endless burgers or fried chicken every day and having to look at hundreds of different people trying not to stare at her eye, and two, it would have been a fuck of a lot of hard work for piss all dough. Besides, she'd had her great business idea—invisible drug dealing—and it had even been fast food related, she'd realised with a grin the evening she stole her first moped. Unfortunately, this wasn't the kind of business for which you could apply for a grant, and even if you could, it also wasn't the kind of business where you got a lot of sole traders, at least, not ones who survived to retirement age.

She'd known that she had to take the idea to a recognised firm and, horrible as it had been to contemplate, Bewlay's lot were certainly that. The first moped she'd used had been nicked from an actual pizza guy and Bewlay had paid the cops and the branch manager off to keep her away from court.

For her first runs, Big Ian had come with her on the back of the bike as security, which looked totally stupid and drew all the unwanted attention to her that she'd wanted to avoid in the first place . . . but she'd been glad of his presence on a few occasions.

The more runs they'd made together, the more she got used to feeling his boner poking into her back and—unwelcome as it had been at first—it became part and parcel of the job.

Anyway, as soon as she'd realised that he wasn't going to do anything with it without her express say so, she didn't mind. A man who waited for permission was clearly a man in love, and she'd banked that fact for future use, reckoning she'd be able to use it one day. What a fucking stupid idea that had been. In fact, the whole thing of getting involved with these fuckers at all had been a stupid idea . . . but, she'd been living in lonesome, benefit misery for too long and she'd wanted to afford stuff.

Despite herself, she had been flattered when Bewlay had admired her 'pluck' as he'd called it, back then when he'd had a full complement of nasal cavities. He smiled and made jokes and was obviously extremely intelligent. University type intelligent, she had thought. He boasted that he had left school at fourteen and that he really knew nothing much of anything and that his brother had really been the brainy one—but she knew that was total pish. From what she'd heard, Tommy was little more than an imbecile. It was Arthur who had the book type knowledge at his command. He spoke the big words and seemed to enjoy being seen to be cleverer than everyone else. She hadn't minded him so much then, but it soon got to be that she hated spending any amount of time with him alone. Even before his illness had started taking a grip, he was clearly not trustworthy in any way shape or form.

She remembered the day she had shown up at the pub to pick up some gear from behind the bar, only to be told to go upstairs. Each tread on each step had made her feel lower and lower in spirit and when she'd gotten to the sitting room, he had shouted for her not to come in but to wait in the hall. She had done so and had heard him humming some tune to himself—it sounded like something classical maybe. Then, he had just stepped in front of the open door, his dick sticking out of his trousers, and had masturbated himself to a climax right in front of her—all the while humming that stupid tune. She hadn't had a clue what to do. He had smiled at her and told her to go back down to get the stuff for her next bunch of deliveries and that had been that. That was when she had known for sure that Bewlay considered himself beyond anything and anybody and that he'd probably been that way for his entire life. She should have left a long, long time ago.

She got out of her chair and swayed slightly as she stood. She'd get some food at the railway station—that would steady her. She'd get away from here as soon as she could and then figure out what to do, permanent escape-wise, when she was fed and sober and sitting on a train.

20

Maryam hadn't expected this.

She hadn't expected to . . . feel like this.

She hadn't expected to feel anything.

Not for real.

All she had expected—all she had dared to hope for—was the ersatz, the *appearance* of love. That would have been enough for her. She didn't deserve or anticipate any more than that. But here they were—out together in the sunshine, walking through the park. The sun was warm on her arms and her simple, thin cotton summer red dress had made him smile. She leaned into him, putting her head on his shoulder and he put his arm around her waist. She felt protected and cared for.

The grass was cool beneath her bare feet and she felt a small thrill when he kissed her on the top of her head just for the sake of it.

She reached over for him, longing to let her fingertips trace a light path down his tanned arm, but she stopped, unable to prevent her lips drawing back from her teeth in horror.

Her hand looked like a withered claw.

She gasped and drew it away like it was on fire, hiding it behind her back.

She looked up into his face. Had he noticed? Had he seen what had happened to her?

He mustn't see! He mustn't! It wasn't real, not anymore! Not here.

'Are you ok Maryam?' he said, smiling pleasantly down at her, genuinely puzzled. She made herself put on the brightest smile she could manage and nodded. Yes. She was alright.he hugged her again and they continued to walk on, the sounds of the children playing on the swings and slides nearby and the music from people's radios weaving through the trees.she dared another look at her arm.

It was fine.

Normal.

'Let's find Grace and go home,' he said. 'It looks like rain.'

She looked around. The green wasn't so busy now. The music had stopped and all the children in the play park distant were silently walking away, their backs to her. Where were the parents? she thought. The sky darkened and there was a soft approaching *shush shush shush* of rain. It began to patter on the broader leaves of the surrounding trees and the wind felt cold. Grace was on a large limb on an old tree. What on earth was she doing up there?

'She's crying,' he said. 'She's stuck.'

He walked away from her then, toward the tree, and Maryam wanted to grab him and pull him back. Just leave her there, she thought. If she's stupid enough to go climbing trees at her age she deserves everything she gets.

Maryam knew that it was insane, but she was suddenly jealous of her sister because she was about to be caught in his strong arms. But she knew that she wasn't really angry, because she knew that Grace was only twelve years old ... and she also knew that she was more afraid than angry. She wanted to leave the park. Right now. If she left right now, none of this would happen and she and he would be together forever.

Why did Grace have to climb a stupid tree? It was all her fault! If she hadn't climbed a stupid tree, none of this would ... he wouldn't have ... she ...

Maryam couldn't concentrate, her head started to hurt.

'Come on, Grace,' he said, 'just move your legs over and dangle. It's not a big drop. I'll catch you.'

But when Grace let go and fell, she landed awkwardly on him. The ground around the tree was a mess of exposed, protruding roots and he stumbled with her, losing his balance and both of them collapsed to the ground, she on top of him, on top of his arm, on top of a root sticking out like a gnarled elbow from the earth.

It was a stupid, inane happenstance. Nothing should have come of it. People fell every day and emerged with nothing more than bruises.

There was a dull snapping noise and Maryam immediately knew that he had broken his arm.

Like he had before.

Like he always did.

Grace was crying and he was trying not to. He was in tremendous pain.

His short sleeved shirt was dirty and wet from the muddy ground and the rain was sheeting down now, hard enough to make speaking or hearing or seeing difficult.

Grace looked down at him and squealed. A jagged haft of bone had erupted from the flesh of his arm and he was unnaturally pale. He was about to faint and when he saw his arm—his blood washing away in the rain like it was being hosed. He started shouting.

'Oh no God no . . .'

Maryam ran to him and she held him and she wished—she wished with all of her might—that he would be better. He started screaming then and she looked down and realised that she was actually gripping his poor arm very tightly. He was struggling to pull away from her . . . but for some reason she couldn't explain, she held him even tighter. After a few moments, he had fainted. But still she held on. She had felt a huge rush of energy, like an endorphin boost after a particularly exhausting sprint . . . she had met him when she'd been running a half marathon, he seemed to know just the things to say to a shy young woman who didn't . . . who couldn't . . . who wasn't . . . why was her head hurting so much?

When she looked down again, his arm was completely healed.

Not a mark. Not a blemish. He smiled at her. He was alright—he was going to be ok.

She had smiled back, her headache gone. But then he had looked down and he had suddenly stopped smiling. She looked at the palms of her hands and saw what he had seen.

She looked up again and it was night time.
It was night time now.
The table had been set and he was coming to see her. He was coming to dinner and to wish her a happy birthday.
She was wearing white opera gloves, but they were stained and unpleasant smelling. She already knew what her hands looked like inside them.
He had been gone for so long and his letters had become fewer and less personal until at times she felt like she was reading dispassionate reports about the comings and goings of someone under observation by the Stasi.
But she treasured them all the same.
He had gone to university.
She hadn't.
She had been making the money for Papa from her gift.
Why did Papa have to spend so much money?
Papa sat at the head of the table, looking at his watch, wanting his dinner—where was this boy?
Grace had made a valiant effort on Maryam's face, copying from the pictures in her magazines.
He'd said in the letters that he understood about her 'disease' and what it did to her and that it didn't make any difference to him. That an extreme reaction to sunlight was just one of those unfortunate events, apparently believing her when she'd told him she had latent xeroderma pigmentosum... and somehow managing to forget about what had happened with his arm. Or choosing to, since the alternative meant questioning every single thing he'd ever known or believed. And who would want to do something like that?
Papa sat at the head of the table, looking at his watch.
Where was he?
She knew that she didn't look right anymore, but she knew that he had loved her once and that he would do so again because it was her that he had loved, not the shape on the outside. She knew that.
Because that was what love was.
Real love.

True love.

Why had Grace climbed that stupid tree?

She'd never have known that she could do this . . . thing if she hadn't had to heal him. And she wouldn't have had to watch herself rot away and rot away a little more and even more yet every time she did it.

He would come and he would take her away. She wouldn't have to do this ever again.

He tried to hide his feelings from her when he at last stepped into the dining room a humiliating two hours late but she didn't care as long as he was here with her at last and Grace was all idiotic smiles and asking him how his arm was even though it had been years since it had happened and not noticing he'd had a drink before coming and he had taken one look at her and she had known instantly.

Finally.

It wasn't what the person was like on the inside that counted after all.

Dinner was quiet and goodbye was forever.

'John . . .' she said, 'John . . .'

She ran to the door . . . she followed him outside—but it wasn't John. It was Joe.

Here they were—out together in the sunshine, walking through the park. The sun was warm on her arms and her simple, thin cotton summer red dress had made him smile.

A man of low morals, making a superhuman effort to pretend that he did not find sleeping with her as revolting as one would with a corpse.

She leaned into him, putting her head on his shoulder and he put his arm around her waist. She felt protected and cared for.

The very things that she had craved in her life—love and trust—the very fact that Joe had synthesised both of those things so well, actually showed him to be *un*trustworthy and love*less* . . .

She forced herself not to think like that. She should be grateful to be receiving anything at all from this man.

She made herself recite over and over in her head: *pretence was better than nothing*. She had been dead inside for so long that even the semblance of living was better.

There would be a price to pay, she knew. He would leave and then reality would hit her. Very, *very* hard.

But that would be then. This was now.

Screw reality.

She jammed her eyes closed, not wanting to see herself as she really was, preferring to stay the person she had imagined she'd been when she had been making love with Joe. She had felt every movement inside her body as they had joined together, feeling her insides changing and blossoming. She wasn't old and dried up *inside* herself, she knew that now.

Every touch of his lips had been a promise made to her that he would stay with her forever and that he would look after her and be there for her and her alone.

That was what she told herself.

That was what she believed.

That was what she knew.

It was summer and the sunshine made the park a beautiful place once more.

The grass was cool beneath her bare feet and she felt a small thrill when he kissed her on the top of her head—just for the sake of it.

21

Someone new was moving into the block. There was a white van, packed full of furniture that looked like it should be in a skip. They'd probably gotten it from one, Skinny thought, as she walked out of the pee-smelling lobby, her black holdall slung over her shoulder.

A greasy looking guy was pulling out a very threadbare armchair and swearing at it as the woman inside was pushing it from the other end. Skinny stopped and watched for a few moments, her eye drawn to the girl's hair. It was a natural, sandy blonde and very clean. Probably still smelt of the morning's shampoo. These two were starting some sort of new life here, she thought; taking up their odd sticks of furniture and probably—despite being in a bad mood with each other at the moment—looking forward to it.

She continued watching the girl who, with a great deal of patience, talked her greasy partner into pulling the chair just so, and with an awkward twist, thus freeing it from the van. The pair smiled at each other then and the girl looked up, catching Skinny's look.

Skinny didn't get the usual reaction she got when someone clocked her—a kind of mild shock and then either a quick look away or a forced smile to show that the person didn't really have any issues about someone with a glass eye. This girl genuinely smiled at her. She must be really happy, thought Skinny. She was truly pretty and looked to be barely in her twenties. She was still smiling at her as the man got busy pulling the chair across the pavement to the lobby of the flats. To her surprise, the girl had a look now that she recognised absolutely. Some women could take one glance at Skinny and just tell what she was and then they either looked superior or pitying. This look was neither. This look was an attraction. Unbelievably, this gorgeous girl was giving her a *look* look. Skinny stood shock still, amazed.

Mandy had been gorgeous, sure, but Skinny had had to pursue her vigorously, plying her with drink and promising a regular supply of Charlie before she would even agree to a date. Even then, Skinny had known, really, that Mandy was a pipe dream and that the most she'd have gotten from her would be sex. And grudging, drug-tainted sex at that. This was different, Skinny could feel it. This girl knew nothing about her, yet here she was giving her a *look*. And it was *quite* a look. She'd seen it on girls' faces sometimes in the clubs—a look given to other people, of course, and not her. Until now.

Skinny dropped her gaze, afraid that by staring over for too long she would jinx this. This couldn't be right, she thought. This beautiful girl was moving in here, with that guy and . . . she paused. Maybe she wasn't, Skinny thought, with a tiny rush of hope.

Maybe the guy was her brother or something and she was just helping him? Or, better yet, she was moving in and the guy was only a friend or relative helping her out? She glanced up again, but the girl had gone back into the van, getting busy with a dilapidated sideboard or something.

Skinny didn't feel dispirited, though. The girl wasn't going anywhere except into Skinny's building . . . and maybe she needed a hand? Skinny could help her. Just go over there and introduce herself.

Hi, neighbour.

Are you moving in?

Even if the girl was married or something, there was definitely an attraction. At the very least, a possible friendship. It was very rare that Skinny felt an affinity like this with anyone at all, ever. She could feel it inside her. Potential.

The police car had pulled up behind her, but she hadn't really been consciously aware of the slight gravelly sound the tyres made when they'd rolled to a halt. The jet flying overhead had seen to that. Sergeant Wendy emerged with a constable who had lumpy, raspberry coloured patches of acne on his face and chin.

Skinny was thinking hard about staying, after all. Just taking the risk. She knew it was stupid, but she couldn't just go and never come back without knowing, at the very least, if what she had seen and felt about this girl was true or not. All it would take would be a quick word, two minutes of conversation tops.

Much later on, just before she died, Skinny remembered these moments—the girl, especially, but also suddenly seeing the two shadows on the ground arriving from behind her.

If she'd been on the ball, she would have fled the instant she'd seen those shadows. No one, after all, creeps up behind you silently to give you birthday cake and a pile of money. But she wasn't on the ball, and they were upon her before the significance of their shadows had occurred to her.

She turned quickly... but even then had relaxed momentarily when she'd seen who it was. But the look on Wendy's face wasn't a good one. Too friendly. Too smiley. Too much. Skinny gripped her bag tightly and threw it at them, to hell with the coke or anything else inside it—she knew why they were here and that she had to get away.

She turned and ran and managed to get about twenty feet from them before the raspberry constable fired his taser and decked her, leaving her twitching and gasping and writhing in the dirt like an epileptic, among the McDonalds cartons and the broken glass.

◆

The blonde girl emerged once more, a creaking and wonky second-hand chest of drawers partly sticking out of the van in front of her, and a look on her face that was keen on asking for help from the unusual boy with the funny eye she'd been looking at moments earlier. But all she could see was a police car, disappearing down the hill, away from the flats.

22

Joe lay wide awake in bed, staring up at edges of the high ceiling; The dark holes in the elaborate mouldings and cornices above reminded him of an old New Yorker cartoon by Charles Addams—it was of a down at heel bass fiddle player, a man who was clearly bottoming out luck-wise, practising beneath a bare bulb in his seedy, rundown flophouse room—his tatty instrument being quite possibly the only thing of value he possessed.

But something had caught the man's attention.

He was looking down into the body of his double bass where, through one of the f-holes, a human eye looked out from the darkness and up at him. It was disturbing, funny and melancholy, all at the same time. The moral of the story being, Joe thought, that having company wasn't necessarily a good thing.

He'd fucked Maryam until he'd ached.

But no matter how hard he'd tried, he couldn't make himself come. It didn't seem to matter what exotic things he'd imagined himself doing with Grace. Famous movie stars (Bette Davis excepted) had also come and gone in his head, but there had still been no completion in sight for him. He'd started wondering how it was that he could still actually be erect. Maybe his dick had just . . . locked? Maybe he had broken it somehow (that horrible moment with the catheter back at the hospital?) and this would be its new default position, sticking out of him at a right angle forever. That would be fun to explain at church socials.

He had plugged on and—having noted that she had already come some time previously—had taken the risk of making the right noises and pretending to ejaculate, hoping she wouldn't notice any lack of semen dribbling from her when he pulled out. She'd gotten plenty wet down there anyway and he reckoned he'd get away with it. He figured besides that her experience in these things was probably not vast. Then, the goddamndest thing had happened. She had spoken very softly, her voice suddenly sounding much younger.

'I love you, Joe,' she had said.

And he knew that, even though this was all part of the big game of pretend, she'd really meant it. He knew, absolutely *knew*, that whatever love was, however it made you feel—even if it were only for a few moments—that at *this* moment, when she thought he was going to come inside her, she was actually feeling it. So then it was time for his part of the bargain and he found that the words came from him completely naturally and that, for that small moment, he could believe what he was saying.

'I love you too Maryam,' he'd said, and it didn't sound awkward or forced to him. She held him even more tightly and she started to laugh softly, sounding surprised more than anything else.

'I love you Joe . . . I love you . . .'

And when she said it again, he came like a train, feeling it go through his entire body—but more than an orgasm, it was sheer joy. All of a sudden, thoughts of anyone else—thoughts of Grace—were unreal and false and irrelevant; the images blew away like paper in the wind because he was in the here and the now of being with this woman and the moment stretched and stretched like slow motion.

He couldn't explain it to himself. The very fact that someone actually and truly not only loved him but was able to express it to him in such a way that he *knew* it was true turned him from a rational creature into a writhing mass of pleasured nerve endings.

It was as if he'd managed to go through some kind of barrier and forgot who she was, what she looked like, what her breath smelled like. He just let go of any conscious thought and enjoyed both the physical, dirty, sexy sensation of slopping in and out of her as she clung onto him—her legs wrapped around his hips, her arms around his back—and a weird, mental one of pleasurable white noise wiping out any and all cynicism in him, an electromagnet against tape. He'd never felt like this with anyone ever before and it was the difference between looking at a postcard of an old master painting and being in the Louvre standing right in front of the real thing. He found himself laughing and crying at the same time, needing to hide his face in the pillow to shade his embarrassment.

They lay there panting for a while and he'd held her tightly to him, the strange sensation of having completely lost control of himself already starting to fade. He tried to hang on to it—it had been so . . . unusual.

Compelling and open.
Breathtaking.
Diminishing.
Gone.

His conscious mind took over again, and it made him sad. But! This was a job and he had to get back to work. He'd just fucked a lady and it was time to knuckle down and start whispering the sweet nothings. He'd realised that he couldn't go the usual route of being complimentary about her beauty—he didn't think she'd be *that* able to suspend disbelief—but had done just as well, it seemed, with saying the things he'd sometimes imagined he might say one day were he ever to actually be in love with a girl. That, along with mild dirty talk and a lot of enthusiasm, seemed to satisfy her.

The murmurings had petered out naturally and sleep began to creep slowly upon them. She had shivered and he'd found himself holding her that little bit more closely, pulling the bedcovers up over her shoulders with his free hand—all quite naturally and instinctively, he was bemused to note. There must be something automatic that kicks in with men in situations like this, he'd thought—your basic caveman protect cavewoman type thing, behaviour that's instinctual. Regardless of what the woman looks like, talks like, smells like, acts like—if you're this close to her and she's cold and uncomfortable; you make her warm and comfortable. Maryam appreciated it as she snuggled her back against him in her sleep.

Not long after, when he had been beginning to drift off, she broke wind under the sheets and spluttered slightly to herself. He found himself stifling a laugh . . . but it wasn't an unkind one. So she wasn't Playmate of the Month—big deal. There were worse ways to be spending your time. Her stiff, dry hair was now sticking in his face and he had to bend it away from him to stop it from tickling. As he was doing so, he found himself leaning forward and kissing her gently on the top of her head. Just for the sake of it.

It was involuntary and natural and he didn't attach any significance to it, because he knew there wasn't any. Not for him, anyway. It was just a nice thing and so what? He was playing his part that was all. Except . . . she was asleep and wouldn't know he was doing it, so why do it at all? Before he could examine that thought in more detail, she made a small, happy noise, as if she'd been able to register the tenderness of his lips as she slept and he smiled, justified now in his seemingly irrational action.

Now he began thinking rationally.

He had a basic template for scamming, a visual metaphor which he kept in his mind to help him through any job. The image he used was that of a small town with a highway running through it. He would imagine himself arriving at one end of this town, on foot and completely naked . . . and leaving the other end in a chauffeured, gold-plated Rolls Royce. Simple, but effective. Mostly he came out the other side as naked as he'd gone in, but not this time. No sir. Maryam was going to be his Rolls Royce.

She stirred beside him. He wouldn't press her on the details of their arrangement immediately. He'd bring her up some breakfast and generally ease her back into it, mindset-wise.

He moved his arm slowly and carefully out from under her, barely breathing as he did so, slipping from her bed naked, his feet warming quickly on the wooden floor. He pulled on his pants and snuck from the room.

◈

Maryam opened her sleep crusted eyes, awake, knowing that she had done something that was terribly, dreadfully wrong.

'*Never mind that!*' the selfish, mean part of her said. '*Just enjoy this while you can!*'

Selfish mean 'part'? She thought everything about her these days was selfish and mean. There seemed to be no 'good' parts left in her.

He wasn't in bed anymore. Maybe he'd left? Maybe he'd had enough and couldn't stand the thought of going through with their game of 'let's pretend' any longer? That would be good, she thought, because if he'd left, then she wouldn't have to face him and tell him the truth.

She became aware that she was feeling tender and a little sore between her legs. She pulled the sheets down and her nightdress up to her waist, looking down to examine herself. The tops of her thighs were livid with small bruises. Joe hadn't been particularly rough with her, had he? Mind you, she thought, she had never been caressed down there by anyone but herself. How would she know what was rough and what wasn't?

She supposed that virgin flesh would tend to bruise at the slightest pressure, like a ripe peach. She quietly laughed aloud at her own presumption. Ripe peach, indeed. Who would ever have thought in a million years that she would have warranted that description?

She now became aware of the strange sensation between her legs and *inside* her.

She wouldn't have known really how to describe the feeling. Achy, but not actually painful. Tingly. Used, maybe?

At last.

She decided that Joe should on no account ever find out how old she really was. She had wanted to be 'loved' for how she was now, not how she should have been because that girl was long gone and never to return. There was to be *no pity*—ever, ever, ever. Pity was a black poison that spread like spilt ink, staining and ruining everything. And self-pity, she knew, was the worst. She was beginning to see now what it had done to her and by extension to her poor sister. There would be no more of that in this house, whatever happened. She found herself smiling and stretching back on to the sheets like a cat, closing her eyes again and caressing herself. The marks on her legs were secret—only she and Joe would know about them. She would tease him about them later when he was in bed with her again. She would scold him that he was too rough for her . . . and provoke him perhaps into apologies and tenderness. She would ask him to kiss it better for her. She felt herself flush at her own dirtiness. Kiss it better. Would she enjoy that? She'd certainly enjoy finding out, she supposed.

Perhaps she should just go back to sleep again just now? She had never had the pleasure of being woken by the warm kisses of a lover and she was sure that Joe would be the sort. She would enjoy that also.

After all, there was no need to tell him the truth straight away, was there?

23

SKINNY WAS LYING IN A FOETAL POSITION, THE BURNT SIDE OF HER face against the worn nylon weave on a stinking carpet, its 1970s style spiral pattern stretching away from her, all the way to her immediate horizon; the skirting board.

She'd had carpet burns before—but never on her fucking face. She felt like her right cheek had been pressed against the nylon bristle wheel of an industrial shoe polisher for a day, and surmised that she had been dragged in here rather than carried. She was fully conscious now . . . but she didn't want to move. She didn't even want to be awake. She had a terror in the pit of her stomach that made her wish that she was dead. She didn't want to be alive in here, in this place, knowing that any second the door could open and that when it did, a nightmare worse than any imagining would begin for her.

◆

Squashed up on the floor in the back of the police car, as Sergeant Wendy had driven, she had been given regular jolts from the Taser by the constable—again, again, again—until she was just a lump of insensate meat, showing signs of life only when the electricity was being spiked through her. Unbelievably she had remained conscious throughout the drive—a design facet of the device, maybe? No matter how much juice was pumped into you, it was never quite enough to give you the respite of unconsciousness? People were very clever about things like that. A lot of time and effort was expended on perfecting torture devices the world over.

When she'd had any chance to think—extremely brief micro moments snatched when one shock was wearing off and another had yet to be applied—she'd clung desperately to the idea that Sergeant Wendy would somehow help her. That Wendy was being forced to do this to her, and that, even now, she was thinking of ways to get her out of this. However, Wendy sounding very pissed off and saying '*She nicked forty quid from my purse, keep pumping her*' ended that notion, so she concocted another desperate fantasy instead.

Maybe, she thought, she was just to be tortured like this, here in the cop car, simply as a warning, and then dumped on the edge of town with instructions never to show her face again. That would be good. Maybe she'd be beaten black and blue and then let go. Or have something broken first. That would also be good. Even being taken into the middle of nowhere and being shot in the back of the fucking head would be better than where, she knew deep down, they were taking her.

And it was when they had finally pulled up at Bewlay's pub and she had been roughly pulled from the back of the car by the constable, that it had really hit her. That place, with its windows all bricked up and its front doorway a pitiless dark orifice leading to hellish blackness inside—she knew that this was going to be where she would end her life. And not in an easy, quick way . . . but slowly and with all the fear that could be induced into her. She felt like a child again, feeling the unspeakable, indescribable terror and sickness she used to feel when her aunt would arrive, dragging her own equally frightened child with her, and mum would pull the blinds down and take the Argos bought video camera out of the bag.

They would make her and her cousin fight each other, egging them on and screaming at them to really, *really* hit each other, spraying them with beer from their shaken up cans and shrieking with laughter, taping them the whole time . . . and selling the tapes in the pub afterward—two small children being made to fight each other like pit bulls in the vain hope that there might be a mother's love and cuddles at the end of their ordeal.

That's entertainment.

The terror of the 'visits' only ended on the terrible afternoon Skinny's mum had given her cousin the chopstick . . . and the poor little bastard had burst Skinny's eye with it.

Even though she had been screaming in pain, mum had kept on filming.

The dreadful feeling that a boundary had been irrevocably crossed, that a door had slammed closed forever on normality and goodness and light—the feeling she had had when her eye had been taken from her . . . that feeling was back now, here, in front of this terrible place. She lay there, head in the gutter and drool collecting at the corner of her mouth, as the tendrils of the Taser were torn from her like jellyfish stingers from a beached swimmer, and she knew that something awful and unfixable was going to happen to her here. And she knew that even if by some miracle she survived this place, that it wouldn't be for very long and that her spirit—such as it was—would be shattered forever. She knew it, and knowing that there was absolutely nothing that she could do about it, her body had shown her the tiniest smidgeon of mercy and she had passed out.

◈

Now the bare lightbulb above her shone pitilessly down, exposing to her this room's story of horror and fear. On the carpet, roughly midway between her good eye and the wall, was a small, yellowy object. She focused on it and saw that it was a tooth, its pulp still attached, gone brown with age and rot. There was a scattering of hypodermic plungers along the skirting board, their insides caked with dried blood.

She slowly put her hands out before her and pulled herself up into a sitting position. The place stank of garbage truck and sewage pipe, its walls smeared with desperate, bloody handprints. The carpet itself was sticky beneath her palms—heavily marked and bloodstained. It had weird, thin black lines spiralling all over it, burnt in circles and loops like someone had been spraying jets of lighter fuel and setting them alight. There was a pile of filthy, plastic supermarket bags in a corner and she could smell them from here; they were full of excrement, and hadn't been tied at the tops. They were simply tossed there, the backsplash from the force of the throws causing tidal marks of brown and yellow to spurt and stain halfway up the wall to the ceiling.

On the floor, partly hidden beneath these bags of filth, was a pair of girls', once pink, underpants. They were torn badly, but she could just make out the Playboy bunny logo on the front and the dull twinkle of the one or two diamante studs that remained on the fabric. Nearby was a cheap, thin, pink belt that had been looped around itself several times in a broad figure eight. That had been wrapped round wrists or ankles, she thought, her vision swimming as her tears started for the girl who'd been here before her. She wiped her eye savagely with the back of her hand, trying to rip her mind away from the story she could see so clearly in that corner of the room.

She looked away, toward the bricked up window, and could make out what looked like roughly torn, small chunks of meat, hanging from uneven parts of the brickwork and grouting sealing her in. It brought to her mind the image of a face being slammed against it and rubbed there, the flesh being torn at and gouged out by the jagged surface.

The rough cement between the bricks was squeezed out in lumps, frozen there, forever capturing the moment in time when the brickie had laid his hasty building blocks and hadn't bothered to scoop away the excess cement to give it a finish.

She wasn't surprised he'd been hasty. Even if this room hadn't looked remotely like this when the windows were originally sealed up (which she presumed it hadn't), the guy probably couldn't wait to get the fuck out of here, given who the pub belonged to.

The room was also hot. Very hot. There must be a heater or a radiator in here, she thought. She turned to look behind her, abruptly wishing that she hadn't. Stretched across the battered, Victorian ornate hot water radiator was the body of a dead greyhound. It was upside down, its chin on the floor, neck bent at a right angle to the rest of its body, which had been stretched out like a canvas, each paw a corner. It had been eviscerated at some point, its insides removed to God knows where, its other fleshy parts drying here against this furnace of a radiator where it looked as if it had been mummified by the heat. Even that wasn't the worst though.

Skinny saw that its coat was absolutely covered in lacerations, hundreds and hundreds of them, and its snout had the remains of some sort of wide, black sticky tape that had been wound around it. The dog appeared to have been slashed over and over and over again and she had no doubt at all that Bewlay had done this and equally had no doubt that he'd done it while the dog had been still alive.

Because what would have been the point, otherwise?

Its eye sockets were dark empty holes encircled with dried matter, but they still managed to appear as if it were looking up at her. No, wait. They weren't both empty. One of the eye sockets had had something put in it. She looked a little more closely. It was a marble.

No, it wasn't, she realised. It was a glass eye.

She skittered backwards, away from the ghastly thing. She wanted to scream and scream and had to force herself to remain quiet. Her hands flashed up to her face, feeling for it—surely to Christ that bastard hadn't taken her eye out and put it into . . . that!

No, she realised, he hadn't. She forced herself to calm her breathing down.

She had to think rationally, realistically. She knew she could do that. She had become a hard realist at a very early age and now wasn't any kind of time to be abandoning that.

Let's start getting a few things straight here, she thought.

She wasn't frightened by a dead fucking dog—she was frightened about why she had been put into a room with one. Was Bewlay giving her a preview of what was in store for her? Was that what the fucking eye thing was about? Then, as her mind regained control of itself and she started to use it to think properly about this situation, a realisation suddenly hit her.

She was fucking furious.

Some time in the last twenty seconds or so her fear had mutated into hatred, and that was something she knew she could be very good at. And it had been the thought of that sick fucker messing with her body or getting in any way personal with her while she was out cold that'd done it. This was just a fucking room, she thought. She was in an ordinary, small room in a pissy, ancient pub that was practically falling down. She was still alive and she was still fucking kicking. She was sorry for whoever had been in here before her—she really was—but she'd cried for them already and that was as sentimental as she was prepared to get. Their part in this story was over, thought Skinny, and it was time for her to pull herself together and get right the fuck out of here. But how? She looked around her again and the glimmer of an idea came to her.

The bricks on the window. The untidy overflowing cement. The brickie had obviously been in a hurry to do his job, so maybe he hadn't been too fussy about how he'd mixed his grouting? Maybe he'd put too much sand in? Maybe not enough? Maybe it would be weak? Maybe she could start to chip away at it? If she had enough time she could scrape the cement from around and between the bricks and start pulling them away—make a hole and get out of here!

She was on her feet in an instant and over at the window, ignoring the retch making stink from the plastic bags. She scanned the brickwork, looking for any likely place she could start. She was looking for anything to get a hold of, anything to dig out—surely somewhere in between all of these bricks, with all of this cement squished out like the filling in a badly made cake, there would be something she could make a start on . . . and there it was. Right in front of her face, behind the biggish chunk of dried hanging skin—there was enough cement wastage sticking out like a small, horizontal stalactite for her to wrap a pinkie finger around.

She first pulled the piece of dangling flesh off and it made a small tearing sound like Velcro as it came away. It was in a rough triangle shape and it looked like a piece of scalp, but then she looked more closely and she could see that the hair on the skin was actually beard stubble. So there had been a guy involved in here too, and this was a piece of his cheek. Or chin. Not that it mattered any more. She noticed a dead tick embedded in the flesh.

'Here Rover, din dins.'

She tossed it in the direction of the dead dog before turning back to the window and grabbing at the cement lump, pulling at it with all her strength. It didn't take much—the piece snapped away easily, exposing a big air bubble beneath. She found that there was enough room in the bubble to stick her forefinger in and she started scraping away, frantically hollowing it out.

The cement came away quite easily as she crooked her finger in and out . . . but she knew that she probably wouldn't be thinking so in a while, when her nail had torn off and her finger was raw and bloody. This was abrasive grit and cement she was dealing with here, not Play Doh. She would have to find some kind of tool to help her do the job.

There, on the floor next to the bags of human waste—the pink belt. She picked it up and ripped the cheap buckle from it, pushing it onto her finger like a ring and using the metal tongue against the tip of her finger to start digging out the cement again.

That was better. Marginally. But any advantage was good.

She smiled grimly to herself. Arthur Bewlay had just fucked with the wrong girl.

This was going to work. She was going to get out of here. And when she did, she was going to come straight back in through the front fucking door, reach right into the hole in that shitfucker's face with both of her bare fucking hands and tear it right the fuck in half.

24

JOE STOOD ON THE BALCONY FLOOR. NOW IT WAS DAY, THE PLACE was brilliantly illuminated by cold sunlight flooding down from the huge, domed skylight high above him. The bright hues from its stained glass seemed to completely fill the place and made it feel odd and disjointed, the huge blocks of colour projected by the sun making it look like the walls and floors were made from wildly variant materials (a massive square of blue here, a hexagon of red there, distorted yellow triangles, massive green star shapes and such all hugely magnified and soft edge blurred by the distance they had to travel from above). The overall effect was quite dizzying. It almost felt like the place was made *only* of colour and any lines that should have been straight—like the skirting or the floorboards or the balcony rail or even the edges of the doorframes—were somehow not.

It reminded him of a cheap Christmas present he had received as a child—a toy kaleidoscope, which had tiny pieces of misshaped, brightly coloured plastic rattling about at the lens. It had fascinated and delighted him, but now it felt like he was actually inside the thing and he didn't like it. Colours so bright should be wonderful, he thought—but maybe that was just a misconception. After all, rainbows were nice to look at from afar, but who would want to experience what it might be like *inside* one? If such a thing were possible, Joe was willing to bet that it wouldn't be delightful at all.

He looked down and was glad of the coffin on the trestle tables below him. It was something geometric and solid, he thought, something with *order*—and on thinking that, the colours all around him seemed less oppressive. They were, after all, just the sunlight filtering through tinted glass—an optical effect and nothing more. Still, he didn't like it. It made him think again of the old shit Brewster—his barn had been full of stained glass too—but of a late sixties kind, just regular, ordinary windows daubed with washed out paint. Cheapjack and barely functional even at the time, either as decoration *or* windows. Age had since made them into something venerable to be treasured and preserved. Age seemed to do that to a lot of things, he thought, apart from people.

He smiled.

His misadventure with Brewster was feeling very far away from him now and he didn't have the spirit sapping doom feeling that had been dogging him since that night. Bad things really were better dragged out into the light.

He even thought that he could admire the old fucker's sheer guts.

Joe walked along, sliding his hand along the polished wooden rail, to the top of the wrought iron spiral staircase, passing closed door after closed door. He slowed. So many doors, he thought, all they were missing was room numbers. So the girls stayed here, along with their father, although he obviously wouldn't need his room anymore. He had a more compact space to stay in now. Joe giggled a little, mildly horrified at his callousness but still unable to stop himself.

So . . . what exactly was inside these rooms? Treasure stacked up to the ceiling, he wondered, or damp, fusty boxes of magazines and old useless household crap? It could go either way, really. The curse and the blessing of the antiquarian world were the ignorant and the forgetful—you had to catch people (and what they had in their possession) at just the right time or else it might all end up either in the hands of relatives or on the garbage dump. The right time was usually, of course, immediately following a death, preferably of a patriarch or matriarch who hopefully owned things that they and the rest of their family had grown so used to that they didn't appreciate their value. He felt a little guilty about thinking this way, but reckoned he could live with himself.

He stopped outside the last door before the turn on to the staircase and reached out for the handle, gripping it gently. He instantly pulled his hand away. What the hell? He reached out again and tentatively touched it with his fingertips. It felt normal now. That was weird, almost like a shock of static charge. He turned it slowly, hoping it wouldn't creak. It was soundless. He pushed in. The room was dark and smelt vaguely of garbage and Joe wondered when it had last been entered.

The floor was bare and the wallpaper looked original to him- late Victorian and densely patterned with a thick, meaty foliage design that twined and turned in and around itself, in the unpleasant vibrant green colour that was all the rage in the drawing rooms and salons of its day. This Victorian speciality brightened the previously dun colored interiors of that age . . . until it was discovered that the 'new green' was killing people. Arsenic based, Victorian green wallpapers and paints were toxic in the extreme. It wasn't even a nice green, Joe thought. It was unattractive and it gave Joe the creeps. The only furniture was a genuine, Victorian brass and iron bedstead with rusted and deadly-looking springage and an ancient, worn and sagging mattress. Its faded blue stripes made him think of concentration camp uniforms. There was a huge brown spurt of a stain that fanned out towards the foot of the bed on the lower half of the mattress. It looked like the archaeological remains of an explosion of blood. Some woman, long, long ago, had given birth on this bed, he thought.

At least he hoped that was what had happened.

There was a small tiled fireplace in the corner, cold and long dead. He stepped closer—always on the lookout for value in fixtures and fittings. All of the tiles had been removed from the surround, crudely chipped or hammered off by the look of things. There were still fragments of them clinging to the cement—jagged shards He stared at the half destroyed fireplace before him and couldn't understand why the tiles had been vandalised in this way. If they were being removed for re sale then whoever had removed them hadn't done any kind of a good job on it. If they'd been removed so that the fireplace could be re-tiled, then the work was definitely not satisfactory. Why in God's name would anyone do this? The beating the surround had taken and the careless way the debris had been tossed about made it look like a truly manic effort had been made here, a fury of smashing. Someone back in the day had been—for some reason—highly unfond of this fireplace. The frenzied effort almost made it look like someone had been trying to escape.

He looked down at the grate, his eye catching more of the tiny, unpleasant green shards still scattered there. There was something in the fireplace grate—what looked like the lumpen mess of a long ago melted candle, its wax looking soured and gelatinous—and charred fragments of whatever had last been burnt. Cloth, it looked like. Or to be more precise, the sort of stuffing one found in an ancient sofa or couch. Horsehair, thought Joe. That's what it is. Had someone gotten bored and decided to immolate every piece of furniture in the room before smashing up the tiles? By Christ they knew how to make their own entertainment in the old days, he thought.

Seeing nothing else of interest, he turned and left the room pausing at the door for a moment to look back at the fireplace grate again where the small, charred clump of fibrous strands lay. He closed the door behind him and headed down the iron staircase for the kitchens.

Horse hair, Joe thought. It had to be.

❖

He placed the tray with orange juice and toast on top of the coffin lying trestled there before him—the elephant in the goddam room. When were they planning on burying this guy anyway? Or maybe this wasn't their father at all, but part of the original fixtures and fittings? A novelty occasional table, perhaps?

He hadn't seen anything of Grace since he'd woken. He'd presumed she would be around . . . and he hadn't been looking forward to seeing her. Well, he corrected himself, seeing her would be no chore but what if she'd heard him and Maryam the night before? Her obvious crush on him might make things awkward and he didn't want anything to foul up his deal. This thing with Maryam was more than just an escape route—it was going to make him for life. Her too, of course. He'd gotten over the spooky feeling he'd had upstairs and figured on carrying on his inventory down here.

Joe looked walked into the dining room. The curtains were still drawn; burgundy coloured and thick and heavy, keeping out any traces of daylight. The ends of their faded gold rope ties were limp and trailed slightly on the floorboards like miniature hula skirts. There was a painting that he'd noticed last night and, now that he was in here, he realised this was what he'd come to take a closer look at.

He shut the door quietly behind him, intending to turn on the light rather than open the drapes. He imagined that they would make a very loud swish with their brass rings every time they opened or closed and he didn't want to disturb Maryam or Grace.

The painting was a figure of a very old man, way beyond the age, Joe thought, to have been a suitable candidate for vanity portraiture. He was certainly past it looks wise. He had a long, horsy face with very deep set eyes, cheekbones of extreme prominence and possibly the ghost of youth somewhere around his not quite smiling, thin lips. The skewed twilit building looming oppressively behind the old man's head was very odd looking indeed. When Joe looked more closely yet, he also saw that there wasn't a straight angle to be had on any of the 'windows' (black, square-ish holes with no attempt at painting glass on them or wooden framing around them) nor on the sides of the buildings. Everything was slightly out of true, kind of forcing the viewer to vaguely angle their head . . . marginally twist their neck . . . almost half shut their eyes—all in an attempt to make the subject of painting look like how it should in 'real life'.

If one of the marks of a successful painting was that it 'drew one in', then this painting certainly had that going for it. It had the strange effect of making the viewer adjust their reality to fit the 'reality' of the picture. And the more Joe looked, the more he could see.

The almost squares of the 'windows' were not quite completely black. He thought he could discern a shape in each one, painted black on black perhaps (a man here? a woman there?). It was strange but it was almost like he *felt* the figures rather than saw them; one of those optical illusions where if you fixed your eyes on something it would disappear . . . but when you let your gaze drift you could catch them (or it) in your peripheral vision. Whoever 'they' were. Whatever 'it' was. This painting was quite possibly a lot cleverer than he'd first given it credit for.

But it could have been Joe's eyes playing tricks on him; searching for meaning where there was none, manufacturing order from chaos because nature abhorred a vacuum and the human mind *had* to have order and meaning—*some* kind of order and meaning—to function.

Or else what? He asked himself.
Or else it would go insane, he replied.

That was why God, in all the varied forms that concept took, had been invented he supposed—to provide structure where there was really none. If you looked at nothing for long enough, you would eventually see something. He was seeing something in the blank, black square windows of this painting right now and he found himself not really liking it. He ignored further thoughts of any 'them' and looked at other parts of the canvas instead.

A giant clock with no hands was at the top of a tower on the distant horizon way behind the building and the old man.

And it looked plain wrong there, thought Joe.

Because although the horizon was distant, the tower sitting on it wasn't. If the artist had had any real idea of perspective, he would not have painted the structure in the way he had, because to be that far away from the viewer, and yet be so big, the tower—in real life—would have to be stratospherically gigantic; a structure so tall, so monumental, as would be impossible to ever build.

It was as if whoever had painted it had really no idea about what an actual building looked like or what perspective was supposed to be. In fact, Joe thought that the best way of describing this would be to say that the structures contained in it had themselves been described—badly—to the artist by a third party. It occurred to him, then, that for something to have been described at all, it would first have to have been actually *seen*. And where in hell would structures like *these* have been seen? Maybe, he thought with a small chill, they had been described *well* and had been reproduced *precisely*.

Looking at the painting was starting to make Joe feel faintly queasy, like he was struggling to read with the wrong glasses on. Joe frowned. The damned thing was also making him think convoluted, confused gibberish. He felt a little like he'd been nodding asleep on a train in a station and had suddenly jerked awake to find that he was now in the middle of the countryside.

Joe decided that he couldn't see much money in this, and backed away from it. No Victorian collectables here, he thought, grateful to be stepping away from the painting's close scrutiny. Correction, he thought, *his* close scrutiny of the painting. He kept backing away until he was in the middle of the room practically, but found that he couldn't seem to stop looking at it. He didn't want to, but he was thinking that perhaps he *should*. Just in case.

(In case what? he thought.)

It made him think of a game he used to play at primary school when he'd still been in Scotland. A kid chosen to be 'het' would go to one side of the playground and turn his back on the rest of his classmates. Everyone would start to creep up on him as quietly as they could. The one who was 'het' would turn randomly and everyone had to freeze where they stood and anyone still moving was out of the game. It was fun... up until the last moments, when there were still at least a half dozen kids creeping towards his turned back and every time he spun around they would be standing perfectly still, their hands outstretched toward him, clutching fingers suspended in mid-grab, their faces in frozen grins, but infinitesimally closer... and each time he turned they would be closer yet... until the final turn when everyone would rush him. At those points, his friends had become *not* his friends—*not* kids in a playground—but ghastly, grinning imps, whose sole purpose was to capture him. He didn't know them anymore... and their steady, unflinching, relentlessness had always scared the living bejesus out of him.

Fuck this, he thought. Every room he'd been into in this goddam place seemed to be giving him the creeps. He was going to get a grip. He deliberately turned his back on the painting, thinking: *Fuck you.* You're just a goddam painting and you cannot affect me in any way whatsoever.

The lights immediately went out.

In the blackness there was a noise... *footsteps from behind rushing toward him...*

He yelped and bolted forward to the opposite end of the room—there was a light switch there, he'd seen it, he'd turn the lights on and...

The metallic clang of the old fashioned brass dome and nipple switch echoed in his ears and he turned to see Grace standing right there.

'Je-*sus*! You trying to gimme a heart attack?'

She shook her head, unfazed by his agitation, looking up at him cow-eyed. She must have come in and tiptoed around the edge of the room, he thought, because he sure as shit hadn't heard her or seen her come in. She was barefoot and wearing a plain, clean white cotton nightgown. It was ankle length and Victorian in its primness. She stood before him and he simply couldn't get over how clean she smelled—she was fresh scrubbed and rosy-cheeked and she clearly adored him. He looked down at her joyful smile. Her teeth were white and even and her breath smelled sweet and warm.

And she was hot.

Not just in the sexy sense (although she was that too), but physically emanating heat. He figured that she must have just had a bath or a shower or something, because when she stood right next to him, he could feel it coming from her, could practically see the *shimmer* around her, like she had a small generator under that nightie somewhere.

'That's who lived here before us, Joe,' she said. 'That's the Architect.'

She was looking at the painting of the old man with the hallucinogenic background. The architect? Joe thought. Architect of what? This place?

'He gave Papa the house for nothimg.'

Obviously not.

'That was good of him,' said Joe.

'He was a doctor too.'

She took a small step closer to him and was still looking up intently into his face.

'Really?' he said. 'A man of many talents.'

He was aware now of her complete nakedness beneath the thin cotton. There was the smallest of gaps between them—the kind through which sparks tended to jump. The kind of gap that promised everything, and Joe found himself greatly wanting to touch the bareness of her arms.

'Why would he give your Papa the house for nothing, Grace?'

Her eyes were sleepy and darker than he remembered—sloe and sexy. He noted that his voice seemed to have gone down an octave or so.

'It was the deal,' she said. 'Papa made mumma do it.'

'What deal? Do what?'

He could see her nipples poking through the nightdress and found that he was growing less interested in getting a proper answer.

'Move imto here,' she said, softly. 'The house.'

She put her arms around him.

'Papa used to ride mumma like a horsey,' she whispered, smiling.

Nonplussed, Joe opened his mouth to speak . . . and then closed it again. He had absolutely no idea what to say to that. She giggled and hugged him tightly and he felt both aroused and vaguely repelled. Abruptly, she jerked her head around to look over her shoulder—so suddenly that Joe also jerked back, following her look to the shadows, vague panic filling him. But there was nothing there that he could see or hear.

'What is it Grace?'

He could feel his heart hammering in his chest. He didn't like this room at all.

'It's . . . I dom't . . .'

'*What?*'

He had automatically held her more closely (that old caveman protection thing again, he thought) and she burrowed her face into his chest. She mumbled and he couldn't make out what she was saying.

'I can't hear you,' he said. 'Say it again.'

She pulled her face slightly away from him and he could make out her words a little more easily.

'My life...'

'Yes Grace, what?'

'It... ism't beimg emriched, Joe.'

He looked at her. Pardon? Enriched? What was she talking about? She smiled up at him and she was *so* pretty. She closed her eyes and blew him a kiss... before placing a warm palm over his crotch.

'You're thimg is big agaim,' she said.

It certainly was, he thought. Somewhere in the back of his mind, though, he found himself dimly wishing that it wasn't. There was something wrong with all of this, he thought. Was it her age? Or rather, her mental age? She wasn't actually mentally handicapped, he told himself... just not very intelligent; at least, not in the conventional sense. She pressed herself into him even more, breathing a happy sigh he could feel against his chest, rather than hear. Her breasts pushed against him and he let himself enjoy the sensation—it felt fantastic. Every part of him was focussing on her, now. She ground herself into him. He could feel heat emanating from between her legs as he felt the pleasant, soft crunch of her pubic hair against his thigh through her nightdress.

He was starting to wonder what he was making a fuss about. To have someone like this—someone who *looked* like this, being so willing for him—what was his goddam problem? She brought her hands up to his face and caressing him gently, eased his head down so his ear was level with his lips.

'Joe... please give me sex,' she breathed.

Oh Jesus, he thought. Who could argue with that? She really was the very definition of irresistible. He gave in. He held her close and brought his lips to hers. Her small tongue responded to his and she felt *so* wonderful pressed against him...

He would quietly take her to 'his' bedroom, laying her down carefully on the clean white sheets. He would be very slow with her, very careful, his fingers gentle and his lips light. He would do everything for her and her alone and—although she wouldn't know any different—he would be really good and when she came, *she* would be crying and laughing at the same time. He could see it all in his mind—it was like watching a film starring himself and Grace . . . then there was a sound, like distant waves lapping on a shore . . . or was it steady, monotonous breathing? The 'screen' darkened almost imperceptibly around the edges and he began to feel dizzy and afraid. Lots of people breathing, all at the same time. Was it the sound of his own blood rushing though his head? An image appeared in his mind with the swiftness of an unexpected train roaring through a station.

It was a TV wildlife show, a PBS special, and there was an island . . . or a beach . . . home only to seagulls and snakes. The snakes lived solely on the birds' eggs, their only source of food. In return, the birds would peck out the snakes' eyes, their most vulnerable and easily attacked part. So the cycle went. The island was dominated by the forcibly blinded snakes and the seagulls. There had been a terrible image of a dirty looking blind snake, its eyes long since pecked away and its sockets full of grey sand and jagged dried out membrane. It was crunching open and swallowing down an egg, which was just hatching a gull chick.

It was an awful thing to see.

An awful thing . . . and now he could feel Grace's tongue squirming around inside his mouth with a greed and rapacity he wouldn't have believed of her. It was no longer small and darting, it felt thick and meaty and . . . *cold*. Another image flashed into his mind then—of Grace's eye sockets black and empty . . . apart from grey, dirty damp sand spilling out from the remains of her eyeballs—looking like translucent egg sacs, dirty . . . empty-eyed . . . dirty . . . the pores on her face were all open, impossibly wide open and full of filth . . . what the fuck? What the hell was he *thinking* about? There was nothing in the least erotic about kissing Grace any more. His erection had long gone and he felt . . . sick? He opened his eyes, not realising that he'd even had them closed.

He pulled away from her with a suddenness that would have been insulting, had Grace noticed it. But she seemed to be in a dreamy land of her own; eyes closed, her body malleable, and she merely sighed. As he pulled away from her he saw a rope of spit connecting between their mouths . . . and it looked to Joe like there was a thread of blood twisting a thin crimson through it.

What?

Grace slurped the spit trail back into her mouth like it was a length of spaghetti and giggled. He swallowed down the urge to heave and wiped his own mouth with the back of his hand. He looked around. They now seemed to be further into the room than they had been a moment ago—a lot further. They were practically against the painting now . . . and there was something else about that goddam painting as well. Just after he'd opened his eyes he thought he'd seen . . .

. . . well, he thought he'd seen a light being switched off in one of the painted apartment rooms. Grace opened her eyes again—and they were normal. Beautiful, bright eyes, sparkling with youth and fun.

'I wamt to live with you forever, Joe. I love you,' she shouted. 'Maryam cam just go *stick*!'

Grace broke away from him then and twirled, her arms outstretched, shouting: 'Go *stick*, Maryam!'

He grabbed her roughly and put his hand over her mouth to shut her the hell up. She started giggling again, delightedly and he felt her tongue jabbing out from her lips and playing against his palm—but there was nothing unpleasant about it now. It was just wet and warm and tickly. The vague darkness around the periphery of his vision seemed to have dissipated. Jeez, he thought, I need a *real* rest. Never mind goddam birds and snakes and dumbass paintings and feeling 'vaguely uneasy'; he was being a complete fucking idiot, *that's* what was wrong with this goddam picture! Jeez Louise, what was he *thinking*? This was going to go down really well with Maryam wasn't it? The golden goose would be over the moon about him fucking her sister, wouldn't she? Where was his goddam head at, for Christ's sake? One of the cardinal rules of life—never shit on your own doorstep. He pulled himself together and gently pushed her away from him.

'Listen, Grace . . . I'm very flattered, but I can't do this with you . . . I'm sorry . . .'

She looked hurt and confused.

'Why?'

'I just can't, sweetheart . . . believe me it's not a good idea.'

'Yes it is . . . are you afraid of Maryam?'

'Honey, there's a lot going on you probably don't get . . .'

'You dom't hab to worry about Maryam, Joe,' she said. 'You domb't owe her emmythimg.'

'Look . . .' he began, but she brought a finger up to his lips, shushing him. Her face took on a sly, petulant look.

'I kmow what Maryam's doimg, Joe,' she said.

There was something in her tone.

'What do you mean?' he asked. 'What is she doing?'

A faint alarm bell began to ring for him.

'First you kiss me agaim . . .' she said in a sing-song. She giggled, wrapping her arms round him once more and upturned her cuter than cute face. The hell with cute, thought Joe. This could go on forever.

'Grace,' he said, the sternness in his voice changing her mood completely. 'You tell me what you're talking about or I'll never kiss you again as long as I live.'

'Dom't say that Joe,' she said, and seeing her hurt and alarm made him feel shitty. He immediately wanted to apologise, to make things better for her. However, there had obviously been a development with Maryam that he needed to know about, so he could live with shitty.

'Tell me,' he said.

'She's a liar.'

'Is she? What is she lying about?'

'She ism't going to let you take her emmywhere.'

'How do you know?' he asked.

Grace said nothing, looking guilty—and then he realised, of *course* she would know. She had her 'gift', didn't she? Grace would know and she would know absolutely and with no hint of error. His suspicion that her 'talent' was more powerful and useful than Maryam seemed aware of was correct, apparently.

'Grace, tell me exactly what it is that you know,' he said, not relenting in his tone.

'I just . . . I saw it from her head . . . she's . . . lyimg,' she said, almost in tears. 'She ism't goimg to let you do what you wamt with the rich people. She ism't going to do emmymore healimg. She hates it amd she was lyimg to you because she wamted love. But you love *me*, Joe.'

He wasn't listening. He was too busy feeling like the idiot he truly was. Maryam was grifting him. Of course she was. The stony reality of his situation hit him hard again, like it should have in the first place. He thought to himself: how could he have been fooled? How could he have let himself be taken in like that? It was Brewster all over again. Christ, no wonder he wasn't a millionaire—as a grifter he was a fucking joke.

So what was he going to do about it?

'We can live together, Joe, you and me,' Grace said, throwing her arms around him. 'We dom't have to have that old poop Maryam aroumd. *You* cam be the healer!'

He laughed, humourlessly. *He* could be the healer? That would be genuinely funny if it wasn't so pathetic. Obviously the finer detail of his and Maryam's conversation about how he made his money had gone in one ear and out the other for Grace . . . then he stopped laughing. It sank in for him that Grace actually thought he was for *real*, just because he said so. She believed that his act was genuine . . . she probably thought that loads of people could do it—and in that instant, a flash of sick, dangerous inspiration illuminated the only way forward for him.

It appalled him, but he knew now that he had no choice—none at all—he knew with absolute certainty. He was alone again. Penniless, alone and still very much in danger of his life and he had to stop pissing away any more time here and start moving immediately.

He became aware that Grace wasn't saying anything anymore but was staring up at him intently, her brow furrowed ever so slightly, like she was concentrating on something—and he knew it wouldn't be a math problem. She was trying to read him. He had to keep his thoughts very far away from this girl. He immediately concentrated as hard as he could on a mental image of her smiling face, imagining it framed by a pink love heart, like some kind of cheesy, customised Valentine card.

'Grace,' he said, grinning cheerfully, 'that's a *brilliant* idea. That's the best idea I *ever* heard, darling. Tell you what though, I need to go away for a while and do something, ok?'

'Do what Joe?'

She was still frowning, but he could see a brightness returning to her eyes.

'I need to get some money so that we can run away together sweetheart, alright? Ok? Then we can go around Europe, Rome and Paris and all over. Anywhere you want to go!' he said. 'And I'll be the healer. It'll just be the two of us and never mind that old poop Maryam! What d'you say?'

The smile on her face brightened to full blazing wattage as, in his mind's eye, the Valentine card disappeared and he made himself see he was running on a hot and sunny beach with her.

'You just need to do something for me though,' he said, 'can you get me some money just now? I need to get a cab some place. Could you?'

The words were difficult to get out, he was concentrating so hard on the happy images he was sending, the vaguely remembered paper sun of some tourist brochure beach coming to giggling, hand-holding, splashing life in his head.

'You promise?' she said 'You promise it'll be just be us?'

He despised himself. This was cruel . . . but he *had no choice*.

'I promise,' he said.

The look on her face told him that all of her Christmases had come.

'I've got lots of poumds im my special box upstairs!' she squeaked, before scampering off.

◈

Grace watched from the door to the apartment as Joe strode briskly down the tiled communal hall to the brass cage lift at the bottom of the corridor. He didn't turn to wave bye bye as she'd hoped.

'Doesm't matter Joe,' she whispered to herself. 'You've come here to marry *me*! I kmow that's the truth! That's why they gave you the accidemt—so you could be with *me*! I've beem waitimg for so lomg . . .'

She went back inside and closed the door behind her. He was hers, not Maryam's. *Hers.*

They'd said someone *very spemcial* was coming into her life to marry her and be with her forever and make everybody happy and give everybody what they wanted and she honestly *couldem't* in a *milliom* years have imagined emmyome better or more beautiful than Joe! She had begun to think that they had just been lying to her all these years . . . but she couldn't wait now to get out of the house and run away with him. She had done everything they had ever told her to and now it was her turn to be free and away from them—forever and ever.

She couldn't believe it was happening at last. At last, at last, *at last.*

◆

Joe was thinking of anything and everything to do with a holiday in the sun featuring Grace—booking flights with her, choosing a hotel together, taking off holding hands on the plane, a scary/fun bumpy landing, and the first wave of heat stepping out of the air conditioned airport and into the baking warmth of a sunny paradise, hand in hand.

He had no idea how far her 'reach' might be, or even if she had such a thing. Nevertheless, he didn't allow himself to think of anything that was *really* going to happen until he was down in the street, well away from her, and flagging down a taxi.

25

The cheap belt buckle had snapped when she'd dug in about half way and she'd had to chuck it, but Skinny had finally managed to pull the brick from the wall. She had dug around in the air bubble and had cleared all of the crumbling, dry cement out that she could. She'd then put her filthy, bloody fingertips on the top edge of the brick and her thumbs on the bottom and had started pulling down and pushing up, in millimetre increments, then wiggling side to side as much as she could, trying to get the fucker loosened without having to dig out any more damn cement with what was left of her nails and the bloody, raggy mess of her fingers.

Pull down, push up.

Wiggle wiggle wiggle.

It had gotten to the stage where the jabs of pain were shooting all the way up her arms.

Pull down again, push up again. Wiggle fucking wiggle.

It had been a long and tedious process, but when she had finally managed to wrest the brick from its place, it'd taken her completely by surprise and she had staggered backwards and fallen heavily on her backside. She'd stayed there for a few stunned, sore-arsed moments; staring down in surprise and wonder at the jagged edged, cement dusted brick in her hands like it was a gold bar.

One brick out.

Hoo-fucking-ray. It had only taken what felt like the best part of her adult life to get it. At least now it would get easier, she thought. There would be more room to work. She could wrap something around the loose brick to keep the noise down and use it as a bludgeon to loosen the other bricks around it. She wouldn't need many and was sure she could make a Skinny-sized hole fairly rapidly.

She was wrong.

Behind the wall of bricks was the wooden frame of the sash window, its glass long gone. And beyond that, another wall of bricks. This one was way more professional—with textbook, centimetre wide cement grouting between the neat rows of red rectangles. No finger holes to be dug there.

She stood staring at it, numb, any despair being held in check by the still searing pain in her fingers and arms. Then her brain caught up with events and started thinking of ways around this. She supposed that she could fit her loose brick long ways into the hole and start to bang at the second wall with it, like a mini battering ram. Maybe she could wrap her T shirt round the front to keep it quiet?

Then she heard the murmured voices approaching from downstairs and realised that she'd just run out of time. She felt the fear starting to creep back again and had to use a supreme effort to keep it under control. Whatever was going to happen was going to happen, she thought, but whoever the fuck came through that door first was in for a surprise because they sure wouldn't be expecting a house brick square in the face. The shock element might give her a small advantage.

After that she would improvise.

◆

Big Ian walked behind Arthur as they climbed the stairs. He was calm—he usually was once he'd made his mind up about something. He remembered the first time he had bought a national lottery ticket—he had been in a churning panic for hours as he'd agonised over which numbers to pick but once he'd done so, he'd felt a very profound calm come over him. Deciding to rescue Skinny now made him feel the same way.

He didn't feel that he was being disloyal to Arthur at all. It was crystal clear to him now that Arthur, as he had known him, simply didn't exist anymore and that the person walking up the stairs ahead of him was not really Arthur at all. He was a sick person, and one who was, as Skinny had already said, not going to be alive for very much longer.

Big Ian just couldn't see the point in it anymore. It was over—so not only wasn't he going to let Arthur treat Skinny badly and then kill her just to find this Yank Bible con man, he wasn't even going to let Arthur get into the same room as her. He'd made his mind up. He could admit to himself that he was very curious as to what the connection between Skinny and the Yank could be, but he was not in any way curious enough to allow her to be destroyed in the process of finding out. So he'd decided that he would let Arthur ask his questions—he had one or two himself—but from a distance. And asking would be *all* that was going to happen. She would either tell them or she wouldn't, and if she didn't want to then that was going to be just too bad for Arthur, because it was time for all this to stop.

They had reached the top of the stairs and Big Ian almost bumped in to Arthur who was blocking the way. He looked at Big Ian intently.

'Have you been listening to anything I've just said, Big Ian?' he said. 'You look very preoccupied.'

'Sorry Arthur. What did you say?'

Arthur smiled a good-natured smile of indulgence.

'I said, that I think it's time I showed you Tommy's writing.'

Big Ian was puzzled.

'Tommy couldn't write, Arthur. Could he?'

'What are you taking about? Of course he could write. Better than you.'

Big Ian took the implied comment on his thumblessness in his stride.

'But he couldn't read,' he said. 'How could he write?'

Arthur sounded a little angry when he replied.

'Of course Tommy could write! How do you think his walls got covered in all his diaries and his thoughts and ideas?'

'I didn't know that they were Arthur.'

'Well that's what I want to show you . . . you sound like you don't believe me.'

'No, no. I believe you.'

Big Ian didn't. He remembered a time when there had only been the one bricked up window in the pub—Tommy's room. He knew for certain that Arthur's brother could neither read nor write because his Da had kept him locked in that room since he was a toddler . . . and with a big bolt on the door. Tommy hadn't emerged until after Arthur's Da had passed away. He had been sixteen years old then and had never received any kind of education at all up to that point. Even after that, Big Ian seriously doubted that what Tommy had been watching on TV up in his room day and night had been the Open University.

'You don't believe me, Big Ian,' said Arthur. 'You think I've gone doolalley with the morphine and the pain and that I'm making all this up. Well come and I'll show you. We can chat with Skinny later—not as if she's going anywhere is it?'

Arthur laughed and led the way down the corridor.

As they passed the door to the spare room, Big Ian glanced at it. Even with the door between them, being this close to her he knew he'd made the right decision. It didn't matter whether she liked him or didn't like him. All he knew was that that freeing her was the right thing to do. In thinking this, he felt lighter inside. In fact maybe Skinny had had a point about taking over the business? Of course, he had no intention of killing Arthur . . . but after he'd died? Someone would have to run things, wouldn't they? Why not him and Skins? Big Ian was starting to feel pretty good about all this now. He would come back and get her out of that room in a minute, once he'd sat Arthur down and explained the situation to him. Tommy's old room would be as good a place as any to do so. Arthur opened the door to Tommy's room so that Big Ian could look and see.

So Big Ian looked. And he saw.

And he kind of realised that Arthur might be beyond reasoning with.

He stared at the severed human head on the bed sheet. There were concentric rings of dried fluid stains circling it, all differing shades of brown and yellow like some kind of tie-dye job from a nightmare. And it smelled absolutely rank.

'Is that . . . is that Tommy?' he said.

Arthur burst out laughing, unable to contain himself any longer.

'I bet you hadn't been expecting that, eh?' he said, delighted, nudging Big Ian in the ribs.

Big Ian slowly shook his head. No. He hadn't been expecting that.

'How did you get his head?' he said, quietly, unable to take his eyes from the squashed up but still just about recognisable face on the pillow.

'It was delivered to the door a while back,' Arthur said breezily. 'Obviously whoever took it had no further use for it, so they sent it back to me.'

'Sent it back?'

Arthur started whispering.

'Listen, Big Ian, don't mention the fact that he's only a head. He doesn't actually, um, know it and I don't know how to tell him. He keeps asking when he can get back down to the pub for a pint, but I have to keep putting him off. I bring him his Guinness up but, whenever I try giving him some, it just goes straight through him. Look at the mess he's made on the bed.'

Arthur slapped Big Ian on the back and walked over to his brother.

'Hey Tommy, look who I brought, eh? It's Big Ian. Thought I'd better start showing you around a bit more. Say hi to Tom, Big Ian.'

Big Ian smiled as best he could.

'Hi Tommy—long time no see,' he said quietly.

Arthur stood by Tommy's bedside, a wide grin on his face. Big Ian wasn't sure what to do. Then he heard a squeaky voice start to speak and the hairs on the back of his neck stood completely on end.

'*Have—you—no'—had—your—face—fixed   yet,   you fat—ugly—cunt?*'

Arthur laughed heartily.

'He's not lost any of that sense of humour, has he Big Ian?'

He turned once more to his brother.

'Don't insult him Tommy—he's been in a funny mood recently and we need him.'

Big Ian stared, stiff as a board, his eyes widening with fright when Arthur started speaking again in that awful, grinding squeaky voice.

'I'd—get—a—facelift as well, Ar-thur if—I—were—you.'

Arthur laughed with gusto at this joke. It was as if he were in a different sphere of consciousness altogether. Another world. A strangely happy one. Arthur spoke again in his own voice.

'Sure Tommy. I'm sure I can get some kind of something rebuilt for me.'

Arthur laughed heartily once more and started chatting to himself, in and out of his Tommy voice, telling the head all about how Skinny was going to spill on where 'Reverend Joe' was. Big Ian looked around the room as Arthur prattled on. It was entirely covered in pen scrawl, the walls floor to ceiling . . . and actually on the ceiling too. None of this had been here the last time he had been in this room. That had been a few days before Tommy's funeral—when Arthur had been looking out Tommy's best suit for the undertaker to put on his headless corpse. The walls had been normal then. The only unusual thing about the room had been that it hadn't stunk of semen anymore, like it usually had when Tommy was in residence. The floor wasn't covered in balled up, crisp dried paper tissues and the DVD player wasn't playing whatever new porn Tommy had obtained.

Tommy had been a horrible, nasty wee shite and had wasted no time using his newfound freedom from his cell of a room to enjoy himself where and when he could. He would only ever leave the pub to go out at night. Arthur had told tales of some of the outrageous shit Tommy had perpetrated and neither Big Ian nor anyone else (apart from Arthur, obviously) had been surprised when he'd gone missing one night on a whore hunt 'round town for some underage action. The fact that his headless body had been found on Glasgow Green one morning, a massive blood spume from his neck looking like it had been freeze framed bursting across the grass, pretty much indicated that he had been killed there.

Nearly everyone had presumed that he'd been done in by a dad gone psycho or the cops. Or both, in collusion. It wasn't unusual, as Tom Jones used to say, it just wasn't usually so blatant. Normally nonce deaths (weighted feet, dropped in Clyde—sometimes dead beforehand, sometimes not) were disguised among missing persons files by the cops in the know and the victims and their families were spared trials and further degradation. Tommy's death, however, had been like a public execution and the filth and the rags, as Arthur called the straight cops and the newspapers, had gone completely bananas over it for months.

Where the head had gone had been a mystery, until now. Big Ian walked over to a wall as Arthur happily burbled away to himself, alternating his jokey banter between voices. The light was dim, but Big Ian could make out what the words scrawled on the walls said. His gaze came to rest randomly in the middle of a sentence and he squinted as he followed the trail backwards with his forefinger to find the beginning.

He'd seen the words: '. . . *blow jobs as well as taking it up the ars . . .*'—which had collided with a sentence written in column form, coming down the way and crossing it like a motorway intersection, which read: '. . . *on the Sunday and it bled hard again but stopped on the Monday . . .*' and then this sentence hit a different coloured pen—red and hard to read in this light—which looked like it spiralled into itself in the centre. Big Ian twisted his head slightly, but suspected he'd know the kind of thing he'd see. This one read: '. . . *only twice but squealed like a fucking pig fat pig fucking pig . . .*'

Big Ian stood back. Tommy, he knew, hadn't written any of this. Tommy had been incapable of writing or reading.

So it must have been Arthur.

And he must have been doing it since Tommy's funeral. That meant two years-worth of this stuff. He looked again and found the original sentence he'd first started following. He found '. . . *blow jobs as well as taking it up the ars . . .*' again and began tracing his finger backwards to find the beginning. He regretted doing so pretty much instantly.

It said: '*Arthur my brother that fucker I hate him that cunt he made me give him blow jobs as well as taking it up the arse for him whenever he came into my room from when I was wee . . .*'

Big Ian jerked away from the writing like someone had set a flashbulb off in his face. His breathing was coming in quick, low bursts. He could feel the blood pounding through his temples and his heart hammering inside his chest—but he couldn't tear his eyes from the writing on the wall. There was so much of it . . . so much. Helpless to do anything else now, he compulsively scanned the wall and caught something else; something worse: '. . . *I said I was sick and tired and I was going to go to the papers I really was and I shouted at Arthur and told him and they would give me money for my true story and I would get away from him at last and Arthur cut off my head and Arthur cut off my head and Arthur cut off my head and Arthur* CUT OFF MY HEAD AND ARTHUR CUT OFF MY HEAD AND ARTHUR CUT OFF MY HEAD . . .'

Big Ian suddenly noticed that the room was now silent—no happy burbling from Arthur or 'Tommy'.

He turned around to look at the bed and had just enough time to see that it was empty of both Arthur and his brother's head before the lights went out with an almost comical 'plink'. From the spare room, he heard a shouted curse and a crash.

◆

Inside the room, Skinny had climbed on to the radiator by the door, steadying herself against the wall with one hand on the top of the doorframe, holding the brick in the other, figuring that she'd have more chance of hitting Big Ian in the face—if he came in first—if she were actually the same height as him. When the lights had gone out so suddenly she had lost her balance and was now tangled in dead dog skin on the floor. Revolted, she ripped the thing from herself and scrabbled to the door to listen. If this was part of some more psychological war on her, she wasn't going to fall for it. She and her raggy-edged brick were ready to rumble, no matter what came down the canal.

◈

None of the lights were working and Big Ian came out of Tommy's room into the mineshaft darkness of the corridor, determined to get to Skinny before Arthur did. He reached out blindly with his big four- fingered hands, shouting.

'Skinny! Are you ok?'

There was silence.

'Skinny!' he repeated.

More silence.

Then: 'You come in here and I'll fucking take *your* fucking eyes out, do you hear me?'

There was an edge of pain to her voice. She sounded like she might have hurt herself, falling over or whatever had happened. Big Ian felt a pang of guilt. He should never have let it get this far and now he had to make sure that she got out of this ok, no matter what happened to him.

'Is Arthur in there with you?' he called.

'If anyone tries to get in here with me, they'll be fucking dead!'

Big Ian reckoned he could assume Arthur wasn't with Skinny. He started to move as silently as he could manage, arms still blindly extended. He called out to her.

'Listen, Skins, Everything's alright. I'm going to just burst your door open and get you out of there. This is all over, all of it, ok?'

There was another silence.

'I'm sorry Skins, I really am. I made a mistake and I should've listened to you and I'm sorry. I'm going to take you out of here, I promise Skins, I promise.'

◈

Skinny stood there in the complete blackness of the room, listening to her own breathing. Was this some new kind of fucking around with her head? She would expect it from Arthur, but Big Ian really wasn't one for that kind of thing. He sounded sincere. She hoped that this wasn't just a question of wishful thinking on her part . . . but if he really had decided to turn against Arthur and help her then she would be out of here and away. Everything inside her was screaming at her not to . . . but she let herself hope.

'Just get the fucking door open, Big Ian. We'll talk about anything else later.'

◈

Big Ian smiled. He knew that she trusted him. Everything was going to be ok. He walked with both of his huge arms extended into the darkness. If Arthur was going to try and get him, Big Ian would expect him to arrive anytime now. *All* the electrics had gone off, not just the lights. Big Ian knew that because the noise level in the place had changed—no background noise of fridges from the bar or buzz from the kitchenette fly zapper. Nothing. Coupled with the total blackness because of the bricked up windows, the place had turned into one great big sensory deprivation chamber.

Big Ian breathed in deeply and slowly to try and lose the sound of his own blood rushing through his ears before pushing himself gently away from Tommy's doorway. Arthur would have to have gone down to the cellar to switch all the electrics off.

That meant downstairs. *That* meant Arthur was—literally—in the dark as much as he was. Arthur would have access to weapons downstairs, of course, all under the bar or beneath the optics. In this pub there was no shortage of 'dangerous ordnance' as Arthur would say, that was for damn sure. The only advantage Big Ian would have would be the total silence. He would hear Arthur well before Arthur would have a chance to take him by surprise.

His back to the wall, he began sidling along the narrow corridor to the guest room door. He was being as quiet as possible, taking his time, and concealing every breath—not wanting to miss even the slightest squeak of an approaching step, a soft rustle on a carpet, a wisp of Arthur's breath.

'Big Ian, are you still there?'

She sounded very nervous and agitated. Like she knew he was close and couldn't stand the wait any longer.

'Yeah, Skins,' he said softly, but loud enough for her to hear.

'Well hurry up you big fanny!'

All pretence at anger or control had gone from her voice now. He knew that she was reckoning he was her only real chance. That something had happened between him and Arthur and that if he didn't get her out now, she'd probably never get out at all.

'Shhhh Skins. I'll be there in a second. Just shoosh. I have to keep my ears open for Arthur.' She was a brave girl, he knew. The bravest. She could keep a grip. She did so now and the place was plunged again into total silence.

Big Ian had to touch his way down the corridor, stretching his arms out pressed flat against the wall, his fingertips travelling over long, worn woodchip paper as foot by foot he moved closer down to her door. His breathing was getting faster. The longer he took to do this, the longer Arthur had to work his way slowly back up here. He knew that there were a couple of loose floorboards on the staircase, loose enough to creak dryly when stood on. But, of course, Arthur knew about those boards as well, and he would know how to avoid them.

In the blackness, Big Ian's eyes began to compensate for the lack of sensory input by playing tricks on him. Small things, little blobs of purple, just on the edges of his field of vision. Weird shapes, faintly swimming before him. He knew he was beginning to lose his sense of distance.

Big Ian froze suddenly.

A noise. Rustling. Faint, but very nearby.

He stood still, trying to keep the sound of his breathing down, but feeling the rise and fall of his enormous chest getting faster and faster. There were no more noises of any kind . . . but he was *sure* he'd heard it.

'Skins . . .' he whispered, 'did you just move about in there?'

'Yes,' she whispered back savagely, 'I hurt my ankle when I fell . . .'

'Try and not move!'

She didn't reply, but he knew she'd taken it on board. He started moving sideways again, tense and feeling the weight of his years on him. He was having trouble getting a full breath into his lungs because he was trying not to be heard. He started feeling a little sick and dizzy and knew that this was because he wasn't getting enough oxygen into his lungs. His legs started feeling watery, because they were so tense and strained from his wall-hugging crab walk.

It was a short distance between Tommy's room and the guest room, but it felt hugely long in the utter darkness. He stopped, judging as best he could that the door should be in front of him now. He stopped and stood away from the wall at his back. Instantly, his body relaxed, un-tensing and he could feel a painful tingle at the sudden rush of blood into his legs. The almost there, *catch me if you can* colour blobs in his vision were jumping about all over the place but he had to ignore them. He had to concentrate.

Tommy's room was now way back there to his left.

The stairs down to the pub where Arthur had gone were to his right.

He extended his left arm outwards to make sure he had Skinny's door in front of him. There was nothing there! Wait, wait, and calm down. The corridor is just a little wider than he'd thought. That's all. The darkness and the silence played tricks on you. He took a baby step forward and his fingertips made contact . . . but with more wallpaper. Fuck it. He wasn't there yet! But he couldn't be far. He kept contact with the wallpaper, now realising he had to crab right once again until he reached his goal. Once he was there, it would be just a question of stepping back against the wall; bracing himself and giving the door an almighty kick with his massive size thirteen's. Skinny had better not be anywhere near it, he thought.

He extended his free arm outwards into space, pointed toward the open end of the corridor, his big meaty fingers splayed out, and started crabwalking once more. His left hand ran along the wallpaper for only a foot and a half before his fingertips met with the doorframe. He hadn't been too far out after all! He decided to keep moving so that he knew for sure he would be centred with the door when he was kicking it. He'd only moved another six inches or so when his extended free hand came into contact with the cold slime of Tommy's face.

'Boo!' cried the croaky voice as a flashlight flicked on, illuminating it from beneath. Tommy's head was floating in the air, pop-eyed and horribly staring. There was foul smelling matter spittering down from the nostrils and all of his squashed up features had elongated, like his face was melting. The jaw had swung loosely open in a mute scream.

Big Ian abruptly found that he couldn't breathe at all. His left arm was suddenly incredibly painful; numbingly, crushingly painful like he was being hit by sledgehammers. He could feel the pain travelling up it, through each and every vein, his chest strapped in a tightening steel vice.

'Arth-ur . . .' he gasped, as he blundered forwards. Arthur skipped back, holding Tommy by the hair and away, turning the flashlight onto Big Ian.

'Please . . . Ar . . .' he breathed, his voice strangling in his throat, the glare of Arthur's flashlight dazzling his eyes, making them ache. He collapsed sideways slamming into the wall and then buckled, falling heavily down onto the floor unable to say or do anything as Arthur kept the light trained on him.

'You ought to know by now that you can't lie to me, Big Ian—you should *know* that.'

Big Ian's spine was beginning to arch backwards as he was clutching at his arm, his breath coming in ragged, hitching jags.

'I saw you change,' Arthur continued, almost sadly. 'I saw it when I opened the guest room door. You looked at those two wretches and then you looked at me, and I knew—like Christ did at Gethsemane—you were going to betray me. You really are an idiot, son. You've wasted your life, completely and utterly.'

Arthur got down on all fours next to him, whispering in his ear as he writhed in agony. 'I think I've figured this all out,' he said. 'It occurred to me when I was watching the oil refinery. I asked myself this question: why would this man McGill come all the way from America just to heal me? I'm sure the US has more than enough terminally ill people inside its borders to keep him occupied. Answer? He didn't come for me. He came to see Skinny.'

Big Ian was making a huge effort to speak, dry clacking noises coming from the back of his throat.

'And why would he have come all the way from America to see Skinny in the first place? Well, I've figured that out too. It's my firm belief that they were once very close. What do you think of that, old friend?'

Big Ian abruptly grabbed for Arthur, but managed only to glance his fingertips along his cheek. Arthur pulled back, surprised.

'*Skins* . . .' Big Ian grunted, and then he began to spasm violently, his eyes losing their focus, his teeth gritting together so hard that Arthur could hear them splitting and breaking in his mouth.

'*Big Ian?*' whispered Skinny urgently from the guest room.

Arthur, with difficulty, got back up and stood again over him, shining the flashlight directly into his face, watching him die on the ground. The big man's years of eating soggy battered chip shop shit, liberally sprinkled with salt of course, had finally caught up with him. Big Ian had lived in the worst area of the worst city of the worst country in the world for heart disease and had now just won its top prize. Arthur realised that he was already thinking of the big guy in the past tense.

Hm. Off you fuck, Big Ian, he thought. He also realised that he wouldn't have to use the kitchen knife he'd brought on tiptoe all the way up here after all. At least, not on the big man. He had stopped moving now and Arthur nudged his head with the toe of his shoe. Skinny spoke up again.

'*..Big Ian?*'

'I'm afraid he isn't taking any calls right now, Skinny,' Arthur said. '*I've* got something interesting for you though.'

◆

Bewlay stepped over Big Ian's body and strode briskly down to Tommy's room, putting his brother back down onto his pillow.

'You take a rest now, Tom,' he said with a wink. 'I'll take care of this. When there's something nice to look at, I'll come back for you, alright?'

Bewlay headed back out again, humming 'Lara's Theme' from Doctor Zhivago.

Inside the room, Skinny's head was buzzing. Bewlay had killed Big Ian somehow. She realised that she felt more than shock—she felt like she'd lost someone close. Totally ridiculous, but she felt tears starting to sting her eye. That fucking cunt Bewlay had somehow killed probably the only person that had loved him and now he was outside with 'something interesting'—God only knew what—for her. And what did she have? She had a house brick. And one good eye. And, of course, attitude.

'I don't care what you've got for me you freak fuck!' she shouted, 'I'll take a lot of fucking lumps out of you before I go down!'

That made her feel a little better, until she heard him humming that tune again. Bewlay had returned to her door.

'Brave talk, Skinny. You're a good, brave, little girl for your mammy, aren't you?'

He enjoyed her sudden silence. When she spoke again, he was pleased to note that she sounded a little less sure of herself.

'What the fuck are you talking about you fucking freak?'

Bewlay put a feminine lilt into his voice.

'Now, all you have to do is play the fight game for mum and Auntie Rae . . .'

Skinny was silent now.

'She's bringing over your cousin, and we'll get you ice cream after.'

Skinny was still silent.

'But they never got you ice cream, did they, Trudy?' said Bewlay, gently.

❖

She was breathing fast. Somehow, he was giving her verbatim dialogue from her childhood. Despite herself, the clawing, scrabbling fear in the pit of her stomach from those days had returned. She could feel herself starting to tremble.

❖

Outside, Bewlay was standing right at the door, his flashlight pointed down, looking for something on the floor by the chipped skirting board.

'Here's a question for you. When you came up that night in your stupid pizza boy disguise, did you not think to yourself: I should be dead now. I come up here, past everyone, I could have been sent to blow Mister Bewlay's fucking brains out so *why am I not dead yet?* Why has he not had me killed?'

He chuckled a little to himself, shining his torch onto the floorboards next to the door, looking . . . looking . . .

'Did you not think that I might be a little peeved and want to make an example of you? Hm? Show everyone what happens when you come up to my house un*fucking*announced and unfucking asked and unfucking wanted? Did you not wonder why the FUCK I didn't do that? Did you think that you'd survived due to the sheer magnetism of your personality . . . you little alky dyke?'

He was standing right at the door now, his ear to the wood, listening in. He couldn't hear anything.

'I guess you didn't,' he continued. 'But as soon as you took that helmet off, I recognised you. Believe me, one-eyed fucked up lesbians your age from this area aren't as common as you would suppose. I recognised you from the vids your mum used to make. Me and Tommy watched them all the time . . . they were brilliant.'

Arthur had found what he was looking for—a tiny trap door in the floorboards. He got his fingernails into the slightly indented groove and flipped the rectangle of wood upwards, revealing nothing beneath it but a dusty hole and the ends of two thick, bare copper wires facing each other. One of these led into Skinny's room, remaining bare, the other was exposed only for a few inches from its very thick, insulating plastic covering. This part of the wire, Arthur knew, ran all the way down the stairs to the cellar. Arthur, a little awkwardly, reached down and started twisting the two bare wires together.

'Tommy used to say he didn't like them, but I knew he did really. I used to sit up here with him and watch them. They were really good to get off to. There were loads of others as well, from all over the world, but the really good ones were all yours. Especially the last one. I think we wore the tape out at the bit where your eye went pop.'

◆

Skinny was standing there in the blackness, completely enraged. Her fingers were gripping her makeshift weapon so tightly it felt like it had become a part of her arm. Bewlay and his fucking freak brother had been watching her on tape and getting off on it. All this time.

◆

'And that's why I didn't have you put down that night,' he said. 'I'd watched you so often, you felt like part of the family. I was pleased to see you all grown up and what a well-balanced adult you'd grown into. I wanted to help you out. What a fool I was, eh? Although I must tell you, I have a little confession to make, Skins. I feel a little tiny bit guilty about your . . . um, accident, since it may have been partly my fault.'

Arthur finished winding the wires together.

'I'm afraid that I had been enjoying your earlier tapes so much that I tracked down where they were coming from. It wasn't hard. Word gets round. I asked your mammy to make me something special—I specified a knitting needle, but I suppose she wasn't a woman much given to knitting, so she threw in a chopstick instead. The results were more spectacular than I could have anticipated. What can I say? I love your work.'

◆

Skinny stood shock still, willing the door to open. She seriously didn't care anymore whether she lived or died because come what may, this fucker was going to suffer first. He was going to suffer in the worst way.

◆

Arthur got himself up from his crouch position a little unsteadily. The pain was starting to return to him and he knew that he would have to take a swig of his medicine soon.

'Listen Skinny, I know you're a resourceful little cunt and I would frankly be disappointed in you if you didn't have some kind of nasty surprise waiting for me in there. There are needles and all sorts lying around, I know. But let's face the harsh truth of the situation here—I am the one outside, whilst you are locked in, so here's the deal. All I need from you is information. Give it to me and then I'll let you go.'

She managed to keep her voice steady.

'Come on in and get it, Arthur.'

Bewlay carried on as if she hadn't said anything at all.

'Where is Reverend McGill?'

Skinny was thrown—what the fuck? Was he *still* going on about that preacher guy? She didn't know and didn't care. All she wanted was a shot at his face. She had to get him in here somehow. She had to offer him something he'd want.

'You and your, um, friends took him from the hospital, is that correct?' he said. 'Where are you keeping him now?'

She turned on the sniffles and started to plead with him, all the while practicing swinging her brick and making sure she had the tightest grip possible. The brick was not leaving her hand until this fucker's face was soup.

'I'm hurt, Arthur,' she whined, adding a tearful sniff. 'I fell and I need help. Please come in. I'll let you do what you want to me. Please, just open the door.'

She made a practice jab holding the brick longways and didn't like the way it wobbled at the end of her reach. Too easy to lose her hold. She changed its position to grip it from the side.

'You remember him, don't you?' he said, ignoring her again, unscrewing the cap from his silver flask.

'I don't know who you're talking about, Arthur,' she sniffled. 'Please just come in. I really am hurt . . . you could hurt me more if you want. I know that you like to . . . please come in and hurt me . . . I like it.'

She was now swinging the brick in short arcs—arm parallel to the floor, palm forward like a slap. That seemed to be working the best—more brick surface area for face impact and easier to keep hold of if blood made it slippery. She would go with that.

'Sure you know who I'm talking about,' said Arthur. 'You're the only phone number on his mobile.'

'I'm sorry Arthur; I really don't know . . . please just come in here with me?'

Arthur took a long swig and shuddered. *Urg.*

'Hm. Alright, let's do it the hard way,' he sighed. 'I'll pretend that I believe you don't know what I'm talking about. Although I must say that a coincidence on this scale really stretches credulity. You knew him as Joe Brady? You surely haven't forgotten your little co-star, have you?'

◆

Skinny felt like she'd been slapped in the face. What was going on? Joe? What did he have to do with this? Was he *here*? *Here*? Her cousin?

◆

'The connection only occurred to me today,' said Arthur. 'I put that down to my brain being a bit fogged by my medication. It's been happening a lot these days. But that *is* the connection between you and the good reverend isn't it? He went to America and you stayed and now he's back? You told him all about me and you both came up with your pathetic plan to con me, yes? I am right, aren't I?'

Nothing.

'But it went a bit wrong, didn't it? And now your accomplices have him holed up somewhere. That's all I want to know little Trudy—where is he?'

Arthur screwed the lid back on his hipflask and dusted off the knees of his trousers, already feeling immeasurably better from the spreading warm glow in his abdomen. It was just the ticket.

'I'll leave you to think about it.' He said. 'I'm just going downstairs to put the power back on—be with you again in a jiff.'

◆

She heard him pad away from the door and for an instant, an insane hope filled her. Was Joe actually here? Had he come back for her after all?

By some miracle, only a few days after she'd returned from the Victoria Infirmary minus her eye, her Uncle Danny—Joe's dad—had also come back; from the horror of Desert Storm to the horror of what had been happening at home. The social services may have believed her mum's story about a bizarre accident . . . but her Uncle Danny hadn't.

He'd beaten the shit out of Joe's mum and then had done the same to her mum and had then upped and left, taking his boy away with him. Her cousin, Joe. He had cried and pleaded for his dad to take her away with them as well . . . but he said he couldn't. He was leaving Joe's mum and marrying a sergeant from the US army and could go to the US with her. And Joe.

No help for Trudy.

The best he could do, he'd said, was report her mum, which he did. He'd said that the authorities would make sure she was looked after. Skinny and Joe both knew though, even at that age, that the best she could hope for was a care home that wasn't too much of a drop in centre for paedos. Joe had promised faithfully and tearfully and childishly that he would come back and get her, but—on all fronts—she had been as luckless as ever. Until now? Did miracles actually happen? *Had* Joe come back for her?

Her lip curled in disgust at her naivety. Get a grip, she thought. It was more likely some psych dope trick Bewlay was playing on her to fuck up her mind, to stop her from thinking straight. A trick. To keep her mind occupied. *Why?* What had he been doing outside the door? She had heard a scrape sound and . . . her breath caught in her throat. He'd said he was going to put the power back on.

Why would he do that?

She re-visualised the strange, almost randomly burnt loops and circles on the carpet that she'd seen when she'd first come to—the ones that had looked like someone had sprayed whorls of lighter fuel and set fire to them. She fell to her knees and ran her hands over the carpet, feeling it blindly with her fingertips in the dark. There. There was something hard and thin that was curled underneath it . . . and it ran in loops. She realised then that the burns hadn't come from the *top* of the carpet—they'd come from *underneath*! It was an electrical wire! The noise she'd heard from outside while Bewlay had been taunting her—it was a floorboard being lifted. He'd been doing something with the wiring!

She was on her feet in a second and scrabbling to climb onto the radiator—but too late. The light came on along with the mains supply, the sudden power surge hitting her like a bolt gun in a slaughterhouse. This was a million times worse than the Taser—this was for keeps. She jerked around, unable even to cry out, before collapsing onto the now smoking floor and having a seizure.

◈

Down in the cellar, Arthur gave the power a good three seconds before he switched off again. It was tiresome to have to wade up and down the stairs to do this, but better safe than sorry. He wasn't as physically strong as he had once been and would rather open the door to a disabled Skinny than one who was terrified and desperate and able to defend herself. He'd go up and undo his copper wires . . . but just might not bother coming all the way back down to get the lights put back on again. He had a big flashlight, after all, and things were more fun in the dark.

Besides, Tommy liked it better that way.

As he turned he saw his kitchen knife, waiting for him. It had been an emergency choice—after he had fled with Tommy away from Big Ian it was the first thing he'd been able to grab quietly for the way back up. But now he had much more leisure time. He could pick and choose what he would apply to Skinny to persuade her into telling him all about the whereabouts of her long lost cousin. The rough sponge, he thought, would probably get him what he wanted from her.

26

Maryam remembered how she had held Grace's little hand and read her stories every single night when they were children. She also remembered when she had been the one regarded as the most beautiful of the pair of them. Maryam couldn't see it herself, but in those days she had been painfully shy and not self-aware. Then, of course, her 'talent' had been discovered . . . and she had become a prisoner in her own house, with emaciated clients limping in (or being wheeled in) every few months or so to keep the pennies coming—each session making her older and more withered until she was the one who looked like she needed healing. Finally, after her 21st birthday and the debacle of the meal with John, she had decided that, in essence, her life had passed a tipping point and had more or less lost any potential it might once have had.

So she had simply given up on it.

She'd thought that she was a strong-willed person. She thought she'd decided to do the only thing possible under the circumstances. She'd been wrong.

She hadn't been strong at all, she realised; in fact, she must have been profoundly depressed to just give *up* like that! To accept what was happening to her body as a fact of her miserable, bitter, sad life and to simply carry on destroying herself.

She wasn't depressed now, though. Not any more. The night in bed with Joe had all been a pretend love (at least for him) but it had shifted her perspective. She was seeing herself differently now. She looked around her room and felt oppressed by it. In fact this whole place was diseased. What the hell were they doing still living here in this mausoleum? She and Grace were both unhealthy in their minds as much as anything else, she thought, and she suddenly felt ashamed. She had treated her wee sister like dirt, and now she would do something about it. They had to move on, get out. She would help and encourage Grace to become better educated to the best of her ability—to find some sort of a simple job perhaps and meet people of her own age. She hoped that it was not too late.

But if she was to have any chance of a life at all she knew that she simply had to stop healing people. Because deep down, she also knew—the real catalyst for change had been when she had healed Papa.

Papa had asked her to free him of his cancer. Naturally. Except that she didn't heal terminally ill people, did she? After all, her logic went, if healing cataracts or untwisting arthritic fingers could have her body withering away—then what on earth would stopping someone from dying do to her? She could see herself instantly crumbling to dust.

In the end though, it wasn't Papa's pain or pleading that had made her change her mind—it was her own nihilism. She had thought to herself—sure, why not take the risk? Just do it. What did she have to lose?

Because what, exactly, did she have to live for?

But the healing of Papa had been a revelation. There had been no strain, no trouble, no ghastly pounding headaches, no bleeding or fainting—no discomfort of any sort for her whatsoever.

Overjoyed, she had supposed that, logically speaking (if logic could be applied to what she did) it made complete sense; healing a few microscopic cancerous cells was bound to be easier than fixing old bones or eyesight or skin. It was almost, Maryam had thought, as if her gift had been specifically *designed* to deal with terminal illness—quickly, easily and painlessly. Papa had practically bounded from his bed, elated and cured, Grace smiling her head off.

It was the first time she could remember the three of them ever being genuinely happy. It seemed to be the solution to all of her problems and she cursed herself for never trying it before. She even began thinking along the very lines that Joe had when he'd made his proposition to her over dinner. That is, find someone very wealthy who was terminally ill, and make enough money saving them to never have to put herself through the horror of healing salons ever again. It was a good plan and it had gently sung her to sleep that night with thoughts of better days to come.

She had been woken by Papa's screams a mere few hours later—high-pitched and unnatural sounding coming from a grown man. She had hobbled across the gallery floor as best she could but Grace was already there at the door of his room, hand to her mouth, staring in at her father naked, jammed into a corner, jerking and trembling uncontrollably, his feet splashing in the growing puddle of his own urine. When Maryam had gone to him he had clung to her bony shoulders, hurting her with his gripping fingers, babbling to get it all out, to *tell* her . . .

'I was supposed to die, Maryam. I was supposed to, and I didn't want to and I made you cure me. I didn't understand that I *had* to die. I was *meant* to and I *should have* . . .'

Maryam was panicked, what on earth was he talking about?

'I don't understand Papa . . .'

He said that he had lost his soul.

'What?' she had asked.

His mouth had twitched with the effort of attempting to look calm—for Grace's sake, she'd presumed—and he had forced a smile. It had arrived at his lips without touching his eyes, resembling the results of a mild stroke.

He told her that when she'd healed him, his soul had gone away . . . and had left him behind.

She and Grace had put a robe on him and had led him gently to the kitchen, where he continued to twitch and look around the room. Maryam had gotten Grace to make him a strong cup of coffee and the smell was filling the kitchen. She could see that Papa was trying not to gag, and when she had held the cup to his lips and made him drink a sip he slapped it from her hands, smashing it against the china-tiled wall above the black iron stove, ignoring the burning liquid spattering across his face . . . in fact seeming not to feel the scald at all, despite the fact that Maryam could see fingernail sized splashes reddening his skin. He'd cried out that it tasted awful . . . putrid. She had shouted at Grace to run for a clean facecloth and to soak it quickly in cold water . . . and had then been left alone with him.

He'd watched Grace dash out, making sure she was gone before grabbing Maryam's wrists, making her wince. She saw that his eyes were duller than they had been before. Polluted, almost, like grey dishwater. And his pupils seemed unnaturally enlarged. She had started to speak, to try and ask him again to explain, but he had shushed her and had begun to talk urgently, almost in a monotone—low and intense.

His proper time had come, he'd said, but he had been healed and . . . what had he become? Just a human body? And what was that without a soul? A husk, made of flesh and bone? And inside, all that was left was consciousness; all on its own. And what was consciousness? Awareness? If that's all it was then what good was it? Beasts, after all, had awareness. *Ants* had awareness. The lowliest damn crawling *thing* had awareness. To be a man you needed a *soul*!

What if the soul was one of those things that you didn't actually realise you possessed until you didn't have it any more? And having lost it—if you were then still able to think and see and breathe and act without it—then what had been the soul's purpose in the first place? What, exactly, had it been *for*?

She had whispered quietly that she didn't know. He had told her that he did.

The soul, he'd realised, was a practical device; as much a part of the body's machinery as a kidney or a brain or, more to the point . . . an *immune system*. A filter, a defence from the formless bad things out there, crawling their way across the world. Things only ever glimpsed in the darkest recesses of the worst nightmares, when the unconscious mind can view reality unfettered. If you no longer have your soul any more, if you no longer have your *protection*, your *ozone layer*—what will you see, no longer prevented from doing so by the soul's *antibodies*? What will approach you? And what will they do when they meet you?

She stared at him, horrified.

'I can see them,' he'd said.

He had started crying then and had bolted from her and into his room.

And that, apart from in passing every time he'd arrived back home with bags of religious gee-gaws, had been the last time she had shared anything other than a few curt words with him. He had lived like that for three days, spitting out food, shrieking that it tasted putrid, forcing himself to drink, praying constantly without sleep—until the morning he had gone out of the house, walked halfway across the pedestrian footbridge and had let himself tumble down onto the motorway below.

It had been easy and pain free for her to heal her Papa of his terminal illness, almost as if the healing of minor troubles was to be discouraged, in favour of healing the dying. That would surely have been a good thing, but if Papa was to be believed, then the healing of terminally ill people had but one outcome—to make them lose their souls.

If that was the case, however, then for what *purpose* was it like that?

Who—or what—could possibly gain from it?

She decided now to stop thinking about it. She had made her decision to leave with her simple, beautiful, sister in tow and it need never trouble her again. She would make amends to Grace and she would apologise also to Joe for making him do what he had done for her last night—it may have been Cinderella for her, but she was aware that it must have been more like Beauty and the Beast for him—with her as the Beast. If he needed money, he would have it; the house ought to fetch a tidy sum.

Her life up to this point had been a piece of grit—and now she would coat it with love and hope and good intention until she had made a pearl of it.

Pleased with this image, she pulled the covers from herself and got out of bed. As she hobbled over to fetch her dressing gown she felt lighter in her steps. A little less like she was walking with iron boots on and, psychosomatic or genuine, she appreciated feeling easier on her feet.

27

The Pretty Blue Fox was an incongruity—a nineteenth century red brick building, marooned in the middle of a 1970's concretion of dark underpasses, overgrown waste ground and damp, grey cube houses with flat roofs. Apparently the gradual makeover of Glasgow had bypassed this particular corner. The area hadn't even been a part of the city originally and the Pretty Blue Fox had once been a coaching house for wayfarers and business traffic on the Great East road to Glasgow, the gentle slopes around it dotted with small cottages.

When the city had spread ever outwards taking over every small town and parish surrounding it, this place had also been absorbed, and all had been transformed gradually from shortbread tin village to satellite slum.

The original building had been burnt to the ground in the mid-1800s and this—a prime example of Victorian Gothic—had been built on its foundations and in its stead.

It looked like a tiny scale version of St Pancras station in London—all weird spires and false towers. It even had a clock face above its doors, but with its hands long gone. There were the remains of weather worn and pollution damaged bas relief shapes at regular intervals around the rim of the clock dial where the numbers should be, but even as worn as they were, one could see that they didn't look like numerals.

More like symbols.

❖

Joe stood outside the pub, afraid. The aggressive, tinny sounds of the area were all around him. Very young children swearing in the distance, a car revving up and racing in circles somewhere nearby.

Behind him, a parade of shops were lined up next to each other, displaying everything the area needed in the way of retail facilities. A Chinese takeaway, a convenience store, a heavily fortified bookmakers, a chippie and—the jewel in the crown—the lawyer's office, which was even more fortress-like than the bookies, with dull, red painted solid steel sheeting covering the window and a thickly barred security gate at the doorway. Joe wondered if there were queues there at Christmas time, snaking out of the door and around the block, as the seasonal shoplifting charges began stacking up. He reluctantly turned back to the Pretty Blue Fox.

Parked beside the pub was a mint condition 1964 S Type Jaguar. Navy blue. In this place it stuck out like a horse in a bowling alley, and Joe had no doubt at all that it would remain in its pristine condition for as long as Bewlay was alive. In fact, Joe doubted very much whether its doors would even be locked. He also knew that he really didn't want to go back inside that dark place.

He had realised however, that he had no other choice. He had to get real—Maryam had screwed him and he still needed money to escape and disappear as much as he ever had and the only way he could get anywhere near the amount he needed as quickly as he needed it was through Bewlay. Except that now he wouldn't be conning him because now he could have Arthur Bewlay 'miracled' for real—*if* he could get Maryam to go along with it. There was no point in actually asking her, of course—she would just say no because she didn't heal the terminally ill did she? But Joe knew that was another lie. He remembered from back in the hospital that Grace had said something about their Papa—that Maryam had '*made him well*'. That meant Maryam *could* cure terminal cases, just that she chose not to.

Well Maryam, he thought, today would just have to be different, wouldn't it?

There was no way he could coerce her into it, he imagined. She wasn't really the type to take orders from anyone, but maybe she would do something for love? Although both of them 'understood' that their love story was all a big pretend . . . he knew now that she loved him. He guessed that he was just going to have to find out how much. In the cab over, he had come up with a plan, of sorts.

Maryam would cure Bewlay's cancer if he could convince her that Bewlay would kill him if she didn't. Then Bewlay would give Joe his money and Joe would be able to leave this place forever. Simple.

As in simpleton, he thought. As a plan, it had more holes than a cheese grater.

He might not get out of that damn pub alive. If he did, Bewlay and his pals might just kill them all anyway. But what the hell else was there to do? Joe thought. What else *could* he do? He needed the money—he needed Bewlay; there was no one else to go to. He had no goddam choice. He had to psych himself up—he had to go on in there with the right mental attitude. Positivity was the key. He walked toward the door.

He stopped.

He *really* didn't want to go in there.

◈

Arthur already had Skinny's jeans gathered at her ankles and was pulling her pants down. He could have just cut them off he supposed, but he thought Tommy would like the look of her better this way.

The flashlight beam from the doorway illuminated a strip of the room, still foggy from the smoking carpet, its powerful light glinting off the sharp highlights of the embedded razor fragments in the palm sized block of wood lying on the floor near Skinny's head. She was still out, but breathing. Maybe he'd left the power on a wee bit too long. Never mind. Electric shocks would be the least of her troubles soon.

The place still smelled of burnt nylon. He'd need to get that carpet replaced, he thought—then laughed at the ridiculousness of having such a notion in this situation.

'Hey Tommy!' he said, 'here I am, going to die, and I'm thinking of redecorating!'

Tommy's head was resting on a pillow against the wall, mute.

'I should go on one of those makeover shows! Maybe get the whole place done up!' He laughed but Tommy didn't join in.

Skinny stirred slightly as Bewlay parted her knees, having to push her feet up toward her body to get her legs as wide open as he could (*she looks like a frog*, he thought) but she quickly fell back into unconsciousness.

'Tommy,' he said, his voice growing a little thicker as he looked at her, 'I think we should just make a wee start on young Skinny just now, hm?'

Tommy remained quiet on the subject.

The door downstairs was knocked.

Who could that be? thought Bewlay. Should he ignore it?

Yes, he would ignore it.

He strapped the rough sponge onto his palm, the broken teeth of the razor blades still stained with the dog's blood.

'A few light strokes to begin with, eh Skinny? That might wake you up, and then we can have a chat.'

Even in her unconscious state, she jerked when he started on her.

◆

So his car was here . . . but that didn't necessarily mean that Bewlay was, thought Joe. He could be anywhere. Or, he could be in there with his whole gang having a Mouseketeer club meeting, looking out at him through spy holes, sharpening axes. Joe hesitated in front of the door.

What did he think he was doing here? Should he go? Just give up on all of this? He needed the money, but . . .

Well, there was no 'but'. He needed the money full stop. He would try again.

◆

The knocking returned, more insistent. Arthur sighed. No point pretending it wasn't happening—hiding your head in the sand never got the breakfast made as Da used to say. Besides, he wouldn't be getting any information from Skinny while she was out like this, so he might as well.

'Tommy, keep an eye on her. Give me a shout if she comes to, would you?'

Arthur removed the rough sponge from his hand. The elastic was tight around his knuckles and he had to pull quite hard to remove it, the snap causing hundreds of tiny pinpoints of her blood to suddenly spit all over him from the crooked blades. Shit.

This shirt was clean on this morning.

Never mind, if it was the cops, he would tell them he'd cut himself shaving. If it was the press, he'd say he was a cannibal and had just eaten the postman. He laughed to himself. The press boys loved all that 'personality' stuff. Made a better story and sold more papers and at the end of the whole thing that's all they were ever interested in really, wasn't it? At least, for as long as papers lasted, he thought—and by the looks of things that wasn't going to be for much longer. He realised then that he wouldn't live long enough to enjoy the humiliating death throes of the conventional press—and it made him sad. He'd reached the front door and pulled it open, and instantly his mood was lifted.

◆

Well, thought Arthur. Of all people. He guessed it was true what they said; sit still for long enough and everything walks past you eventually.

◆

Joe's heart jumped when the door had suddenly opened . . . it creaked and screamed like a vault in an old horror film. It was completely black inside the pub and Bewlay chose not to step into the daylight. Joe could just make out his face in the gloom—aside from the putty coloured flesh of his cadaverous face, the dark shadows of his eye sockets and the actual deep hole above his thin-lipped mouth, it looked to Joe like the bastard now had measles as well, or something like it; there seemed to be dozens of tiny dark spots pinpointed across his cheeks and forehead. Good, he thought. There wasn't enough misery in the world, as far as Joe was concerned, that could be heaped on this wretch.

◆

Bewlay instantly took in Joe's physical appearance. The boy was standing on his own two feet, looking strong as an ox and ruddy with health. Unless Big Ian had been hallucinating, then some sort of miracle had actually happened to the good reverend. Bewlay cursed himself for a fool—what a rash idiot he had been.

'Reverend Joe,' he exclaimed in a chummy manner that set Joe's teeth on edge. 'Believe it or not I am genuinely delighted to see you again.'

He extended a hand that Joe ignored.

'Notice anything different about me?' said Joe. 'Anything unusual?'

'You've lost a few pounds?' Bewlay replied. 'Had a haircut maybe? Give me a clue.'

'I'm standing up. I'm speaking. I'm able to walk.'

'You've been on a motivational course.'

Bewlay laughed at his own joke. Joe didn't.

'How much money have you got right now, in cash?'

Bewlay grinned. Joe wished that he wouldn't.

'Don't fucking do that,' Joe said. 'Your face looks bad enough when there's only one open hole in the middle of it.'

Joe was pleased to note that Bewlay's grin faltered a little.

'Sorry I'm smiling,' Bewlay said, 'but I can't help it. All joking aside, son—you *do* have the gift, don't you? I was wrong and you were telling the truth all along, weren't you? I knew, deep down, that such things were possible, of course, but to find out that it was right there in front of me! And I threw it away like an idiot! I really must apologise for my rash behaviours . . .'

Joe held his hand up.

'Shut up and listen to me,' he said. 'You can be cured, but I want money and I want it now.'

'Straight to business. That's fine Joe,' said Bewlay. 'Just you come on in and let's get everything settled and done, no funny stuff.'

'You're kidding, right?' Joe shook his head. 'I'm not going back in there. You have to come with me.'

'Explain.'

'I'm not the healer,' Joe said. 'But I can take you to her.'

'Her?'

Bewlay didn't say any more and Joe could see distrustful little wheels turning in his mind.

'It has to be right now or not at all, Bewlay,' Joe continued. 'Do you want to live or not?'

'It's one thing me trusting you to help me,' said Bewlay, eventually, 'here in the safety of my own home. It's another thing entirely to . . . well, after all, I caused you some harm. Or at least I *thought* I did.'

'Believe me, you did.'

'Did I?' said Bewlay. 'I didn't see you after the accident. For all I know reports about your injuries were exaggerated and you and your friends have come up with this scheme to lure me away somewhere—for revenge.'

'You saw me being cut open in your shithole bar, didn't you?' spat Joe, 'before your merry fucking men took me away to murder me? Well, have a look now.'

Joe raised his shirt and Bewlay looked. No scars of any sort.

'This is genuine,' Joe said. 'I couldn't even go to the cops about what you did to me, because there's no goddam evidence anymore that you ever did *anything*!'

Bewlay knew for a fact that Joe's torso had been lacerated multiple times with broken glass, enough in some areas to expose strips of raw, bloody muscle. He had certainly seen *that*. Now it was smooth and clean and scar free. Bewlay suddenly grinned again.

He was going to live.

'I have close to five hundred grand in cash in a gym bag upstairs. Will that do?'

The turnabout was so sudden, Joe was unsure whether or not to believe him.

'You must know the kind of business I run, Reverend Joe,' he said. 'You'll know that five hundred thousand isn't an unlikely amount for me to have lying about. Otherwise, why come?'

Why come indeed? thought Joe. He hadn't been expecting quite that amount though . . . *if* Bewlay was telling the truth.

'I'll give you three minutes exactly,' Joe said, 'starting now, and then I'm out of here. And don't forget, you try fucking me around or sending anyone out here to get me—you don't get anything.'

'Well I'd get *you*, wouldn't I?' Bewlay smiled.

Joe stared at him.

'I'm joking, son. Relax,' said Bewlay. 'What's involved? What does she do?'

'She puts her hands on you and then you're fixed.'

'Simple as that?'

'There's a certain amount of pain.'

'A 'certain amount'?'

'A lot,' said Joe. 'You've got two and a half minutes left.'

Bewlay smiled graciously and went back into the gloom of his pub. A slight breeze blew and made Joe realise that he was drenched in sweat.

◆

Arthur carried a black holdall full of the money and McGill's mobile, switching it on as he carried Tommy back to his room. Something was puzzling him. Reverend Joe hadn't mentioned Skinny or his scam with her—not once. If they had been in league together against him, Joe would surely have been at the very least curious as to his partner in crime's whereabouts. He would have made that part of his bargaining for the money . . . unless he really didn't give two hoots about her. That was, of course, possible, but there was something that was now starting to seem even more likely.

What if there hadn't been any scam between them after all?

What if Reverend Joe had no idea that Skinny worked for him?

Arthur was beginning to wonder whether he'd gotten the whole Skinny thing completely wrong in the first place. Maybe it *had* all been a coincidence? After all, if you take a trip back to the old country—as Reverend Joe had—why *wouldn't* you intend to contact long lost relations? And was that really all it was? As innocent as that? An *intent* to make contact with his cousin after all these years and maybe have a good old natter about all that interesting history they shared? He checked the call log on Joe's phone and found Skinny's number . . . but there had been no calls actually made to her by Reverend Joe.

Oops.

He maybe should have checked that out first before jumping to conclusions—chalk another one up to that pesky, old morphine induced absent-mindedness. Poor Skinny, he thought, amused. Poor luckless Skinny. She hadn't had a fucking clue about *any* of this. In fact, he thought, never had the sun shone on her once in all of her miserable young life. Not once.

It occurred to him then that the reverend might just become cheesed off at what had been happening to her—*if* he found out. And he seemed cheesed off enough already, so he'd better not find out, had he? That would really not be useful at this stage in the proceedings. Better to just lock her in here and let her bleed out?

Best thing for her really. It would be doing her a kindness, he thought—she wouldn't be able to have any real kind of quality of life now anyway. He'd only intended for a light touch, but had gotten a bit carried away. He set Tommy down comfortably on his damp pillow.

'I have to go out for a while, Tom,' he said. 'There is a miracle about to happen to me—I *know* it.'

But Tommy said nothing. Arthur frowned, a catch coming into his voice as he tried to jolly his brother along.

'Now you keep an ear and an eye out for the little dyke in case she comes to, ok? I'll lock her in, but if she says or does anything—anything at all—you shout me, ok?'

There was a faint groan and Arthur bent his ear to his brother's lips.

'*You can be easily disposed of Arthur,*' the voice croaked. '*What would* you *do if you were the American cunt?*'

Arthur saw all at once that he could be *very* easily disposed of, should Reverend Joe decide to take things in that direction—he was a frail, ill, elderly man now, after all, not the 'big man' of old. And why shouldn't the reverend go that way?

He might have been desperate, Arthur thought, but he wasn't stupid. If he *really* thought that Arthur was all alone in here, any notions of a service rendered for a fee paid would fly out the window and Arthur would find himself suddenly 500k poorer, unhealed and possibly dead.

'Thanks Tommy,' he whispered, but Tommy seemed to have said all he was going to on the matter. That was fine though, as far as Arthur was concerned. This little exchange had sharpened his mind wonderfully, reminding him what it was like to be in a genuine combat situation with a potential adversary who was neither simple-minded nor beholden to him in some way.

Maybe though, he thought, Skinny could help him out? He left Tommy's room, intent on heading to the cellar and retrieving that kitchen knife. Looked like he could get some use from it after all.

◆

Joe was waiting nervously outside. The few shoppers who were at the parade paid him no heed. In fact no one he'd seen around here so far had looked in the direction of the pub at all. Learned behaviour or instinct, he thought, wondering if Bewlay really was alone in there. And in wondering that, a whole new way of looking at the situation started to form in his mind.

There really was no need to put Maryam to the trouble of healing this insect, he thought, because if he and Bewlay *were* alone ... then something else could be done to get the money. Joe certainly couldn't imagine any passers-by on the streets, the few there were, rushing in to aid Bewlay if he were to be crying out for help. And it wouldn't really be a murder either, he thought, it would be more like pest extermination—a mercy killing for the benefit of the world in general and for himself in particular. Thinking of the physical shape Bewlay was in, Joe didn't imagine that it would take too long.

'*Besides, you've done it before, haven't you . . . ?*' a voice said inside him.

Yes, he thought, I goddam have.

◆

He approached the pub and stepped just inside the front door as quietly as he could. He could just about hear some shuffling about upstairs, but other than that, the place did seem totally empty. He let his eyes grow accustomed to the darkness. He had no intention of moving any further inside unless he could make out exactly where he was and the direction of the exit.

What he could see of the bar room around him gave him the shivers. Lightning strike glimpse moments of it had been seared into his mind forever. He noticed that his hands were shaking. Then, he heard Bewlay speaking and stopped dead. The bastard wasn't alone after all, he thought.

Joe moved quickly and quietly back a pace, one foot almost out of the door, and waited to see if he could work out how many others were in here—but there had been no replies, just more of Bewlay talking. Maybe he was talking to himself? More likely he was on the phone calling for reinforcements. If that was the case then it was a combination of good news and bad news. Bad news because he would be overrun by a bunch of psychotic mutants—but good because it meant that Bewlay was currently alone, and if he was quick enough . . .

He took a step inside the pub again, letting his eyes become accustomed once more to the dark before he went for the stairs. That was when his theories went flying out the window because he heard Bewlay shouting his head off at someone to 'stop hurting the girl', and he heard struggling and a heavy thump on the floor. Joe didn't know what to do. What the fuck was going on? He knew he should turn and go immediately, but a question had been planted in his mind and he knew that it wouldn't go away.

What girl?

◆

After plunging the long blade deep into Big Ian's chest and shouting his head off, Arthur idly shone the flashlight onto Skinny's prone body and waited. Her face was looking puckish and sooty from the burns she had received. He moved the beam downwards. He really had gotten a little carried away down there, hadn't he? The human body was an amazing thing, though. After all, who would ever have imagined someone in his state of health would be still able to achieve an erection without Viagra? Seemed a shame to waste it—he wasn't getting any healthier and who knew when he would next get one?

He regretted being so hasty about making his noise to attract Reverend Joe. He could easily have waited a few more minutes and lain with her awhile, as they said in the Bible. Although . . . maybe the reverend hadn't heard? Or was too afraid to come up? That would give him a bit of time . . .

'*Oh my God* . . .'

It was Reverend Joe behind him, in complete shock at what the relentless beam of the flashlight was revealing.

Arthur sighed.

Too bad.

28

GRACE WAS IN THE KITCHEN ON HER OWN, HANDS IN HER LAP. She was nodding seriously at someone across the table and Maryam opened the door fully expecting to see Joe sitting there . . . but there was no one. Maryam looked around.

'Where is Joe?' she said.

Her eye was drawn to a glass of water sitting in front of Grace.

'The water you semt me for's gottem a bit warm, Maryam,' Grace said, pointedly. 'Sorry.'

Maryam sighed, feeling absolutely dreadful. She decided to ignore whatever childish nonsense Grace had been up to. She obviously hadn't been nodding to someone across from her because there was no one there to nod to. Maybe she had been agreeing with herself about something or maybe she'd been doing nothing and Maryam was just going insane and seeing things. She didn't care. She wanted to get everything off her chest and try to make her new start with her little sister.

'I'll come to the point,' Maryam said. 'I did something very bad last night. You know it and I know it. You have a crush on Joe and I deliberately made sure that he went to bed with me. I forced him to tell me that he loved me. I'm sorry, but that's all there is to it. It was something I needed to do and I'm afraid your feelings on the matter didn't trouble me. Not until today. I would like to say I'm sorry. And I am. Truly.'

She took a deep breath before continuing.

'I do love you, I really do. I've been blaming you for something that wasn't your fault and I'm sorry for it. I don't expect you to forgive me, but I'll keep on saying I'm sorry until the day I die. I'll make it up to you, I promise.'

It had all come out in one great big blurt and she looked at Grace, wondering how much of what she'd said had gone in.

Grace shrugged, a small smile playing on her face. Something had changed with her sister today, Maryam thought. There seemed to be a slyness to her, and something else too. What was it . . . an intent?

'He didm't wamt you Maryam,' said Grace. 'You made him. But he had to have me im his head whem he was doimg it with you. He had to pretemd it was me amd it wasm't you.'

Maryam opened her mouth to speak and then closed it again. Well *that* was a slap in the face, for sure. She'd known that she was no great erotic muse for him, obviously, but still . . . to be confronted with the actual mechanics of how he had made their mutual lie work for him stunned her a little. Also, she didn't like him using Grace like that. If he'd used her in his head, how else might he have used her? What had this man—whom she realised in the clear light of day she barely knew and who could have been telling her nothing but lies from the moment he opened his mouth—what had he been doing whilst she was asleep?

'Did Joe have sex with you Grace?' she asked, as neutrally as she could.

Grace stared her out for a few moments, but finally had to shake her head. No. Maryam found that she was more relieved than she would have expected to be at this news, and not just for her sister's sake.

'Then did Joe tell you what he was thinking about when he was . . . with me?'

Grace shook her head again.

'I saw it im his head,' she said.

Maryam almost laughed.

Of course you did, she thought. She was disappointed in herself for being disappointed in him, but what else should she expect, after all? There were two Joes—the Joe she had fallen in love with, truly and for real, the Joe who said that he loved her and would care for her for the rest of her days . . . and then there was the real Joe—rootless con man and deceiver of young girls. Thinking that way caused a small ache in her heart and she wished she could make the imaginary Joe real. But then what? The thought was bitter. What in God's name would he ever want with me?

'Do you know where he's gone?' she asked.

'To get us lots of poumds so we cam go away . . .'

Maryam groaned inwardly, cursing him. What the hell did he think he was playing at, messing with Grace's head like this? She knew that Joe had no intention of running away with Grace; he was using her for some scheme of his own.

'Where was he going to get this money, Grace?' Maryam asked, tersely.

Grace shrugged and looked at the frosted glass of the kitchen window.

'Where did he say he was going to get this money for you to go away Grace? Look at me.'

'He didem't say.'

'He has nowhere to get any . . . unless . . .'

The obvious thought struck Maryam then. *Damn* him! The game of pretend was well and truly over now, she thought, wasn't it?

'Did Joe say anything about bringing anyone to the house to be healed?'

'You're just im our way now,' Grace said, ignoring her question. 'You're all used up amd he doesm't wamt you amd I dom't emmymore amd you're *all—used—up!* I wamt to live with Joe. *Joe* will be the healer.'

This wasn't getting any better, thought Maryam. Only yesterday she would have laughed in her sister's face and no doubt treated her to a verbal shit hosing as well. Not today, though. Today, Maryam would let Grace down as gently as she could.

'Grace. Darling . . . this is what you want to happen rather than what really is happening. It's unhealthy and you deserve better than living for make believes and never wills,' she said. 'Like me.'

This seemed to give Grace pause.

Maryam saw then, by the door, a small child-sized suitcase. It was brightly coloured pink plastic and had a little bit of what she could see was one of Grace's dresses squeezing out from it. Oh dear Christ, Maryam thought. She's all packed and ready to go—to run away with 'her' man. She recognised the case from her sister's twelfth birthday—it was a toy she'd been so delighted by she'd cried inconsolably when she realised that it wasn't for real and that Papa wasn't about to start taking them anywhere. She'd wanted to go away so *badly* when she was a child, Maryam remembered. A holiday . . . anywhere away from the apartments.

Maryam felt truly sorry for her.

'Listen Grace . . . Joe isn't a real healer. He's not like me. No one is.' Maryam continued, keeping emotion as far from her voice as she could manage. 'He said so himself, don't you remember? He just pretends . . . so he can make money from sick people. He wants money, darling, that's all, and he would do or say anything to get it. Do you understand what I'm saying? It's like him thinking of you when he was having sex with me—that's the kind of thing he does. When he says he wants to run away with you, he doesn't mean it . . .'

'He *does!*' said Grace. 'I saw im his head . . . we were at a beach . . . amd we were im the samd . . . .'

Maryam thought to herself: I have to not cry. I can't indulge myself in sadness for her, I can't. I have to be kind and explain as best I can. Oh dear sweet Jesus. Grace Grace Grace . . . the bastard had been using her ability against her. Maryam thought that even her imaginary Joe was getting further and further away from her now.

'Sweetheart, he can't do what I can, you know that, don't you? And I'm *not* going to be healing anyone he brings here, if that's what he's planning . . .'

Grace laughed. An honest to goodness amused laugh.

'You'll see, Maryam. You'll see whem he comes back, you'll see! You aremt goimg to be hittimg me agaim,' she shouted. 'I dom't hab to put up with that emmy more! Joe will be the healer amd *we dom't have to have you emmymore!*'

'Grace—it doesn't work like that! Joe can't heal . . .'

'Yes he cam Maryam! Because I wamt him to! We'll live together and he'll love me amd he'll look after me amd he'll stop them from speakimg at me all the time!'

Maryam felt like she'd had that glass of water on the table suddenly thrown in her face. In all of the time she'd had experience of Grace's episodes, her sister had never once made mention of any 'them' speaking to her. It made her think immediately of Papa and *his* 'them'.

'Stop *who* from speaking, Grace?' she said. 'Who is 'them'?'

Grace looked as if she'd been caught out doing something naughty.

'Please talk to me darling,' Maryam insisted. 'This is very important . . .'

The entry phone buzzer went off then, making Maryam jump. Grace laughed aloud and clapped her hands together.

'It's Joe!' she shouted, and ran from the room.

'Grace, get back here!' Maryam shouted. *'Tell me what you're talking about!'*

Maryam began to hobble as quickly as she could after her.

'Grace, don't let him back in if he has anyone with him! I am not going to heal anyone else ever again!'

Far away, at the other end of the great hall, she heard Grace respond to the buzzer . . . and then a distorted unintelligible shouting from the street entrance down below . . . and she had a bad feeling in the pit of her stomach. Whatever control she liked to think that she had over her life . . . this house . . . her sister—she had the distinct feeling that she had just lost it.

Grace giggled happily as she let Joe and his guests in to the building.

29

Bewlay and Joe held Skinny between them as they ascended in the brass cage lift. The floor of the elevator was marble—black and white like a chessboard. Blood drops the size of large coins plopped onto it from between Skinny's legs. Her pants and jeans had been hastily pulled up, the zip still open and the button not done because a huge wad of sheeting had been stuffed into the crotch like a giant nappy. But still the blood had soaked through. Joe was just about managing to hold it together, desperately trying not to think about how much blood she had lost and was losing still. Oh Jesus, Jesus, Jesus, he had to get her to Maryam—that was all. If he could do that then everything would be alright. *There was no need for panic.*

She had lost a lot of blood, sure, but then so had he in his own accident and look what Maryam had done for him. She had given him back his legs for Chrissakes, so she sure as shit could fix Trudy up no problem. This would be a breeze for her. A goddam breeze!

He cursed the slowness of the lift.

◈

In the pub, it had been several moments before Joe was able to take in what he was seeing. From the top of the stairs he had seen Bewlay standing in a doorway, vaguely silhouetted by a flashlight's beam. And then, after taking another step up, he had seen something else—the prone body of the big scar-faced guy at Bewlay's feet, a huge knife sticking out from his chest.

He had approached swiftly, his need to find out about this 'girl' overriding any caution. He drew level with Bewlay and his eyes followed the beam of light. When his mind had assimilated what the bloody mess sprawled on the floor actually was it had made him want to throw up. He had said something—cursed or shouted in disbelief, he couldn't remember—and had pushed Bewlay aside, forgetting all about killing him, forgetting all about the money—realising that if this poor wretched thing lying bleeding on the floor of this hell hole was still alive, then he had the only means of saving her.

Get her to Maryam.

Joe knelt by her, grabbing her wrist and trying to take a pulse. Yes. There. She was still alive. He searched around, trying to find something, *anything*, to put over her wounds and staunch the pitiless bleeding . . . but the room, now that he was looking at it properly, held nothing which could have helped him in any way. It was like a sewer. It smelled vile and he saw that not only had the girl been grotesquely cut but, from what he could make out in the dim light, she had been badly burnt as well. Jesus Holy *Christ* . . .

Bewlay had reappeared at his side, holding something.

'*I* didn't do this, incidentally,' he said. 'It was that dead fellow out there—you remember him Joe? His name was Big Ian. He was going to do the same to you when he visited you in the hospital. You had a lucky escape.'

He held out a clean white sheet.

'I was all for letting the whole thing go; you'd already been punished enough was my feeling. But he'd developed reasons of his own for wanting to harm you further. Jealousy, believe it or not.'

Joe grabbed the sheet from him, frantically tearing it into strips.

'It's clean,' said Bewlay. 'Is she alive?'

Joe began using the strips as wadding against her terrible, ragged wounds, trying to stem the constant oozing of her blood as best he could. He had tears in his eyes and his voice was cracking as he spoke.

'You lying bastard. You said there was no one else here.'

'And you said that you weren't coming in. What happened? Did you decide just to pop up for old time's sake?'

Joe said nothing and hastily pulled the girl's jeans up as far as he was able over the wadded sheeting. They wouldn't fit over her but they would hold the cloth tight against her. He would have strangled the life out of Bewlay with pleasure there and then—but this girl was more important to him now and he didn't want to waste another second. He shifted his position and crouched by her side, easing his hands beneath her and hoping not to hurt her any further by picking her up.

'Big Ian was a bit of a psycho, Reverend,' Bewlay continued. 'Very *much* the jealous type. He had a bit of a thing for young...'

Bewlay paused to enjoy the word.

'... *Trudy* here. It was when he found that you had her telephone number on *your* phone, that he went into his terrible, jealous rage.'

Bewlay sighed at the tragedy of it all.

'This is the sad result.'

Joe's competing thoughts of revenge and rescue immediately stopped dead. He felt a sudden deep chill. What had Bewlay just said? *He* had this girl's telephone number?

No, he didn't.

He didn't even know who this girl was—so...

(*he said her name was Trudy*)

...why would he have her number?

Bewlay had said Trudy.

His unconscious mind was already way ahead of him, waiting patiently for his rational thoughts to put this all together and catch up so that they could scream in despair together. This couldn't be her... it *couldn't* be.

Trudy.

'He was going too far with her,' said Bewlay, keeping the smile out of his voice. 'I had to kill him with his own knife. I was very fond of her—she'd had a very unfortunate childhood and I took her under my wing a few years ago...'

Joe grabbed the flashlight from Bewlay and shone it onto her. She'd been badly burnt all down one side and her eyes were puffy and jammed closed, her face filthy... but he could see in the adult face, traces of the child he had known—and he knew immediately that *it was her*.

Joe let out a strangled moan. He was shaking so badly he had to clasp his hands together.

'How do you know her, by the way?' said Bewlay, 'I was meaning to ask.'

Joe suddenly leapt up and onto Bewlay, slamming him against the wall, hard enough for loose plaster to snow down on them from the ceiling.

'You mother*fucker*!' he screamed.

'Please! Reverend Joe—I'm not a well man . . .'

Joe banged him against the wall again, harder.

'You were just going to *leave* her here? Let her bleed to death in this goddam cesspit? Just fucking stroll away with me and not say *anything*?'

Bewlay started whining now, a poor old geezer being mugged for his life up an alleyway.

'This is nothing to do with me, I told you! I interrupted Big Ian here and *I* dealt with him, as you can see. I thought that she was dead already.'

Bewlay began to cry.

'Listen Joe, I've been a prisoner in my own home for years because of this man. I'm no saint, I admit that, but doing something like this? I am hard but fair, not a psychopath. Look at the size of me and the size of him! This man held me virtually prisoner in my own home. He was the one in charge all the time, not me! I was just a front, pretending to go along with him! He was a sadist and we're all well shot of him.'

Joe knew he was lying. The whole thing was a total lie, but he knew that he didn't have time to unpick it right now. He had to get Trudy out of here and get her to Maryam.

'Keys.'

'Listen Reverend, it'll be easier if I drive you.'

'Give me your keys or I'll fucking kill you.'

Joe slammed him against the wall again. He heard something crack and Bewlay winced. Good.

'*Where are they?*'

'Where are you taking her? To be healed?' Bewlay said, gasping but still unable to keep the eagerness from his voice. 'I have your money right here. Why don't we take it with us, as a sign of good faith?'

Every nerve ending in Joe's body was screaming for him to get Trudy away.

'New deal, Bewlay—I take your money, I take her and I leave you here to drown in your own pus. How d'you like them turnips?'

He felt the blunt jab in his stomach and realised that the crack he'd heard had actually been a click.

'Not much,' said Bewlay, pushing the barrel of a gun into Joe's abdomen. 'I gave you a chance to take me voluntarily, Reverend Joe. You didn't take it.'

'You kill me,' said Joe. 'You don't get anything.'

'Then neither does she.'

Bewlay smiled and pushed again with the gun, making Joe back off.

'Besides, you were going to kill me, weren't you?' said Bewlay. 'You were coming up here to kill me and take my money and just fuck off. Well now you can't, because there's a damsel in distress here, complicating things, and you want to take her to your healer. Well that's fine, isn't it? Because now Trudy and I can both be healed at the same time, can't we?'

Joe glared at him.

'Well?' said Bewlay. 'Are you going to stare at me 'til lightning comes out of your eyes or are you going to get me and your girl here fixed up?'

Joe decided—pragmatic.

'She gets helped first, understand?' he said.

Without another word, Joe had let Bewlay go, wheeled round back into the depraved smelling room, picked Trudy up from the floor and carried her out to the stairs. He would wait until she was fixed, *then* he would kill Bewlay.

◆

The lift clanked. On the drive over, Bewlay sat next to him with the gun pointed at his hip. Joe had come to the conclusion that if he'd been able to swap his life for hers then he would have. Not just because he knew that his life was essentially worthless anyway, but because she had deserved every break that he'd ever thrown away, fumbled or dropped. She'd never had any breaks as a kid and he just knew that her adult life hadn't improved on that average. And now holding her unconscious in his arms in this clanking, prehistoric elevator, he knew that every single thing he had ever done since he had last seen her had counted for nothing. *Nothing whatsoever.* Everything between leaving her as a lonely, broken child in this desperate, blasted, hell hole city and right now was like some sort of a stupid movie—just something to waste his time until the important stuff came back into his life again.

And now here she was—the important stuff.

In their time of trial she had been mother, father, sister, brother to him, and he was ashamed that he had ever allowed himself to forget it even for a moment; ashamed that he had ever allowed her to fade in any way into the background of his mind. He had made her a promise and she had believed him, and he had failed her. As soon as he was old enough he should have done anything and everything he could—swum across the goddam Atlantic if necessary—to come back for her. *He'd made a promise!* He wondered how long she had waited for him, waited for his return, waited for him to keep his promise and burst through the door of whatever ghastly cess pit they'd stuck her in to take her away with him. How long does a child wait? And what happens to them when they give up? She was all that mattered now.

Bewlay started speaking again and Joe fought back the urge to lay Trudy down and rip the bastard's lungs out.

'This building is amazing, Reverend,' he said. 'Do you know, it's world famous? And in all the time I've lived in this city, I have never once been inside here?'

'Shut up.'

'Don't be like that. If this miracle woman you've been telling me about can do all that you say, then Trudy'll have no worries, will she? And neither will I. You'll get your money and then *you'll* have no worries either, eh? Besides, we can't go any faster than we already are doing so you might as well not give yourself unnecessary stress.'

Joe said nothing. She was so small and light in his arms . . . *so small*. Bewlay spoke up again. 'I actually looked into the history of this place several years ago. It's fascinating.'

Joe reached forward and jabbed the shining brass dome button for the top floor again, smearing it with more of her blood.

'Don't you want to know why it's fascinating? Why I bothered looking into its history?'

'No, I fucking don't.'

'Because this building is supposed to be by the same architect who designed *my* pub. The Pretty Blue Fox used to be very grand when it was first built would you believe? Those were great days for architecture weren't they? Rennie Mackintosh . . . Alexander Thomson . . . .no one builds like that now. Labour's too expensive I suppose, and then there's the health and safety . . .'

'I don't care.'

Bewlay spoke now in a faux whisper, obviously greatly enjoying himself.

'Now apparently, this architect cunt was a bit of a mystery man-part of some kind of a secret society—doctors, lawyers, professional high faluting gentlemen and ladies, all very 'involved' with each other. You know—shagging and that. Mad stuff. What your granny couldn't teach you, eh? Is this us?'

The lift ground to a halt and Joe managed to wrench the sliding cage doors open, shouting down the corridor at the top of his voice.

'Grace! Open the door, get Maryam! Now!'

He'd expected her to be there waiting for him already. He had buzzed the apartment from downstairs and had practically screamed for her to let them in. He hitched along with Trudy, pulling away from Bewlay, who sauntered along behind him, apparently fascinated with the details of the tiles on the walls. Aside from the repeated ornate jungle plant type pattern, there was a recurring snake swallowing its tail motif.

'I think this would be a swell place to live,' he said.

Grace came out into the corridor just before Joe reached the door, dressed in another gingham day dress and smiling as if she were receiving guests for afternoon tea.

'Hello Joe,' she said, 'I'm glad you're back.'

Bewlay let out a surprised bark of wet laughter.

'Is Pollyanna here the one who's going to fix me?' he asked.

'Just shut the fuck up,' spat Joe. He pushed past her straight through the apartment's small entrance lobby and into the grand hall. 'Grace, get Maryam; whatever she's doing tell her to drop it. I need her to help this girl right now!'

Bewlay arrived behind him, looking around in genuine wonder.

'Wow,' he said.

Joe was looking for somewhere to lay Trudy down. He couldn't face the idea of negotiating her up that narrow, winding iron staircase to one of the beds. It had been bad enough getting her down Bewlay's cramped and crooked stairs to get out of that coal mine of a pub. He strode into the dining room. He would put her on the table in there—speed was what was important, not comfort.

Bewlay lingered outside in the grand hallway next to the coffin, genuinely puzzled.

'Is this meant to be encouraging?' he said, running a finger down the polished wood. 'It's not much of an advert for her services, is it?'

Joe ignored him, tearing himself away from Trudy to shout through the house.

'Maryam! We've got an emergency! Where are you?'

'Why dom't *you* heal her Joe?' Grace said, smiling brightly.

Joe stared at her.

'What? What are you talking about?'

Her smile wavered slightly. A tiny doubt crept into her eyes.

'You agreed . . . you would be the healer amd we would go away. Together . . .'

Bewlay had followed them quietly into the room.

'That's sweet,' he said. 'Love's young dream. There's nothing like it, but I'm afraid I want to be fixed now, so arrange it please Reverend Joe.'

'Fuck *off* Bewlay. You'll get your turn!'

Grace was staring at Bewlay's face now. Up to that point she'd had eyes solely for Joe.

'Take a picture, Heidi, it'll last longer,' Bewlay said.

He stepped closer to her, bringing his face right up to hers.

'Or would you like to smell the rot up close?'

She looked petrified and he laughed. Joe grabbed Grace by the shoulders.

'Go fetch Maryam. I have a very sick girl here and she's her only hope. Please Grace.'

Grace was now smiling again.

'Joe. We said you'd be the healer. It's *easy*, you just put your hamds om her amd . . .'

'For God's sake shut *up* Grace!' he shouted. 'This is serious! Go and get Maryam!'

She flinched away from him as if he'd just slapped her. He turned to the door—he'd just go fetch her himself—but she was there already.

'Maryam!' said Joe. 'Thank God.'

Bewlay took it in—her worn dressing gown, stick thin arms clad in soiled, yellowed opera gloves and her legs. They were just as thin, and looked like they were barely supporting what little weight she had. Her hair was Bride of Frankenstein crazy and her eyes pink-hued and gummy looking. He turned to Joe.

'Don't tell me,' he said. 'The coffin's hers.'

Maryam ignored his remark and took in his ravaged face, drawing her conclusion immediately. Cancer. She turned from him and gave her attention to the broken girl splayed across her dinner table. Maybe a road accident? She seemed to be in a very bad way indeed. What had Joe been doing, she thought—trawling for customers round terminal wards and emergency departments? Joe pushed past Bewlay and grabbed her arm, pulling her over to Trudy.

'You have to help this girl here Maryam, she's . . .'

Maryam resisted, pulling away, interrupting him.

'You have no right to do this,' she said. 'Who are these people? And what have you been saying to Grace about going away?'

'It doesn't matter just now!' he said. 'I'll explain everything later, will you please just get over here . . .'

'*Let*—*go*—*of*—me!' she shouted, her temper suddenly erupting. 'I healed you and I gave you a place to shelter and this is how you repay me? You make advances to my sister behind my back? She's no more than a child! And you bring these . . . *strangers* here demanding that I heal them! Take these persons and get out of here and never come back!'

'You don't understand,' Joe pleaded, 'please come and look at her, please just heal her! I promise to God, I promise faithfully on everything that I'll do whatever you want for the rest of my life, but please just come and fix her, please!'

'I said get out! You ungrateful, lying *whore* of a man! Get out you . . . *nothing*! Get out!'

'No!' Joe shouted right into her face, but she didn't flinch. 'You will heal this girl right now Maryam! I gave you everything you wanted last night and if I'm a fucking whore then I want my fucking payment! I want my payment, right now *goddammit*! You call *me* ungrateful? After what I fucking did for you last night? Get those fucking mummy's claws you call hands the fuck over here and fix her up right—the—fuck—*now*!'

'Get out, GET OUT!' she screamed, her arms now flailing at him

There was a deafening bang and everyone jumped as bits of ceiling showered down onto them.

'Ah,' sighed Bewlay, the acrid gunsmoke making the air feel greasy and his features momentarily hazy, his voice ringing tinny in everyone's ears. 'It's like you've been married all your lives.'

He strode with surprising speed to Trudy on the dining table, and pushed the nose of the still smoking gun barrel against her cheek. Joe could see the hot metal burning her face and he instinctively moved forward . . . but Bewlay clicked the hammer back and stopped him dead in his tracks.

'Now then,' he said, 'I don't really care about you two and your relationship—although I am encouraged at how seriously you both seem to take it. From what I know about couple counselling, that's a good thing, but I am running out of time, so unless I get my miracle right now, Reverend Joe . . .'

Bewlay pushed the gun barrel savagely upwards into Trudy's cheek, completely closing her already puffy eye.

'. . . then I'll blow this little street rat's brains out the top of her nasty little head and then the whole fucking thing becomes academic, doesn't it? For her, anyway.' He grinned.

'And then after that Joe, you will be next and then after *that*, if your better half there doesn't heal me, I'll kill this one . . .' He indicated Grace with a nod of his head. 'And if the desiccated landlady still refuses to heal me after *that*, then I will kill *her*. All the little ducks in a row. After all, what have I got to lose? Abso*fucking*lutely fuck all. Yes?'

Joe glared hatefully at him.

'And don't go giving me the Clint Eastwood, son. I've pushed out harder jobbies than you.'

For a few moments the only sound was the steady hum of the traffic on the street below.

'What have you brought into my house, Joe?' asked Maryam. She could barely choke out the words.

'I'm sorry.' Joe said. 'But, you weren't going to help me, were you?'

'Are you saying it's my fault there's a man in here with a gun threatening us?'

'No.' Joe sighed. 'I made a mistake . . . one in a long line. I'm really sorry . . . You'd better just do what he asks.'

'And then what?' she said. 'You think he'll just go away?'

'Yes,' said Bewlay, 'I'll just go away. If you can possibly do what he says you can, I'll be only too happy to fuck off home and not shoot anyone at all. So let's just get it over with and then you can all sit round this lovely rosewood table here and have a cup of tea and a nice chat about whether or not to heal the little stinking cunt who's bleeding all over it, ok?'

Grace looked between them, frightened. Joe began trying to calculate the odds on his least worst case scenario. It would be a question of how to get the gun. If he moved for it, Bewlay would hopefully swing it up at *him* and therefore away from Trudy or Grace. On the downside, Bewlay would definitely get at least one shot fired before Joe could get his hands on him . . . .but even with a bullet in him, Joe thought, if he was lucky his momentum would carry him on to Bewlay and he could then put all of his—possibly at this point now dead—weight on the bastard, bringing him down. He was certainly heavier than Bewlay that was for sure. After that, it would be a question of how many more shots Bewlay would be able get off before Maryam and Grace could possibly manage to get the gun from him. *If* they could.

They should hit him with something.

From the dining table, Skinny moaned softly. Bewlay brightened.

'I think young Trudy is waking up,' he said. 'That's lucky, Joe, she'll get to see you one more time before she finds out what happens to someone when they die.'

Joe prayed he'd be able to stay alive long enough to shout some instructions to Grace, who was seriously the only one who had any chance of getting Bewlay once he was down. Something like 'hit him with a fucking chair!' would do, he thought, anything, just so that Maryam and Grace weren't both standing there like dummies as he bled to death all over Bewlay. He realised he was equivocating. Fuck equivocating. Ban*fucking*zai! He moved . . . but Grace grabbed his arm and broke his step. He twisted and looked at her. What?! He pulled away and misstepped again. Bewlay, surprised but recovering well, swung the gun up at him and then . . . well then it was all over. It was all too late. Fuck it! She'd 'read' what he was going to do . . . and she'd stopped him. All over in a second.

'Whoa, easy Tex,' said Bewlay. He kept the gun pointed at Joe as he walked around to the other side of the table, not taking his eyes from him until he was standing next to Skinny's head again. He grabbed her jaw and pulled her mouth open, thrusting the gun barrel down her throat, not bothering too much about chipping her teeth. She groaned again and Joe glared at Grace. She shook her head, looking terrified.

'To be frank, Reverend Joe, Skinny'll be much better off dead,' said Bewlay. 'D'you not think?'

That was it, Joe thought. Whatever small opportunity there may have been had evaporated. He didn't think that Maryam would be able to heal someone whose head had been turned into particles and vapour.

'Please Bewlay,' said Joe. 'Don't.'

'You wouldn't know, of course,' Bewlay continued, 'but she's quite an independent person now that she's all grown up. Quite . . . feisty. She'd be crippled for life if she survived this—and she wouldn't want that, I can guarantee you.'

He used his free hand to lift the stained and matted sheeting away from her for a moment. It made an unpleasant ripping sound as the dried blood pulled away from her skin. Bewlay drew in a breath with a theatrical hiss and made a face.

'Ouch,' he said. 'No . . . that wouldn't do for the girl I know at all. She wouldn't want to be feeling like a watering can every time she went for a piss; hobbling about the place with her toot toot hanging down in strips like the dog's been at it. In fact I wouldn't even feed her to a fucking dog, the state she's in. Don't take her to a hospital, she won't thank you in the long run. Best just say bye bye, Reverend Joe . . . .'

'Please, Maryam!' shouted Joe. 'Please, for God's sake! She can't die! She can't! Not like this! Please just fix him and help her!'

'If she's going to die anyway, Joe, it might be better that it's quick,' said Maryam quietly.

Joe stared at her, open mouthed. What?

'Oh, in the name of Christ,' said Bewlay, 'tell you what, Reverend— since nobody but you seems to give a bat's fucking testicle whether Trudy lives or dies I'm going to try a radically new approach.'

He indicated Grace.

'I'll stick my gun up Heidi's fanny instead. Maybe that'll get things moving a bit faster round here, hm?' Bewlay continued, 'How'd you like to see your little pal get a bullet up her box, Maryam? *That* something you could heal? Bit of a challenge? Or maybe it wouldn't bother you, since she seems to be trying to get her hands on Joe here. I'm sorry to say, but she does have youth on her side. What do you think? Shall I just go and do it anyway?'

'Joe?' Grace said. 'He's goimg to do it . . . I cam see it imside his . . .'

'I *know* he's going to do it, Grace,' he snapped. 'Just fucking shut up!'

She flinched away from him again, but he knew he had to shut her down. Christ knew what Bewlay would do if he thought that there was someone who could see into people's heads. Take her home with him and keep her in a cage probably. Maryam stepped forward and placed her hand onto Bewlay's. After a brief moment, he allowed her to gently pull the gun away from pointing at her sister.

'You are terminally ill, mister . . . ?' she asked.

'Bewlay.' He smiled at her. 'Yes, Maryam. Currently, I am.'

She smiled back at him, breathing an understated and sadly resigned sigh, and Joe thought she looked like a well-rehearsed ward sister preparing to give bad news to some regular schmo. That would be a mistake. Bewlay was not a regular schmo.

'Maryam . . .' Joe said.

'I wasn't speaking to you, Joe,' she said, polite but firm. She turned her attention again to Bewlay.

'I'm sorry,' she said, the very acme of gentleness, '. . . but I really can't help you.'

'Really?'

'Yes,' said Maryam. 'Really. I honestly can't.'

'I see,' said Bewlay, his voice flat. 'Forgive me for saying so, but it hasn't in any way been sounding like that for the last few minutes. In fact it's sounded to me like you could very much help me but you were just not wanting to. Tell you what—why don't you search in that big, soft, old heart of yours just a little more. For me.'

'I'm afraid, Mister Bewlay, that I'm completely unable to be of any assistance in your sort of case whether I search in my heart or not.'

'Hm—'my sort of case' . . . so, you *are* saying that you can help people but you can't help me, yes?'

'Yes.'

'May I ask why it is that you can't help me?'

'I am unable to cure terminally ill people,' she said.

Bewlay blew air from his cheeks.

'Well, right . . . gosh,' he said. 'I suppose that's that then, isn't it? No point flogging a dead horse, is there?'

'No,' she said. 'There isn't.'

'It's a real shame though,' he sighed. 'I seem to have come all this way for nothing, don't I? Hang on though . . . Joe? Can she heal me? Truth, please—you know what I'm like when I'm annoyed at someone.'

'I can do nothing for you so could you please leave now?' Maryam said.

Joe's heart sank. Oh Christ, what was she doing? She was obviously lying and Bewlay could see it. He didn't know why Maryam didn't like fixing terminal cases and right now he didn't give a holy fuck.

'Yes, Bewlay,' he said. 'She can heal you.'

He turned to Maryam. He'd expected her to be glaring at him, full beam infuriation,but she was just standing there looking down at her gloved hands crossed in front of her.

'Listen Maryam,' Joe said 'right now the only chance any of us have got is if you fix this motherfucker, so please just get on with it!'

Bewlay rattled the gun barrel against Skinny's teeth.

'Ting a ling! Not got all day, Maryam,' he said, 'last chance.'

She spoke without looking at him.

'How do I know you won't just kill all of us if I heal you?' she said.

Bewlay shrugged.

'Beats me. Or was that a rhetorical question?' he said, 'because I do know that if you *don't* heal me, you'll definitely be dead.'

'You're truly giving me no choice, Mister Bewlay, are you?'

'Not in any real sense, no,' he said, amused.

'Just as long as I have that absolutely clear.'

Bewlay's mind was squirming with excitement at the very possibility of what might be about to happen to him. Joe could see it—the ill-disguised avarice in his eyes. Bewlay had seen Joe's remarkable recovery and he wanted his own share of miracles. All of Maryam's refusals and reluctance had only made him the hungrier for it. It was like a really good con, except that this wasn't any kind of con at all.

'Let's get it over with,' said Maryam.

She moved toward him, her mind looping round and round—she had no choice, she told herself—she had no choice! She had refused again and again and he'd *made* her do it. She'd waited until the last minute—risking other people's lives—and now she had no choice in the matter, her conscience would be clear. Whatever happened now, it was this man's own fault.

'Do I have to lie down?' said Bewlay. 'Take anything off?'

'I would rather you didn't,' said Maryam.

Maryam began to place the palm of her hand over Bewlay's face and he jerked away.

'Stay still!' she commanded. 'If I could do this long distance, I wouldn't be receiving such charming visitors all the time.'

He stood still. Joe noticed that the gun had come out of Trudy's mouth. It was still at her face, but resting on her chin. That would have to do, he thought. Maryam replaced the palm of her hand over the hole in Bewlay's face and closed her eyes. Joe tensed—he was ready. When Bewlay started getting the sweats or the heebie jeebies or whatever the hell it was that happened when Maryam ran her magic fingers over the afflicted, he was going to leap over that goddam table and pull the ugly fucker down, regardless of Maryam or what she was doing. Then he was going to stamp on the bastard's face until he broke his foot.

He glanced at Grace, then down at her fingers tightly gripping his arm. He glared at her and she dropped her arm. Good. He looked back at Maryam and Bewlay, waiting for the magic to kick in . . . but Maryam only trembled slightly. Bewlay's eyes watered, his cheeks flushed red, then he gasped like a man who had just come . . . and then it was over. The whole thing must have taken about three seconds, thought Joe. What the hell?

Maryam stepped away, seemingly unaffected by the whole thing.

'Was that it?' said Bewlay, rubbing the wetness from his eyes with his free hand.

'What were you expecting?' she said. 'A brass band?'

'Well some sort of song and dance, at least. That's *all*? Really? It seemed effortless.'

'Are you complaining?' she said.

'Joe said it was going to be painful.'

Bewlay had seemed unchanged, Joe thought, until right now. He could see that the man's irises were already losing their dead greyness; the dirty ivory around them becoming whiter.

Maryam shrugged.

'Severity of treatment depends on the affliction,' she said. 'Joe had smashed bone and pulped flesh and massive loss of blood, all you've got are a few cells gone wrong.'

'Is that so?' he said. 'Then why were you so reluctant to do this for me?'

'There are side effects,' she said.

'Now you tell me.'

'Not for you,' she said. 'For me.'

She looked at Joe and fought back the tears . . . but there was to be no self-pity. Not anymore. Not in this house.

'Imagine the amount of energy that was required to break Joe's body like that. The same amount was required to fix him, except that it was all coming from me.' She smiled. 'You'd think I belong in a coffin.'

Bewlay gazed at her very carefully for a few moments, something slowly dawning on him.

'How old are you Maryam?' asked Bewlay.

'How old do you think I am?' she asked. Bewlay shrugged.

A weird chill went through Joe. Maryam was too old to be Grace's sister, he realised. It would be impossible . . . just impossible—but he *had* accepted it as a fact when she'd told him. Why? Why had he not even questioned it in the face of the extremely obvious age difference between the women? He had a terrible feeling that he was lagging behind on something.

'I'm twenty-six-years-old,' she said.

Joe's eyes widened. What? That was impossible! Impossible! . . . but now, that she'd said it he suddenly knew that it was true. In bed, she had moved like a much younger woman . . . she had felt, when he was inside her, like a much younger woman. When she had told him that she loved him, her voice . . . her voice . . .

He didn't notice Grace letting his arm go and just standing back, chewing her knuckles, eyes downcast.

'My so-called healing gift has done this to me,' she said. 'Every time I lay my hands on an afflicted person, a little bit of something precious goes from me. It sucks the life from me—it's like a law of nature. You don't get something for nothing . . . for every action there is an equal and opposite etcetera—whatever you might want to call it . . .'

Bewlay whistled.

'Well I'm sorry about that Maryam,' said Bewlay. 'That is the shit end of the stick.'

'It doesn't matter,' she said.

'Maryam . . .' Joe said, going to her. 'My God, Maryam . . .'

Maryam turned sharply and glared at him, her eyes sending him an urgent signal—*just shut up*. He shut up.

'So . . . what's done is done,' she said 'and I would like you to leave us all alone now, if you wouldn't mind. That was the arrangement after all, wasn't it?'

Bewlay felt his face, his fingers tentatively exploring the open hole in its centre. He frowned at her, the question in his eyes.

'I'm a healer,' she said, 'not a plastic surgeon. Your cancer is gone forever, never to return, but then so is your nose. I can join things together that are broken, but I can't make things appear that aren't there. You'll have to pay a more conventional practitioner for any work you might want done on that.'

'For Christ sakes Bewlay, hasn't she done enough?' said Joe. 'You're healed aren't you?'

'I do feel different,' he said. 'I feel like . . . something has left me . . .'

Maryam cleared her throat.

'Yes,' she said, 'your cancer. You are healed. You know it inside of you . . . you suddenly feel good don't you? Better than you have for a long time, better than you can ever remember even from when you were well, isn't that right?'

Suddenly he nodded, his face breaking into a wide grin. After a few moments, he laughed again, long and hard and hugely good-natured. He uncocked the pistol. Maryam glanced over at Joe and looked quickly away again. He was shocked at the bleakness he could see in her eyes . . . and then the look was gone and she was giving her attention back to Bewlay.

'So before you leave us, do you have the money?' she asked. 'That is the case, isn't it Mister Bewlay? Joe went to you and offered you my gift in exchange for your money?'

'Maryam!' said Joe, 'The money doesn't matter! Please . . .'

'Yes it does, Joe. Very clearly so,' she said, 'otherwise you wouldn't have gone to see Mister Bewlay, would you? And we would not all be in each other's company right now, would we?'

She turned to Bewlay again.

'We're operating on a business level only, Joe and I. We'll discuss our new arrangements once you have given me whatever fee you promised him.'

'Left it back at my place,' Bewlay said breezily. 'We were in a bit of a rush. Though I'm not so fucking sure about paying up anymore actually because I'm going to be needing lots of money for my rhinoplasty, eh? I mean really, really *good* surgery. Maybe

I'll have to go to America to get it. They can fix all sorts out there, better than here, I hear. Ha!'

He was sounding manic and too loud now, Joe thought. Babbling. Colour had returned to his face and he also seemed to have filled out a little. Health was pouring itself back into him as each moment passed. Another miracle from the house of Maryam. Joe was willing Bewlay to leave—to just get the hell out so that she could get on with fixing Trudy. Just *go*, Bewlay . . .

'There's a man out in . . . Florida? Arizona? Alaska? Anyway, he fixes blown up kids from war zones,' Bewlay continued, speaking faster and faster with each utterance. 'You know, kids with *completely* melted faces, but he's private practice too and makes a fortune as well I saw it on TV. Wow, fucking hell, I really feel different. Really good. Really, *really* good.'

Je*sus*, thought Joe. Get a goddam grip and fuck off.

'So you aren't going to pay?' Maryam said. 'I personally don't really care; it was for Joe's sake that I was asking. I just want to know that every piece of your business here is completed and over, so that you can go away and leave us alone for good.'

'Don't be like that,' said Bewlay.

He stared at her for a moment, pop-eyed and unblinking, and then broke into a huge grin.

'You know,' he said, 'I can tell you this—in my entire life I have never felt as good as I do right now! I feel so fucking amazing. *Amaaaaaaazing!*'

'It'll pass,' said Maryam.

Bewlay was laughing out loud again. It was an ugly sound, thought Joe, coming out of two holes simultaneously. Bewlay turned his newfound manic enthusiasm onto Joe, who felt his hand being grabbed and shaken vigorously . . . although Joe noted that the hand holding the gun was still pretty steady, the barrel pointed straight at him.

'Thank you for this, Reverend Joe,' Bewlay said. 'Really, genuinely, thank you. You might not believe it, but I actually liked you! Really! For real!'

Joe stared at him; the hanging tumours in Bewlay's nose had completely gone and the hole in the centre of his face looked cleaner.

It made him think of the body cavity of a gutted chicken that had been very thoroughly washed out, but he thought he wouldn't say so. Joe flashed to an image in his mind for a moment of punching Bewlay down and strangling him to death, the bastard's eyes popping out of his purpled and blackening face . . . but all he wanted right now was to get Trudy fixed. He really didn't care about anything else.

'Please just leave us,' Joe said.

He got the impression that Bewlay's eyes were shining now, something about the electric wall candelabras reflecting in them, making them look . . . not right. His face was flushed and ruddy, but it was his *eyes* . . . the pupils seemed to be expanding and contracting—from one extreme to the other—almost every time he blinked. Joe wondered what the world looked like through such eyes.

'Listen, Reverend,' he said, 'I . . . about the money. You come by and I'll make sure you and Maryam here get something worthwhile for your trouble. I made a deal, yes? It'll be honoured, ok? It will, it must be, because honour is what separates men from beasts, hm?'

Maryam's heart jumped. What? What had he said? Men and beasts? The coincidence gave her a chill, like someone had walked over her grave. Bewlay was still jabbering on.

'. . . so I'm fixed up, so Skinny'll be right as rainbows as well, won't she? So let's let bygones be bygones and start a new chapter, hm? Hm?'

He let go of Joe's hand and turned to Maryam.

'Beautiful place you have here Maryam—I've got a beautiful place too. Same guy behind it all, yes. Maybe we can start up a wee business venture, eh? Tours? Historic Glasgow kind of thing? Hm? It's a subject I've been getting into a lot . . .'

He stood there, clearly aware that he was babbling but seemingly unable to stop himself. His face flushed.

'What do you say to the person who's just saved your life?' he said. 'I don't know. Good luck, I suppose. You come by for that wee bit money there Reverend Joe, do you hear me?'

He took Maryam's hand and shook it also.

'Once I've had my face fixed up, I'll call back and see you again.'

'You won't,' she said.

He stopped then for a second, about to laugh and then . . . there was something now in the back of his mind. A feeling he was growing dimly aware of. Not so much a worry, but a worry about a worry . . . a nagging feeling . . . left the gas on . . . forgot to pay a bill . . . missed an appointment at the dentist . . . a feeling there was something important missing from somewhere?

But then it was gone.

Still, he wanted to get out of here, it was starting to feel a bit hot. Embarrassment, probably. He knew he'd been gibbering pish like he'd just won an Oscar. He really wanted to get himself home and start tidying up. He'd need a clean HQ if he was going to start getting his business back together again—and that meant absolutely no dead Big Ian lying about the place, that was for sure! He'd do the polite thing and thank Maryam again—she really was the seventh wonder of the world. He supposed that he'd been too wrapped up in his problems . . . too concerned about his mortality . . . maybe even too morphined up to realise what a world shattering thing this was that had happened to him. For fuck's sake, he thought, you could in theory live for fucking ever! He looked around and found that he was now in the tiled communal hallway outside the front door of Maryam's apartment. How the fuck did he get *here*? He had no memory at all of walking out.

He had become aware of a weird sensation and it took him a few moments to realise what it was.

It was his posture, of all things—he was standing up straight again. He hadn't realised how stooped he had become! My God, he thought, I've just added another five or six inches to my height!

Delighted as a happy child, he clapped his hands together and went down the stairs two at a time. That fucking lift was way too fucking slow for a man who had lots to do.

◆

Joe was looking at the doorway. One second Bewlay had been standing there dribbling nonsense at them, the next he'd clammed up completely, turned on his heel and had practically skipped out of the apartment without another word, or even an acknowledgement that they were there.

Maryam looked awful, he thought. Whatever little life or animation she'd had in her face seemed to have completely drained from her. She felt her way down the length of the table to a chair.

'Here,' said Joe, 'let me help you . . .'

She waved him away, looking distraught, and sat herself down heavily. She was wheezing like an iron lung. What had happened to her was heartbreaking—truly terrible and he felt such pity for her. But he also knew any attempt to try and comfort her would be hypocritical in the extreme, because he also knew she would soon have to do it again, or that he would have to *make* her do it again. For Trudy. She wouldn't want to—and looking into his own heart, he knew that *he* didn't want her to either, but . . . she would *have* to—and soon. He hated himself, but he had to get to work on her.

'Look Maryam,' he began, 'I know it took a lot out of you . . .'

She looked up at him then and he shut up, shocked at the bleak hopelessness on her face.

'It took a lot more from him,' she said quietly. 'Oh God forgive me, what have I done? Before . . . it was ignorance—*I didn't know*—how could I? But this time . . . I knew . . . and I still did it . . .'

Then she began to weep. Joe went to her.

'Maryam, you have to help this girl now,' he said, 'I'm sorry, but you have to help just one last person before you stop. Please . . .'

She pulled back from him and sat up, wiping her tears away with the back of her gloved hand.

'Do you love her?' she said.

'It's not like that . . .'

'Not like what? I only asked if you love her Joe. Do you?'

'Yes.'

'What is she to you?' Maryam said.

'She's family. From a long time ago when we were kids,' he said. 'She's my cousin and we went through . . . we went through a lot together. I promised to look after her and I didn't. I want to now. I have to.'

Grace was playing with her hair beneath the portrait of the old man. She sniffed loudly and Joe glanced over at her. She too had been crying, he could see. Maryam was managing pretty much to get herself back together again.

'Family. That's important, yes, of course.' She wheezed. 'It's the most important thing.'

She stood up and Joe began to lead her back to Trudy, but she gently shook him off.

'Is she going to die Joe?'

Her voice had a lost, hollow quality to it that he didn't like. Because Maryam didn't help people who were going to die, did she? Unless it was at gunpoint. He thought fast. He really had no idea whether Trudy was going to die or not, but he wasn't going to take that risk. To get Maryam onside, he realised, there was only one simple answer—Trudy *wasn't* going to die.

'She'll only die if we let her, Maryam,' said Joe. 'She's just like I was when you fixed me, I reckon. Badly injured, but not fatally.'

'In that case, you'd better take her to a hospital as soon as you can.'

'But you could heal her right here and now . . .'

'I'm tired, Joe. This takes more out of me than you appreciate.'

'You have to heal her, Maryam, for God's sake you have to!'

'I don't have to do anything! Why should I? Because you say so?'

She turned away and Joe grabbed her roughly, half dragging her over to the raggedy, bloody mess on the table.

'Because *look*!' he shouted. 'Look at her! Look what he's done to her!'

Joe pulled Trudy's jeans down and pried back the dark, wet sheet. Maryam looked and Joe could see on her face her shock as she registered the full awfulness at what had happened. That was good—it meant she would bend her stupid rules for him. Grace had come over too and timidly stepped closer for a peek. She gasped. After a few moments Maryam spoke again, her voice now shaky.

'I can't help her, Joe.'

He stared at her, incredulous.

'What do you mean? Maryam! You have to!'

'If she means that much to you, I especially won't help her,' she said.

'Why?' Joe said. 'This doesn't make sense . . .'

Maryam walked away from the girl on the table. He followed her like a supplicant but she couldn't look at him. The image of what had been done to the girl had been seared onto her mind.

'It makes perfect sense,' she said. 'I will not heal her, for her own sake.'

'Maryam . . . please . . . I'll go back, I will, I'll go back to Bewlay and get the money for you . . . please . . .'

'Don't you dare go near him, Joe! Don't you dare! It isn't anything to do with money!' she shouted. 'I won't heal people who are meant to die.'

'What if she's not meant to die?' he yelled back.

Maryam rounded on him, furious.

'You don't know that! And if she *is* meant to, then believe me, you don't want me to lay one finger on her.'

'Why not? What could you possibly do to her that would be worse than this?'

'You are wasting time, Joe!' she shouted. 'Call an ambulance! Now!'

Joe got down on his knees and grabbed Maryam's hands.

'Look,' he said, 'is this some kind of jealousy thing? Is it? She's my family, Maryam—family!'

'Joe, please don't . . .'

'I'm begging you, *literally* begging you. What I did for you last night? Our arrangement? You don't owe me a thing. Ok? Not a thing, no money, no deals, no damn all. I don't want anything apart from this one thing for her. I'll do anything for you. I'll stay here with you for the rest of my life but please for the love of God, please help her . . .'

Tears filled Maryam's eyes. He could see the compassion in them. He knew that she was going to help, she was . . .

She was shaking her head.

No.

30

THE SKY WAS A VERY DARK GREY—ALMOST BLACK AND ROOFTOP low—but Sauchiehall Street, particularly here at the Charing Cross end beneath the huge clock on the corner of the Mansions, was being blindingly illuminated by the low sun like a floodlight's beam. It was a beautiful, atmospheric look that Arthur found unique to Scotland and which he loved, with the light giving everything a glamour otherwise lacking in this stupidly overlong, drab road of fast food, chemicals and cheap booze.

He had come to his senses, the brightness of the sun reflecting this new clarity of thought. His cancer had started shortly after he had killed his brother, specifically after Tommy's memorable funeral, and now he knew that it had been the mark of Cain. The poison that he'd been repressing from that dreadful time had been slowly hatching out of him and killing him . . . until Maryam, the miracle woman, had taken it all away. He was feeling overwhelmed still by what had just happened, in many ways it was almost too incredible to take in fully. But he was going to be starting a new life now, and he decided that he had to begin with a clean slate. There was to be no more lying to himself, no more subjugation of unpalatable facts for his convenience . . . he didn't want anything else festering away inside him to cause any more fucking tumours. He was going to stare truth in the face.

Starting now, he thought, leaning against the red sandstone of the building as passers-by criss-crossed in front of him on their way to and from the ordinary, dull places which defined their lives.

It was a terrible thing, he reflected, to have one's faith in someone comprehensively destroyed by the chance hearing of an offhand remark. Arthur had grown used to hearing Tommy talking away to himself in his wee room as he had grown up. Years locked away from anyone but himself and Da couldn't have done anything but taken their toll on his mental health, but hearing Tommy falteringly rehearse a statement to the *police* about him and his *strictly personal and private* activities, had been the shocker, and the reason that Tommy had to go.

There had been no junky whores the night Tommy had died in the middle of Glasgow Green—none that he had seen in the darkness on his way to the big tree with his brother at any rate.

Tommy hadn't at all been on a whore hunt for underage action the night he'd died. Tommy hadn't and wouldn't have wanted anything to do with them anyway because Tommy was completely incapable of sexual behaviours, and always had been. Tommy hadn't been the watcher of any kind of tapes either, it had been Arthur.

Tommy had just been Arthur's cover story.

He had taken his brother across the grass in the intermittent moonlight to the large trunked tree. It was a location Arthur had used before on the occasions when he'd felt like outdoors fun. He would tie someone up naked and leave them there when he'd finished with them, their laughably small, but hard-bargained for fee stuffed into whatever orifice he'd been greasing most, and there they would stay until the parkies or the cops came to cut them loose, usually in the morning. It was an activity, Arthur thought, especially to be enjoyed in the winter. No prosecutions ever followed. They were desperate, these girls or boys, but they weren't stupid.

On reaching the tree, he had sat Tommy down gently on the thick, gnarly root that stuck out from the ground like a big, bony elbow.

It was a bad place this.

People injured themselves around here, tripping over these exposed roots. Little climbers fell from big branches. There had been broken limbs and such. Arthur was always careful to watch his footing whenever he was here after dark.

Tommy had asked him what all of this was about and Arthur had stood behind his brother and without another word to him had cut right across his throat, right down to the wee man's vertebrae, with his mother of pearl and ivory handled antique Victorian long-scalpel—a long-winded description, for sure, but that was exactly as it had been painstakingly labelled when he'd bought it.

The metal had sliced easily and very quickly through his brother's thick , fleshy neck, instantly severing all of Tommy's main cables and tubes. His head had suddenly jerked backwards like a flip top and there had been a geyser spume of hot blood that erupted upward and out from him. It had been like lifting the lid from a pressure cooker while it was still boiling away on the hob. Tommy's blood had spurted so high, in fact, that it had been still dripping from the leaves overhead when Arthur had eventually left, the falling drops sounding like the soft pit-pat of an approaching summer shower.

Arthur had never seen anything like it.

It was probably due to Tommy's smaller stature, he had thought. Maybe blood was more densely packed in people of restricted height. Did they have the same eight pints swilling around inside them as regular people? If so, then no wonder Tommy had burst like a ripe zit.

Arthur had never used his scalpel before that night. It had felt appropriate that he do so for this occasion though—it was a solemn and serious act and his brother's specialness had warranted its use. Practically cried out for it, in fact.

It had a blade as long as a bread knife's but with a straight edge—a remarkable instrument and one that Arthur had just happened upon one rainy Sunday afternoon whilst looking through the more diseased and obscure stalls at Paddy's Market. The rheumy old fella who had sold it to him had clicked open the long, velvet lined mahogany and jet inlaid case and had told Arthur that the blade had never been (and would never need to be) sharpened. To do so would ruin it, apparently.

The sales fella had smelt bad, *really* bad, which was saying something since his barrow was right at the very back and in the darkest corner of the damp and mouldy railway arches that served as home for this poorest of poor markets. Arthur had left with his purchase as soon as he could, after noting that there was absolutely nothing else of interest on the man's stall. It had seemed to be covered in swathes of mouldy, red velvet curtain material with gold ties still attached, looking like for all the world like little hula skirts.

Tommy had bled out almost instantly, which Arthur had been glad of. He had been disappointed in his brother, but hadn't wanted to make him suffer unduly. He'd still, however, had to wrench the head back and forth and side to side in order to finally separate it from the spinal column. In the end, he had pulled so hard—and Tommy's greasy hair had been so slick with his own blood—that once separated, the head had slipped out from his fingers, away and gone flying from Arthur's grip, hitting the tree trunk behind him. With a *thu-thunk* sound, followed by a *crackle* once it landed on the dried leaves on the ground, it had started rolling back toward Arthur over the gritty earth.

Arthur hadn't liked that sound.

Thu-thunk.

Crackle.

The head of his precious brother whom he had genuinely loved so much should not be rolling around on the ground where the used condoms and stray dog shit littered.

Thu-thunk.

But Tommy had been planning on betraying him, hadn't he? Arthur had *needed* to do something.

Crackle.

It was amazing how much honour, Arthur reflected, was involved in the mindset of the scumbags he employed and associated with. Honour was, of course, a flexible term, but 'honour' certainly wouldn't have included the sexual molestation of his own brother from infancy. Had *that* gotten out via Tommy's faltering, barely literate 'statement' he'd been rehearsing for the cops, Arthur would have lost his reputation ... and the losing of reputation was the start of a ride down the slippery slope to mockery and betrayal and premature death. The junkies and the dealers, the whores and the petty grifters—those plankton at the bottom of the great money chain—they didn't have much going for them as individuals, but as a whispering, chattering, mocking mob they would be pretty effective at undermining one's authority, and once that was gone, you were fair game. For when common knowledge became public knowledge, it was the beginning of the end. No matter how terrifying one was, everything could fall apart in the face of open mockery.

Even Caesar had been afraid of the mob.

That was why, on the walk back to the car, small splots of blood from Tommy's raggedy neck dripping in arcs onto the grass as Arthur had gently swung it, Arthur had explained to his brother that he felt very strongly that *he* couldn't be seen as the type of person who watched the kinds of films he made Tommy sit and watch with him. Regular porn, yes. But not this stuff—not the kind of stuff which would give people license to believe that they had some kind of insight into his psychology.

He'd found an old, plastic Co-op bag in the boot of the car—it had actually been completely full of gram wraps of coke, but Arthur just emptied them out to make room for his brother's head before putting it in, driving home and popping it into the freezer.

◆

The rattle of a passing cab shook Arthur from his dwam and he jerked his head up, suddenly back in Sauchiehall Street. He shivered violently, feeling very cold now, all of the glow he had felt only moments ago, the shiny brightness of the world was suddenly all gone. Everything looked ordinary. It looked dull and grey and colourless.

Why was he was feeling down when he should have been on top of the world? He had faced down the facts of what he had done—he had, more or less, 'confessed' to himself, and confession was good for the soul was it not? So why wasn't he happy? Why was he being a loser instead of a winner? He had to do something about this . . . this . . . whatever the fuck 'this' was. It needed sorting—but *how*?

And then Arthur had his epiphany.

He needed to do more than just face up to what he had done to Tommy—he needed to *atone*. He laughed; genuinely, openly and with good heart, for now he knew *just* what to do to make it up to his brother.

He turned around and headed straight back in to the Mansions.

31

'Ring an ambulance please Grace,' said Maryam.

Joe shuffled, dazed, over to Trudy. What else could he possibly do to persuade her? The simple answer seemed to be absolutely nothing. There weren't any options.

'I need to wash her...' he mumbled. 'I need to get her cleaned up... she's a...'

He tried to look away from her but couldn't. He embraced her as gently as possible, amazed once more at how light she was. 'She's in a mess...'

'Grace,' said Maryam. 'Telephone, *please*.'

But Grace was simply staring at the girl on the table and at Joe trying to care for her.

'Very well,' said Maryam, straining to sound like she was in control. 'I'll do it myself. That young woman needs medical attention as soon as possible.'

She hurried out of the room, away from the heartbreaking sight of Joe and the poor, wretched thing in his arms, rushing away as swiftly as she could, before Joe could see her tears and think he could use them to bend her to his will. Before he could work on her and persuade her to heal. In truth she would have done anything for him—she *would* give this girl the very last of her strength—if she could only be sure she wasn't supposed to die. But she couldn't be sure of that. And if the girl *was* dying and she healed her... it would not only destroy her, it would obliterate Joe utterly.

Grace went to the door and quietly closed it before rejoining Joe. He was standing over his cousin now, gently wiping away some smuts that were spotted across her burnt, filthy face. She looked so extraordinarily small to him, her features so different and yet still so recognisable, like she'd left his side as a child and returned several seconds later as an adult. There were no in between days. Not anymore.

'I couldn't help her, Grace,' he said. 'Not then, not now.'

He was determined now to get Trudy cleaned up; he could at least do that for her before abandoning her to the paramedics. He couldn't go to the hospital with her, too many questions would be asked. The grotesque things that had been done to her would be all over the papers and so would he and besides, what would be the point? What could he possibly do for her that would make any of this in any way 'better'? Killing Bewlay wasn't something he particularly had any heart for any more either, the heat and the anger had left him, replaced by an awful damp blanket of depression and dread.

He felt defeated and unutterably sad. After this, what point was there to anything? He realised that he had screwed up the one and only important thing in his entire life that he was actually supposed to do—come back for her. That he hadn't done so, that he had wasted his so-called life on himself and his own selfish and stupid wants and desires and hadn't made good on his promise to her, scoured at his insides like bleach. He could have done it. He could have made it back to her; even if he hadn't any money for anything else, he *could* have . . . and maybe have made a difference to her rotten, desperate life. But he'd told himself that people grew up, that they forgot promises, and that things sorted themselves out, and had ended up only finally coming back because he was on the run and had no other motherfucking place left to go.

What a fucking hero.

Grace took his hands in hers, squeezing them gently. He barely noticed. She tugged at him and when he looked up she smiled and he managed a small twitch of his lips in return, starting to get a grip. What the fuck good was he doing standing here like a prick feeling sorry for himself? he thought. He had to start doing what he could for her. He realised that Grace had taken his hands and had placed them palm down over Trudy's wounds.

'What are you doing?'

'You be the healer now, Joe,' she said.

Oh for Christ's sake, he thought miserably, this just got better and better didn't it? What had he done? To Trudy, to Maryam . . . to poor Grace? What kind of a man was he? Was there any way of bringing Grace down gently? He sighed.

'I'm not a healer Grace. I'm sorry I lied to you . . . about everything. But I can't do what Maryam does . . .' He felt his eyes tearing up . . . and he hated himself for it. What right did *he* have to cry about anything?

'I kmow you arem't a real healer Joe,' Grace said. 'Of *course* I kmow that! But that doesm't matter, because Maryam ism't either.'

He had to strain to hear her now, because along with an ever brightening light, there was a huge rushing sound, like a train coming into a station, and he remembered from when Maryam had laid her hands on his wounds at the hospital. He could feel Trudy's flesh beneath his fingers knitting together, like a bag full of small, live things. Everything was getting brighter and brighter . . . Grace was smiling, her beautiful face made even more so in this golden light that was pouring *out* from him and into Trudy.

❖

Maryam stood leaning on the kitchen table for support, determined not to cry or do anything that would show any sort of visible upset to Joe. He would never be able to understand why she had refused to heal his cousin because she had decided that she would never, ever tell him. Now he would simply hate her and she would simply live with it, and she could comfort herself with the knowledge that she would not be healing *anyone* again for as long as she lived.

She stopped her mind from jabbering to itself any further. Aside from it being pointless and annoying, she had noticed that there was something different about the room. The full glass of water that she had left untouched on the table was empty now. Had she drunk it? When? She cursed under her breath. Was she to be receiving the gift of Alzheimer's now along with everything else that was wrong with her? Well too bad, she thought, and to hell with whatever new and interesting afflictions she did or didn't have. She had to see about getting proper medical attention for the poor girl next door.

She pushed herself away from the table and loped as swiftly as she could over to the old-fashioned dial phone that lay beneath the good plate cupboard, but hadn't managed to reach it before she heard the door closing softly behind her. She sighed to herself. Joe had obviously come sneaking in to be alone with her, to attempt to persuade her to change her mind. She must be strong, she thought, she must be. She would scream and shout at him and break his heart and make him hate her—hate her more than he already did. She must make him despise her, so much so that he would never ever be under the impression that he could somehow make her do this thing for his cousin, or indeed, for anyone else ever again. She braced herself—she could be very hard, she knew *that* for sure, and now she would be the hardest she had ever been with anyone.

She spun around and he stepped halfway out of the shadows at the far side of the kitchen and her heart missed a beat. He was between her and the door.

'You have to help me again Maryam,' he said.

His voice was gentle, and all the more awful for it. Maryam noticed now—too late—the puddle of water on the worn linoleum by the table. He must have spilled it, she thought. She could have seen it from out in the hall if she'd been paying attention! Then she would have known something was wrong and she would not have just blundered in here. He saw where she was looking.

'I spat it out . . .' said Bewlay, 'I was thirsty. But the water . . . it tasted off, to be frank. You need to get your supply looked at, dear.'

It's started, she thought. Everything had tasted foul to Papa after being cured, hadn't it? She made a superhuman effort to stay calm and focused on the mundanity of the small puddle of spilt water on a floor that needed cleaning, and not look to the kitchen door and risk giving away the only plan of action she had. The door was only a few feet behind him and if she could somehow get past him to the sink, she'd make it. She'd be able to run into the tiny, white-walled connecting passage outside and slam the door over. There was a very, very old, oversized iron key in the further connecting door out into the grand hall and she might be able to lock him in. How long the lock or its surround would be able to withstand bullets from a gun was beyond her imagining, but she could only take things one step at a time. She was slow, but then, so was he. She bit down on the bizarre thought of two decrepit wrecks struggling to best one another in a life or death two-metre race to a fucking door.

'I'll get you another glass of water, if you like,' she said, her voice calm and her manner still. 'That one was old and stale probably. It was lying there for ages . . .'

She began to move forward, away from him, but he stepped out from the shadows, raising his head to look up at her, and she knew that all bets were off as far as who would get to the door first. She gaped; frankly amazed at the transformation her healing had wrought upon him. She had fixed lots of people, but had never seen a result as spectacular as this one. He looked at least ten years younger—his hair was not only lustrous but seemed to have grown back. His hands looked strong, the skin no longer saggy and liver-spotted, his face ruddy with good health. He also looked rather incredibly to have grown in height by a good few inches, although that was probably due to his body not having to collapse in upon itself in its constant fight against the cancer. He had filled out, especially around the shoulders and chest. He had obviously once been—and now was again—an imposingly big man and the only thing that looked in any way wrong about him (apart from the gristly hole in the middle of his face) was that his pupils appeared unnaturally huge and black.

He was pulling a tiny aerosol from one of his pockets.

'I need you to come with me,' he said, giving his nose cavity a brief puff with antiseptic spray. 'I appreciate that you're frail—believe me, I know what that's like Maryam—but you need to help someone for me and that's all there is to it. If you start causing a fuss and calling for help or any other nonsense, I'll walk straight out there and shoot our nice young Reverend Joe point blank in the gut. He'll live long enough in a lot of pain to watch me being very bad to your sister. She's so *pretty*. Isn't she?'

He smiled.

'I wonder what she'll be thinking when I'm peeling the skin from her face in strips? She's simple, but how long d'you think it would take the penny to drop that her looks were going to go away forever? I'd need a mirror for her so she could see it happening, but I'm sure she'd have one handy. Pretty girls always do.'

He put his little spray back into his pocket, still smiling at her.

'I don't expect you have much use for them.'

Maryam began to shake uncontrollably as he approached.

'And after that, I'd use one of your kitchen knives here to make new holes in her to fuck.'

He brought his face right up to hers, the smell from his nasal cavity like spoiled meat doused in cheap perfume.

'So what's it to be?' he said.

◆

Grace helped Joe onto a chair—Trudy's wounds had gone, her burns had gone, her breathing was steady. Whatever it was that had been gushing through him had suddenly stopped, like a tap turned off, and he didn't have the strength anymore to even stand upright. He had begun to feel pains of his own and thought that he was crying, but when he wiped his eye with the back of his hand, he saw that his knuckles were smeared with blood. His eyes were bleeding, just like Maryam's had bled after she'd healed him.

Or thought she had.

He turned his now aching, trembling hands over and saw that his palms were the colour of cooked lobster. They felt like he'd just used his full weight to press down on top of a hotplate, and they had a wet, suppurating sheen on them. He was also exuding some kind of fluid—gelatinous and translucent but shot through with very fine threads of red, like his veins were escaping through his pores. Grace took hold of his hands again and laid them down, palm upwards, across his lap for him, making him feel like an old-fashioned invalid being put to respite in a bath chair. She skipped away, bright and sing-songy.

'I'll go get cleam stuff out of my suitcase Joe,' she said. 'I'll take her dirty clothes off'm her amd wash her amd dress her like a big dolly umtil she cam do it for herself! Them we cam go away.'

He recognised the damp, sickly odour coming from his hands—the one that he had thought unique to Maryam.

It wasn't though, he thought. Was it?

'I've got cleam dresses amd she's omly a wee bit smaller tham me, I made them myself . . .'

He stared at her—the blood in his eyes misting his vision pink—as she reached the door, vibrant and without a care in the world.

'How long have you been able to do this?' he croaked.

She stopped, her fingers on the door handle, and remained still for a long moment, her head bowed.

'Maryam's never been able to heal at all, has she?' he said, breaking the silence.

She said nothing but turned to him, head still bowed, a naughty little girl caught. Which in a way, he thought, she was.

'Dom't be mad . . .' she said softly.

'I won't be mad—just tell me.'

She stared down at her feet for a few more moments before sighing heavily, an unpleasant duty to be performed.

'I'm omly beem doimg it from whem I started my periods,' she began. 'Maryam's boyfriemd catched me fallimg out the big tree im the park amd he fell amd broke his arm bad sore. Maryam was cryimg amd shoutimg amd holdimg him amd she wamted him to be better so *much* . . .' She blurted out the rest in a gush. '. . . amd I did too amd I wished it, I wished it so hard amd he got better amd that was the emd.'

No, thought Joe, it wasn't the 'emd'. Not by a long way.

'You wished him better but Maryam was the one holding him,' he said, 'like I was holding Trudy here? And so she thought *she'd* done it.'

Grace nodded.

'And you didn't tell her the truth.'

Grace said nothing, still staring at the floor.

'. . . and this . . .' He held up his raw hands to her. '. . . this stuff that's happened to me—it's been happening to her, isn't it? Every time you do this through her, it makes things more terrible for her, doesn't it?'

She lowered her eyes.

'Grace, you know that it's killing Maryam, don't you?' he said softly. 'Why didn't you tell her?'

She shrugged.

'. . . ascause . . .' she said quietly.

Joe waited, but there wasn't any more. He lost it; he couldn't stop himself, anger propelling him upright from the chair, knocking it backward to the floor. She stared at him, terrified.

'Because *what*?' he shouted. 'Why did you do this to her? Why do you let her destroy herself like this every damn time she heals people? *Why didn't you tell her the truth?*'

'Ascause whem Johm got fixed, I saw what happemed to her!' she cried. '. . . amd it diddem't happem to me ascause I did it through her! *I diddem't wamt to look old, Joe!*'

She began to weep and threw herself against him. The anger in him dissipated immediately.

Of course you didn't, he thought. Who would?

He realised that Grace had acted selfishly, but only in the simple way that a small child might—see cake, want cake, have cake. No malice whatsoever.

His heart felt hollow. The sadness of it all . . . the waste.

'But Grace,' he said, 'you didn't have to 'look' *anything*! Don't you know that? You could have stopped that first time. You did not have to keep healing people and making Maryam worse and worse!'

She looked up, fright in her eyes.

'Papa said I was asposed to.'

He stared at her, aghast. *What?* Their father knew?!

'For Christ's sake why would he let this even happen? Any of it?'

'He said it was omly goimg to be for a few years amd them I would meet someome special . . .'

She buried her head into his chest again.

'He said I had to stay pretty . . . ascause I was asposed to get married . . .'

'We're not getting married Grace . . .'

'Yes we *are*! We—*are*—*asposed to*!' she cried. 'Papa *said* so! Amd *they* all said so. They *promised*!'

Joe's head was spinning. What the fuck was she talking about now?

'Who are 'they'?'

'The Ladies amd the Gememtlemem!'

'The *who*?'

'I cam't explaim! It's too complimated ! We just hab to go away! Let's just go away—you said we would!'

'Grace we have to tell her.'

He strode out in the grand hall now, almost bumping into the coffin in the failing light beneath the glass dome. Joe wanted to kick the damn thing over.

Grace was pulling at him desperately.

'Please please please . . . let's just go . . .'

'What are you so scared about Grace—these 'ladies and gentlemen'?'

She shook her head vigorously.

'Then why do we have to go away so urgently?'

'Ascause we *have* to!'

He lost it, grabbing her and shouting into her teary, reddened face.

'*Why* do we have to for Christ's sake!?'

'Ascause whem Maryam fimds out what she's got she'll tell you!' she screamed. '. . . amd you'll wamt to stay with her!'

'What has Maryam 'got' Grace?' he demanded. 'When Maryam finds out *what*?'

'*That she's pregmamt!*'

There was a long beat before Joe was able to speak. The world spun around him. Grace was sniffling. He realised he was holding her too tightly. Her soft arms would bruise for sure, he thought.

What did he think he was doing, grabbing and shouting at Grace? Of all people. He released her.

She spoke falteringly, her breaths hitching.

'I felt it—imside her—whem I healed the bad mam through her, I felt it. She's got a baby startimg to grow imside her from you. It's omly startimg but I felt it.'

He shook his head. No, no, no. Shit, no. She couldn't be . . .

She spoke again, her voice a sad whisper.

'. . . you wamt to stay with her now dom't you?'

And then it struck Joe. He realised Maryam should have heard all their shouting by now. She should have heard their shouting and she should have been out here reading the riot act. *So where was she?*

'Where would Maryam go to phone, Grace?'

Grace pointed to the kitchen doorway at the other end of the great hall. He jerked away from her, shouting Maryam's name, his heart sinking each time he called and didn't get a reply. Grace ran after him, silent now. He burst through the door and saw an empty glass on the table, a small puddle of water on the floor. No major disaster here. Maybe she'd phoned the ambulance for Trudy and gone up to rest? Maybe. But . . .

He caught a faint trace of that goddam antiseptic spray still lingering in the air.

Oh Jesus.

Joe felt like he'd been dropped from a height. Bewlay had taken her, for God knew what diseased reasons (. . . *maybe he thought he could make money from her?* the small, treacherous voice in his mind whispered). He got a grip. This required action, not hand wringing.

'You have to listen to me carefully Grace—the man who was here before? The bad man?'

She nodded, wide-eyed.

'He's taken Maryam away and I'm going to get her back. It's going to be very dangerous and I'm going to have to hurt him. Maybe even kill him, if I can.'

She looked terrified now. He didn't want to do this to her . . . but there was no choice.

'...and you have to come with me,' he said, quieter now, 'because if he's... if he hurts Maryam then you'll have to fix her. Yes? You're the only one who can do it.'

She looked into his eyes for a few moments, then reached out and touched his arm.

'It's too late for us to go away on a hoddly emmymore, ism't it?' Grace said.

He nodded. Yes, it was.

'I'm frightemmed Joe.'

'Me too honey,' he rasped. 'Me too.'

◆

At the last sounds of their echoing footsteps rushing along the communal hallway to the lift, Skinny stirred briefly before descending once more into her troubled sleep. Her dream was of a terrible device, savage and thirsty for blood—scouring between her legs and making an irreparable bleeding mosaic of her private parts. She saw pale faces looming out from the darkness around her, watching her endure this with keen interest, their skins white as leprosy, their mouths open in a red-lined, frozen and horribly diseased sexual 'O'. She heard the excited, wet sounds they made as they all breathed simultaneously in and out, hypnotic like the wash of an incoming night tide against a distant shore.

If she'd been conscious, she might also have heard the sound coming from within the coffin in the grand hall outside.

She might have thought it sounded a lot like crying.

32

Arthur was registering the passing streets now almost in wonder as the cab drove home.

After they'd left the apartments, he had gotten her all the way to his car, having to carry her for some of it, before he'd realised that Reverend Joe still had the fucking keys! But he couldn't face going all the way back up for them, he couldn't spare the time. He needed to get Maryam to the pub and up to Tommy as soon as possible—she was the only solution to his problems! Only she could help him atone for what he had done.

He had the unmistakable feeling that all of his senses had somehow been heightened since his cure. Even in the few minutes they had stood on the street corner waiting for a cab, his arm tight around the wizened stick that was Maryam, he'd been staring with fresh eyes at the world around him.

A weather-beaten old taxi had rumbled into view and he had flagged it down, pulling her even tighter to him and warning her to keep quiet whilst they had to share their company with a stranger.

He had no compunction about killing taxi drivers.

She was quiet now, lips clamped together like a closed purse. She looked like she wanted to scream. Probably was screaming on the inside, he thought, she seemed the type to repress her emotions. Well fuck her. She'd have something else to occupy her mind, something *much* more important, when he got her back to the Pretty Blue Fox.

❖

Maryam found a crumb of comfort in the passing streets outside, where people were attending to their lives, getting into cars, stepping from buses—all of it only the width of a taxicab's window away from her.

People did lead normal lives. They did have normal relationships. They could function and contribute to the world at large

She had pulled away from Bewlay as far as she could in the enclosed space of the cab, jamming herself against the door and unwilling to look at his face. She was terrified of his obvious insanity, but glad that with every moment travelled, every unfamiliar street driven down, they were getting further and further away from Grace and Joe. Bewlay was staring apparently fascinated out of the cab. But apart from this—which may well have been normal behaviour for him—he had not exhibited any other symptoms like the ones Papa had shown after his healing. She could only hope that when he did, he would start feeling suicidal too because as far as she could see, her own prospects were limited.

How was she going to die? Quickly or slowly in some twisted, horrific way? She found that she didn't actually care. Not about herself anyway. If she was to die then so be it, it didn't really matter how to her anymore. What mattered was that if she got the chance, she would do everything in her power to somehow kill this rotted, inhuman wretch sitting squirming beside her, so that he would never be able to harm Grace or Joe or anyone else, ever again—and she would do it even if she had to die trying.

If Bewlay was going to do the job himself first, of course, then all the better.

It was amazing how one could adapt, she thought. Emotionally, that was. Maybe that was how mankind had *really* evolved through the ages—not through physical mutation into better physical specimens, but via thought and attitude. Because an hour ago she'd almost had a breakdown at the thought of healing Bewlay.

And now?

If she'd had a gun she'd have shot him point blank in the face.

33

Joe had suspected that at most all a search of the apartment would yield might be a big knife of some kind from the kitchen—and he'd been right. Blunt and useless except possibly as a bludgeon, there had been no point in even taking it out of the drawer. Bewlay had a *gun*, for Christ's sake! And as he and Grace had run for Bewlay's car, he'd prayed that somewhere inside it, there would be some kind of weapon he could use. The guy was a fucking psycho, after all—a *gangster*—surely there'd be *something*?

And lo, Joe thought when he opened the trunk, there was.

He saw what he'd first thought was a sort of long, mad bread knife lying embedded in hillocky mounds of ossified, off-white powder and torn plastic carrier bags. He pulled it out from the chalky heap like a cut price Excalibur and, along with the sudden whiff of damp, hardened, mouldering cocaine, he saw that the 'knife' was actually some kind of precision instrument. The clumped powder debris fell easily from it and he realised it was, in fact, a scalpel—very old, its handle finely tooled ivory, mother of pearl inlaid. The blade was beautifully tempered and almost as long as his forearm. It looked like a miniature samurai sword. The steel was blemish free and cold to touch, but shone in the streetlight as warm as white gold. If he'd ever been lucky enough to get something like this to auction at Barrington's he'd have made a small fortune in commission. Late nineteenth century—had to be, with that inlay work—and of such a size and heft that it must surely have been designed solely for amputations.

Joe didn't want to think about what the fuck Bewlay was doing with it.

So this was all he had, but if anything was likely to slay a dragon, he'd thought, this sucker was it. Grace had stared, goggle-eyed, as he had placed the huge blade carefully onto the backseat before bundling her into the car.

Now, driving as fast as he dared and hoping he could remember the route to The Pretty Blue Fox, Joe's mind struggled. What the hell was going on? These mysterious people Grace had mentioned—whoever they were—seemed a good enough place to start.

'Who are the ladies and gentlemen Grace?'

'They live im the apartmemts,' Grace said softly.

Her tone was flat. She was clearly unenthusiastic about this conversation. Too bad.

'Where sweetheart? On one of the other floors?' he asked.

She remained quiet for a few moments before sighing heavily.

'They live im *my* apartmemts,' she said. 'They died all together a lomg time ago.'

There was a beat of silence. Joe's grip on the steering wheel tightened enough that his palms were making squeaky noises against the leather.

'Died?'

She nodded, glumly.

'They feel thimgs through me,' she whispered.

'What do you mean? What things?'

She stopped talking. Joe glanced over, and even in the dark of the car could see her face was flushed.

'Grace?'

'They like it whem I touch myself . . . dowm there.'

She indicated her crotch.

'Ascause whem it makes me feel good it makes them feel good as well.'

Joe stayed silent.

'. . . like whem I was kissimg you,' she added shyly.

Joe suddenly remembered the ghastly feelings he'd experienced when he'd been kissing Grace. Had he actually been kissing *them*? He felt sick.

'But whem I wamted to hab sex with you they all spoiled it up amd made you scared amd your thimg got small agaim. They spoiled it reliberately,' she said. 'They diddem't wamt me to have sex with you.'

Why not, he thought . . . if these *things* could 'enter' Grace and get off on her getting off, then why not go the whole hog?

'I'm asposed to wait umtil I get married,' she said. 'Just like a fairy tale.'

Some fairy tale, Joe thought.

They were interrupted by the loud, regular bass thump of music from a car drawing level that was full of Asian boys—it was lit up like a mobile nightclub. One of them noticed Grace and told the others and Joe saw them all, even the driver, staring at her—the expressions on their gaping faces saying it all. She was so beautiful. They banged their fists on the windows, shouting. He glowered over at them, annoyed . . . and realised that they were booing him. He looked at Grace. She was crying and trying not to let him know. The boys drove on, one of them still glaring out of the back of the car disapprovingly at Joe as they disappeared down the off ramp.

He shouldn't be treating her like this.

'Listen, Grace . . .'

She reached over then and ran her fingertip down the bridge of his nose. When she spoke, her voice was strained.

'You dom't really love me do you Joe?' she said.

Oh Christ, he thought. It was bad enough taking her to this place never mind crushing her dreams along the way.

'I do love you,' he said. '. . . just not in the way you want me to. I'm sorry.'

She nodded, sniffling.

'It's ok Joe. Really. I kmew really, really whem you were thimking about hitting the bad mam im the apartmemts. You love her I kmow you do.'

Joe said nothing. *Did* he?

'I dom't mimd Joe I dom't mimd. We cam all go away together evem your cousim whem she wakems up if she wamts to. Let's *all* go away! It's ok. We cam all look after the baby like two mummies amd a aumtie amd a daddy . . . it's ok I ummerstamd. But let's stay away from the apartmemts. I cam get a better hoddly case im a shop amd we dom't hab to go back for it.'

If they survived, he would make this up to her, he swore he would.

He looked at the clock—they'd been on the road ten minutes. By his reckoning it would be another fifteen before they hit the Pretty Blue Fox. He had to try and get a handle on all of this, because there was a lot more to it than going to fight Arthur *goddam* Bewlay, that was for sure.

'Why do you think you're getting married to me Grace?'

'Ascause your nose was rokem,' she said.

Joe was nonplussed.

'Um, yeah . . . so?'

She spoke to him as if the answer was obvious.

'The Architect told Papa I'd marry someome whose nose was all wromg. '

It took Joe a few seconds before it hit him.

When it did, he nearly ran the car off the road.

34

Skinny felt peculiar.

She was staring up at the ceiling, glad the dream had gone. It had made her feel clammy and sick. The hole above her was in the middle of a spider web of cracks and there was a tiny nub of dull, splayed metal at its centre. A bullet? That meant a gun—definitely a must have item. She abruptly sat upright—sick and tired of waking up in places she didn't want be in.

This was a huge, old-fashioned dining room, and she was on top of someone's big, antique table. Her clothes were covered in filth and smelt like they'd been on a bonfire . . . and her jeans were pulled halfway down her legs. What the fuck? Her fanny and arse didn't feel particularly different from normal. It didn't feel as if she'd been fucked in her sleep in other words, like the priests' vodka parties at the care home. Well, maybe whoever had brought her here hadn't started on her yet, she thought. Maybe she'd woken up in the nick of time. Who knew? She certainly wasn't going to stick around to find out.

She swung her legs off the table and slid from it onto the floor, pulling the jeans up in one swift movement. The crotch was stiff and crusty and she recognised the dark stains on them as blood. Lots of it. But whose? She had a vague remembrance of her nightmare with a multitude of jagged, slashing blades, but there wasn't a mark on her. The last thing that had *actually* happened to her, she remembered, was being shot through with a trillion fucking volts of electricity back in Playboy fucking Mansion. He must have joined up some wires under the fucking floorboards or something, because she'd felt like she was plugged in to the national fucking grid. He must've brought her here after he'd fried her.

Or... had someone else done that?

She thought of Joe for an instant... but then told herself that Bewlay had been fucking with her head. If Joe *had* come back for her, then where was he? He could be dead for all she knew; Bewlay was a total cunt who would use anyone and anything to get what he wanted. No—she was in some complete stranger's house and whoever it was; she instinctively didn't trust them. Who the fuck would want to have *her* as a houseguest? Sprawled across an antique table with her naked arse on display? Get real, she told herself. Bewlay had very probably sold her on to some degenerate friend of his for something even more fucking horrible. Snuff porn maybe—she'd heard vague rumours about people he 'kept' in flats and boltholes around the country, people who should by rights have been drowned at birth. It was the kind of thing Bewlay would be in to.

As she stood, cinching up her crusty jeans as much as she could, her eye fell onto a painting on the wall furthest from her. A creepy looking old guy with a stoop and a long, horsy face stood in front of a big building with lots of dark windows and a crazy looking clock tower. His skin looked too white, with unpleasant bumps all over it like cottage cheese. He was, she thought as she headed round the table to the door, no oil painting. The picture was also, she noticed, one of those optical illusion/eyes follow you round the room jobs because... well, his eyes *were* following her. The longer she looked at it the more she also thought that the guy's face was... was it slowly expanding? She stared at it dumbly—it looked to her like a face drawn onto an inflating balloon, the eyes were ever so slowly separating from each other, the nose was elongating and the grin widening... she felt light headed and closed her eye for a moment and when she looked back, the effect—whatever it was, whatever it had been caused by, hunger, fatigue, stress—had gone and it was just a portrait of some piss ugly old twat with bad skin. Except that now there *was* something different about the damn thing.

In one of the windows in the building behind him, a light had come on.

Skinny cursed herself. Of course it fucking hadn't! She just hadn't noticed it before, that was all. She was seeing things. Nevertheless, she was careful not to look at the bloody thing again on her way out of the room. She stepped cautiously into a huge hall, the last of the day filtering weakly down through a stained glass dome way above her head . . . and illuminating a coffin resting on trestles. She stood in the doorway and gawped.

What the fuck was going *on* here?

Her gaze darted round the place. There didn't seem to be anyone at home. No noise, no movement, nothing. She decided to check for exits before she went looking for a weapon—there was no way she was going to tolerate another locked-room scenario in her life ever again.

At one end of the huge hallway an arched doorway led to a smaller vestibule with a coat stand and a boot rack . . . and what was clearly a front door with a letterbox—in fact everything but a sign saying 'Exit'. Bingo. The front door was closed, which she didn't like much, and she bounded quickly towards it, ready to break it down with her bare fists if it was locked.

It wasn't.

She turned the huge, old fashioned brass handle and pulled the heavy door open. She stuck her head outside briefly and saw that the flat she was in was part of some kind of humungous ancient apartment building—high ceilings, wide corridors with pristine, period tiles on the floors and walls. Posh Glasgow. Old Glasgow. There were a couple of doors with numbers on them much further down the communal corridor and beyond them a very old-fashioned looking lift.

She retreated inside and looked at the stuff hanging on the hooks in front of her. This was obviously some kind of cloakroom. How quaint. There was a long dark fur coat, of all fucking things, hanging there like a recently executed bear. She could wear that, she supposed, it would cover her messed-up clothes and keep her warm until she could get home and change into pants that didn't crunch when she walked and take what she required from her flat to deal with Bewlay.

She hoped he liked surprises.

She searched the pockets of the coat and found a crumpled knot of twenty pound notes and some loose coins. Things were looking up. No fags though... and she found that she wasn't actually craving one. Perhaps she'd accidentally discovered a sure fire way of quitting—*Get Yourself Wired to the Mains and Then Go Sleeping Bare Arsed on Someone's Dining Table*. As a title she didn't think it would catch on in the bookstore self-help sections and barked a small, surprised laugh.

She was feeling surprisingly good. Had she been shot through with some kind of drug or something? Even the constant, dull ache she'd had inside since Big Ian had punched her was gone.

But the thought of Big Ian—how he had tried his best to save her and what Bewlay had done to him for it—wiped the grin from her face.

No more grinning for her.

She grabbed the fur coat from its hook and pulled it on, feeling an odd comfort in its weight, and found that she suddenly couldn't stand the idea of stepping foot back inside that apartment, gun or no gun. She had clothes, she had cab fare and this place gave her the utter creeps. Time to go

Skinny pulled the door wide open and left without a backward glance, fur coat flying behind her like a cape as she ran, her Doc Martens thumping indelicately on the marble staircase as she bounded down them several steps at a go; she was in a hurry and Christ help anyone who got in her way—she had an appointment to keep with Arthur Bewlay.

There was no one else left in the apartment except for the body of Georges Clemenceau.

Everyone had gone to the pub for the evening.

35

'He'd been doing fine until recently Maryam,' Bewlay said. 'But then, he suddenly just stopped talking. Clammed up completely. He's been in moods with me before, but I know this isn't a tantrum; I think there's something seriously wrong.'

Maryam had decided to act as normally as was possible under the circumstances. Whatever it was that he had brought her here to do—whoever she had been dragged to see—she would normalise the experience. He was treating her like a visiting GP, so she would act like one. Behaving as if this were anything other than ordinary risked bursting his current 'bubble' of sanguinity and upsetting him and her goal now was to stay alive for as long as it took for a solution to her problem to present itself.

This pub building looked horrible to her; it was Victorian red brick, and in the Hansel and Gretel style she found so disgusting in her own building. Surrounded as it was by low-lying 'modernist' municipal housing, it looked like it had been dropped here by accident from elsewhere, like Dorothy's house in The Wizard of Oz. It had looked, in fact, as the cab had driven them down from the top of the incline leading to it, that it was in the centre of a huge bowl. Or crater.

It made her think of the gnarled and jagged tree where all of this had started for her—that was also in the centre of a natural 'bowl' in the park. How strange, she thought. What on earth had forced that sudden association into her mind?

Bewlay pulled her inside and turned on the saloon lights at the old brass switches by the storm door entrance . . . and of course the place remained in total darkness. He sighed to himself. He hadn't plugged the fucking fuses back in yet, had he? What to do?

Best just go up and get the flashlight first, he thought, rather than go straight down to the cellar—it would be as black as shit up an arse down there and it would be a shame to go haring off in the excitement of a cure for Tommy to end up breaking his stupid neck. He wasn't confident that Maryam would come rushing to heal him again.

'Why don't you just take him to a real doctor?' she asked politely.

Bewlay thought about it for a moment before replying.

'It isn't an NHS sort of thing.'

He moved on, pulling her by the wrist. From the moonlight spilling in through the open doorway behind them, he was just about seeing the bottom of the stairway to the upstairs flat ahead, the steps gradually disappearing into the gloom above. He gripped Maryam's wrist tighter, ignoring her involuntary whimper of pain; there was no way he was letting go. The steps up to the flat were old and uneven and he didn't want her tripping and breaking her neck either—not before she had a chance to help Tommy out at any rate.

Dragging her upstairs after him was like pulling a wee bag of nothing and he thought idly that he'd very probably be able to crush her skull with just one hand if he so desired. He would bear that in mind should the time ever come to dispose of her. It would be novel.

They were halfway up the short flight to the landing; ahead, the glow of the fallen flashlight was like the first blush of a tiny, artificial sunrise on a horizon. He reached eye-level with the floor at the top of the stairs and stopped, antennae twitching. He could see that the light was coming from just inside the doorway of the guest room. Had he left it on? He obviously had, although he couldn't remember. Nor could he recall having left it *inside* the guest room either . . . but he supposed he and Reverend Joe had been in a rush to get out. He moved on again, and could now see Big Ian's prone figure looking like some kind of mountain range silhouetted by the dawn. Maryam gasped when she realised what she was looking at.

'I apologise,' Bewlay said, 'the cleaner's not been for a while.'

He stifled a laugh and walked on; pulling her behind him and she found herself stepping over the body of the huge man in the hall like it was the most natural thing in the world. She'd gone beyond shock, she supposed. The only thing she could think now was that she'd like to get hold of the knife that was sticking out of him. She had strength enough, she was sure, to extract a blade from a corpse.

Bewlay, still holding her wrist, bent over and ducked his arm inside the guest room, reaching onto the floor and pulling out the flashlight. Maryam recoiled, resisting being pulled even a centimetre closer to that room. There was an awful stench coming from inside and without the illumination it looked black enough to stretch to infinity. It made her shudder. She tried to calculate how much time Bewlay had left before the adverse effects of the healing process started affecting him; would she live that long? Papa's visions and babbling paranoia had happened within a few hours, but Bewlay was most definitely not falling apart yet. She tried to fight against extinguishing what had been her only glimmer of hope. She had to believe that Bewlay would succumb to whatever effects her powers had on the terminally ill. As far as she was concerned, it was the only chance that she or anyone else would have against him.

Bewlay was back out of the stinking room now and shining the torch beam down onto the dead man's horribly scarred face, tapping the side of the huge head with the toe of his shoe, and Maryam looked away.

She jumped slightly. Staring into the dark was playing tricks on her. She thought she could see a dog, of all things, at the back of that room padding silently across her line of sight, its head turned balefully toward her as it loped through, deep black holes where the eyes should have been. But Bewlay was pulling her again, his examination of the dead body apparently now finished.

'Sorry Maryam, he was an old friend and I really didn't say a proper goodbye. I was just contemplating how to get him out of here, what with him being the size of a tractor. I actually think I'll just heave him over my shoulder, because you know what?'

'No, Mister Bewlay. What?'

'I feel like a million dollars, thanks to you. I could run a mile and uproot a tree. I can't wait to see what you'll do with Tommy.'

He dragged her further along with him until they were outside a closed door, its wood scratched and carved with the words 'Tommy's Room' in what struck her as a hideous, negative antimatter version of a child's room nameplate. Bewlay pushed in, shining the flashlight inside.

'Tommy!' he shouted. 'You've got another visitor! This one's going to help you . . .' He gently tugged Maryam inside with him.

The grotesque severed head propped against a stained and rank smelling pillow on the child-sized bed stared pop-eyed at her in the flashlight's beam. She could feel Bewlay looking at her. She knew what the expression would be on his face without even seeing it. It would be the expression of all of those who came to her for help, for healing, for the execution of the impossible. He would be looking at her with the only thing about him she could use to her advantage—his desperate hope.

'I won't lie to you Mister Bewlay,' she said briskly. 'This isn't going to be easy.'

36

Joe was staring out of the windscreen at the paper and plastic bag debris blowing around outside. *What the fuck was he supposed to do now?* It very clearly hadn't occurred to Grace until this moment that Bewlay's nose had been *way* more not 'quite right' than his had ever been.

'It's ism't him . . .' Grace breathed, disgust and horror in her small voice. 'It cammem't be him Joe . . . it's *you* . . .'

She began to cry and he held her tightly.

Once he'd exited the motorway, Joe had pulled off the road at the first opportunity he could, and was now at rest in a cement cloister of flyover columns. He couldn't take her to Bewlay's now for God's sake . . . but he couldn't leave her here either—it was a very long trail back to the apartments at Charing Cross. Even if he did take her back home, what then? It was the biggest 'if' of his entire life, he thought. Because *if* he was to fail against Bewlay, the bastard would just come looking for her anyway. It wasn't like she had the nous or the 'braims' to run away and hide; at least, not for any longer than a twelve year old might. She wouldn't survive on her own.

'I'm dom't wamt to asvive om my owm!' she cried, angry. 'I'm asviving with you amd Maryam. Amd your cousim if she wamts to asvive with us!'

His smile was weary, but genuine. He supposed he should have ceased being surprised at her mind reading tricks by now.

He jammed his tired eyes closed. *Fuck fuck fuck fuck!* He was in a lose/lose situation because he *couldn't* take Grace back to the apartments—Maryam might be dying and in desperate need of her sister *right now* . . . but who knew what the fuck this goddam Bewlay 'marriage' shit meant for her?

He had to think.

Things were happening like there was some kind of reason for them to. He remembered thinking in the hospital . . . he'd needed rescue—he'd gotten it. He'd needed healing—he'd gotten it. He had a terrible sensation that he was racing through some kind of maze, that somehow everything that had happened so far had been meant to. Well fuck that, he thought. He would not be driven toward any poisoned fucking cheese if he could help it. This 'architect' would have to be at least a hundred and fifty odd years old to have both designed that building *and* to have advised Grace's goddam 'Papa' on who she was to be married to. Jesus, he thought, for every box he opened there was another one inside . . .

You know what, maybe everything was connected? he thought. But he wasn't going to waste any more motherfucking time agonising about it. Fuck this.

He started the engine.

'When we get there, stay inside, keep the doors locked and don't get out for anyone or anything except me, do you understand?'

'It isn't him I'm to marry Joe,' she said. 'It *isn't*.'

He pulled out onto the road telling himself he shouldn't make promises he wasn't sure he could keep.

'You won't have to,' he said. 'I promise.'

Georges III

THE 'GIFT' HAD BEEN DESIGNED FOR HEALING THOSE WHOSE TIME it was to die, but it removed by stealth their shield and protection from the universe as it really was, and it made them lose their only inoculation against the ghastly truth of everything which was all around. It made their souls fly away without them.

But for what purpose?

An empty vessel was useless unless it was to be filled, surely?

They had tried entering people, but soon discovered that sentient beings were driven insane by their presence and quickly degenerated into hopeless obsolescence—ending up in the jail, the asylum or with their necks in a noose at the end of a washing line. Insane people had their uses, of course, but for the Architect's purpose, a very particular sort of person was required—intelligent certainly, but also innocent and unquestioning. Able to accept the presence of the Ladies and the Gentlemen and—especially—himself, in the same way as a child accepts abuse—because it knows no better.

An empty vessel was useless unless it was to be filled.

Grace was gone away into the worst place imaginable for her and to even think of what was coming would be unbearable.

37

Bewlay looked down at Maryam, his breath a little ragged. She was cowering in the corner beneath the toppled over yellow stepladders where he had tossed her like a rag doll. He saw that Tommy was still clutched between her palms, and felt a bit . . . well, ashamed, really.

What must Tommy think of him?

Within about ten seconds it had become very obvious that Maryam was not going to be able to fix his brother's speech problem—she'd begun spouting some new age horseshit . . .

'Well, I'm sure you appreciate Mister Bewlay that normally I have the whole person to work on. It's very different in your brother's case. The healing comes from the whole essence of the living being and the auras have to be able to float freely from one part of the body—the healthy part, for want of a better description—to help the others—the . . .'

He had lifted her up by the back of her loose-skinned, scrawny neck and shaken her like a cat, a *bad* cat, her feet not touching the floor, and as she'd screamed he had bellowed at her that he was not to be taken for a mug—that *no one* got away with taking the piss out of him, *no one* . . . and had thrown her across the room.

He'd been out of control, he would admit that, but she'd given Tommy false hope and that upset him terribly.

He lifted his left hand now and splayed the fingers out in front of his face examining them dispassionately. There were three of them and a thumb able to operate normally but the pinkie finger had been bent over completely backwards—broken, obviously—and was currently swelling up like an inflating rubber glove. It was starting to become painful—an unusual condition for him; it had been a long time since he'd felt any pain other than the morphine muted chainsaw of his cancer.

He looked over. Maryam was obviously hurt, but wasn't crying, he was disappointed to note. A tough old bird then—Big Ian would have liked her. She looked almost tender sitting like that, he thought, with Tommy's head still in her shaking hands. She could very easily have just dropped him when flying across the room. Accidents happened, after all. But she hadn't dropped him. She obviously had some inherently decent qualities to her.

'Did you ever think that you might have made a good mother, Maryam?' he asked, pleasantly.

'Go—fuck—yourself . . .'

Hm. He forced himself to keep a grip on his temper, at least in front of Tommy, and looked her over a little more carefully. He didn't think he had damaged her too severely; he hadn't actually struck *her*, after all, only the wall. After she had flown from his grip, his swing had hit the plaster with enough force to crack it. And break his finger. It had been the muted sound of bone breaking and the weird sight of the digit going in a direction it was clearly not meant to go which had stopped his sudden rage from becoming all consuming. It would have been sort of amusing if it hadn't been so fucking sore.

'Sorry about that Maryam,' he said calmly. 'I realise that you're delicate . . . but I *do* have a temper. You're not used to living with me and Tommy yet, so we'll let it pass.'

She stared up at him, appalled, as his words sank in.

He reached down and took the head from her, about to apologise to his brother for getting his hopes up about Maryam and a cure—perhaps when he'd had a private word with her in the guest room she could try again . . . harder—when he noticed that the flesh was coming loose from Tommy's skull.

A result of all the recent to-ing and the fro-ing Arthur supposed—scaring the bejesus out of Big Ian and such like—but as he watched, a torn piece of his brother's scalp detached itself and began sloughing down from his face revealing the bone underneath. The torn part flopped over and covered Tommy's left eye in an awful, leering wink. The occurrence was so logical, so ordinary, so matter of fact almost, that its meaning just kind of slipped through into Arthur's consciousness without a ripple or fanfare . . . because of *course* flesh would begin to rot—from something which was fucking *dead*.

And in the simple act of thinking that, he knew that things had changed between him and Tommy forever. He felt tears pricking his eyes. For Tommy. For himself. All things must pass, he thought, and his brother wasn't ever going to be speaking to him any more, was he? The time had come to let go.

He had known deep down that this day would come, and perhaps it was just as well that he depart now, when Arthur was beginning his renaissance. He simply didn't need Tommy anymore, did he? He suddenly felt grateful to Maryam—it looked like she had served a useful purpose after all. It was funny, he thought, how one's life could change direction just like that.

'Don't worry about your failure with Tommy,' he said to her, 'it was my fault. I'd obviously left things too late. He's gone now, and I accept that, so there's no need to take things out on yourself.'

He kissed his brother on the forehead—some of the sheen of slime from the putrefying skin coming away on his lips—and sat back on his wee brother's bed. Maryam was beginning to raise herself up from the floor. He didn't offer to help.

'If you're finished with me, perhaps I could go now Mister Bewlay?' she said.

He observed her discomfort getting up until she was on her feet—unsteady, erect, but clearly in pain. Tut, thought Arthur. He'd gotten away with it this time but, no two ways about it, he *had* been a tad rough with her. He'd have to watch that—no good killing the golden goose. She began to hobble away as best she could.

'I'll see myself out.'

Bewlay reached out and put his hand around her wrist.

'Is this what it's going to be like for our relationship all the time Maryam?' he asked sadly. 'Hm? I mean really—do I have to put you in handcuffs and lock you away in a quiet room? Because I will.'

'I'm sorry that I couldn't help you Mister Bewlay, but I'd like to go home now please,' she said.

'You are home.'

She didn't look at him.

'You know what?' he beamed magnanimously, 'I realise that you're probably feeling down about not helping Tommy, but you can still contribute! Especially as regards my injured co-workers still in hospital. I'm afraid that I need them quite urgently if I'm to get my business back on an even keel. In fact, we can go visit them, hm? Out of hours—you must have done that with the Reverend, hm?'

He was smiling pleasantly at her, genuinely at ease, and Maryam realised that Bewlay had not only failed to succumb to any hallucinations or terrors, he appeared to have become more rational, in his own particular way, than he'd been before . . . so what had happened? Was he immune? Maybe he didn't have much of a 'soul' to begin with? Maybe Papa was the only one who reacted in the way he had to being healed? But Bewlay had spat out the water . . . he'd said it was horrible.

But horrible wasn't 'putrid' she thought, was it? Maybe 'stale' was all it had been?

Had she read all of this wrongly? Had Papa's reaction been the exception? Oh God . . . Joe's cousin . . . that poor girl lying across the table like butcher meat . . .

She felt as if a hole had opened up inside her.

'Maryam,' Bewlay said, 'I'm finding that this pain in my finger is distracting.'

Bewlay lifted his injured hand in front of Maryam's face.

'Here,' he said, 'fix it.'

She stared at his broken finger. Was this to be her life now—healing whatever injuries this beast and his 'co-workers' suffered in the course of their labours? She could imagine. The slashings or stabbings or whatever . . . these low people would be able to leap gladly into whatever conflictions they got mixed up in, believing in their own indestructibility . . . because now they would have their very own pet miracle worker to go to.

'Please,' she said, 'you have no idea how much this takes out of me, Mister Bewlay . . .'

'But it's such a small thing Maryam,' he said. 'You've just cured me of cancer—surely to fuck you can sort out a broken pinkie?'

'You can't make me . . .'

'I can, and the reason that I can is called Grace. You scratch my back and she remains unscratched. It can all be perfectly civilised. And if you miss her company, I'm sure we can arrange home visits for you and days out and such. I'm personally fond of Troon as an awayday destination, although not for golf.'

The thought struck her then . . . maybe Bewlay hadn't actually been *meant* to die of his cancer? Was that why he wasn't reacting like Papa? Maybe something else was supposed to kill him before the cancer did?

What the hell was she supposed to do now?

'Please,' she said, 'even small things, it's all the same. It all takes a lot out of me . . . this is the sort of thing you could take to a casualty department.'

Bewlay laughed at her.

'That isn't the fucking point, Maryam, is it? That's why you're here. Look, I'll give you a head start, how's that sound?'

He grabbed the finger and with a swift movement tried jerking his pinkie back into its socket as best he could. His eyes watered, but he didn't cry out. Its angle was slightly less odd, but it still stuck out awkwardly, three times the size it should have been, pudgy and bluey-black with fluid.

'Right, you cranky old bitch,' he said, without rancour. 'It's set. Heal it properly for me. Now.'

Maryam had two options as far as she could see. One was to get hold of that damn knife outside by whatever means necessary and try to put an end to this creature by herself. The other was to agree with him and his plans . . . and at least that way, she realised, she'd get out of this bricked up prison he'd brought her to. She could go to the hospital with him and scream and cry for help.

'Hurry up dear, we've things to do,' he said.

She put out her hands, wrapped them around his broken finger, closed her eyes—and waited for her own pain to begin; the cramping, the jagged searing jolts like electric shocks in her gut, the horrible, screaming rushing sound, the bleeding from her eyes, the dizziness . . . she hated doing this more than she could ever express. She tensed, the dread in the pit of her stomach making her nauseous.

Moments passed.

'I'm not feeling I can play the Moonlight Sonata yet,' said Bewlay.

She opened her eyes. Nothing was happening.

'What's the problem, do you think?' he asked, sincerely puzzled. 'Too minor an injury? Surely not.'

She closed her eyes again and *pushed* with her mind . . . but still nothing. She thought furiously. What was wrong? Was it being in here? But she had healed outside of the apartments before—the hospital; the tree where John had fallen . . . maybe it was just this particular location that was somehow preventing the process? She felt him gently uncurl her fingers from around his pinkie.

'It's actually more painful with you squeezing it like that, Maryam.'

'I don't understand . . .' she said.

A cold chill went through her that had nothing to do with Bewlay. What the hell was *wrong*? Why could she not perform this simple healing? Had she run out of whatever power had been the bane of her life these last years? Had she somehow just . . . used it all up? She felt both elated and terrified.

'I don't think I can do it.'

'Can't or won't?'

'You have me here against my will,' she said. 'You are threatening my sister—what possible advantage could I gain in antagonising you over this? As you say, it's only a broken finger.'

'Hm,' he said. 'So, what to do?'

She felt gloriously free for the first time since she could remember.

'There is nothing I can say or do to convince you so I'm not going to waste energy trying. You're going to kill me or you're not. I don't have long left to me anyway so do what you want.'

'Maybe you can only do it in your apartments?' he said. 'You know, maybe it's built on ley lines or something?'

Maryam shook her head.

'I have healed people outside of my house, Mister Bewlay. If there are any variables, that isn't one of them.'

She turned toward the door and started heading away from him.

'Maryam . . .' Bewlay said, his voice darkening.

'I think you could class what I do as inexplicable, Mister Bewlay,' she interrupted. 'Supernatural, even. Applying logic or rules to it may well not work.'

She stopped.

'I'm going to leave now, so you can let me go or you can kill me.'

Bewlay thought for a moment. Hm.

'Maryam listen, if you really can't do what you used to then there is no point in you being here is there? And there is no point in killing you either, so of course you can go. I'm a businessman, not a monster.' He grinned broadly. 'I'll even call the cab for you, ok? I just have one more question. Call it scientific curiosity. An inquiring mind.'

She turned slowly and awkwardly in the space between the bottom of the bed and the door to face him.

There was something about the way she held herself, he thought. The posture still had traces of a young woman in it. He wondered how . . . flexible she might be. He allowed himself a moment of pleasure at that. She really was quite a wit, he thought. He might just let her get all the way down the stairs to the front door before bringing her back up again to fuck her until she broke. However, he did have an important question for her.

'Tell me—has there been anything at all with you when you were healing? Something that was there all the time? Something I could fetch for you to help you? A glove? A brooch?'

'I don't use magic charms . . .' she said

'I meant more something that makes you feel good—sometimes a favourite object helps people with their confidence. Like a comfort blanket kind of thing . . .'

'I can categorically state Mister Bewlay that every time I healed, there was not one thing you could possibly pin down and say was with me each and every time.'

'What about Grace?' he said.
She looked at him.
'It's a theory, isn't it? Worth checking out, at least, hm?' he said.
'What are you talking about?'
'Little sister. She was in the room when you healed me. She is not in the room now; ergo sum . . . '
'*What*?'
'Maybe you can't heal without her. Maybe it needs both of you together in the same room, a Ying Yang type of deal. Her Piglet to your Pooh?'
'That's ridiculous,' she said. But he could see that the wheels were turning in her mind. Maybe he was onto something. He smiled. He was always good at getting to the bottom of things.
'Maryam . . . there's a simple test. Ask yourself, and please answer honestly, have you ever healed anyone when the wee one has not been in the same room as you?'
Maryam glared at him. That was *stupid*, she thought. Of *course* she had . . . but then she realised—
Bewlay could see the answer on her face.
'You haven't have you?' Bewlay cried, thrilled.
She scrambled desperately around in her memory for an occasion—any occasion at all—where Grace had not been with her, dutifully by her side, when she had healed . . . and she couldn't recall a single one. Her little sister had been there every damn time, hadn't she? *All* of them, from John's arm onwards, through the grisly parade of all the stinking, shuffling, pleading, arthritic, coughing, half-blind pathetic vultures who'd arrived at her door for their morbid 'salons'—*all* of them, all the way up to Joe . . .
Especially Joe.
Grace had insisted to the point of hysteria that she stay in the room during his healing, hadn't she?
Why else would she do that except to make sure that he *was* healed?
Oh God. Did that mean . . . that Grace *knew* about this? *All this time*? Had Grace kept this from her . . . but why? It was all too much—she couldn't think straight . . .

Bewlay watched her reacting to his theory. He sympathised—a sibling keeping secrets from one made the world seem a different and disturbing place, that was for sure. He understood she needed sensitivity at a time like this, and interrupted her thoughts, squeezing her shoulder gently with an avuncular hand.

'Looks like I need a matching pair to make this work. I think we'll be going back to your place to fetch over another little houseguest Maryam, don't you?' he said. 'We'll rain check the hospital visits for the moment. It'll be safer if I just bring your patients here to you two. And it won't really matter if my boys get a little jiggled about en route, because the pair of you'll be fixing them up for me anyway, won't you?'

Maryam looked toward the door. What Grace did or didn't know didn't matter anymore. She knew what she had to do.

'Accommodation will be a little Spartan to begin with,' Bewlay continued, 'but I promise I'll personally make it a top priority to have new lodgings in the cellar constructed for the pair of you as soon as possible.'

Her thoughts felt like they were moving in slow motion. All she had to do was take a few short steps to the dead body outside.

'We'll get a king size bed put in so I can come down and snuggle in between you both on the cold nights, eh? You can pick the wallpaper,' he said. 'But I'd advise you to choose with care. You'll be looking at it for a long time.'

She heard the sound of the car screeching to a stop outside. Until then Maryam hadn't realised how deep and stagnant the silence was both inside this wretched building and in the streets around it. The engine noise cutting through the unnatural stillness seemed to be the only thing in an age that she'd heard apart from Bewlay's voice.

Bewlay heard it also and sighed. It was not a young car, and he would recognise the sound of its twice yearly tuned, four stroke, six cylinder, three point eight litre engine anywhere. There was certainly no other sound like it around here, he knew.

And there really only was one person it could be behind the wheel. Excellent.

'We've got a visitor Maryam,' he said, brightly. 'You'll need to wait in here with Tommy while I assess the parameters of the situation.'

She had no reason to suppose that it wouldn't be Joe arriving and her heart warmed a little at the thought he had very probably come to rescue her. And who knew? He might even succeed in overcoming Bewlay . . . but she wasn't going to rely on that being the case. Too much was at stake with Grace now for her to take any chances.

Whatever happened from this point was in her hands only.

Maryam hobbled her way weakly to the door. Bewlay sighed theatrically.

'Is this you being brave Maryam?' he asked.

She didn't reply and he watched her steady herself against the doorjamb for a second before continuing out into the darkness of the hall.

'I mean *seriously*, do you actually think you'd even make it to the end of the corridor before I got a hold of you?'

He appreciated the fact that Tommy was gone from him, but he still placed his brother's head carefully onto his pillow—although less carefully than he might have done in previous times it must be admitted—before picking up the flashlight to follow her.

She'd made it surprisingly far along the corridor and was now stooping over Big Ian. This must be what it was like having a small child, he thought. You have to keep your eye on them all the time. Bewlay observed her having difficulty pulling the kitchen knife from Big Ian's body.

'It must have gone straight through him and into the floorboards.' he said. 'Here, would you like me to give you a hand?'

She didn't reply, concentrating hard on her task.

'I was once assaulted, Maryam, by two men simultaneously—one of whom was wielding a machete, the other a straight razor. As you can see, I'm still here, so unless you're planning on chopping us some veg for dinner I think you should give up on the knife, hm?'

With a final grunt she managed to get it out and staggered backwards. She straightened up and faced him, unsteady and frail, but with her head high, the knife—its blade black with the big man's dark, dead blood—pointing toward him.

'Even if you managed to nick me with that, which you won't,' he tutted, 'I'd only make you heal me afterwards. I'd keep young Joe around the place as collateral. I know that you're both fond of him.'

She ignored him.

'I'm serious, Maryam. I've got a visitor to greet and you're just being silly,' he said, not unkindly. 'Please drop the knife—I can't have you hurting yourself.'

She smiled then.

'I know.'

In the brief moment it took for him to realise what she was doing, Bewlay leapt as swiftly as he could toward her, but it was already too late. The only resistance her gentle push met was when the tip of the blade eventually touched her spine. She didn't even cry out—it was a strange sensation, both cold and hot at the same time. She looked down in quiet amazement at her gnarled, old lady fingers wrapped around the handle of the blade sticking out from her abdomen, as she and Bewlay stood perfectly still for a moment, facing each other like a mechanical couple on a Swiss clock meeting in the middle to confirm the time.

'You lose,' she breathed.

Then she felt an awful, warm sensation and looked down again and saw the red, liquid darkness rapidly blotting the front of her nightgown. She let out a very soft moan and, furious, he pulled the knife out of her. There was a fan spray of blood and a whiff of body gas from Maryam's stomach. The wound gurgled wetly for a brief moment, like a pair of baby's lips making a fart noise, and then the blood really began to bubble out.

As she fell, he caught her by the head with his good hand, and held her up before him, her body now limp, the blood literally pouring out from her like water spilling from a jug onto the floor. He heard the car door closing none too gently outside and threw her into the guest room where she landed—a cotton sack full of bones, not a sound escaping her lips. He sighed, irritated with himself. He wouldn't be getting any more healing out of her and her sister, that was for sure.

Mind you, he thought as he pulled his pistol out and headed for the stairs, he *was* getting his car back—which was a plus.

38

EVERY STREETLIGHT AROUND THE PRETTY BLUE FOX HAD BEEN smashed and the moonlight was making the carpet of tiny, broken glass fragments on the road twinkle like frost. To trip and fall on this would flay your skin off, Joe thought.

He was staring at the entrance to the pub, his breath misting in the air, the ground crunching beneath his feet as he strode quickly from the car. In the cold, harsh moonlight every shadow looked painted on—like a flashbulb had popped with everything suddenly frozen in a micro moment of forever, black and white and completely sterile. He glanced up and noticed that although there wasn't a cloud in the sky, he couldn't see any stars at all. It gave him the feeling of being somehow under glass. Whatever was up there might have been a billion miles away . . . or within arm's reach.

This building. The Mansions . . . made by this architect about whom Joe knew nothing and frankly cared less. The who, where, what or why concerned him not a fucking jot; all he knew was that these locations were poison and that he was going to take the girls—Grace, Maryam, Trudy—as far away from them as possible. Whatever power was behind all of this was in some way heavily connected to these places and who knew how many other buildings or locations were involved. But he thought that if he could get through whatever was going to happen next, then he might just have found a way out for everyone.

Grace stared out, terrified, from behind the windscreen as Joe stood in the threshold of the pub for a good few moments, arms by his sides, hands empty, before stepping quietly inside.

In the bar the spill from the moonlight was weak, the darkness overwhelming, but he was confident of the geography, imagining that not much had changed since he'd last been here. In his mind's eye he saw the jagged flashes from his assault once more, but they didn't terrify him. He used them as markers—edges of bar stools with ragged thread hanging from the worn seats like mutant spider webs, silvery beer pumps throwing dancing shadows across ghostly optics, twisted chair legs, the low circus midget part of the bar that had nearly lost him his tongue . . . he negotiated his way steadily toward the stairs to the upper part of the building, knowing their location by the smell from the toilets nearby, their rank ammonia stench more savage and piercing in the dark.

There was absolutely no noise that could have warned him . . . but he did catch in the corner of his eye a sly darkness being raised against another darkness—blobs of shape distinguishable in the black only of his mind's eye because he could *feel* a disturbance of the air around him . . . but Joe didn't need to see. He could fill in the visual for himself.

A raised arm extended toward him.

A loaded gun.

Bewlay was standing right behind him, he realised, the gun pointed straight at the back of his unsuspecting head. Joe was a fish in a barrel, but he knew the bastard wouldn't shoot. Not right away at any rate, because there was no need was there? He would want Joe to know he was fully in his power—he'd maybe even want to torture him again—making sure he knew that it was Arthur Bewlay alone who called the shots around here.

After all, who decided the time and place of someone's death? Arthur *goddam* Bewlay, that's who, so why get it over and done with when you could take your time and enjoy it? From everything Joe had experienced so far, it was the man's M.O. And it was now his downfall.

Hopefully.

In the car Joe had realised that there was no way in Hell he could surprise Bewlay in his own fortress, so he'd decided to announce his arrival instead. Bewlay would have heard Joe pulling up outside the place, as Joe had meant him to. He would also have observed Joe's silhouette in the moonlit doorway, where he'd stood long enough in the only light available so that Bewlay could see he had no weapon.

There was a click . . . but no explosion, and Joe saw his own shadow suddenly appear, huge and fractured, against the wall opposite. Bewlay had turned on his flashlight. He should have pulled the trigger.

'Reach for the sky, Tex,' said Bewlay, amused. 'You saved me the bother of coming to you . . .'

'Where is she?'

'I thought I'd put her in Skinny's old room. She's dead, or should be, considering the rate the blood was pissing out of her. I didn't do it, by the way—you'll like this, she—'

Joe simply dropped down and swung his arm gracefully round in one move, the long scalpel instantly sliding out from inside his sleeve and into his hand, the handle suddenly gripped tightly in his palm, the still swinging blade's unstoppable silvery arc meeting what felt like no resistance whatsoever, slicing through clothes and flesh with equal ease like light passing through glass. The sharp steel was so swift and keen that Bewlay's blood had the chance only to smear its tip with one, tiny droplet as it passed through him—a small elegance not witnessed by either of the men.

A quiet gasp was heard, the trigger of the gun was not pulled and Arthur Bewlay's innards splashed out from him and down onto the tacky, stained pub floor, emitting a stench of yesterday's supper turned to bile. Lumpy ropes of intestine were heard by Joe rather than seen, bouncing as they struck old linoleum with strange, indescribable wet clumping noises. Joe finished his deadly pirouette—a ballet dancer who'd just executed the greatest move of his life—dropping to a squat on the floor at the same time as Bewlay's eviscerated body fell heavily onto his knees, one of his kneecaps making an awful, muted pop sound as it burst open on a careless nail head sticking from a floorboard, before he fell again, forward into the mass of his own viscera, gun arm still extended, finger still curled around the trigger, brain too surprised to command it. Joe immediately was up again and running to the door, not willing to waste a single second more on the filthy wretch who lay gurgling on the floor behind him.

Not while Maryam could still be saved.

Joe stuck his head outside, shouting desperately for Grace. Maryam needed to be healed! Now! He screamed for her to get in immediately and ran back inside, grabbing up the flashlight, already halfway up the stairs before Grace had even slammed the car door closed behind her.

The only sounds after that, apart from Joe's shouts for Maryam as he made it to the landing, were of Grace's small, light footsteps clicking swiftly towards the pub from outside and Arthur Bewlay's wet and gasping, dying breaths.

◆

Skinny had seen the young man stick his head out of the door and shout for the girl in Bewlay's Jag to come to him. Her heart had lurched, because she knew immediately . . . it was Joe. Even at this distance, after all of this time, a glimpse was all it had taken—he was older, obviously, his voice was the voice of a man . . . but she could see the child in him—the way he stood, the way he just *was*. And that stupid face of his, broader somehow, and used-up looking, but still so handsome that it bordered on ugly. No one else could look like that. She'd had to practically bite down on her tongue to stop herself from calling out to him. He *was* back! Jesus, *what the fuck was he doing here!?*

The stupid cunt had better not be fucking anything up for her.

Then, the young girl from the car scampered over to the Pretty Blue Fox after him, running like a skelly twelve year old, and Skinny, her moped's hairdryer engine already switched off to aid her silent approach, lifted her feet and coasted down the incline past all of the squat concrete housing to the pub.

◆

335

Joe shone the flashlight into the rank smelling torture room.

'Maryam . . .'

She was slumped against the wall beneath the bricked up window like a broken and discarded doll, and Joe gasped when he saw her from her abdomen down. It was like her lower half had been dipped in red dye . . . Jesus, he thought. His shoes made tiny splashing sounds as he paddled through her blood to reach her. She was only just breathing, but not dead. Not yet. Thank God.

'Grace!' he shouted. 'Up the stairs!'

He heard the sound of her feet shuffling about. Dammit, he should have put the lights on.

'Grace!' he shouted, 'follow my voice!'

He felt her neck for a pulse. It was very weak, but still there—Christ knew how. She was obviously as tough as she acted, he thought, hot tears stinging his eyes.

'Grace, she's not dead, but she's going fast! Just keep following the sound of my voice—can you hear me?'

No reply.

'Grace, dammit can you hear me, go to the stairs, if you're at the door they're to your right . . .'

No reply. He didn't like this . . . Jesus what if . . .

'Joe!' she called.

She was near, at the top of the stairs he reckoned.

'Follow the light Grace, we're in the room with the light, you're only a few feet away, just keep coming . . .'

He heard her arrive at the doorway.

'Thank Christ, come here she's been bleeding really heavily, lay your hands on me and I'll do it . . .'

'Joe . . .'

'. . . through *me* Grace, please ok? I *want* to, now get over here be quick . . .'

He looked up. There were two shapes in the doorway. The smaller one—Grace—cried out as her hair was savagely yanked, pulling her away from the door.

'You're a sneaky little fuckshit Reverend Joe,' said Bewlay.

◆

The passenger side door was open and the car empty. There seemed to be no one about on the streets at all. It was like high noon, Skinny thought, leaving the bike on its side and hidden behind the car, careful not to make any noise.

Joe could be good news or bad news.

She didn't have time to think about it too deeply—he was either friends with Bewlay or here because he had to be—but the basic result for her was a simple one. If Bewlay had guests, willing or not, it meant he would be preoccupied, making her task a little easier. The door was open and there was no light coming from inside as far as she could see. He could be anywhere, but was most likely upstairs. That would be good—there was a sawn-off in the old-fashioned, flip-down oyster grate beneath the pie and bridie warmer at the 'wee' end of the bar—Tommy's 'special' end.

If it was still there and *if* it was loaded.

She stopped in her tracks, swinging round, the fur coat swirling about her. What the fuck was that? She could have sworn she heard a baby cry—right behind her. But there was nothing. In fact no activity around the Fox at all. She cursed. She'd been feeling weird since she'd left the apartment, but it had been getting worse. She felt empty inside, like something had gone from her—a sensation that was like having a tooth out—and only *just* out; that sudden hole where a part of your body had been moments previously. A strange sensation—you could feel the hole with your tongue but because you were still anaesthetised, you couldn't *feel* yourself feeling it. You had no idea how big a hole it was. Something had drained from her—had *been* draining from her—slowly at first, when she had been in the apartment, but getting faster and faster . . . it felt worse here.

Fuck it, she thought, get a fucking grip! She felt in the pocket of the fur coat for the things she'd brought for Bewlay from her own flat and smiled, feeling instantly better, before making her way carefully toward the black maw of the open door.

◈

Joe could only stare.

'I'll fill you in, shall I?' Bewlay said. 'I was lying on the floor with all my fucking guts around me. You were at the door, shouting like a hysteric for young Heidi to come help Maryam here. Well Joe, do you know what? I was on my way out, but I had enough life left in me to put two and two together *just—like—that*!'

He laughed, genuinely delighted.

'It's amazing how the shadow of the guillotine concentrates the mind, hm? I realised they're not a double act after all, are they? It's a ventriloquist show, and Maryam's the fucking dummy isn't she?'

Bewlay shook Grace violently.

'Tell him what happened Heidi. I can't wait to see his pretty face all happy when he knows how big a help to me you were.'

'He grabbed my amkle Joe . . .' said Grace, crying. 'I'm sorry. He grabbed me amd tripped me amd said he'd shoot me amd if he shot me Maryam would die as well cos I'd be shot amd I couldm't save her emmymore . . . so I fixed him.'

'With moments to spare, as they say,' said Bewlay, dryly. 'And when she did it, it was like being hit by a comet, but you know what? I was right as rain in two seconds flat—look at me.'

He used his gun hand to briefly expose his midriff. Joe stared— Jesus Christ, Bewlay's guts had been all over the floor and now there wasn't a goddam mark on him. Grace had accomplished it with ease in a matter of seconds. The sheer, raw *power* that must come flooding out of her when she wasn't channelling through someone else! It was the difference between a nuclear power station and a twelve-volt battery.

And that meant Maryam could be fixed in an instant!

'Grace, get over here!' he cried. She started but Bewlay pulled her back.

'I'm curious about the other details of this set-up, Joe, but I'll have plenty of time to get that info from young Anne of Green Gables here as our relationship progresses. Now, slide me over the flashlight before I blow your fucking brains out.'

'Let her go Bewlay, Maryam needs her . . .'

'Believe it or not Joe, I truly and honestly don't want to shoot you—'

'Please Bewlay, she's going to *die*, just let Grace . . .'

'But I fucking will, and I'll blow the old bitch's face off first if you don't slide that fucking light over to me.'

Joe slid it over to the door where Bewlay eased it into the hall behind him with one foot.

'Now let her in here Bewlay!'

'Don't you want to know why I don't want to fucking blow your stupid American fucking brains all over the fucking walls you double-dealing, backstabbing Yank piece of *fucking shite*!?'

'Please, I'm begging you . . . you can do anything you want to me after . . . just let Grace in here for God's *sake* . . .'

'Here's the fucking news Reverend, I can do anything I fucking want to you anyway . . . and have I got a hot surprise for you. Nighty night Joe and Maryam. Sweet dreams.'

Joe leapt for the door too late. The key turned and he and Maryam were left in the blackness of the foul smelling room. He battered at it with everything he had as Grace screamed at Bewlay outside: *'You said you'd let me fix her! You said I could fix her!'*

'What's the point?' he said, and Joe could hear he was already dragging her away. *'We don't need her, do we dear?'*

Grace screamed again and Joe heard a slap and the awful sound of her little body falling onto the floor. He attacked the door in a renewed fury, screaming at the top of his voice. He had brought her to this—*all* of them to this. Oh Jesus, what had he done?

He heard a tiny gasp behind him. Maryam. He went to her and sat down by her as carefully as he could, his hands sticky with her blood, and held her thin body to him, seeking to comfort her, knowing that he was feeling her die in his arms.

. . . the cat had been run over. Joe had heard the tyres squeal and the small thud and had run outside across the yard and seen the only thing he'd loved in the few months since he'd been brought to the US lying twisted up on the asphalt in a spreading pool of its own, metallic red blood. He wanted to help it so badly, he wanted to heal it like Jesus did the lepers and the dead guy and he couldn't do it. Why couldn't he do it? How come Jesus got to do it and he didn't? He'd hurt Trudy and he couldn't do anything to help her and now he couldn't do anything about this either . . . and he

wanted to help, he wanted to be able to fix things . . . He sat on the kerb with the little creature trembling in his hands and it died, yellow, icky stuff leaking from its mouth onto his clothes and he didn't care about his clothes or what his stepmom would shout at him, he just cared about his cat . . . and then he'd felt the frantic activity in its belly. She was pregnant he realised, and he cried and cried and couldn't stop crying as he felt each and every one of those little living things inside her struggle futilely and die one by one . . .

The memory had sprung unbidden into his mind. He seemed to be very prone to that since he had been healed. Perhaps it was a side effect, he thought. The past and the present touching each other in ways he might never have realised before . . . Maryam suddenly shifted, breathing sharply and gasping for air like she'd just surfaced from a dive. Her legs began to jerk spastically and she twisted and wracked in his arms, her back arching up from the floor with more power than he'd have thought possible. Her body was struggling to stay alive, like Brewster, like anyone who was dying—even as it was fading away he thought, clinging to her. And then she collapsed, all the fight gone from her.

He felt her lips moving weakly against his cheek and through her shallow breaths he could tell she was mouthing his name silently, over and over. He pulled her to him, the only Bible quotation he'd ever found meaningful now on his lips—about the huge and terrifying power that love could wield over those caught unawares by it.

'Thou art terrible o my love,' he breathed. 'As Tirzah. Terrible as an army with banners.'

As a prayer for the dying, it would do.

◆

She'd quietened down when they reached the bottom of the cellar steps, but as he marched Grace over to the fuse box, she suddenly kicked off again, ten times worse than before. She screamed and screamed at the top of her lungs for him to stop, trying to pull him back—it was as if, he thought, she knew what he was going to do and the little squealing brat wanted to stop him getting to the power switch.

'Stop it Grace,' he said, 'I'm just going to turn the lights on, that's all . . .'

He twisted her hair even more tightly round his fist and pushed her down onto her knees on the dusty concrete, giving her head a wee sharp bang against an iron support column to stun her and hopefully shut her up. It didn't.

'Dom't! *Dom't!* Please, you'll *burm* them dom't do it *pleeeeassse* . . . .'

She was hysterical, her face contorted as she tried to keep him away from the power supply. How unusual, he thought. Did she know? How? He'd have to ask later, but at the moment it was getting on his nerves—in fact he'd been feeling more and more peculiar since she'd fixed up his tummy. It felt almost a bit like not everything had gone back in—like there was a hole in the middle. Mind you, there were bound to be *some* sort of physical or mental repercussions to all this miracle stuff, he thought, as he reached into the open fuse box and pulled down the mains switch.

There was a bang as every light in the place suddenly came on, and there was a distant, brief tattoo of thumping from above that soon stopped . . . along with Grace's screaming and struggling. He looked down at her—all the moxie seemed to have been knocked out of her and she slumped at his knees, empty of resistance, her torn and dirty hair covering most of her tears and dirt-streaked, little pretty face.

He had an erection.

He pulled her up from the floor. Her body pressed against him and his arm around her small waist, and he told himself that he wasn't going to hurt her.

Not really.

Not *hurt* hurt.

'Grace,' he said softly, his face centimetres from hers, 'we're going to be together for a long, long time, dear. We're going to be close and comfortable with each other like an old husband and wife for the rest of our lives, you and I. Won't that be something? Hm?'

She stared at him, open-mouthed in horror, making him the most turned on he could ever remember being. He hoped she would at least cry.

'If it helps,' he breathed, 'think of this as our wedding night.'

◈

The light had come on suddenly and although it was only a bare bulb, fly specked and very probably as old as he was, the abrupt change from pitch blackness to illumination had seared Joe's eyes like paint stripper, hurting enough for him to have to jam them closed. Some cowardly part inside him had wished that he could just keep them that way forever.

'Joe?'

Maryam shifted in his arms. He opened up his eyes. Illuminated now, the room was a lot smaller than it had seemed before, and infinitely more disgusting. He looked at her. She was . . .

'Maryam?'

◈

Maryam was looking at Joe's face inches from her own. He was beautiful and . . . and he looked concerned for her. That was nice, she thought. She smiled back at him, dopey and half dreaming like she'd been just after they'd made love, about to tell him that she was alright. They had had a wonderful night together and she wanted him to kiss her better . . . and then, emerging from what felt like a woozy dream, she remembered what had happened—with Bewlay, with the knife . . .

She realised she was seeing shock in his face—she must be as near to death as one could be without actually being dead, she thought, furious that he'd had to see her like this. Bad enough normally, but her body must be bled white by now.

She found however that she had strength left in her to run a finger down his soft cheek to thank him for coming for her. She expected to see her hand look fish-belly white and bathwater wrinkled . . . and when she saw it she cried out, terrified. Her hand was smooth and soft, her fingernails clear and healthy. Her palm didn't have a mark on it. It was the hand of a normal, healthy, young woman.

She pulled away from him and looked at herself. Her clothes were covered in blood . . . but she was fine.

More than fine.

She leapt up from the floor, pulling her nightgown up to look at her legs—they were strong and healthy, the skin smooth. She ran her fingertips down her face—there was *nothing wrong with her*. Joe stood, staring at her, speechless.

'Joe . . .' she said, 'what's happened? Joe?'

◆

He thought that something had gone wrong with his eyes. He thought they had been damaged in some way. He thought that he had died with her and they had gone to some sort of spiritual waiting room because *Holy Jesus*, she was absolutely beautiful.

He stared, stunned, at her face. Her soft skin was flawless, her huge, violet eyes clear and healthy. He tried to take in every detail he could about her but he was overloaded. He was looking at the most beautiful young woman he'd ever seen in his life. What the fuck?

'I don't know Maryam . . .' he said, 'I . . . I really don't . . .'

◆

Blown halfway down the hallway, her neck cricked at a painful angle—Skinny had come round and was staring over at the hole in the floor by the ragged skirting boards next to Bewlay's 'guest room'. She held her burnt and blistering palms away from her body, biting on her lip to prevent crying out.

She'd entered the Fox in time to see Bewlay dragging the young screeching girl through the bar to the cellar. There was frantic shouting and banging from the room above.

Joe, she thought. Had to be.

He was locked in upstairs—in *that* room, for sure—and Bewlay had come down here to the cellar taking the kid with him, and she could guess why on both counts.

Fuck it, fuck it, *fuuuck it*! The bastard had a flashlight and he had a hostage and he had a gun to threaten her with and keep her at bay while he did what he pleased with the power supply *and* the kid. There was *no other choice* for her. Run for Joe, leaving Bewlay with the girl . . .

(Fuck it shit shit shit shit *shit*! She *could not* worry about that!)

She'd belted up the stairs, three a time, leaping over Big Ian's body, sliding along the floor on her belly to the hole she'd heard Bewlay fiddling around with before *she'd* been fried. She collected a hedgehog's worth of splinters on the backs of her hands as she'd jammed them into the hole and grabbed at the two twisted, bare wires and, unwilling to waste time unwinding them, had wrenched them apart with all the strength she had . . . letting go just as the juice came on.

She'd conducted the power for a fraction of a fraction of a second, but it had been enough to send her body skiting against the wall and her feet to bang out a brisk drum solo on the floorboards.

Her breathing was steadier now, and she had a blistered spot in the centre of each of her palms, raised and burnt and weeping, but liveable with. She heard Joe's voice coming from the room, so he was alive, at least. Good . . . now she had to shut him up before Bewlay heard him and the whole thing got fucked.

◈

Joe was repeating himself, stunned, asking if she was ok and how did she feel and generally acting like a man in shock. Maryam was staring at her hands . . . of all the stupid things. She'd been dying and she'd been healed—but all she could do was stare dumbly down at her hands, moronically grateful to see them so normal, so clean. It was absurd and it was pathetic.

'I was dying Joe, I know I was . . . and you came here. Bewlay said that I couldn't heal without Grace . . . did Grace . . . did she fix me?'

'No. Maryam, she wanted to, but she didn't even get the chance.'
'So how did *this* happen? *And where is she?*'
'Joe?' said a voice from outside. 'It's me, Skin . . . Trudy. Is that really you Joe?'
He ran to the door.
'*Trudy!* Jesus! Yes, it's me, are you ok? How did you get here? What's happening?'

◆

Skinny rested her head against the door, the pain in her hands no longer a concern to her. She had never expected to feel like this again in her life. Happy. She spoke softly and urgently.
'Listen Joe, shuttup ok? He doesn't know I'm here so keep quiet. I'll get you out when I can . . .'
'There's a young girl, she's called Grace, he's got her . . .'
'Shush! I saw her and I'm going to get her, ok?' she whispered. 'Just you stay quiet and stay safe, alright?'
She turned away from the door . . . and turned back again almost immediately, touching her fingertips to its surface.
'You came back for me, didn't you?' she said.

◆

He thought he could hear her trying to not cry.
'Yes, I did. I'm sorry I took so long . . . Please for Christ's sake get me out of here now, you can't do this alone. I don't want you to die Trudy . . . *Trudy!*'
But there was no more.
Maryam and Joe looked at each other, as if for the first time.
'I've got a lot of stuff to tell you,' he said.
The lights went out again.

◆

Arthur was emerging from the cellar, his flashlight's beam pointing up through the narrow doorway like a searchlight, Grace sniffling as he dragged her up behind him. He was proud of his self-restraint. He intended to keep a very sharp watch on his baser instincts from now on—Grace was a girl with whom he could not under any circumstances play with too roughly, as much as he might want to. He would continue to lay with her in the conventional manner, as he had just demonstrated to her, and thought from now on it should be on a bed too—quietly, calmly, nicely. Horizontally. He would have to treat her well; she was now the most precious commodity he had and she was going to ensure his good and continued health for quite some time to come. He wondered in fact, as they emerged up into the pub proper, if there was a statute of limitations on the number of times a fellow could be brought back from the brink of death? He'd been saved twice today already.

'Omce,' Grace said tonelessly, staring at the floor.

'Pardon?'

'Omce. Just ascause you've got camser doesem't meam you're asposed to die of it first. You were asposed to die from what Joe did to you with the scampel.'

Arthur stared at her bemused. Had he spoken aloud? He didn't think so . . . so how did she know what he was thinking? And—again—*had* she known what was going to happen when he flipped the switch? How? When he'd been dragging her down the stairs, in his mind's eye he'd certainly been transposing the fantastically colourful burns he'd given Skinny onto Joe's face, but . . . good God . . .

'Can you . . . can you read minds *as well*?' he said.

'Sometimes,' she said quietly. 'It depemds.'

Arthur laughed, joy in his heart. He not only had his very own perpetual life support mechanism, she could also read the minds of any bastard who might want to betray him. How much better could this *get*?

There was a rap on the bar top.

'Service,' said Skinny.

Her.

Arthur fired straight to the voice over the bar; the muzzle flash illuminating the exploding optics and fragmenting woodwork . . . but Skinny was already rolling over Tommy's half-sized section and firing the twin barrels, knee-height, point blank at him. The twirling white beam of the falling flashlight turned instantly pink with bloody vapour as tiny chips of kneecap and leg bone shrapnelled everywhere, the sharper pieces embedding themselves into both the woodwork of the bar and Skinny's face. The rest of Bewlay spun around on the spot like a huge top and he screeched in agony, whirling and collapsing onto a table, smacking heavily against its surface and laying there, steam coming from the ragged end of his leg, blood erupting from newly shredded and exposed veins.

Skinny was up from the floor in a beat, shotgun discarded, a handful of filthy bar towels grabbed from where she'd placed them moments earlier, and began to tie off the end of Bewlay's leg as tightly as she could.

'You ok Princess?' she shouted over her shoulder to Grace. She caught a glimpse of the girl slowly shaking her bowed head.

No.

'I'm bleedimg.'

Skinny felt sick.

'I am so, so, *so* truly fucking sorry,' Skinny continued. 'I had to make a choice about who was in most trouble . . . and you lost. But you're still alive, and that's something.'

'S'ok,' Grace said softly, 'this was all asposed to happem emmyway.'

Skinny didn't have time to ponder this, Bewlay was literally hosing out blood. She'd meant to cripple him, not saw him the fuck in half. This was fucking up everything; she did not want him to die. Not right now and *not—like—this*! Fuck it!

'I cam help,' said Grace.

She stepped forward and placed her hands on the end of Bewlay's leg and the blood flow instantly stopped.

Skinny stared. Wow. A lot of things started coming into focus for her . . . but she'd ask later. Bewlay was groaning and writhing on the table top. Skinny tipped it over, landing him heavily on the floor before searching in his pockets.

'You're Grace, aren't you?' said Skinny.

'Hm hm.'

She produced a key and threw it to her.

'Here,' she said. 'Go get Joe and whoever's with him . . .'
'S'Maryam. My sister . . .'
'Whatever; I'm going to be busy here for a wee while. Tell him I'm fine and not to come down here ok? Got that? It's important—he is *not* to come down here until I shout that it's ok—that is very important. Tell him he's to look for Bewlay's money. I know for sure there's a stash planked here. It'll probably be in his room. Tell him I need money and he's got to find it for me. It's very important ok? You guys are not leaving here empty-handed.'
'Amd you too.'
Skinny stared at her.
'Just go. I'll get the lights back on.'
Grace darted off.
'Princess!' Skinny called. Grace stopped at the bottom of the stairs.
'Don't touch any loose wires.'
Grace rushed up to the flat above and Skinny began to drag Bewlay over to the bar, propping him up against it. She could care fucking less about money. What she needed was for Joe to not see what she was going to do to this slug. If he came down here, he'd see a side to her that . . .
That I don't want you to see, she thought. I've got you back now Joe, and I like that you haven't known me since we were kids. I like the fact that I can start again all over and be someone else. I like it and I don't want you seeing me the way I really am. And it's just for the next wee while, that's all. Just let me do this and it'll be over and I'll be a normal person and we can go off and do fun stuff and we'll have money and we can bring along your girlfriend and her wee sister and we can play at being happy families and who knows what'll happen. Good stuff . . . but please only if you don't watch what I have to do . . .

◆

They were still hugging each other when the lights came on.
'You're so beautiful Maryam. I'm so sorry,' Grace said.
Maryam shushed her.

'How did you fix me? Can you do it from a distance? Is everything else—the laying on of hands or anything like that—was that *all* false?'
'I didm't heal you Maryam.'
Maryam looked at Joe.
'Then how?'
'It was your baby,' she said. 'Whem I healed the bad mam's camser through you the power wemt through the baby as well . . . it made the baby be like me maybe.'
Maryam gripped Joe's hand tightly. He had told her the news; she'd really had no idea what to say or do and she had put it to the back of her mind. There were way too many other things to worry about—but now? Now it was *the* thing.
Grace continued. 'You were goimg to die up here amd the baby didm't wamt to die, so *it* fixed you. From the imside . . .'
'How do you know this? Can you . . . 'read' it?'
Grace nodded.
But it's *not* a baby, thought Joe. At the minute it was barely even a set of subdividing cells for God's sake . . .
'It ism't sells Joe,' Grace said. 'It's a soul.'
Joe and Maryam stared at each other. Jesus. That was radical. Joe thought of Brewster's acid-tinged vision of The Universal force that arrives in the world when you do and leaves you when your time's up. Maybe there was something to it. He broke from the girls reluctantly. To hell with whether Trudy wanted him to stay away from her for longer or not. He was going to look for Bewlay's money so they could all get out of here as soon as possible.
Maryam held her sister, grateful to be doing so without the usual aches and pains in her body. And she thought . . .
I was meant to die and I was saved. That means that something bad is going to happen to me . . . am I to lose my soul like Papa and scream and cry insanities?
She stopped herself. That was not necessarily the case, was it? Bewlay hadn't 'lost his soul' when she, or rather Grace, had stopped his cancer, had he? But if Bewlay wasn't meant to die of his cancer, then how come healing him of it had been so effortless? She should have been in agonies, like when she'd healed Joe.
Unless . . .

Maybe the losing of one's soul had nothing to do with what one was dying of at all? Maybe it had to do with the *date* of one's death? Was it that the *day and the time* of one's passing was *preordained*? It made her think of fortune tellers and astrology, and star signs being able to predict one's future.

It meant that someone who was dying *could* be healed, and the pain and effort expended on that healing would be minimal, beneficial to both parties . . . just as long as it didn't happen on the day of their death.

But that meant that timing was everything?

What had happened to Papa meant that she must have healed him on the *very day* he was supposed to die . . . and she would only have been able to do that if he had known and had intentionally asked her to heal him on that day.

But he *had* been insistent that day.

He must have known when he was supposed to die—it was the only thing that made sense. But he hadn't realised—or hadn't been *told* by whoever or whatever had wanted him to lose his soul—about the terrible consequences of doing so.

Who or what would do such a thing and for what reason? It was terrifying. Something, some force or power seemed to know when things were going to happen and was making sure that events happened around those things.

But what about Bewlay? He had been healed twice on the same day, so his time was probably not up . . . no, she thought. No he hadn't. She realised that it was now after midnight. He had been cured of cancer yesterday. Today, he had been healed of Joe's assault on him. With luck, she thought, today was the day Mister Bewlay was supposed to die.

She smiled grimly to herself as she held Grace closer to her.

It took a few seconds before she remembered with a cold chill.

Joe's cousin.

◆

He could hear her returning from the cellar. The gun was on the floor only feet away from him. But even if his hands hadn't been bound by manky, blood-drenched bar towels to the brass footrest at the bottom of the bar and he'd been able to grab it, he wouldn't have used it unless it was absolutely necessary. It was time for some common sense to prevail here.

She'd stopped moving. Through teary, pain-blurred eyes he saw her standing in front of him, wearing some kind of fur coat.

'Ok, Skinny, you've got me. What do we do now?'

'What do you suggest Arthur?'

'Things are different,' he said. 'I shouldn't be alive, you shouldn't be alive. That girl *fixed* us.'

'So?'

'So I'm *thinking* differently now, and that's the truth. We're special. We were special anyway, and you know it. You thought you could run my show and you were right, you absolutely could, but you know something else? Between us we can run the whole fucking *country* if we play this right. We *need never die*!'

He tried not to flinch when she leaned closer to him, but he couldn't help it. She had a paper towel or a hanky or something and she wiped the tears from his eyes before she settled back into a squat in front of him. That was better, he could see her clearly now.

He grinned.

'We should put the past behind us and *exploit* this girl. I promise I won't do any of them any harm. What we've got here is too precious to be fucked with. She'll need a twenty-four seven minder—you can play mother, ok? You can all live together in a lovely house and you can keep your hands clean and I'll do all the hard stuff, but we'll be partners fifty-fifty. It's the only sensible way to go. I apologise unreservedly for my behaviour—I genuinely and honestly mean that Skinny—you gave me a wake-up call and I have absolutely no grudge against you now. Sincerely.'

'You know what Arthur?' she said. 'I believe you.'

And she did.

'So?' he said 'I've lost a leg, you've had your revenge. We're quits, hm? Let's talk business.'

'Yes, let's,' said Skinny, reaching into the fur coat's deep pocket and producing two chopsticks.

◆

There was no furniture at all in Bewlay's room apart from an ancient iron bedstead with a worn, sagged mattress. The open sports bag filled with what looked like banknotes lay on the scraggy blanket... but Joe didn't want to step in there to get it. He could feel his hands shaking. He'd already looked in the room across from this one—with its floor to ceiling, insane scrawls and the severed head—and that had been *bad*...

This, however, was something else entirely.

'Joe?'

Maryam was down the corridor at the door to Bewlay's sitting room, holding on to Grace. She mustn't see this.

'I'll be with you in a sec,' he said, straining to keep his voice steady. 'Just stay there. Won't be long.'

Joe stepped in, intending to swiftly snatch the bag up and get out—and once gone, make a very special effort to try to not think about what was inside Arthur Bewlay's bedroom.

◆

Skinny looked down at Bewlay. He was moaning unintelligibly, the chopsticks poking out from his eye sockets, the liquid and the blood running like dark, thick tears down his cheeks. There was a little over a third of each stick poking out, the rest having been pushed into his eyes and as far into his brain as she could get them.

The tips must be touching the inside of his skull, she supposed.

His body was jerking in spasms—his hands clenching and unclenching spastically at his sides, like little electric currents were running through him. And maybe they were, thought Skinny. Maybe what was left of his mind after she had inserted the chopsticks and vigorously wiggled them about inside was trying to reconnect its minced up wiring. His brain must look like it had been through a blender, she thought. He hadn't said a word though, not after his last frankly confused 'no...' to her. She wondered how much brain damage had been done and if he could remember the last thing he'd seen—her smiling, happy wee face—just before she pushed the chopsticks in. How long did he have left to live? He wouldn't bleed to death that was for sure, not from these wounds. If she were to ring for an ambulance she supposed they might get to him and do something or other with him in a specialist unit. He could well survive for a long time like this.

That would be nice.

But she knew she wouldn't phone an ambulance. She would leave him here to rot and if someone found him, blind, minus a leg—and a nose, she reminded herself—and permanently brain damaged, then fine, because if anyone had a way of sorting all *that* out then the cunt deserved to live. She heard the approaching footsteps coming down the stairs.

'Keep back Joe. You don't need to see this.'

'You're right. I don't—'

Skinny stepped away from Bewlay and looked at Joe. They stared at each other over the gulf of the years that had come between them. There was too much to say, so they said nothing. Instead, they spoke.

'What should we do?' she said.

'Leave. I got the money so let's split.'

'Is it that simple?'

'Yeah. I think so. If we want it to be.'

'I want it to be.'

'Then it's that simple.'

They smiled together and Skinny looked at the two women by his side.

Jesus, she thought. *Good genes run in that family, that was for fucking sure.*

'You're Maryam?' she asked.

Maryam nodded. Even in a blood-soaked nightdress she looked a million dollars, thought Skinny. But she also looked tense enough to snap in half.

'How are you feeling Trudy?' she asked.

'I don't know,' she said. 'How do I look like I'm feeling?'

'You either know exactly what I'm talking about or you don't,' Maryam said, and Skinny frowned at her brisk manner. Maryam saw this but ignored it.

'Well?' she said. 'How are you feeling? Inside? Does it feel different from usual? Do you feel like . . . like there's something missing? *Inside?*'

'What the fuck are you talking about?' Skinny smiled nervously. 'Joe?'

'Just tell her Trudy, please.'

'I'm *fine* Maryam, thank you very much. Nothing 'missing'.'

'Oh thank God . . .' Maryam cried, '*Thank God.*' And before she knew it, Skinny was being tightly embraced by this gorgeous, crying, happy woman. She looked over Maryam's shoulder to Joe, who was glancing nervily behind him at the stairs.

'C'mon Trudy, let's go,' he said, 'I'll explain in the car. This isn't a good place to be.'

At the door she hesitated, letting the others go on without her for a moment, looking back into that disgusting place for the last time.

She smiled. An explanation, if Joe had one, would be nice she supposed, but it wasn't compulsory. She thought she could hear a noise from upstairs, like long fingernails clacking lightly together.

Skinny walked out, not bothering to close the doors behind her.

She might not know about everything that had been happening but she knew that she wasn't going to die.

At least, not today.

Georges IV

IT WAS CLEAR TO HIM NOW.

Georges realised, he had served his purpose, hadn't he?

He had been healed on the day the Architect had told him to be, and he had been entered by the 'Ladies and the Gentlemen' and driven mad by their squirming and whispering and had been goaded by them into killing himself for real, believing he could erase his mistake by taking control of his own death. And he had landed on that car . . . so that everything else could happen.

They had amused themselves with him for sport, the attack dogs that they were for the Architect but had then left him once more, like so much waste.

He had served his purpose and now he was being left alone. Forever.

39

THEY WERE FOLLOWING SIGNS TO LOCH LOMOND, ONE OF THE most beautiful places in the whole world—only twenty miles from Glasgow and none of them had ever been there in their lives.

The bag of money had proved a pointless acquisition—the notes had all been torn to shreds. Savaged would be a better description, thought Joe, like a dog had been at them. Useless mulch. They had made a swift inventory of everything else they had of value and he and Trudy had come to the conclusion that even cocaine, which had been lying damp and spoiled in a car boot for God knew how long, was still cocaine. She hadn't wanted to try selling in the city—too many faces there to ask too many questions—but she knew of a guy who was pretty rich who lived out by the loch somewhere. She'd delivered 'pizzas' to plenty of parties he'd held in Glasgow hotels and was sure he'd be up for a sale. They were going to make an approach and see if they could squeeze enough from what they had to get them all out of the country.

In the meantime, the balled-up wodge of money in the fur coat pocket had been enough to get them all booked in to one of the dun and sterile budget hotels in the centre of town and they had all filed into the cuboidal sleeping space—or 'room' as the management would have it—cramped, but glad to be close to each other. And at least it was brand new, clean and more importantly as far as Joe was concerned, not in any way architecturally interesting.

No one said much of anything—Maryam and Trudy had passed guarded, but essentially funny and self-deprecating remarks about taking turns wearing the coat. They had both been very solicitous of Grace, who in turn had been quite happy at being the object of their affection. But despite Joe's attempts, the subject of Bewlay and everything else that had happened was avoided.

'No one's ready for a post-match analysis yet, Joe.'

That was how Trudy had put it. That was fine by him, he supposed, they had plenty of time to work through what all of this had meant. But that didn't mean he could stop his brain picking at it. All of the disparate elements that they had experienced *had* to come together somehow, he thought.

The girls had slept—the three of them bunched like spoons, protecting each other—on the smallest double bed Joe had ever seen. He had sat in the chair, waiting to use first light as the alarm clock to get out of that cheerless place, his mind turning over and over and trying to make some sense of everything.

Something, some force, connected Bewlay's pub and Maryam's house . . . he knew that for sure. He felt far enough away now from what he had seen to take another look at Bewlay's room in his mind. Apart from the bed and the fact that the window had been bricked up, it had been identical—*identical*—in almost every respect to the room with the broken green fireplace that he had walked into at the Mansions, even down to the matted, burnt-looking fibres in the grate. He was sure now that they were the *same* room. It gave him a horrible feeling, like being inside an Escher drawing.

But the creeping feeling hadn't been the worst. There had been one major difference between Bewlay's room and the room in Maryam's house. The blackness inside the fireplace itself seemed to stretch back forever . . . and on the tiles in front of it was a baby's arm. It stood erect like an obscene candle.

As he'd stared at it in disbelief, knowing full well that it was not a fake, he could swear that . . . the fingers were moving. He'd grabbed the money and bolted for the door, which had been closing silently behind him. He saw it swinging closed and he knew that he had to stop it and get out because if he didn't, when he opened it again he wouldn't be in Bewlay's pub anymore. He'd be somewhere that really didn't have a name or a way of describing it because it was somewhere the Ladies and the Gentlemen lived. And 'Papa'. And the goddam 'Architect' . . . and God knew who or what else. The place Brewster—and countless others on LSD—had caught the tiniest of glimpses of when their fully opened up minds felt the full weight of The Universal . . .

He'd grabbed the handle and had pulled the door as wide as he could, relieved to see Bewlay's cramped corridor outside. He'd risked one last look over his shoulder and saw that the baby's arm had gone and that the blackness on the inside of the fireplace seemed to be alive, millions of black things crawling—awful, awful *crawling*—all over each other . . .

Joe shuddered at the memory.

He wouldn't tell the girls anything about that. They were away from both of those places now and they would not under any circumstances be going back again. This hotel they were currently in may have been a shithole, but there was no feeling of dread here. It was just a place like hundreds and thousands of other normal, safe places all over the country.

All they had to do was stay in those sorts of places.

Bewlay had said, hadn't he—this 'Architect' had built both his pub and the Mansions, so whoever this person was or had been was somehow responsible for all of the bad stuff going on in these places. Who knew how many other buildings he was responsible for?

He went to the tiny bedside table and opened the drawer, shallow enough to have doubled as a jeweller's tray, and pulled out a small 'tourist pack' for visitors. He thumbed through all the flyers for curry houses and nightclubs and found what he was looking for—a little map of the city. It wouldn't be ordnance survey standard but it might do for his purpose. He lifted the hotel pen from next to the phone, sat down and scanned the map by the light of the orange hotel sign outside the window.

He made a small circle around the Mansions at Charing Cross before running his finger eastwards, along the old London Road and beyond to mark where Bewlay's pub lay. This was all he had—a straight line.

But what if there *were* other buildings—how many points would *they* make on the map? Five? Pentangle? Pentagram? Was there some kind of ley line shit happening with these buildings? He thought he'd try a pentacle first, remembering an entire evening spent with Brewster giving him an impromptu talk on occult geometry, and both of them coming to the conclusion that even the weirdest of mystical shit couldn't come close to what was possible in real life mathematics. He marked a nick on the side of the pen with his thumbnail for the distance between the Mansions and the Pretty Blue Fox. He then held the bottom of the pen in place over the Mansions and swivelled it down wards, trying to roughly judge the second line of his notional pentagram, hoping some landmark would appear to him as a stop point, that some clue would manifest itself . . . and it did.

The equidistant point from both the pub and the Mansions was the Victoria Infirmary—where he'd been taken after the accident and where he'd encountered those creatures in that awful cellar corridor.

Well that certainly made a shape, didn't it?

And it wasn't a goddam pentacle or pentagram or any other more obvious magic shit.

It was a triangle.

Joe used the business end of his pen and drew the lines between the points and joined them up, his mind already ahead of his shaking hands, remembering a detail from one of Brewster's arcane mystical books.

The equilateral triangle was also known as a thaumaturgic triangle—that is, *thauma* from the Greek equivalent for miracle, and *ergon*, for work.

Miracle working.

The thaumaturgic was also otherwise known as the Devil's Doorway, the portal through which demons, apparently, could enter the world. There was undoubtedly something very bad happening with all of these buildings, so Joe had no doubts that the triangulation of them had been intentionally achieved at the time of their planning and construction. Jesus fucking Christ, this was big, he thought.

But was he missing something?

He looked into the centre of the triangle. It was slap bang in the middle of Glasgow Green. He wasn't familiar with the place, but he had little doubt that where that centre point was he would find something.

Like what?

He suddenly crumpled up the map and tossed it into the waste bin.

Maybe he'd find a fucking tree. Who the hell cared?

Because what the fuck, if anything, was *he* supposed to do about it?

He stared out of the window, waiting impatiently for the morning to come. They would stay away from the city, in fact they would stay away from any cities if they could. He would go with Trudy to get the best deal possible for the drugs and then they would all leave this damn country, by whatever means necessary, and stay away forever. There was nothing and no one to keep any of them here, and no way in hell was he ever going to let any of them near anything that remotely resembled one of the Architect's buildings. They'd find a way of living, the four of them together, and to Hell with the rest of the world.

It could live without them.

◆

The sum is good amd warm, thought Grace, as they stepped out of the car and onto the wet sheened surface of the deserted car park. They were at the big posh shops next to the loch, where Joe said they had emough to buy breakfasts amd some clothes for Maryam whem the stores opemed.

Grace loved Joe amd he loved Maryam . . . but that was ok.

Maryam deserved it after all the trouble she'd had. Grace was sad but happy at the same time. Life was full of sadness and that was a part of beimg a persom. She was away from the Mansions now amd the Ladies amd Gememtlemem could go take a rummimg jump as far as she was concerned. Her amd Maryam amd Joe's cousim amd Joe would all live together amd be a big family. It made her feel warm imside. Papa'd told her about her operatiom she had whem she was a baby amd she kmew she diddem't have a sole, but she diddem't mimd. She never missed it amd diddem't kmow what it was so what difference did it make? They were all goimg to be a great *big*, happy family. And there would be Maryam's baby to love im a while too.

Grace knew that the baby starting inside her wasn't like Maryam's.

Not like Maryam's at *all*.

Hers was stramge.

40

Arthur was standing outside the door of his room, and he realised that for the life of him, he could never, ever remember what it looked like. His Da had made him sleep in there since he was wee and he told him it was special and that if he wanted to keep the pub then he had to sleep in that room. That was fine by Arthur. But every morning when he left it he had no memory of what it looked like, and every evening when he went to bed he had no idea what he was walking in to. It was unusual, he supposed, but at least he wasn't locked in like Tommy. Da had always said Tommy was locked away for his own safety, but Arthur knew he was a lying old bastard.

He heard the sound of his own car driving away.

Where was Reverend Joe? What had happened to Grace? Then he heard noises from the pub downstairs and decided to think about all that later—it sounded like he had something urgent to deal with. In fact it sounded like the pub had become populated in an instant; the air was full suddenly of that sound so familiar to him over the years—bodies moving and feet shuffling, but instead of banter there was just a murmur ... instead of clinking glasses there was a sound like clacking nails.

The pub wasn't open for business, so who could possibly be downstairs?

The rival gangs obviously knew of his weakness and had probably heard tales of his state of mind. Those things, coupled with the fact that the few soldiers he had left were now in hospital, might mean that some harm was going to be visited upon the person of Arthur Bewlay, and that was not on.

Arthur cursed himself for being so careless with where he'd put the gun. His scalpel was in the car... or was it downstairs? He'd seen it recently, he was sure... or was he remembering it from somewhere else? The shotgun was downstairs behind the bar, so that was no fucking good—there seemed to be nothing up here to help him—except maybe the rough sponge? That was in the guest room. It was sharp enough to wield indiscriminately against even a group of attackers, and now that his strength had returned, he could certainly make a mess of the first few who tried anything with him. And that would be enough, he thought. Fear would do the rest.

He smiled. He was in the mood for something like this. In the mood and *fit* and *capable* of doing something about it. In fact, he thought, if whoever it was that'd come to hit him was expecting a clapped-out, cancer-ridden wheeze bag then they had another thing coming. He had the total element of surprise! And something like this would be perfect for re-establishing his dominance on the scene.

A bloody scrap with a bunch of invaders?

The single-handed dispatch of a rival firm's war party?

Word would spread among the plankton and he'd be back on top before midnight's chimes tonight. He strode down the corridor to the guest room and only then noticed something he had failed to before. Where was Big Ian's body?

The jukebox downstairs suddenly ground into action and the house lights flickered on and off and he thought he could see shadows on the walls in the intermittent flashes, two figures lumpen and misshapen, one with a topknot like Big Ian's wee junky niece...

Arthur suddenly wanted to leave, and whoever was in the bar he would deal with as best he could, because he didn't like being up here anymore. By wielding the rough sponge, he might be able to push through whoever was down there and reach the shotgun... but it would certainly be trickier now, because of his missing leg and all...

His what? He looked down—his legs were fine. What the hell was that about?

From inside the guest room, a dog growled.

Hard men he could handle . . . but what was the sketch here? Psychosis? Fucking hallucinations? It could be any of those, but Arthur thought that if he were only able to get out of here, the question would be academic because, deep down, he knew that there was something about this place. The things that were happening to him needed these walls around them. If he could just get outside he would be safe. He would have time to try and figure a way out of this. But of course . . . there *was* only one way out of here wasn't there? He had made sure of that himself hadn't he? The place was bricked up!

The only way out was straight ahead, walking downstairs and through the bar. He was a big guy, after all, and he was a strong guy again. He'd fought a guy with a razor barehanded and another with . . . he felt strange. He'd said this before to someone . . . .what was wrong with him, why was he feeling like this? He was cured wasn't he?

The jukebox powered down and Cher's 'If I Could Turn Back Time' wound slowly to a ghastly, slo-mo complaint before it ceased its squawking entirely. The reedy, murmuring ululation started up once more . . .

He couldn't stand it, he needed light. He decided that he *needed* to see them, at the very least to be able to see where to hit them and push them to get them out of his way. Fists, feet, head, he could only use them if he could see what he was doing!

. . . there was still the flashlight on the floor of the guest room . . . he could grab that . . . he could just run to the doorway, quickly reach in and run out again—all over in a moment, not looking, not seeing whatever was inside there now. He'd already left the flashlight in there, hadn't he? Had he? Had he? Had he? Had he? Had he? Had he?

What was *wrong* here? He'd come up the stairs with Maryam and he'd seen the light was on in the guest room, but he'd known then—as he knew now—that he hadn't left it there. He hadn't. That meant it had been put there by someone else . . . but before now ... before he lost his leg ... he looked down and the stump of his leg was dripping blood onto the floor. He fell against the wall, gasping and found that he was fine again. Both of his legs were present and correct. What was wrong with him?

He took swift strides to the room, pausing momentarily for a deep breath before grabbing the doorframe with one hand and reaching in to snatch the flashlight from the floor with the other. But what he saw made him freeze his grabbing hand in mid-air.

Standing there huge and looming was Big Ian, or, at least, it was Big Ian's body, and jammed onto his ragged, bloody neck was the squat, shrunken and squashed head of Tommy.

'Hello Arthur', Tommy said.

A substance glurted from between his lips as he spoke. It was glistening and almost clear in a dirty sort of way, like raw egg albumen, but it also had long, scarlet thread veins of blood roping through it. It was slowly running down his chin and dripping lazily onto the chest of what used to be Big Ian and it made his voice glutinous and thick-sounding, like he was speaking with a mouth full of cooking oil.

He heard awkward, shuffling steps. Emerging from the darkness next to Big Ian/Tommy was a smaller person ... a *much* smaller person—one who was about only as high as Arthur's waist. Tommy's height, in fact.

It had Tommy's body and was dressed in Tommy's suit—the one he'd been buried in, its dark weave now covered in mould, its long stay in the grave's dampness making it spongy and as thick as flooring felt. The body was shuffling about from foot to foot like a child needing to pee, the stubby hands fidgeting with each other in that shy way Tommy had ... but Arthur could see it really wasn't a person at all. Sticking out of the frayed shirt collar, with its tie still knotted, was the head and neck of the dead greyhound, its teeth bared in a silent snarl, rags of black sticky tape hanging down in tatters from its jaws—and a pair of eyes bulging from its sockets.

Arthur noticed they were the same colour as Big Ian's.

The dog growled, low, deep and frightening, its eyes swivelling obscenely.

'Say hello Arthur,' gargled Tommy. Tommy/Big Ian was looming over him, his giant arms outstretched as if getting ready for an embrace, the tiny head grinning down, with its translucent bloody mouth, dripping goo in oily slo-mo onto Arthur's face. It burnt where it touched him like acid, and he jerkily wiped it off with his sleeve.

The midget dog head creature was now nosing aggressively at Arthur's crotch, growling louder, its teeth bared and its jaws slavering out the same translucent substance below the panicked, staring eyes swivelling wildly in its skull. Tommy's little hands were nipping and pinching hard at Arthur's legs. Staring up at him from the dog's face, Arthur thought he could see fear and misery in Big Ian's eyes—a mute, trapped witness to what was happening here.

'You were always a special child, Arthur,' Tommy glurted. 'You were always so perfect for your purpose . . .'

'What do you mean?' he asked. 'What purpose?'

'Your lovely Da—did you never wonder why he got so drunk all the time? Why he kept telling you he was sorry? He wanted a pub, Arthur, and when I met him he had no money. So I said he could have what he wanted if he gave me you. So he did.'

The jukebox jerked into life again, but so slowly that the sound was an awful, grinding abstraction, so painfully loud that Tommy had to shout.

'Of course, I couldn't use you until recently. You know, until Grace had healed you when you should have died?'

'You . . . *you're not Tommy!*'

'That's right Arthur,' the mouth glurted. 'I'm not Tommy. I'm just borrowing him for a while.'

The head of the dog began to bark.

'Temporary accommodation, you might say, whilst I'm waiting for my next home to become available to me.'

Arthur began to cry.

'Who *are* you?'

'I'm a lot of things. I've been a soldier, a surgeon . . . an architect. I work for . . . well let's say I represent an administrator, who is returning after an absence. I plan things. I make sure everyone does what they're supposed to—that everything happens when it should, that people meet when they have to, be where they have to be. There are always random elements, of course—but I've had a lot of time to plan. A *lot* of time. They do say that the best laid plans etcetera etcetera . . . .but you know what Arthur? It's all going very well, so far.'

'What is?'

'Why . . . everything that has to happen. The main thing is, you don't have to worry about it because you've done your bit.'

'I have?'

'We have met before you know,' the head glurted. 'I sold you something that was very important for everything to happen as it should.'

Arthur shook his head.

'I can't remember.'

'The scalpel? Do you remember me now Arthur?'

Arthur nodded . . . the old man in Paddy's market.

The head grinned. His wide, flat teeth looked like they were made of brass.

'It's a relatively tiny cog in the machinery, but just as an example of the sort of thing I do. Think about it this way—if you hadn't bought it you wouldn't have killed Tommy with it and left it in your car, and if you hadn't left it in your car then Joe would not have found it and you would not have been fatally injured by him, and if that hadn't happened then Grace would not have healed you and you would not have been made perfect for your purpose. Only a man with no soul left in him could give Grace what I need. Everything means something, Arthur. Everything.'

'*What purpose?*'

'Things are going to change in the world. They've been changing since this place, and all my others, were built. It's one of the reasons *why* they were built—so that I always have a place to go whenever I'm . . . temporarily homeless. That's a situation which has just been remedied, however, and I'm expecting to be able to occupy in about nine months or so.'

The head grinned. The barking got louder and louder and the little hands were pinching Arthur harder and harder.

'So thank you for your efforts,' the head said. 'You've done your part in what was required and now you're seeing the world as it really is. The way that *everyone* will be seeing it, eventually. Now, stand up straight. You have guests wanting to come up and visit.'

'Guests?'

'Why are you repeating everything I say like a dummy? Have you suddenly lost all your intelligence? *Guests*, man! You know them already—they made you what you are. Don't you remember? Every night they would take turns to give you a good, old-fashioned, solid Victorian education. Why do you think you're so erudite? It certainly wasn't from attending your local comprehensive, was it?'

Tommy's head was inches from his own face now. It opened its mouth and the sound of a baby crying came out, loud and shrieking and in pain. Arthur started to shriek himself now, like he once had as a small boy—when Da had continually shoved him into his room every night.

Now Arthur could remember what his room looked like and why, when he had been securing the pub for Tommy's return, he had chosen to brick it up himself. He knew that he hadn't wanted anyone else to see what it was he saw inside it every night, in the fireplace. Every single night.

Tommy stopped his shrieking.

'They've all been watching you since you were small and they've been champing at the bit to get their hands on you for all these years. They are literally *starved* of entertainment and I want to keep them happy. They'll be doing a lot of work for me soon enough and they deserve some distraction. So, Arthur. What should we do now?'

'*I don't know* . . .' Arthur said, almost inaudibly.

'Well . . . you like your blow jobs, don't you?' it said. 'Why don't we start with that?'

And as the dog at Arthur's crotch suddenly lunged forward, its jaws snapping and tearing, he could hear the frantic rush of feet hurrying upstairs to come have a look.

❖

If anyone were to go inside the Pretty Blue Fox and take a walk up the old, slanted, narrow staircase that led to the flat, they would be following a trail of blood smears and hand prints all the way to a foul-smelling room where, laying against a bank of plastic carrier bags full of human waste, Arthur Bewlay twitched—two sticks black with blood protruding from his eye sockets—slowly dying. How he could possibly have made his way up to this room would be a complete mystery to them, given his physical condition and the fact that he had no brains left in his head to speak of.

That's if anyone were to go inside the Pretty Blue Fox.

That's if anyone were to notice that there was even a pub there.

41

She remembered the time in the supermarket whem she'd heard that baby cry imside the girl ascause it didem't wamt to die. But it had to, she supposed, because the girl was still im a school uniform amd she wasm't evem old enough to have boobies, never mimd look after a baby so the girl's baby had to die im ama borshom.

The same as her baby had to die.

Because she didem't wamt a baby from the bad man. Amd she didem't wamt a baby for the Architect to stay imside of amd to grow up im amd for the Ladies amd Gememtlemem to look after umtil he got big emough to look after himself.

She was glad she'd seem the schoolgirl now. It had beem sad at first, but now she had givem Grace her idea. It had meamt somethimg.

Everythimg means somethimg, she thought . . . and ran over to her sister and Joe and Trudy, laughing as she splashed her way through the deepest puddles she could see.

Laughing at the bright son of the morning.

Jim Shields is a director/producer living and working in his home town of Glasgow. His work has been BAFTA nominated and he has spent much of his career killing people who aren't real and blowing stuff up. *Baby Strange* is his first novel.